# MIKE MAIHACK

# CLEOPATRA
## IN SPACE

### BOOK FOUR
### THE GOLDEN LION

AN IMPRINT OF

**■SCHOLASTIC**

All rights reserved. Published by Graphix, an imprint of Scholastic Inc.,
Publishers since 1920. SCHOLASTIC, GRAPHIX, and associated logos are
trademarks and/or registered trademarks of Scholastic Inc.

Library of Congress Control Number: 2016944743

ISBN 978-0-545-83871-9 (hardcover)
ISBN 978-0-545-83872-6 (paperback)

10 9 8 7 6 5 4 3 2 1    17 18 19 20 21

Printed in China   38
First edition, July 2017
Color flatting by Dan Conner and Kate Carleton
Edited by Cassandra Pelham
Book design by Phil Falco
Creative Director: David Saylor

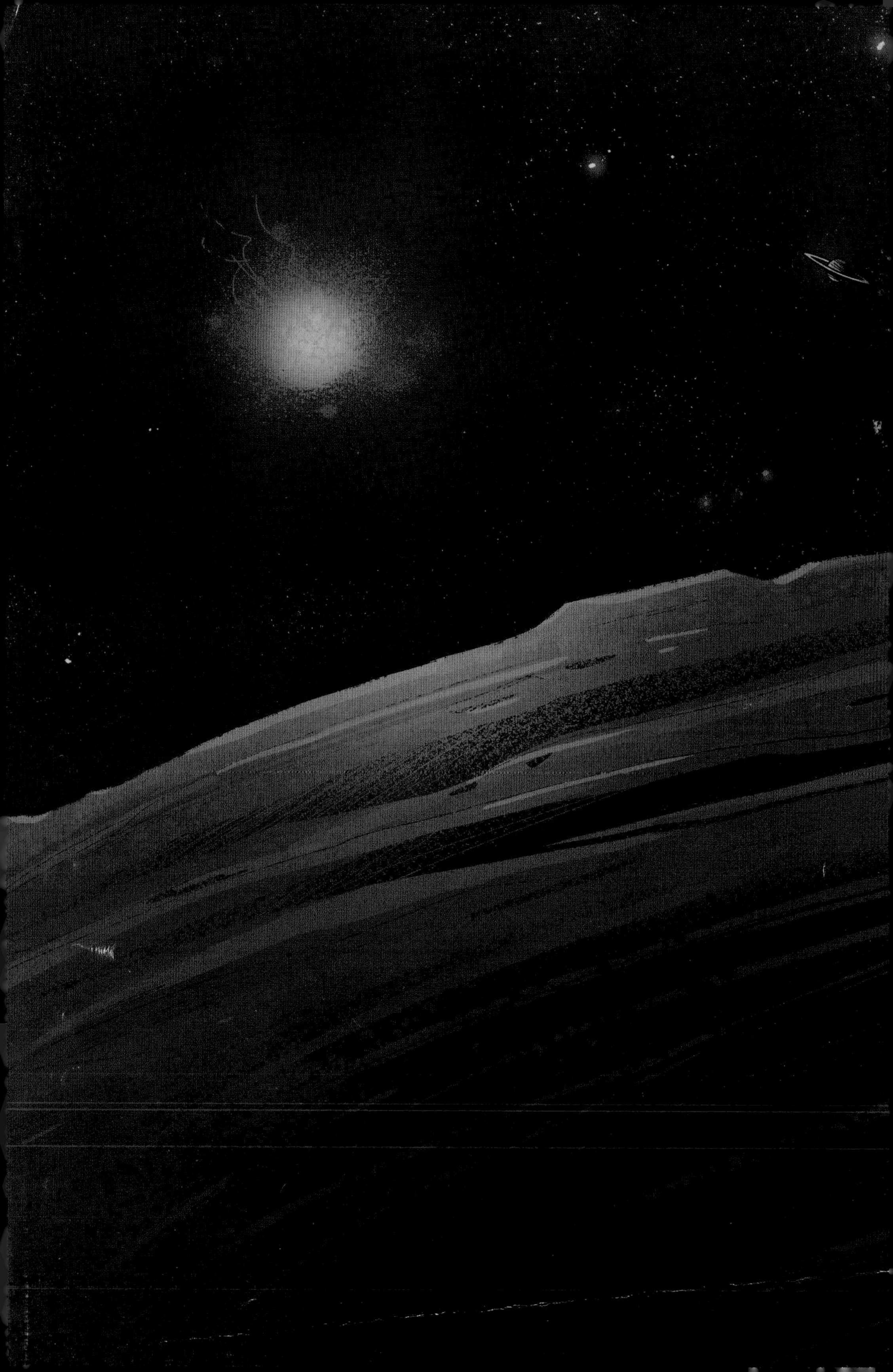

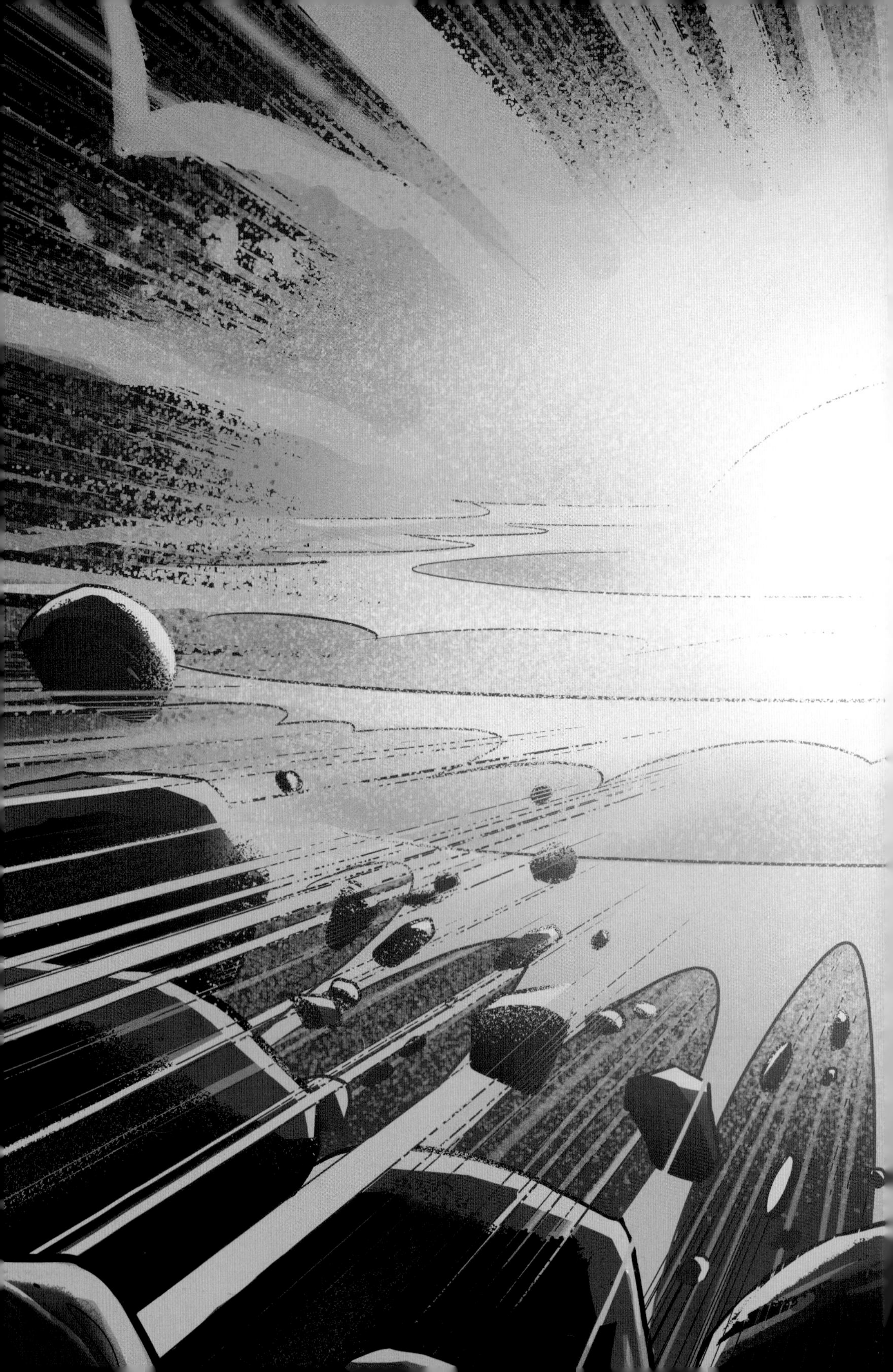

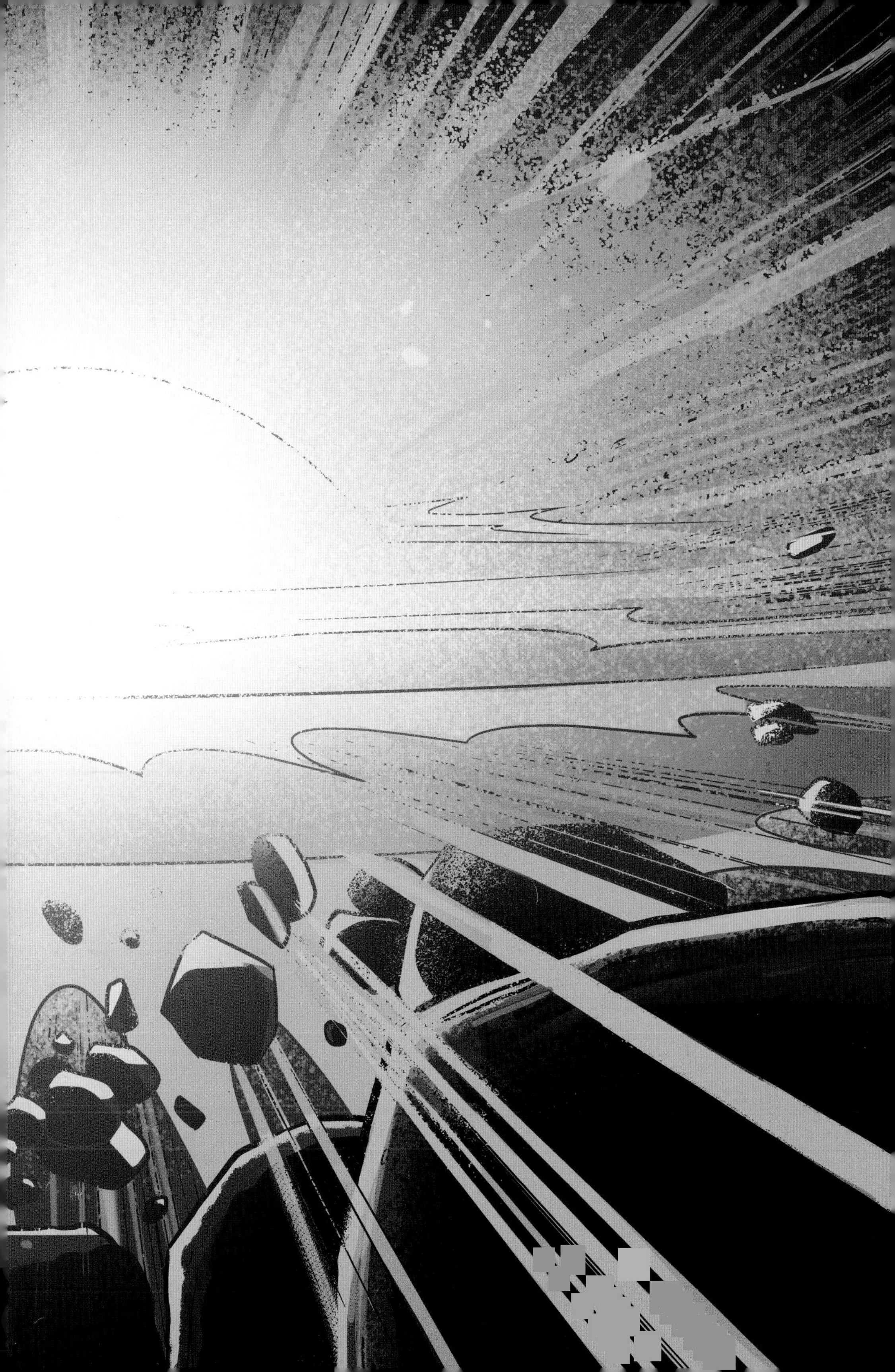

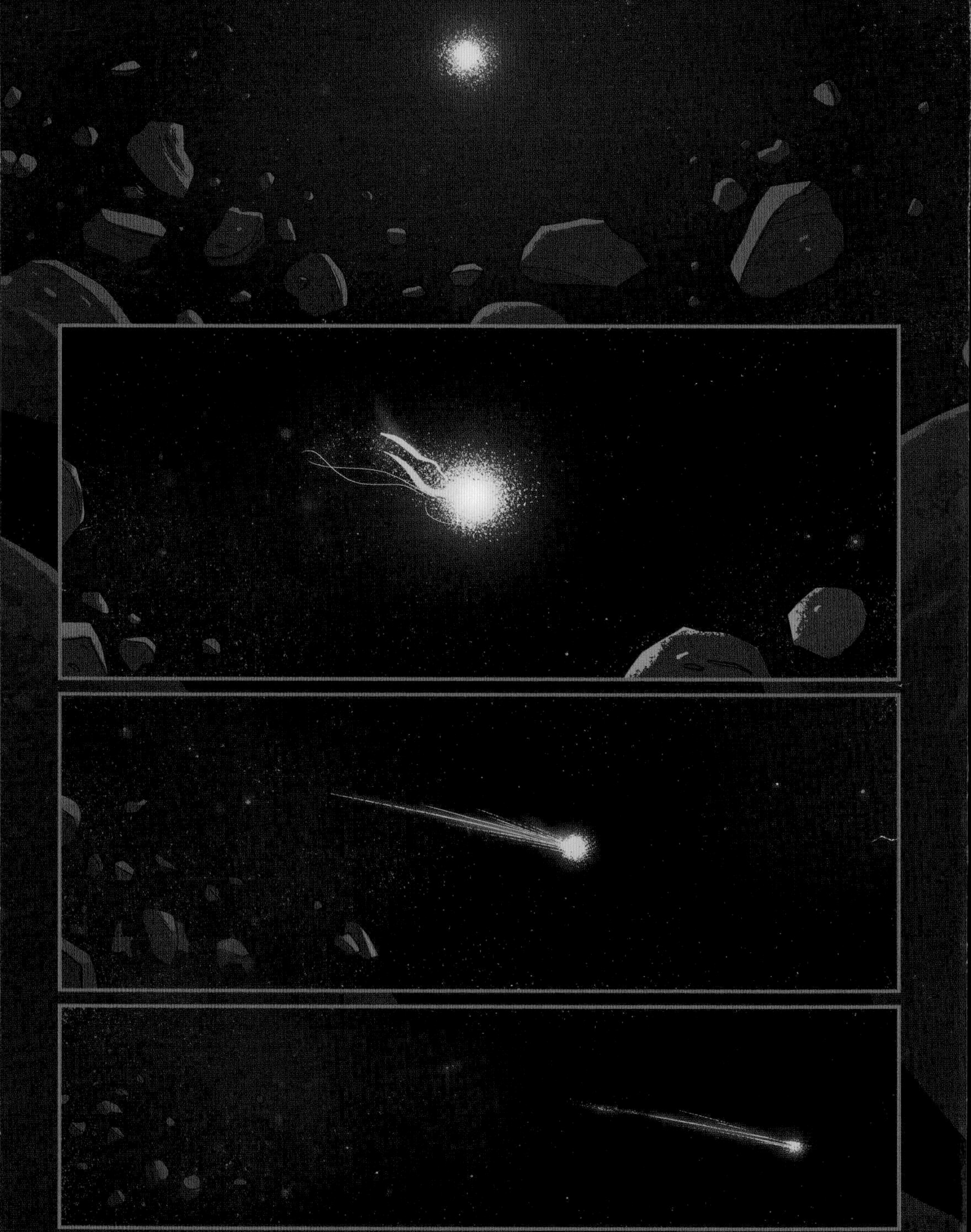

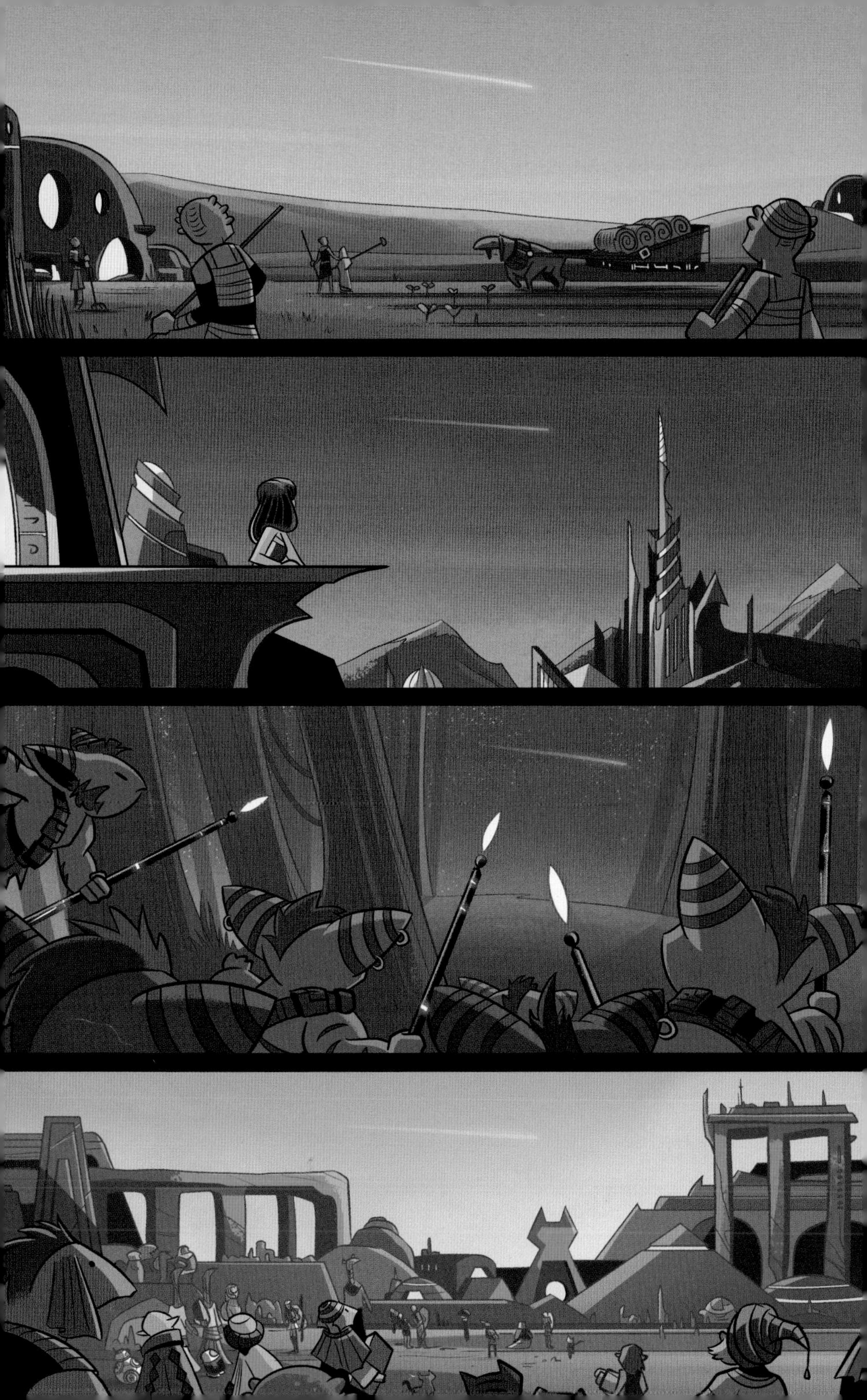

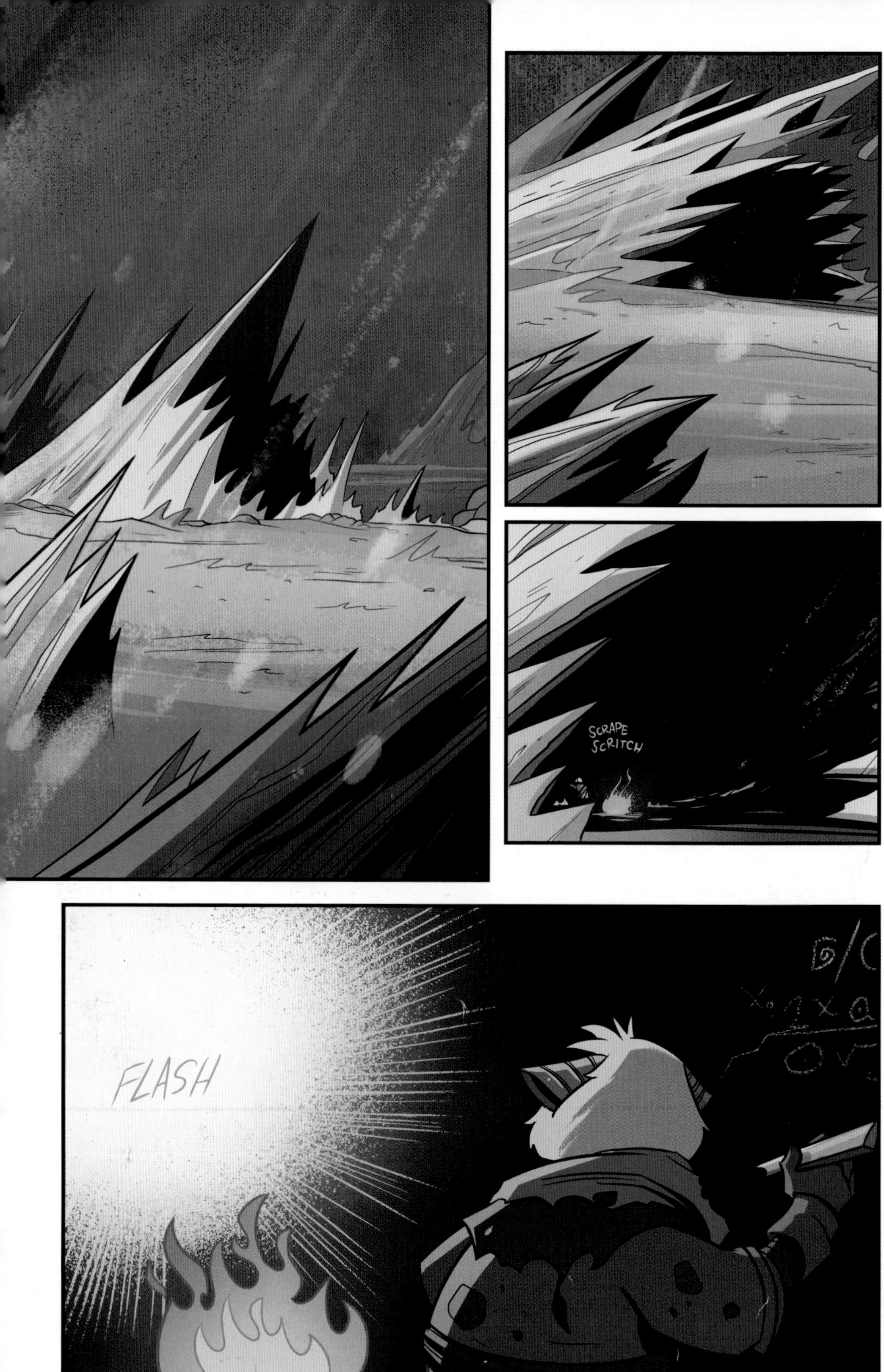
SCRAPE
SCRITCH
FLASH

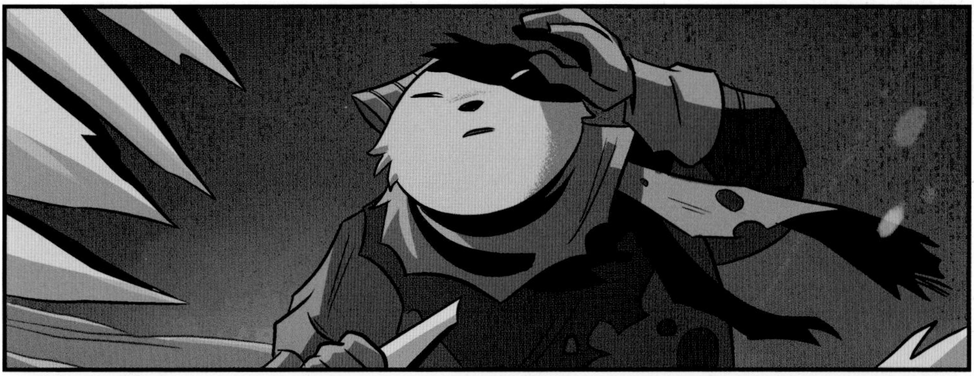

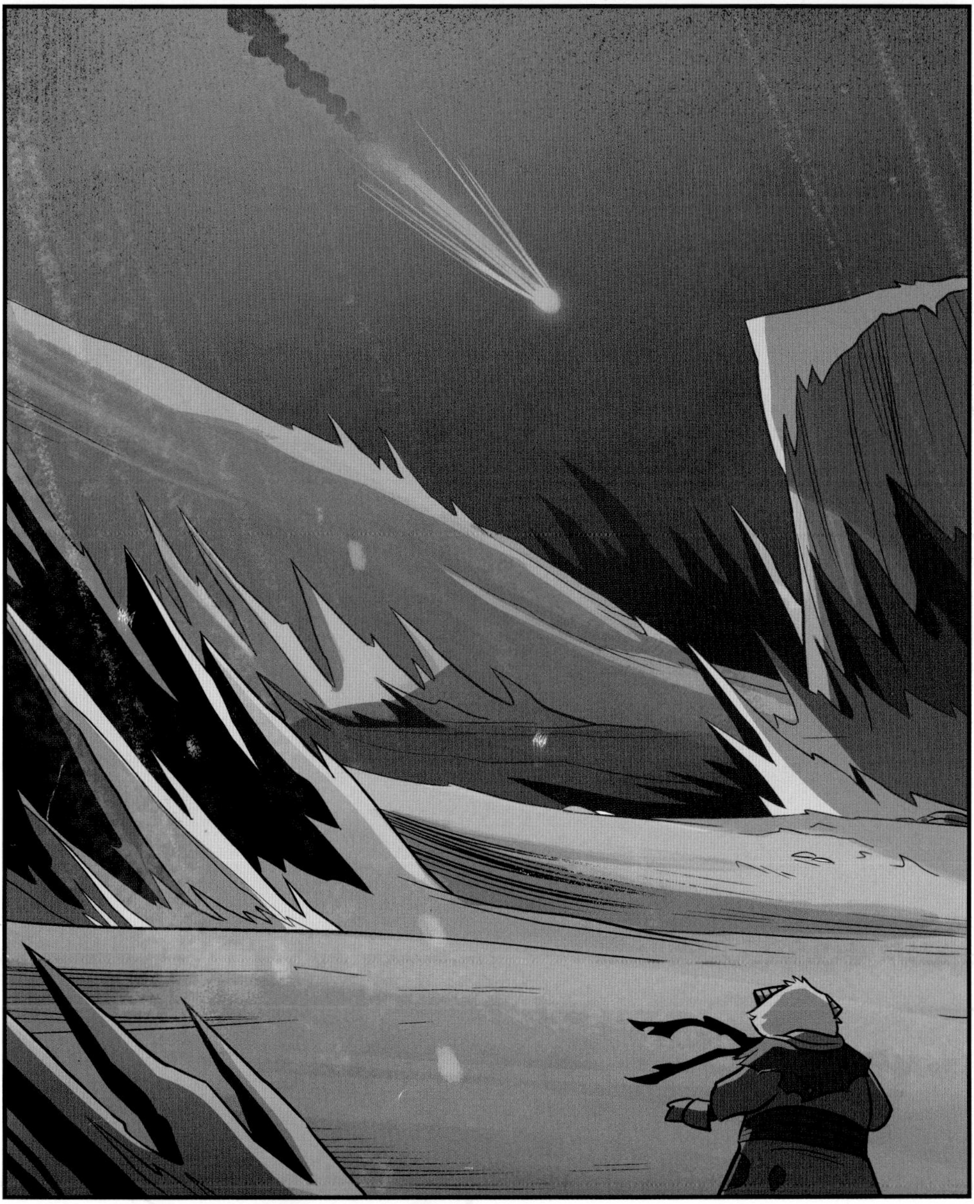

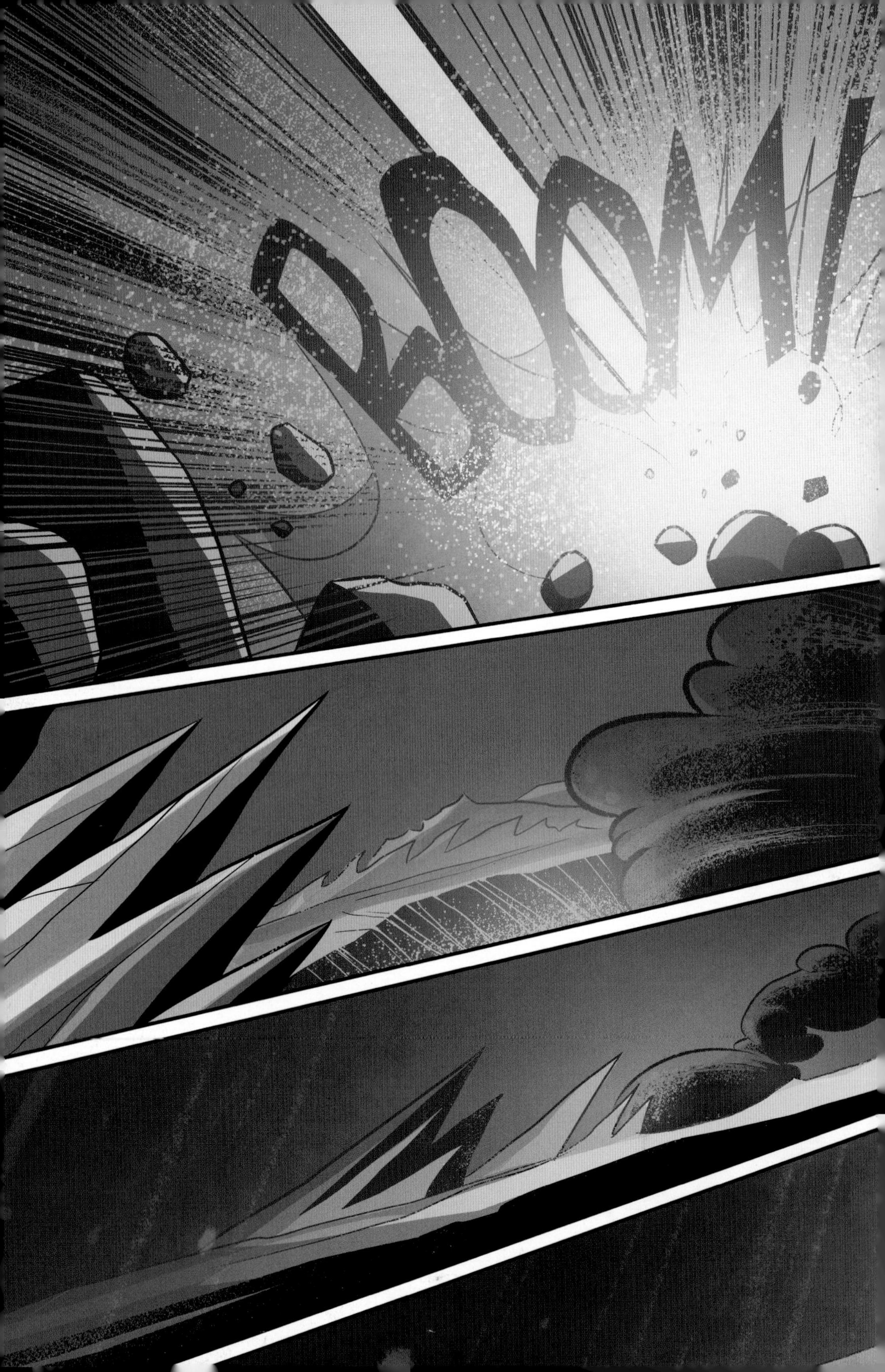
BOOM!

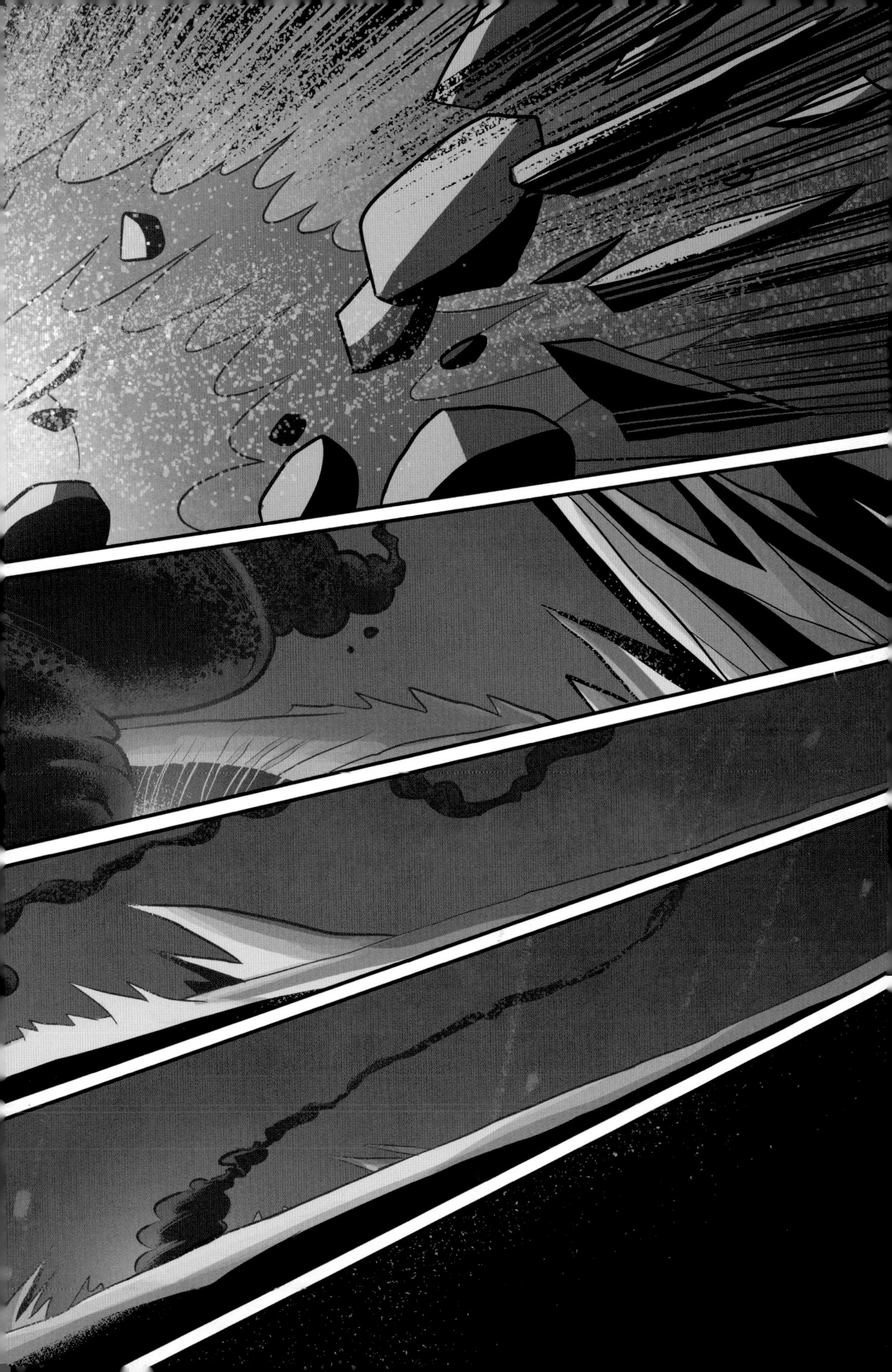

# CHAPTER ONE

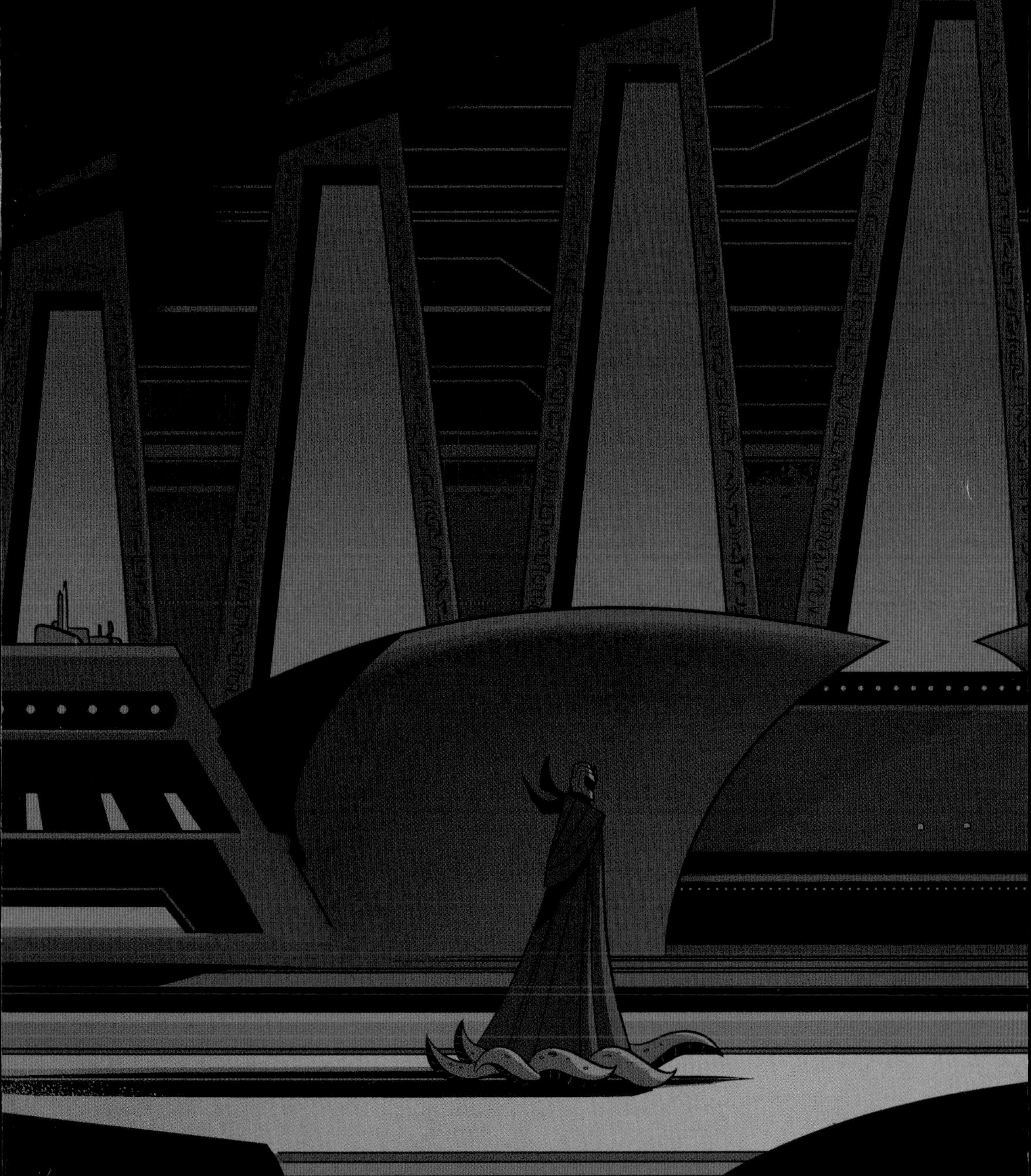

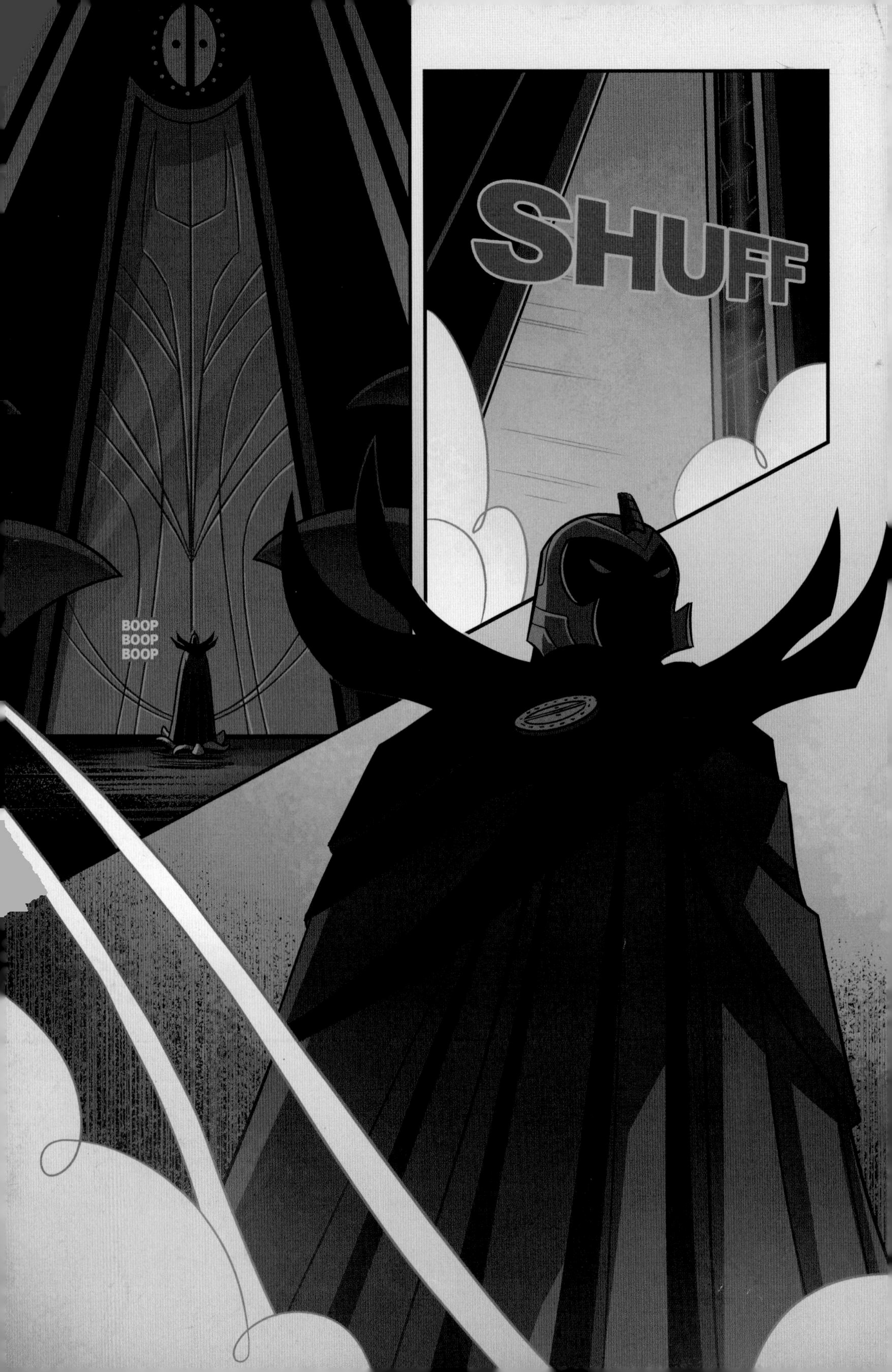
BOOP
BOOP
BOOP
SHUFF

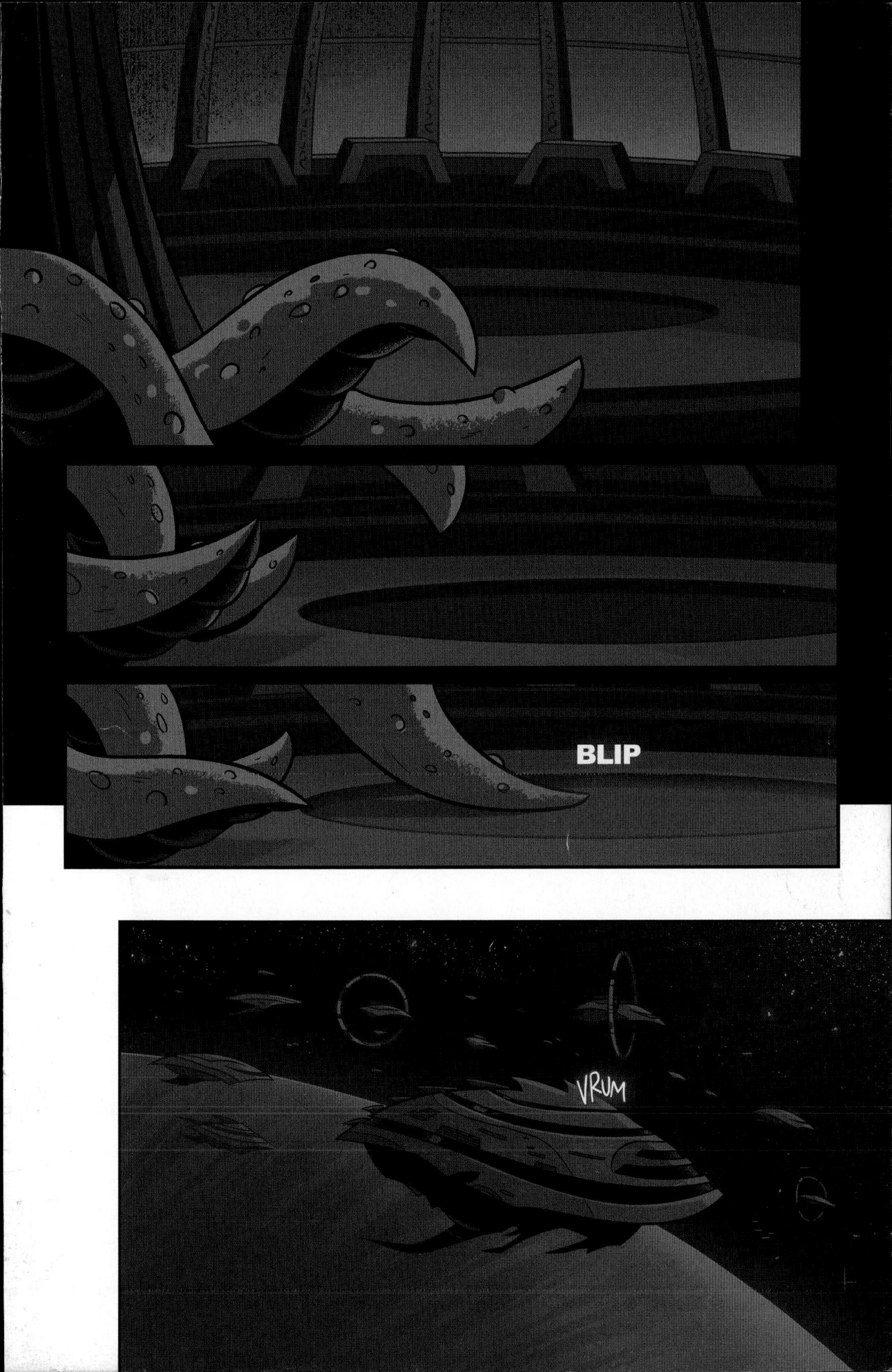
BLIP
VRUM

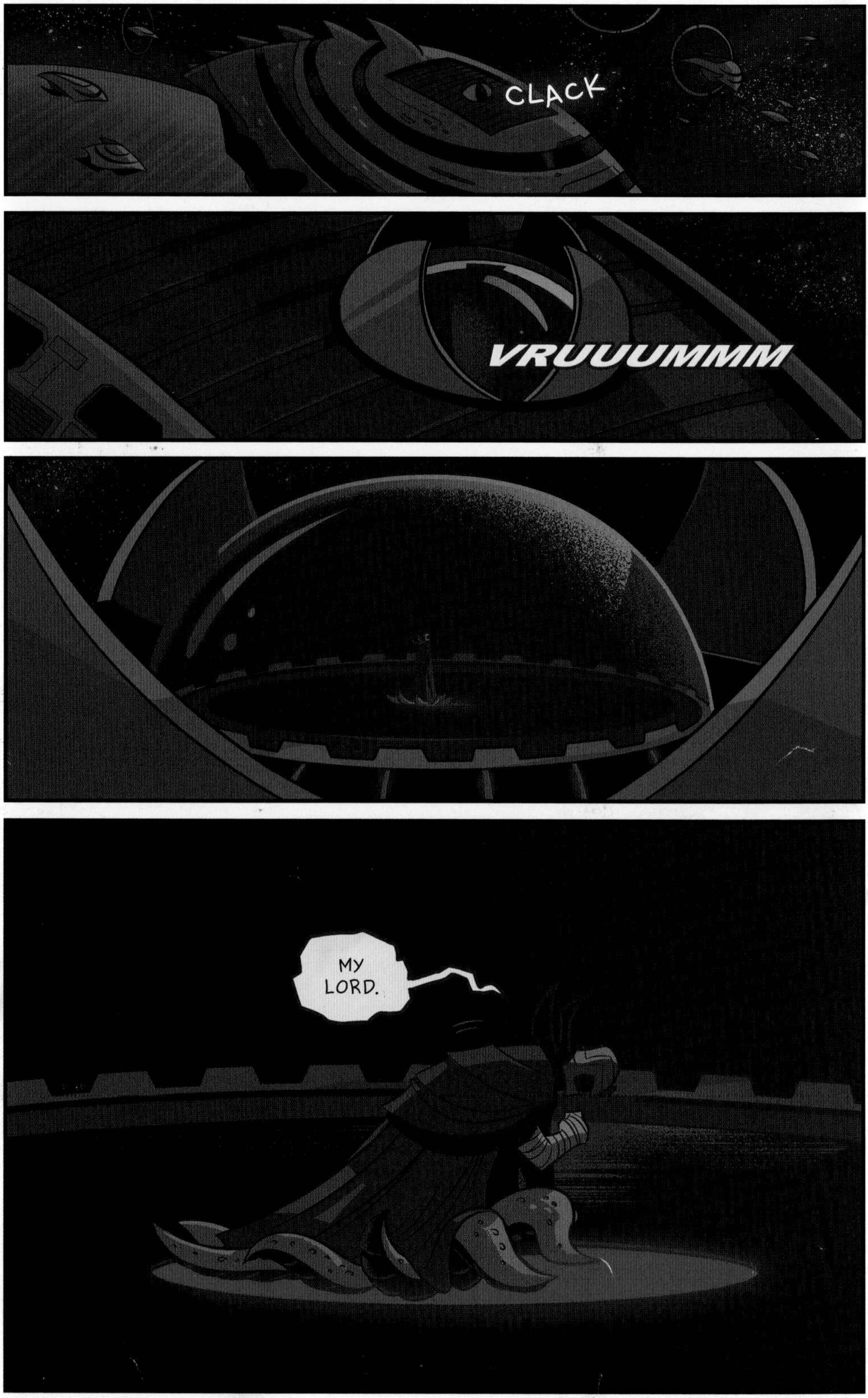
CLACK
VRUUUMMMM
MY LORD.

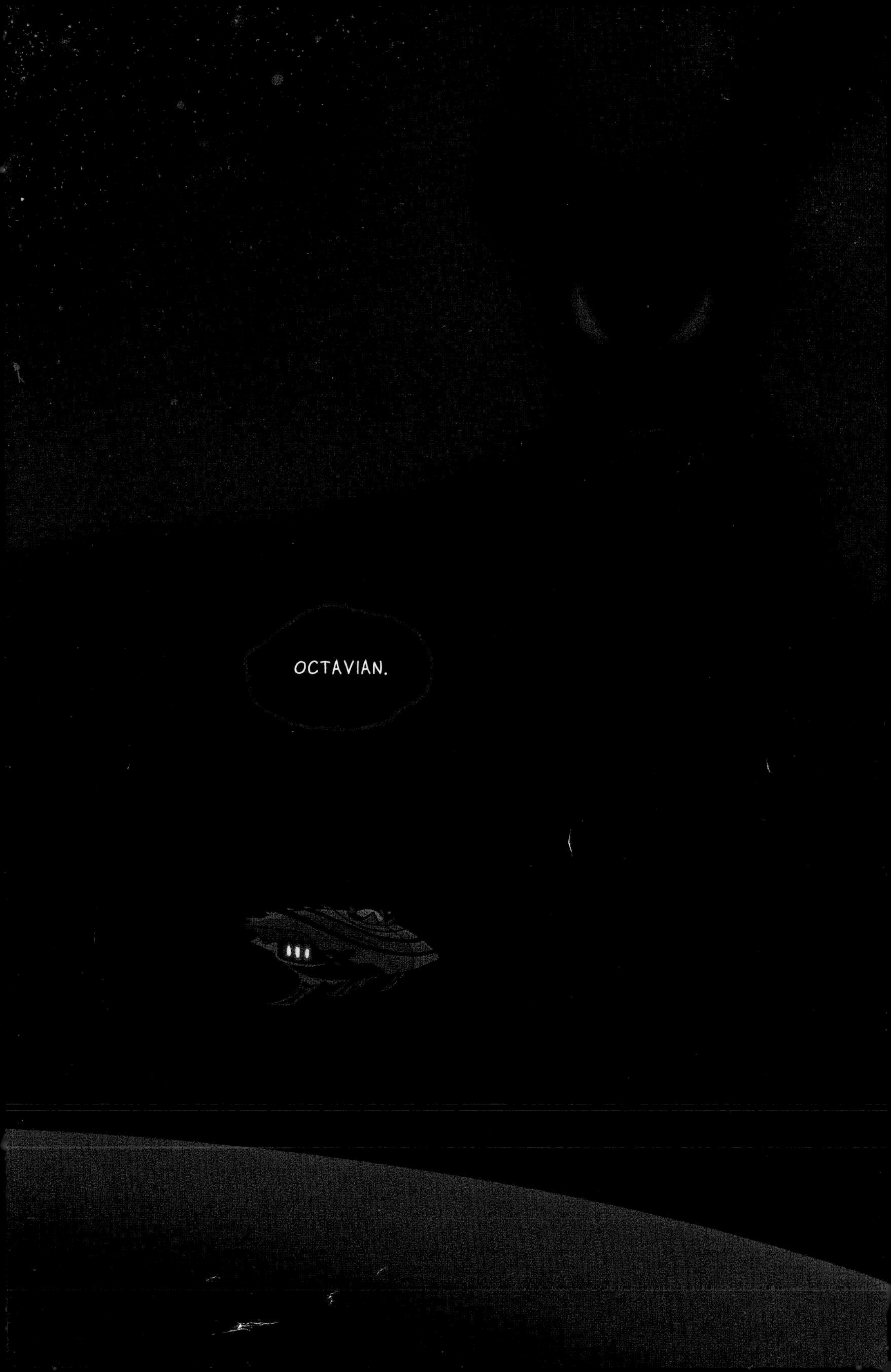
OCTAVIAN.

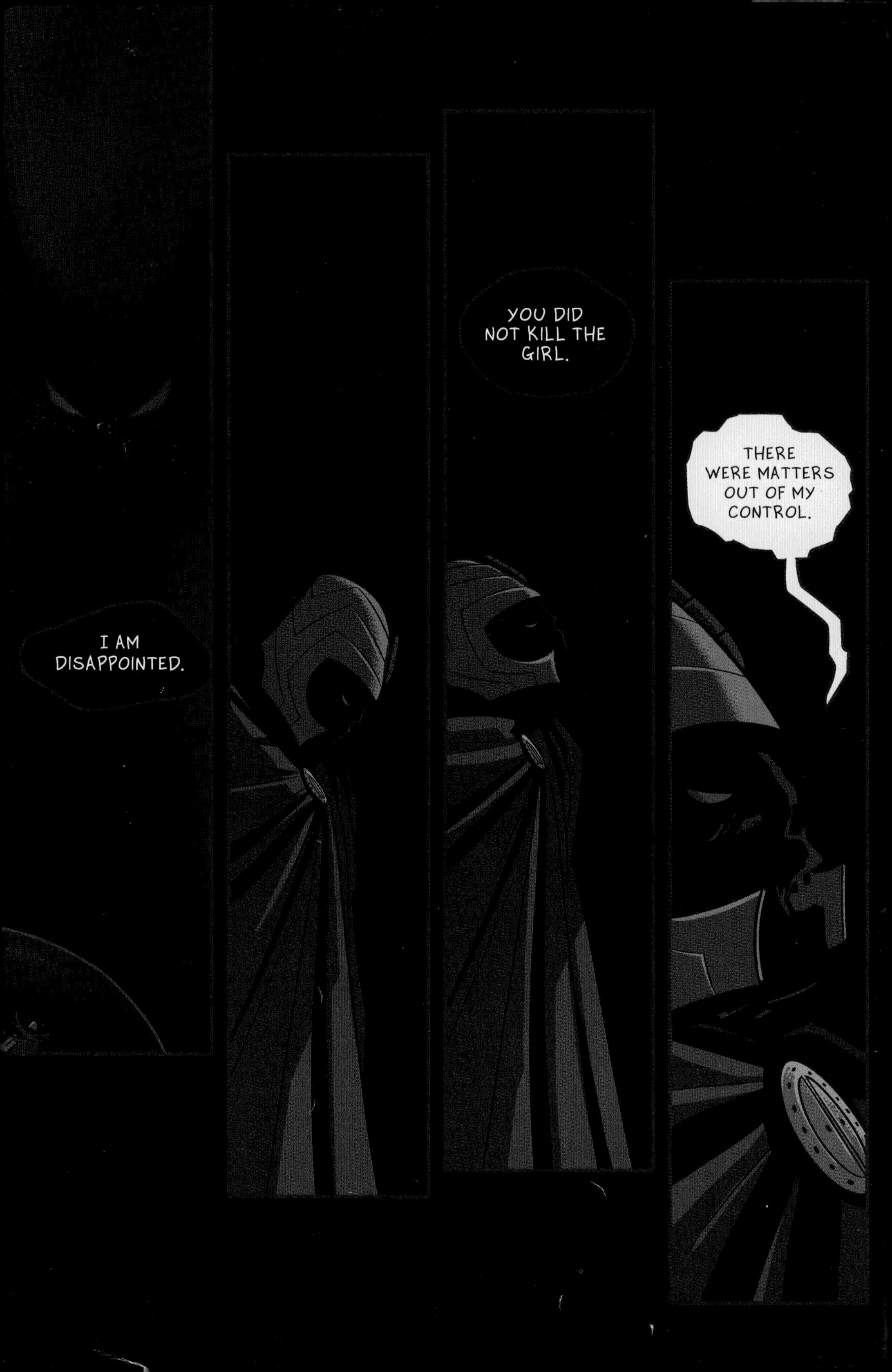
I AM DISAPPOINTED.
YOU DID NOT KILL THE GIRL.
THERE WERE MATTERS OUT OF MY CONTROL.

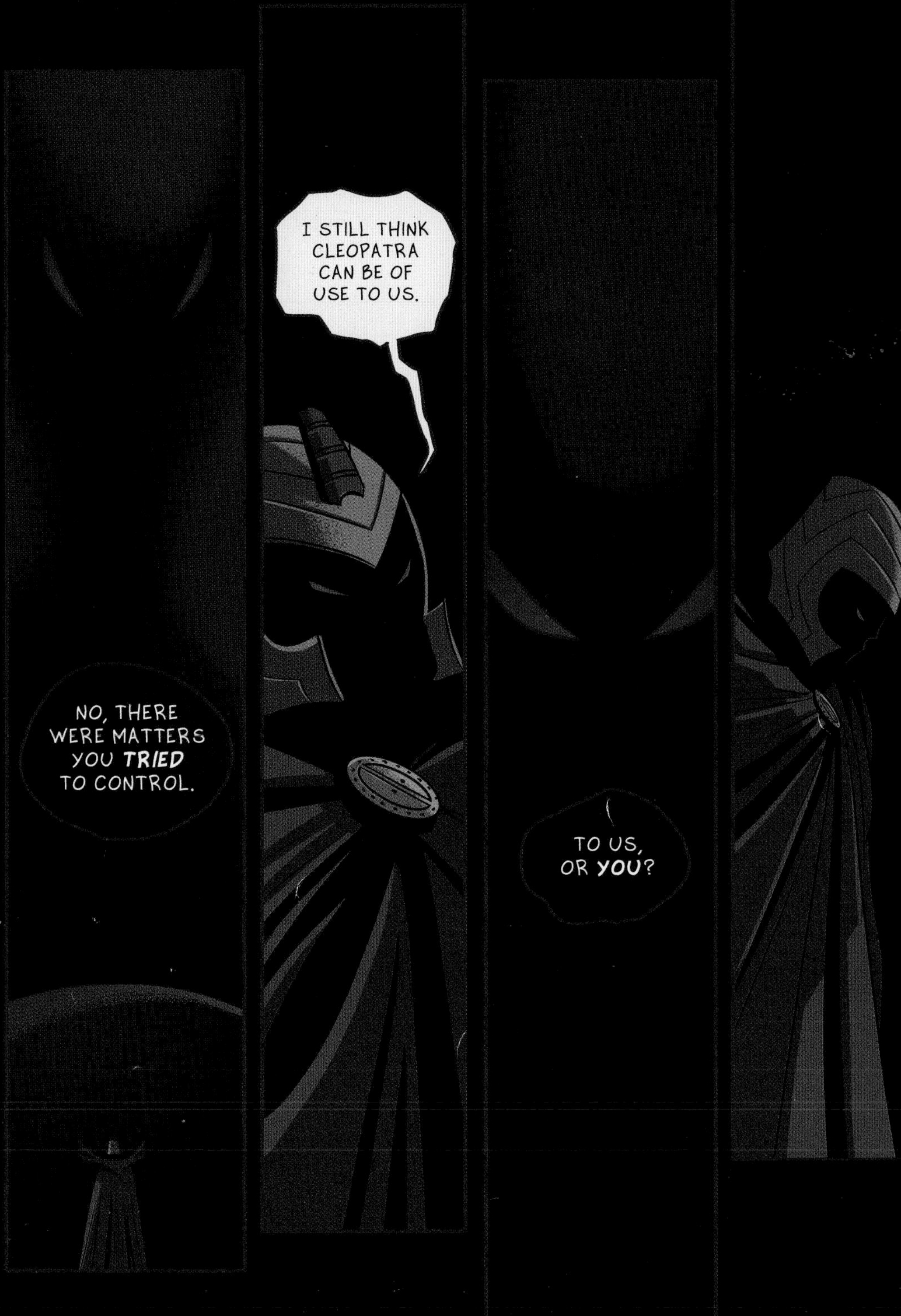

I STILL THINK CLEOPATRA CAN BE OF USE TO US.
NO, THERE WERE MATTERS YOU **TRIED** TO CONTROL.
TO US, OR **YOU**?

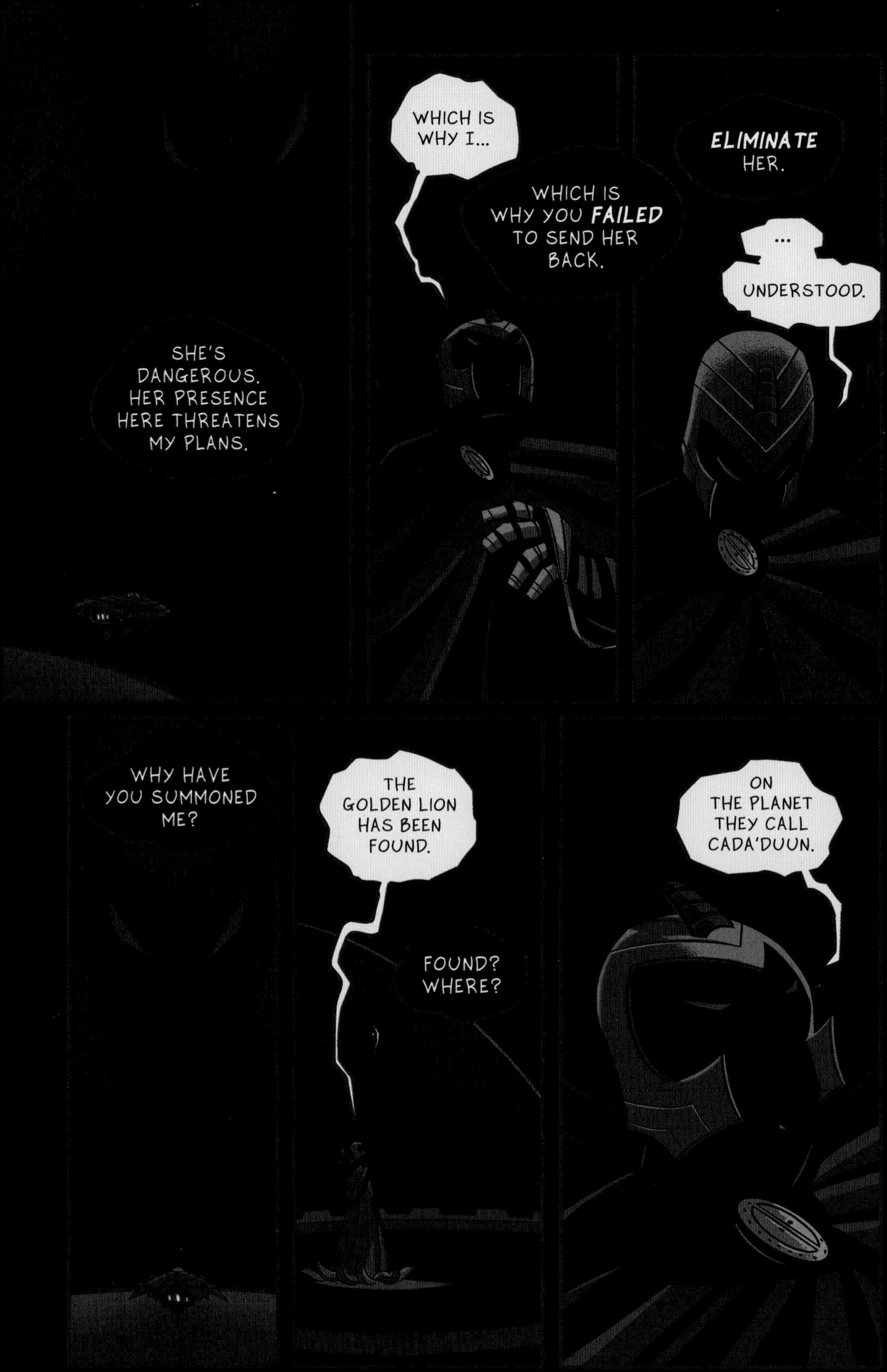
SHE'S DANGEROUS. HER PRESENCE HERE THREATENS MY PLANS.
WHICH IS WHY I...
WHICH IS WHY YOU **FAILED** TO SEND HER BACK.
**ELIMINATE** HER.
...
UNDERSTOOD.
WHY HAVE YOU SUMMONED ME?
THE GOLDEN LION HAS BEEN FOUND.
FOUND? WHERE?
ON THE PLANET THEY CALL CADA'DUUN.

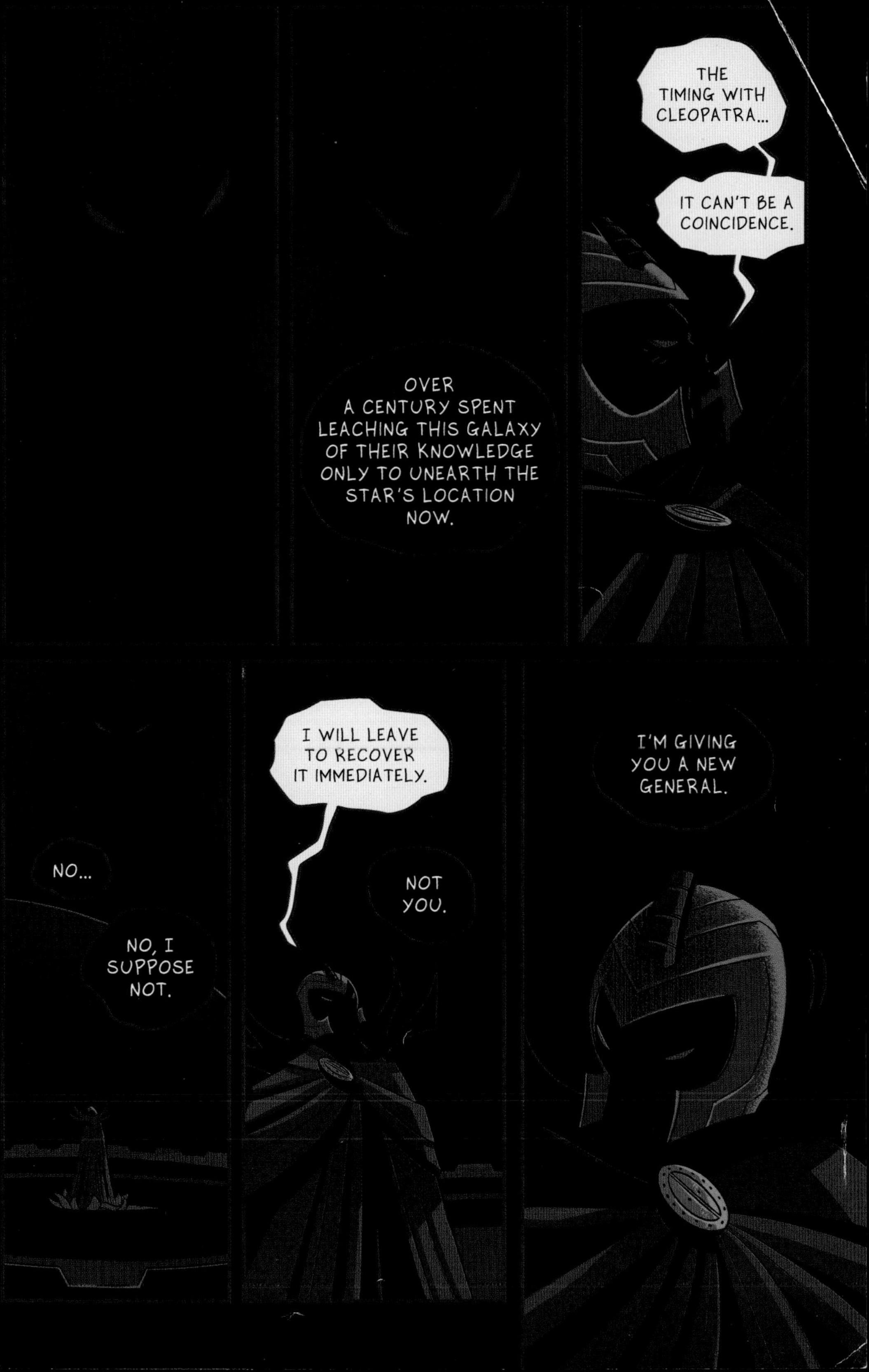
THE TIMING WITH CLEOPATRA...
IT CAN'T BE A COINCIDENCE.
OVER A CENTURY SPENT LEACHING THIS GALAXY OF THEIR KNOWLEDGE ONLY TO UNEARTH THE STAR'S LOCATION NOW.
I WILL LEAVE TO RECOVER IT IMMEDIATELY.
NO...
NO, I SUPPOSE NOT.
NOT YOU.
I'M GIVING YOU A NEW GENERAL.

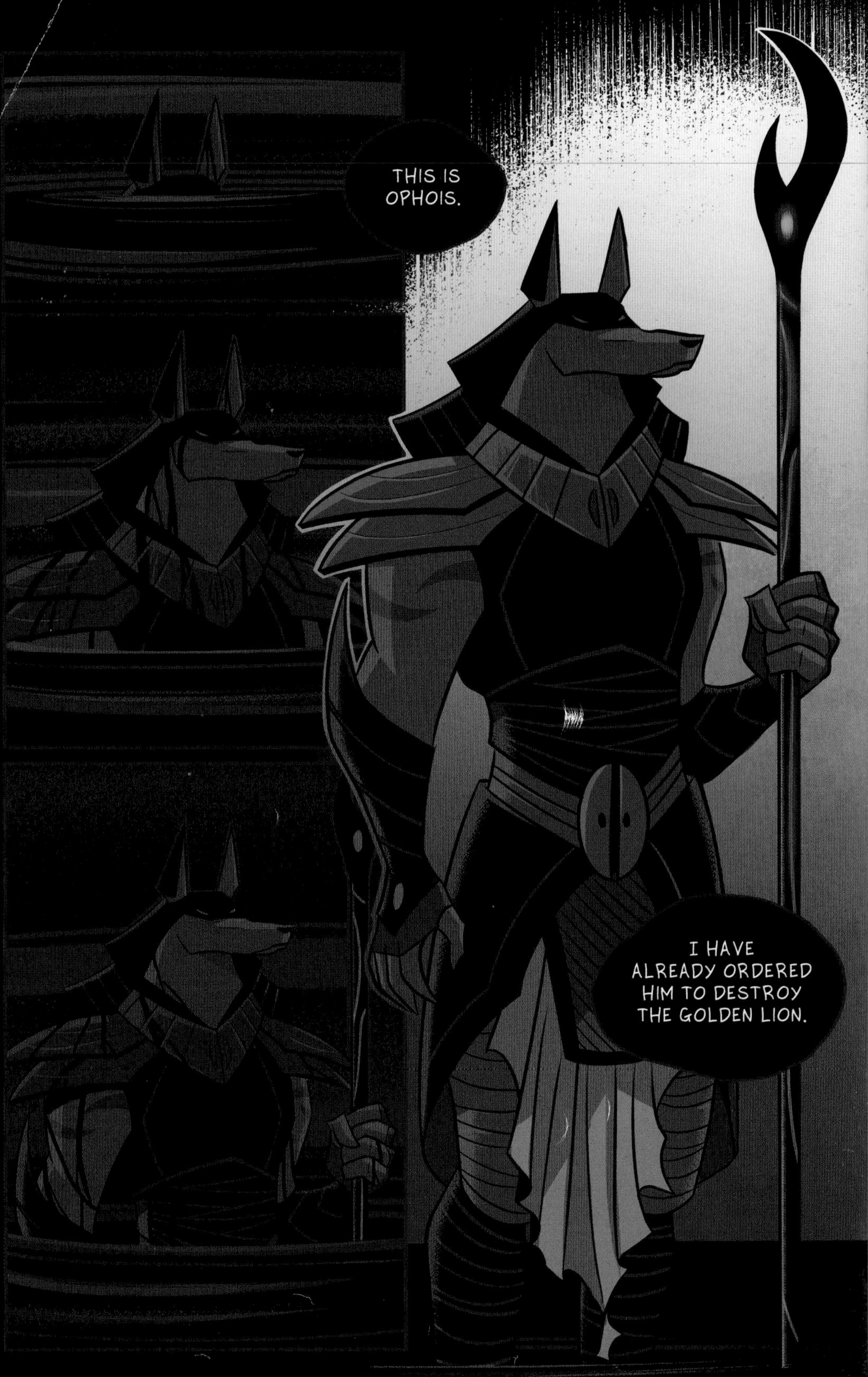
THIS IS OPHOIS.
I HAVE ALREADY ORDERED HIM TO DESTROY THE GOLDEN LION.

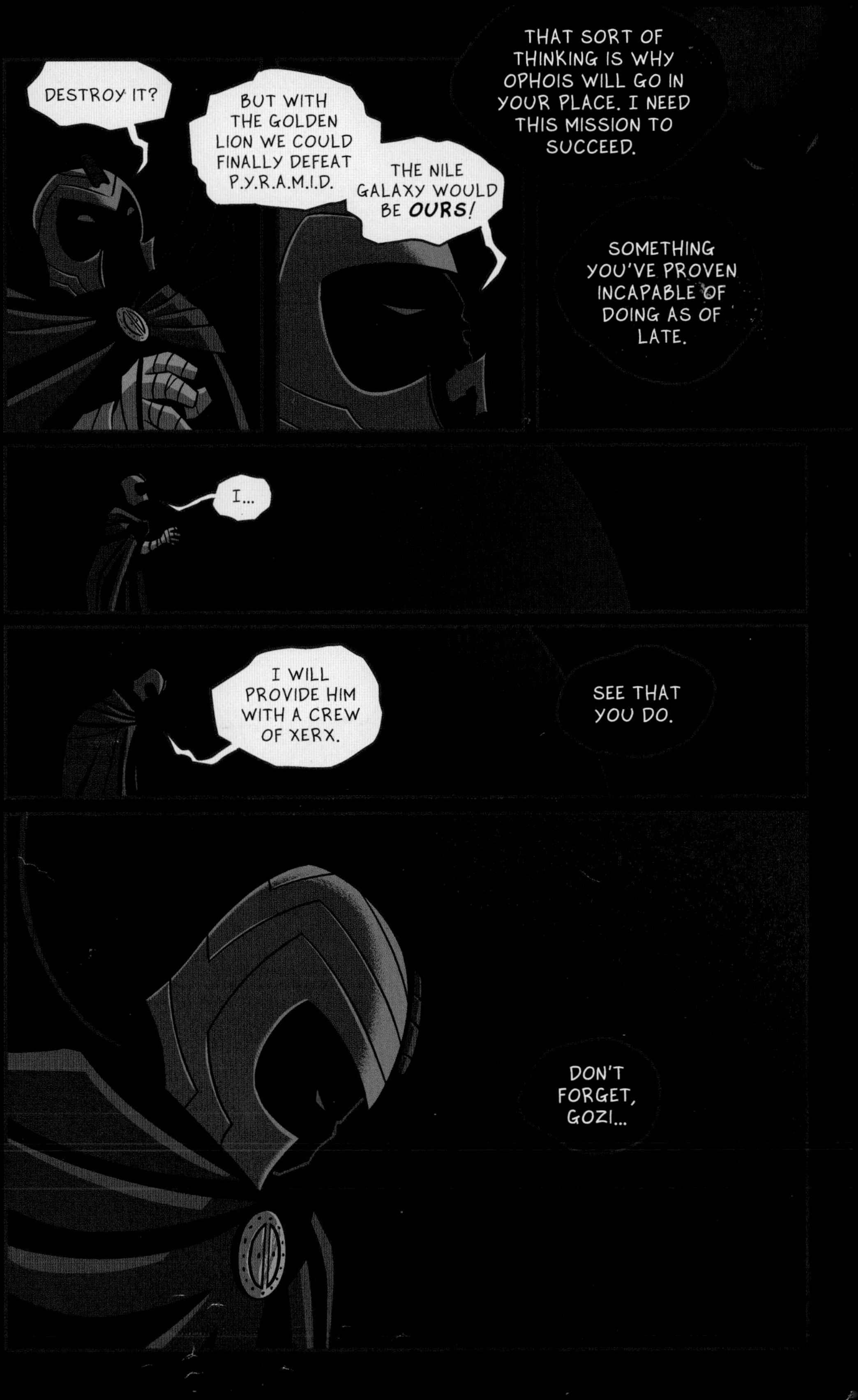
DESTROY IT?
BUT WITH THE GOLDEN LION WE COULD FINALLY DEFEAT P.Y.R.A.M.I.D.
THE NILE GALAXY WOULD BE **OURS!**
THAT SORT OF THINKING IS WHY OPHOIS WILL GO IN YOUR PLACE. I NEED THIS MISSION TO SUCCEED.
SOMETHING YOU'VE PROVEN INCAPABLE OF DOING AS OF LATE.
I...
I WILL PROVIDE HIM WITH A CREW OF XERX.
SEE THAT YOU DO.
DON'T FORGET, GOZI...

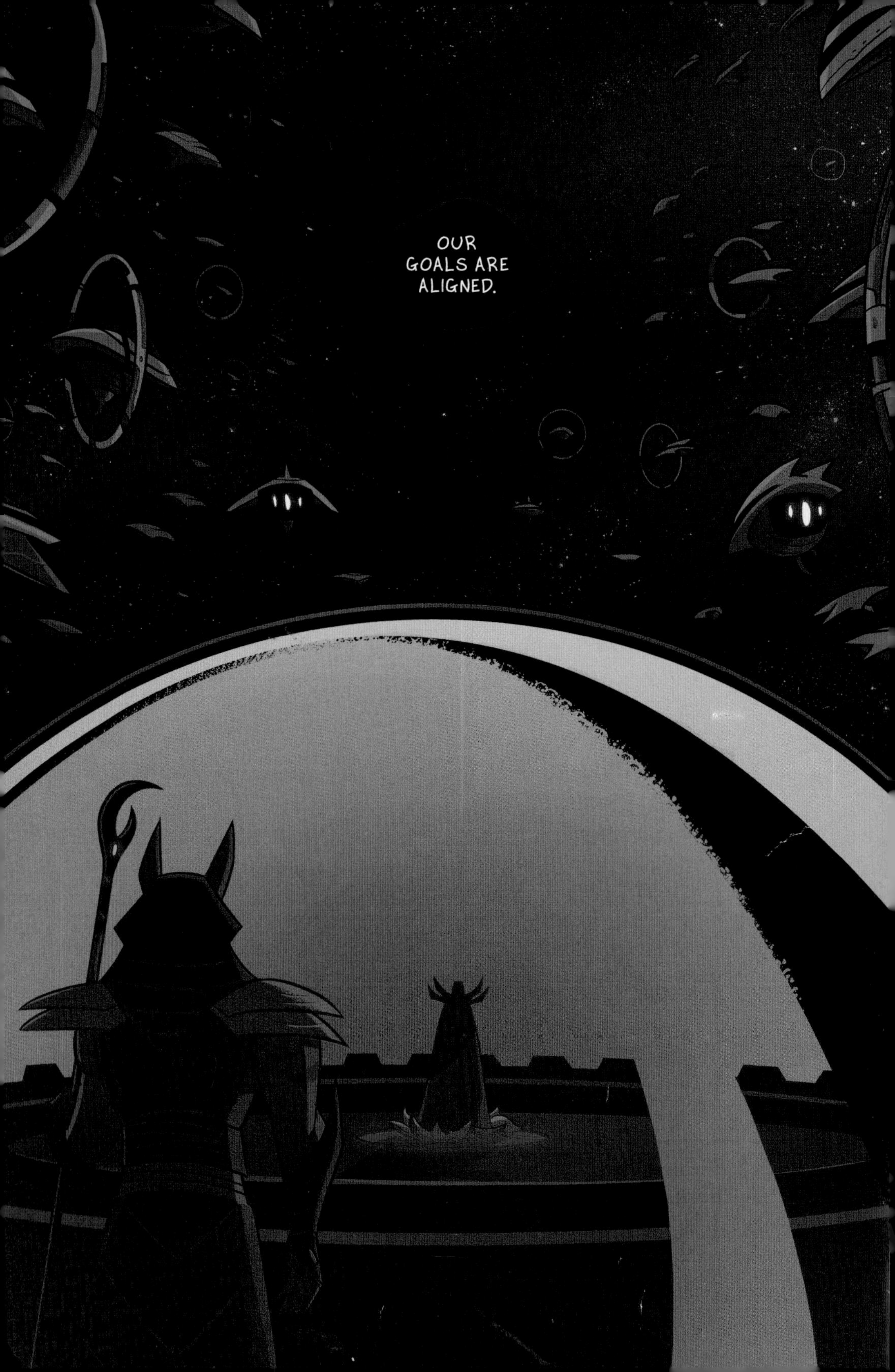
OUR GOALS ARE ALIGNED.

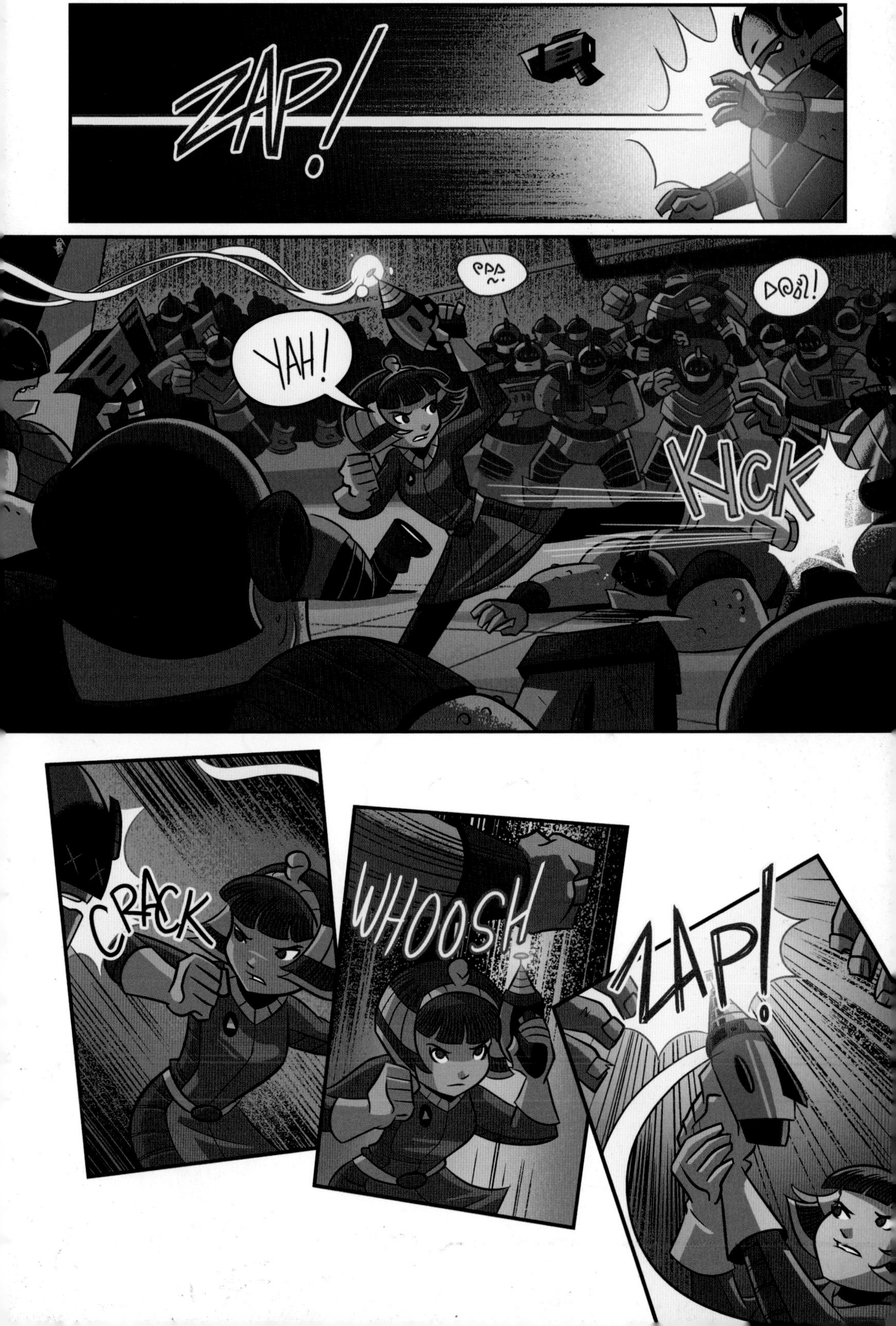
ZAP!
YAH!
KICK
CRACK
WHOOSH
ZAP!

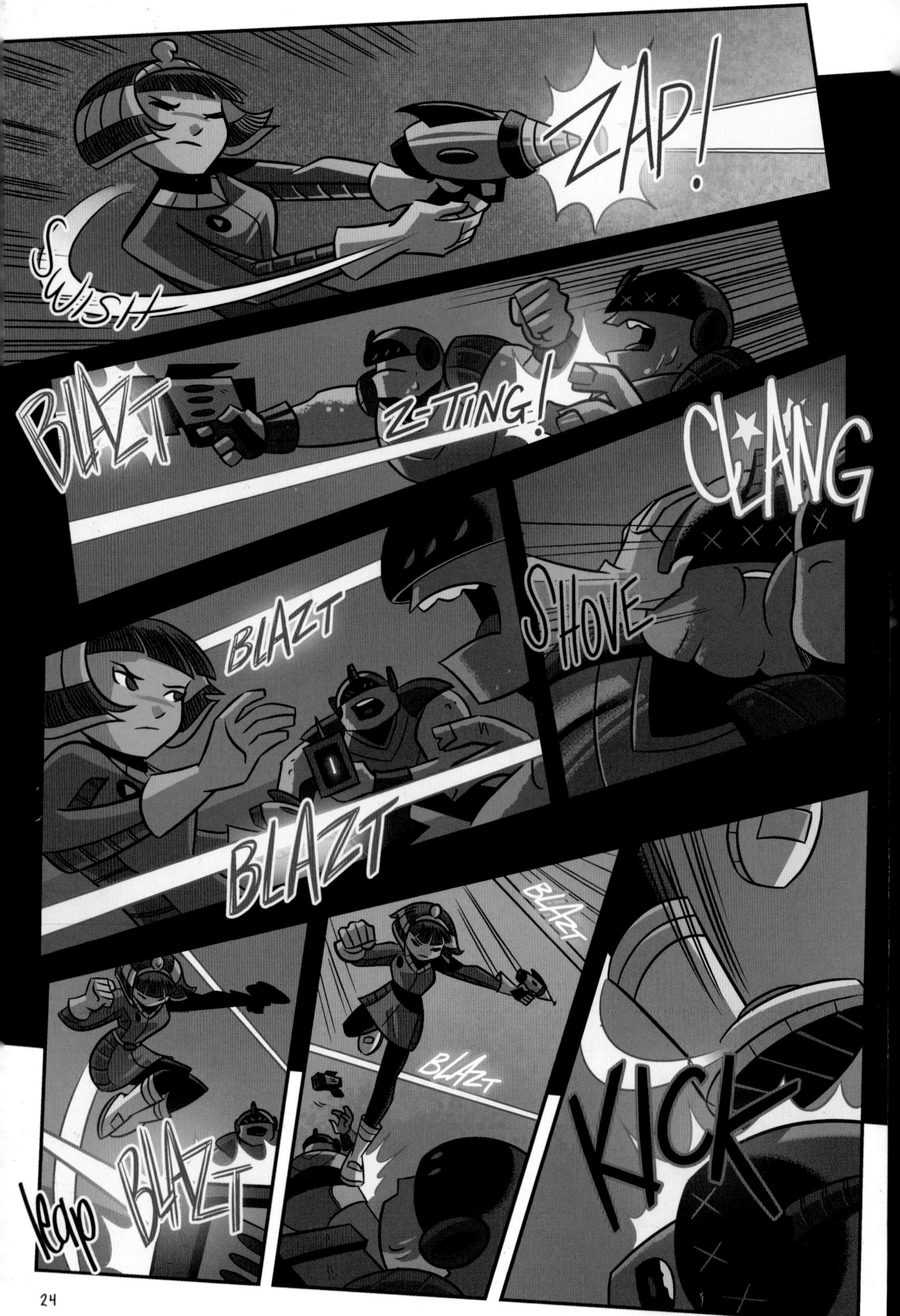
ZAP!
SWISH
BLAZT
Z-TING!
CLANG
BLAZT
SHOVE
BLAZT
BLAZT
BLAZT
leap
BLAZT
KICK

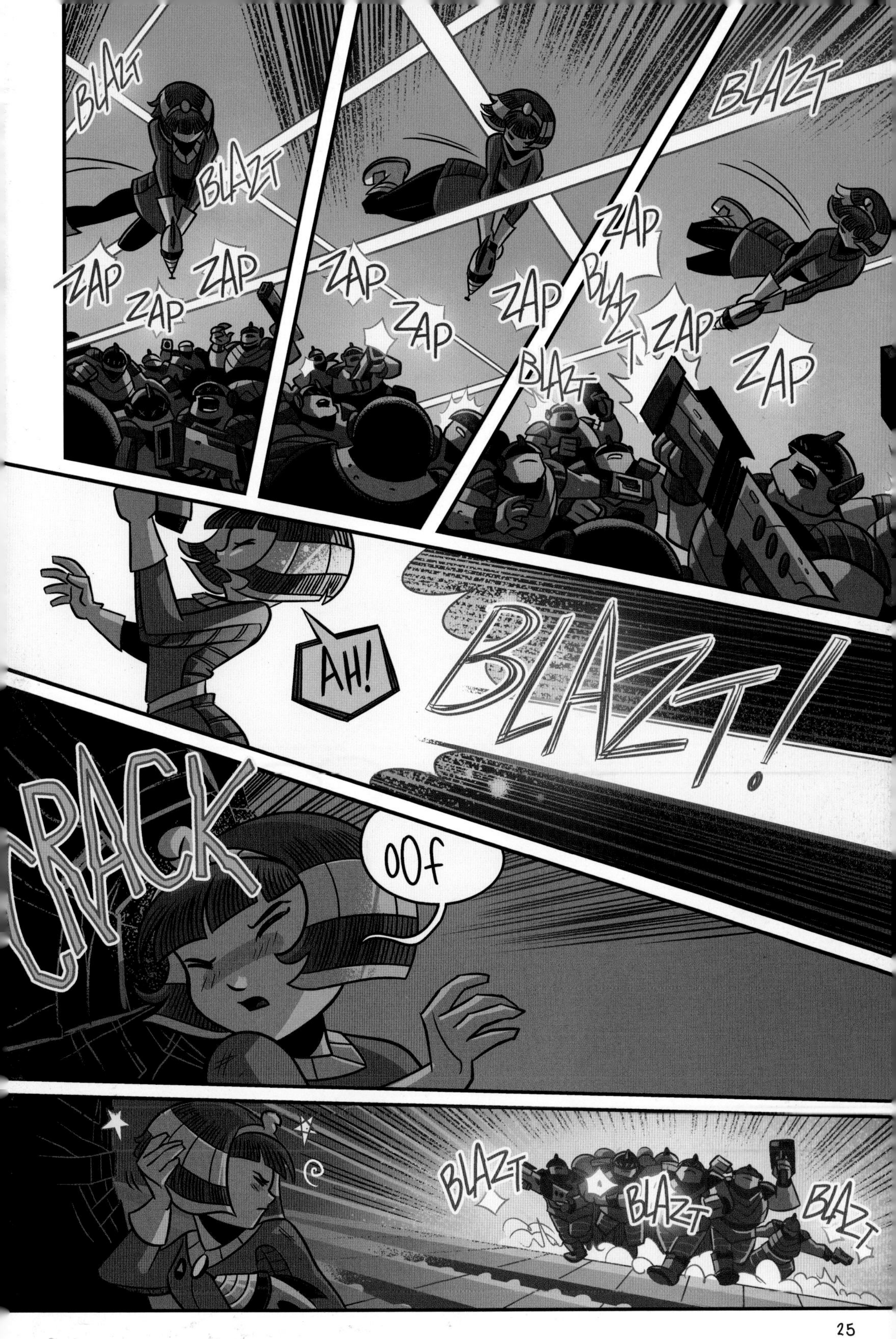
BLAZT
BLAZT
ZAP
ZAP
ZAP
ZAP
ZAP
ZAP
BLAZT
ZAP
BLAZT
ZAP
BLAZT
ZAP
AH!
BLAZT!
CRACK
OOF
BLAZT
BLAZT
BLAZT

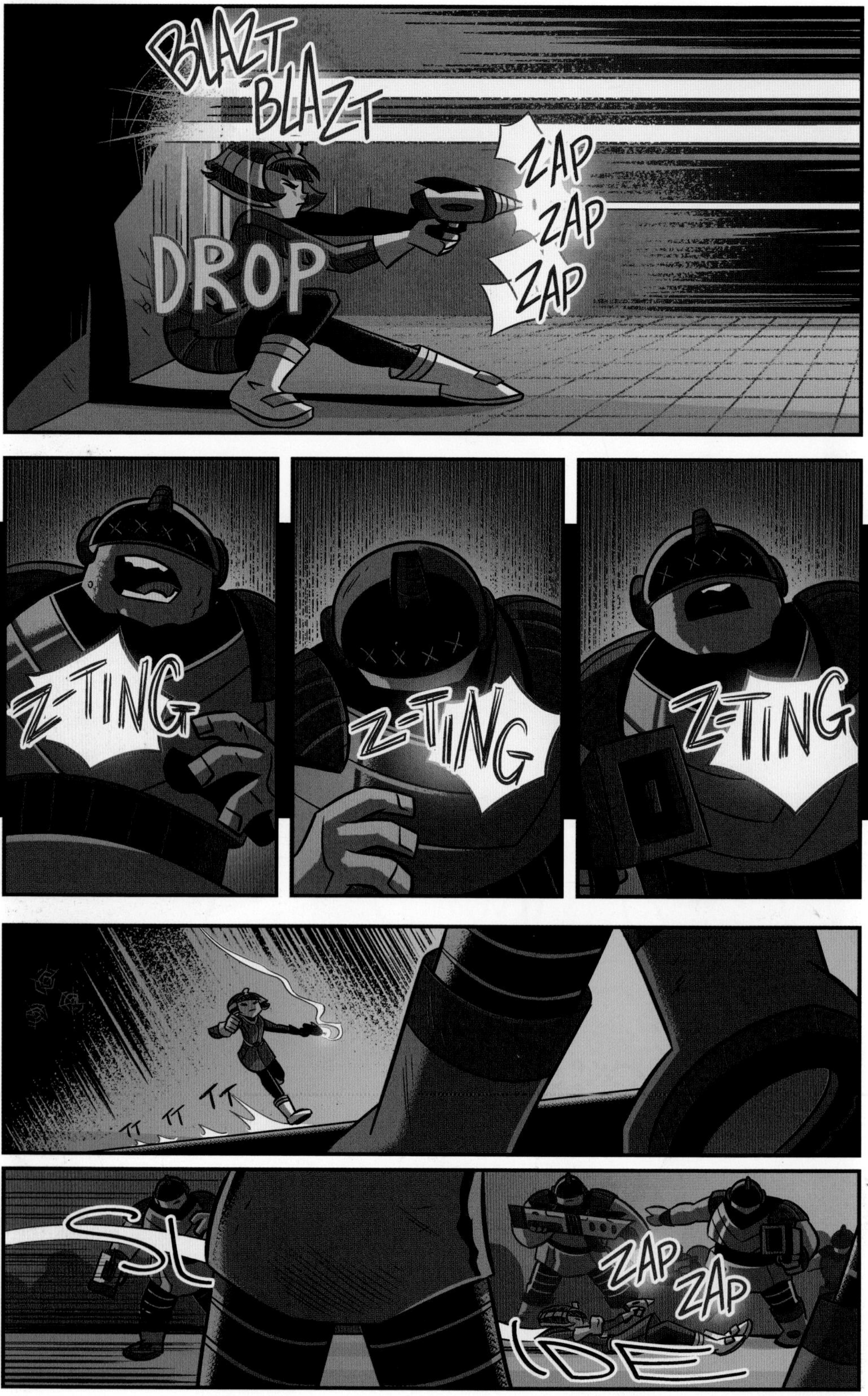
BLAZT
BLAZT
ZAP
ZAP
ZAP
DROP
Z-TING
Z-TING
Z-TING
TT TT TT
SL
ZAP
ZAP
IDE

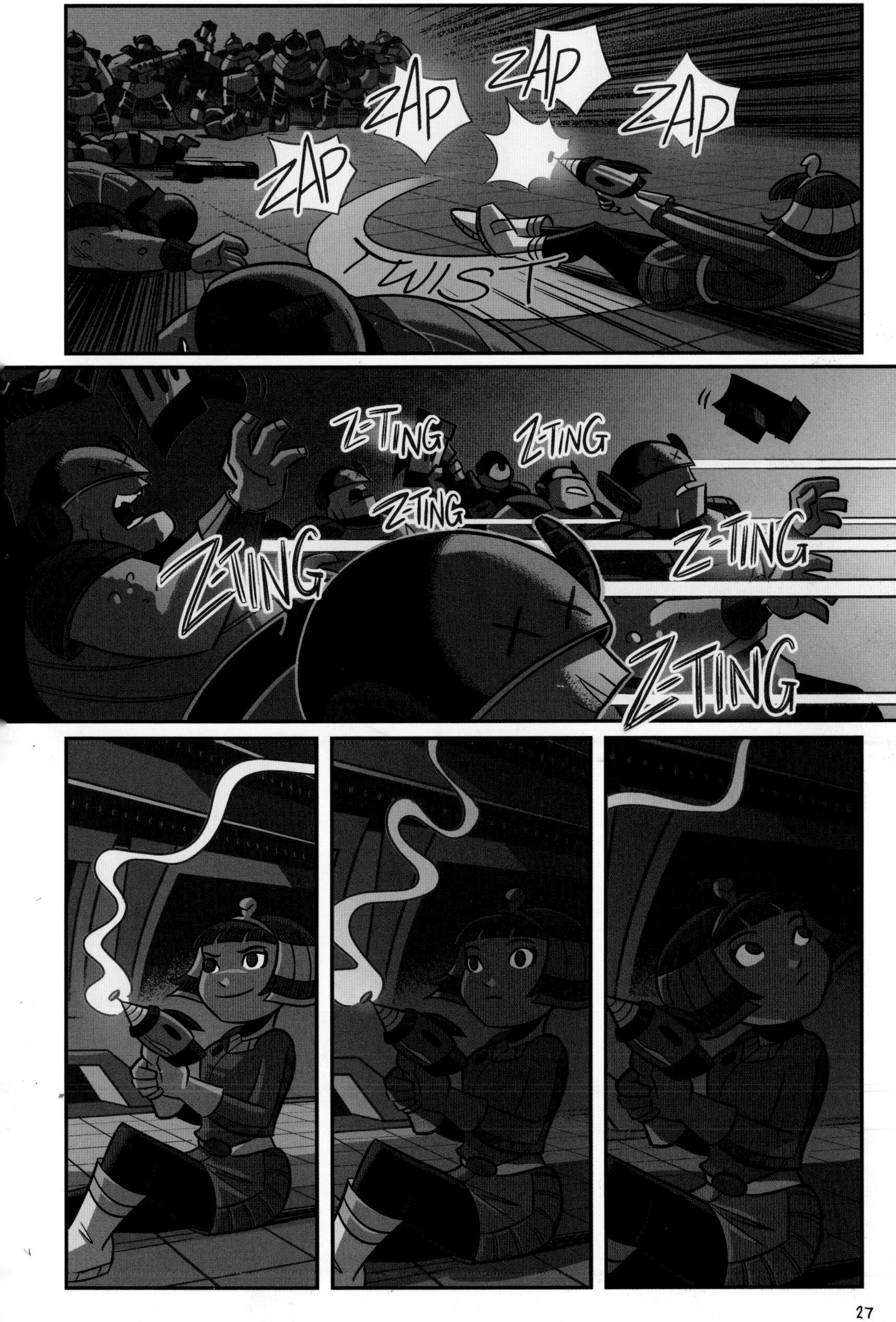
ZAP
ZAP
ZAP
ZAP
TWIST
Z-TING
ZTING
ZTING
ZTING
Z-TING
ZTING

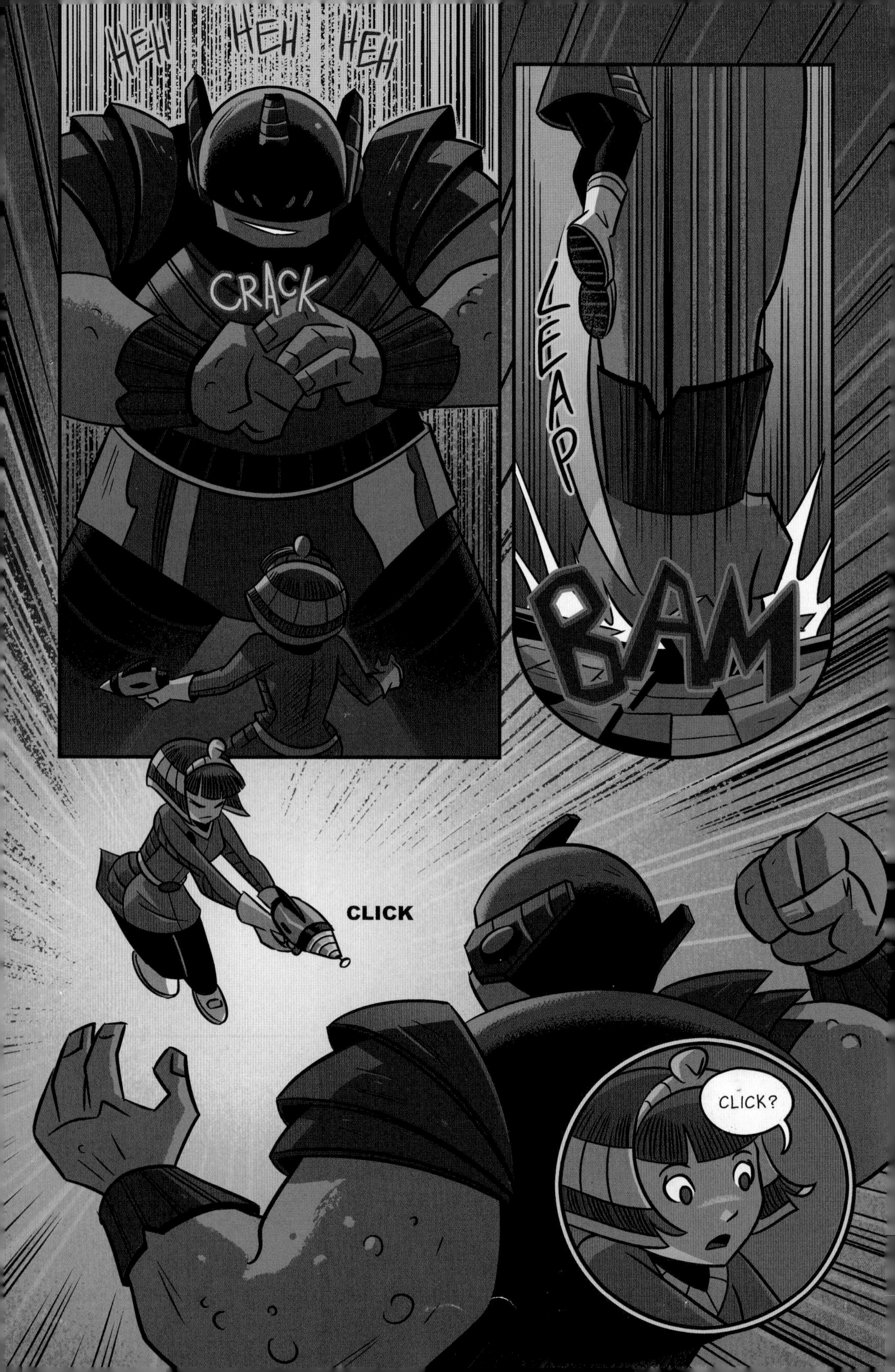
HEH HEH HEH
CRACK
LEAP
BAM
CLICK
CLICK?

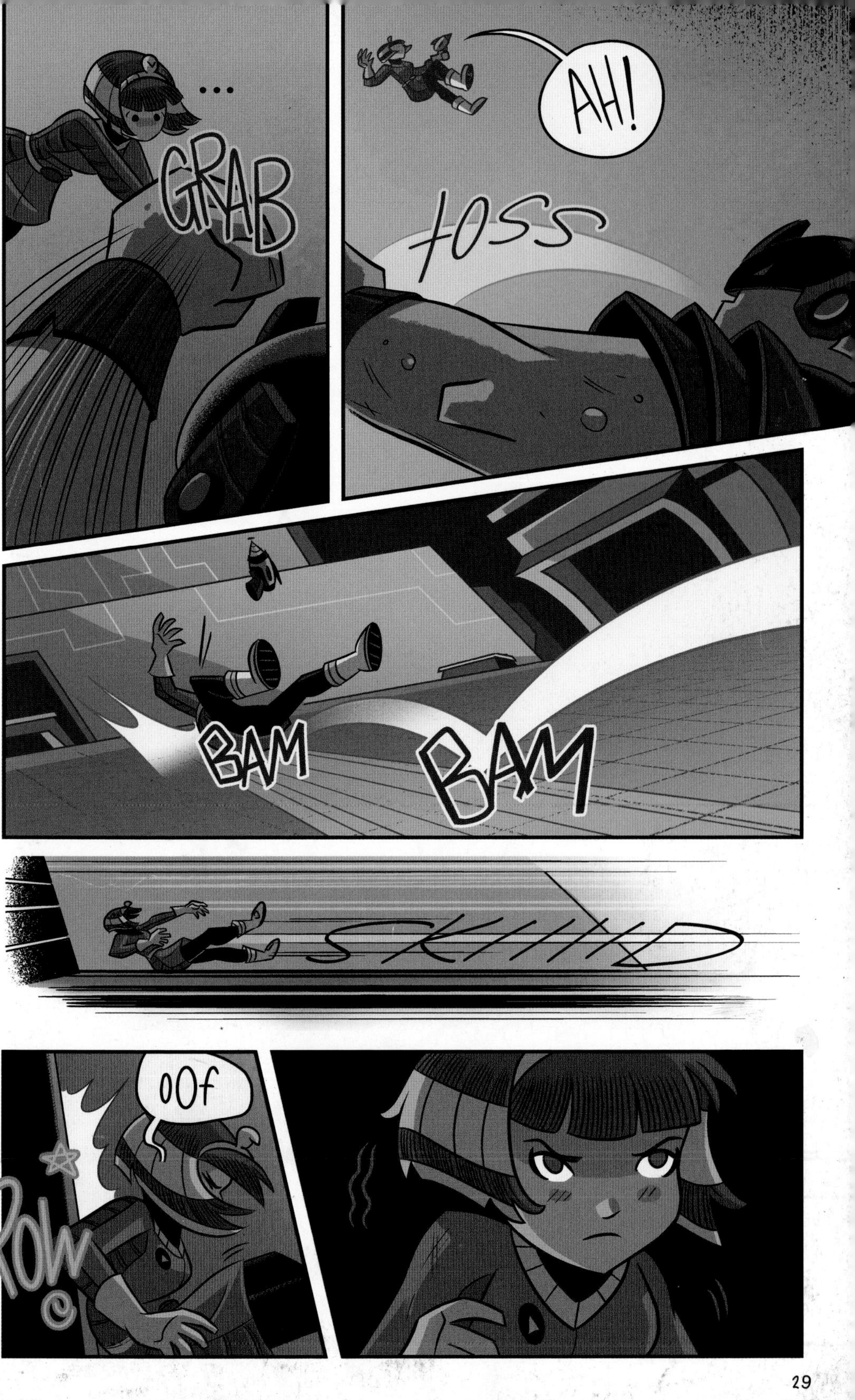
...
GRAB
AH!
TOSS
BAM
BAM
SKIIIID
OOf
POW

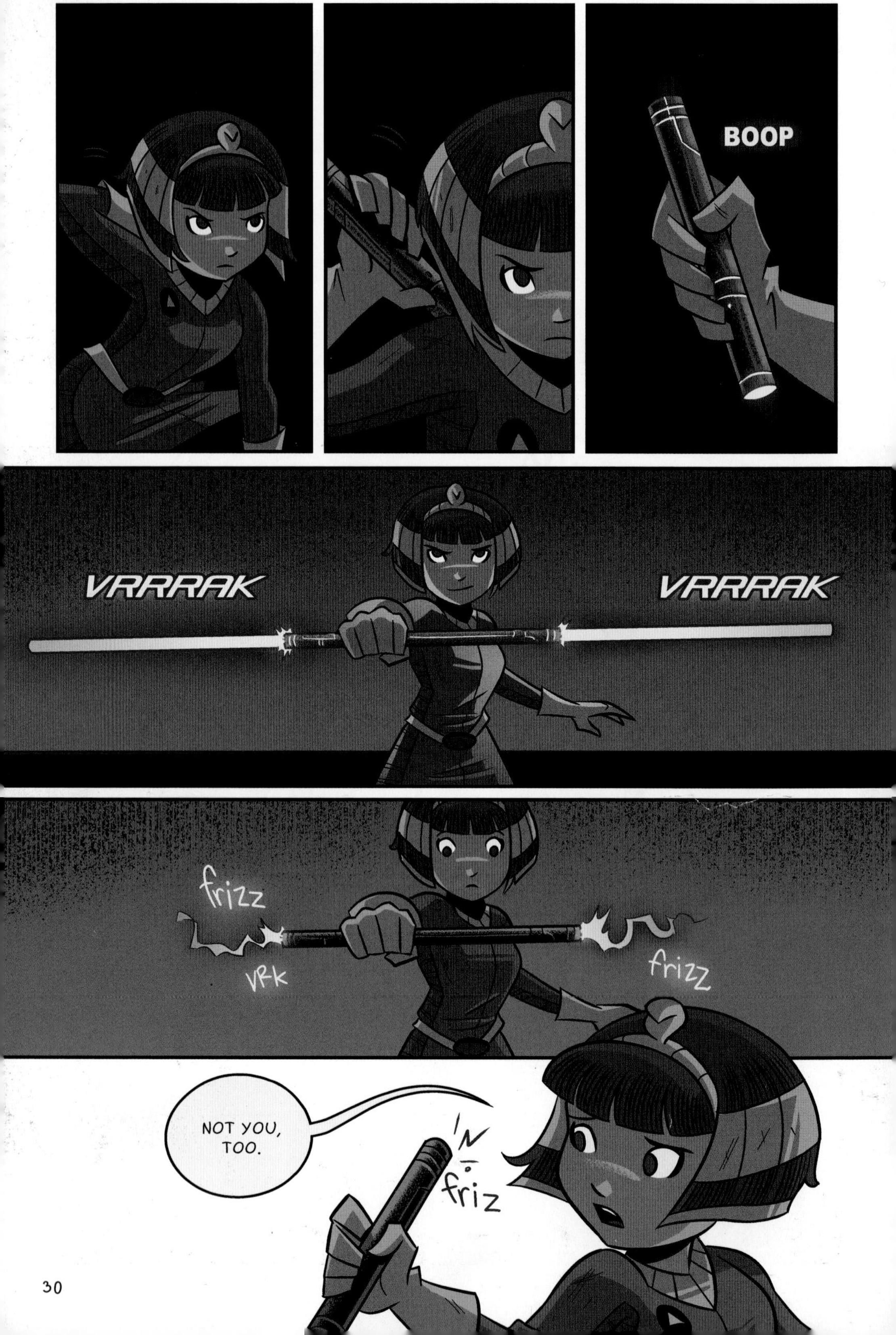
BOOP
VRRRAK
VRRRAK
frizz
VRK
frizz
NOT YOU, TOO.
friz

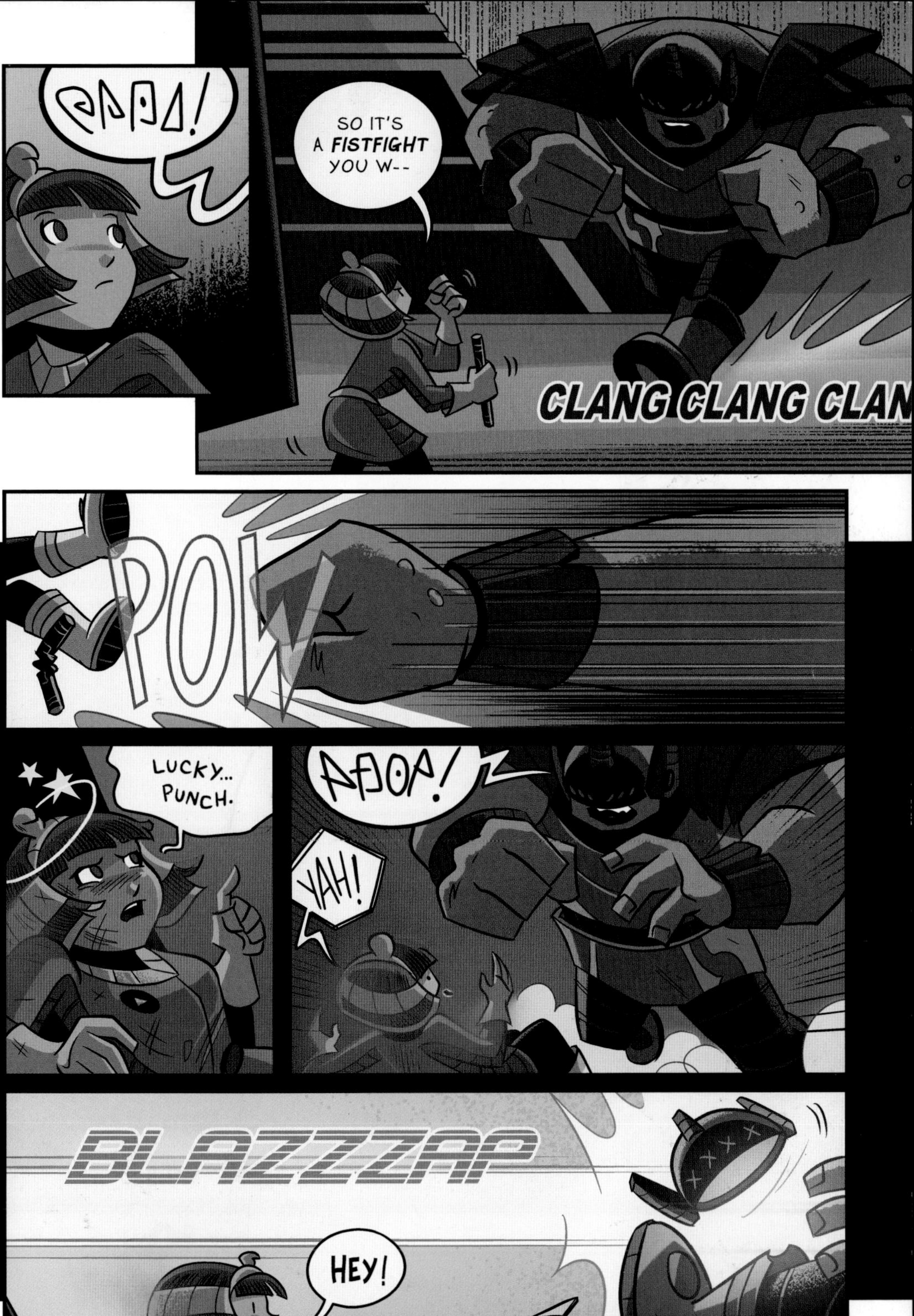
SO IT'S A **FISTFIGHT** YOU W--
CLANG CLANG CLAN
POW
LUCKY... PUNCH.
YAH!
BLAZZZAP
HEY!

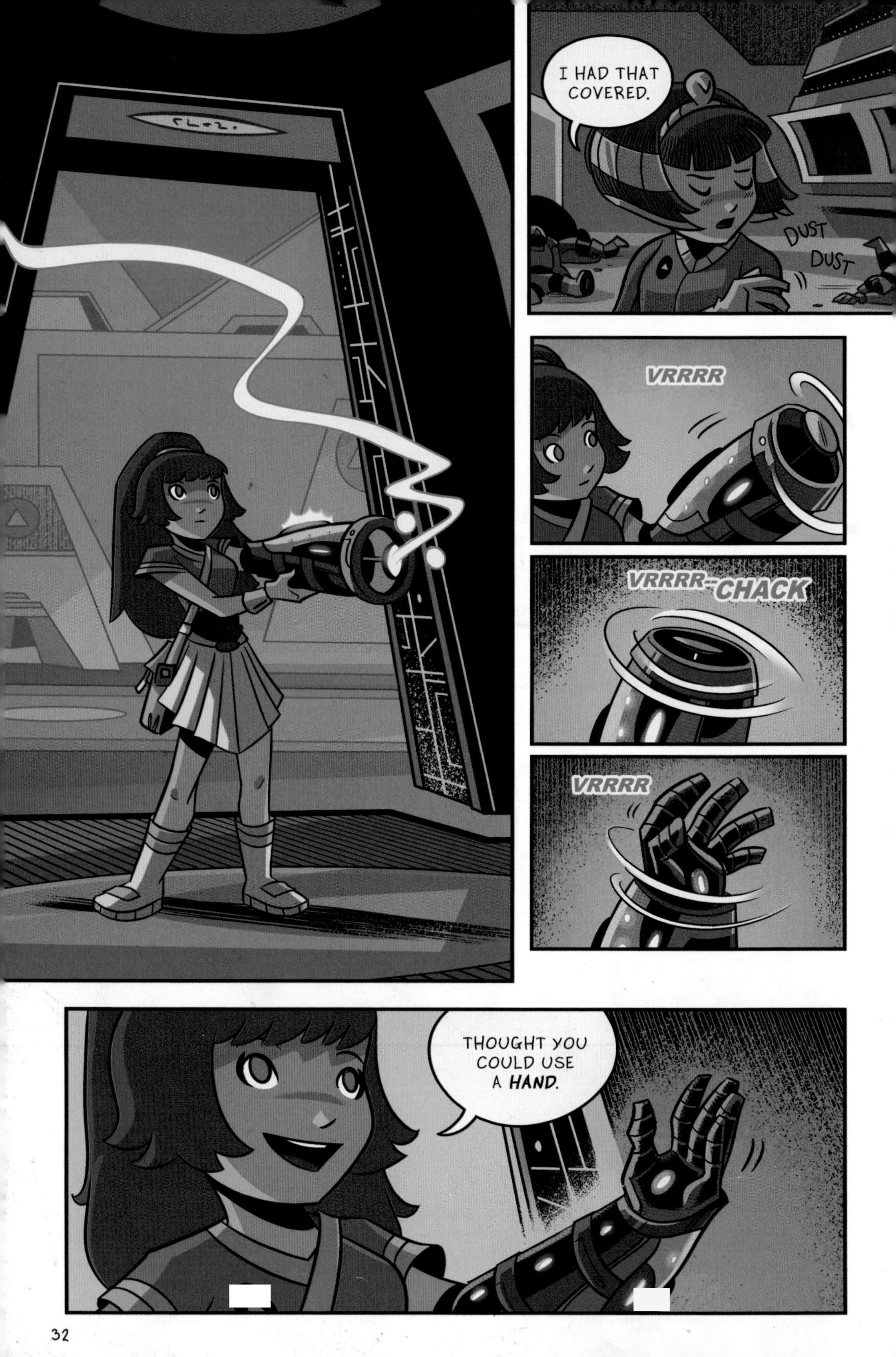
I HAD THAT COVERED.
DUST
DUST
VRRRR
VRRRR-CHACK
VRRRR
THOUGHT YOU COULD USE A **HAND**.

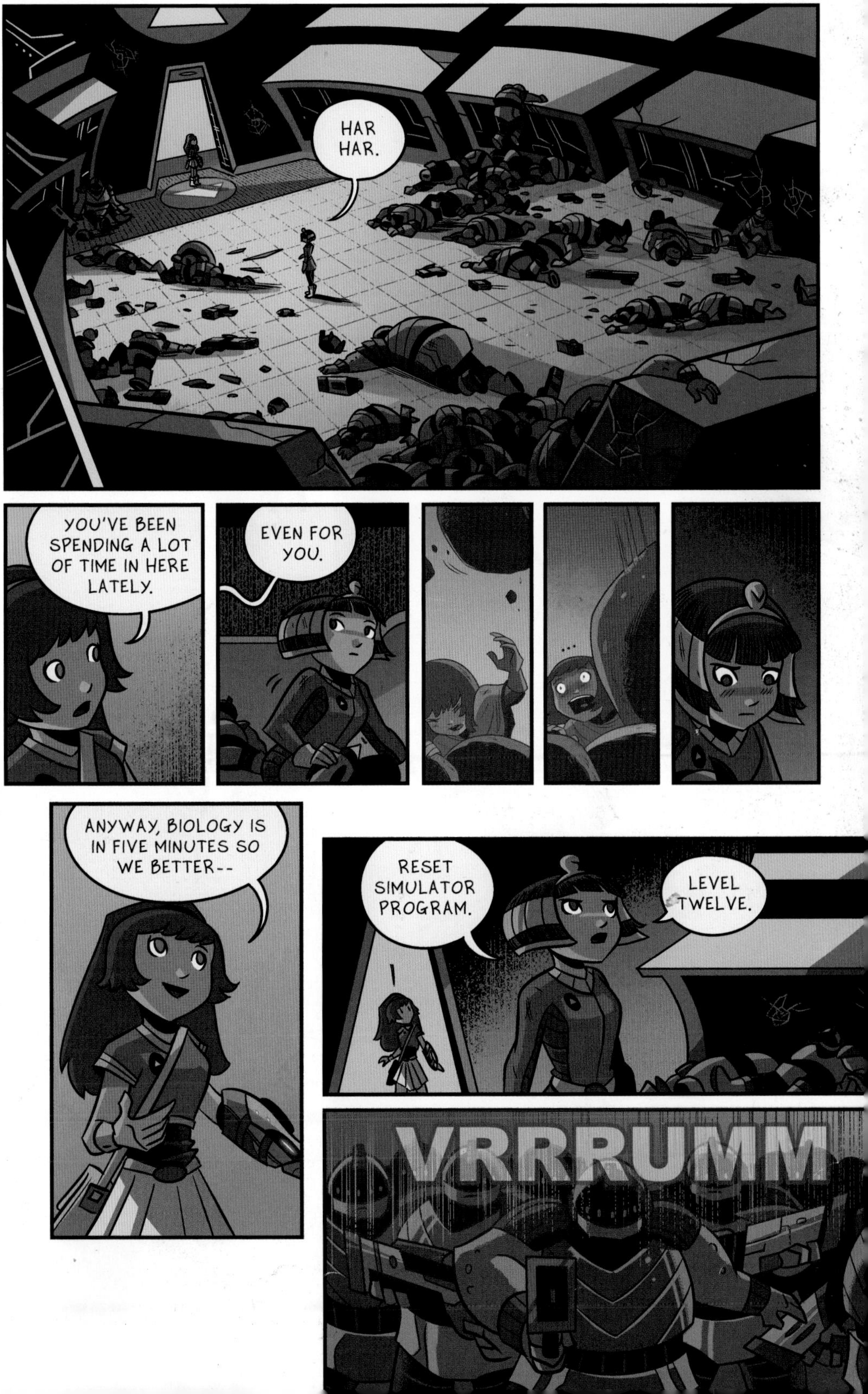
HAR HAR.
YOU'VE BEEN SPENDING A LOT OF TIME IN HERE LATELY.
EVEN FOR YOU.
...
ANYWAY, BIOLOGY IS IN FIVE MINUTES SO WE BETTER--
RESET SIMULATOR PROGRAM.
LEVEL TWELVE.
!
VRRRUMM

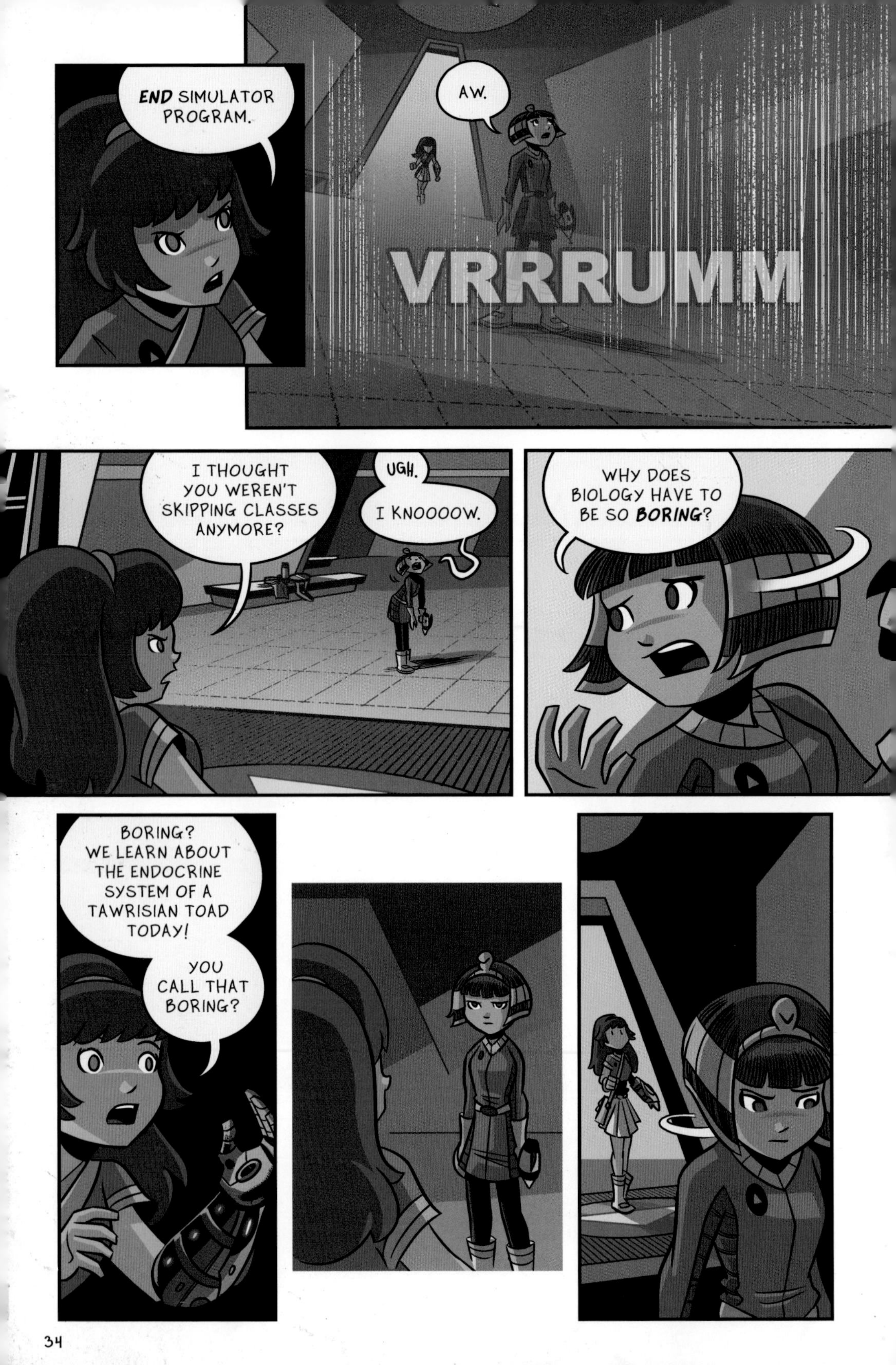
END SIMULATOR PROGRAM.
AW.
VRRRUMM
I THOUGHT YOU WEREN'T SKIPPING CLASSES ANYMORE?
UGH.
I KNOOOOW.
WHY DOES BIOLOGY HAVE TO BE SO BORING?
BORING? WE LEARN ABOUT THE ENDOCRINE SYSTEM OF A TAWRISIAN TOAD TODAY!
YOU CALL THAT BORING?

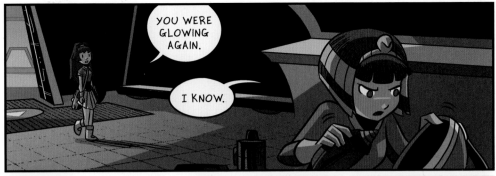

YOU WERE GLOWING AGAIN.

I KNOW.

KHENSU'S BEEN OFF PROBATION FOR A WEEK NOW. MAYBE...

MAYBE WHAT?

YOU GOING TO *SEE* HIM?

WHAT DO YOU THINK?

fizz

STUff

I KNOW YOU'RE ANGRY ABOUT HIM KEEPING THINGS FROM YOU, BUT IT'S BEEN SIX MONTHS SINCE HYKOSIS, CLEO. YOU CAN'T AVOID TALKING TO HIM FOREVER.

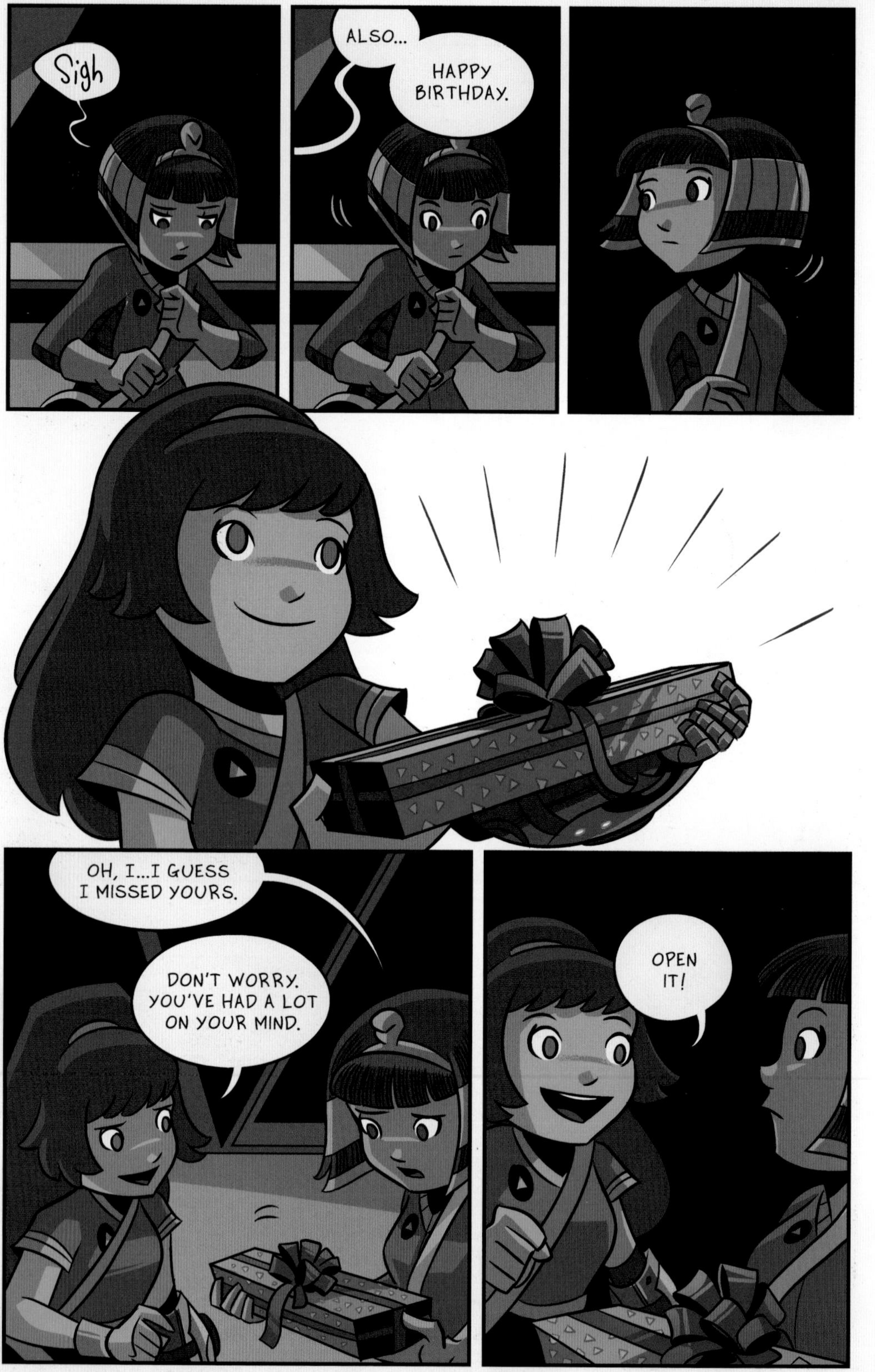
Sigh
ALSO...
HAPPY BIRTHDAY.
OH, I...I GUESS I MISSED YOURS.
DON'T WORRY. YOU'VE HAD A LOT ON YOUR MIND.
OPEN IT!

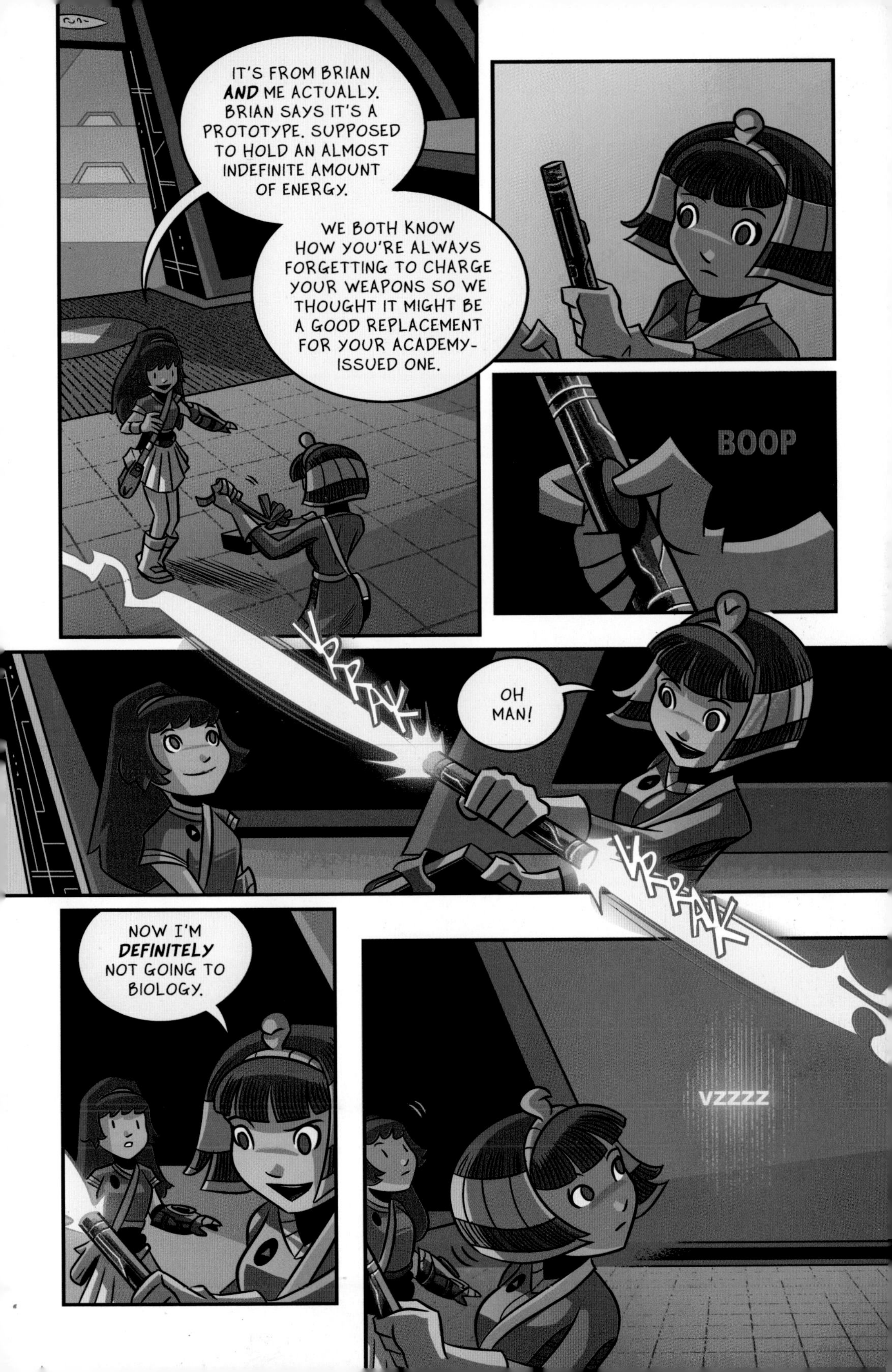
IT'S FROM BRIAN **AND** ME ACTUALLY. BRIAN SAYS IT'S A PROTOTYPE. SUPPOSED TO HOLD AN ALMOST INDEFINITE AMOUNT OF ENERGY.
WE BOTH KNOW HOW YOU'RE ALWAYS FORGETTING TO CHARGE YOUR WEAPONS SO WE THOUGHT IT MIGHT BE A GOOD REPLACEMENT FOR YOUR ACADEMY-ISSUED ONE.
BOOP
VRRRAK
OH MAN!
VRRRAK
NOW I'M ***DEFINITELY*** NOT GOING TO BIOLOGY.
VZZZZ

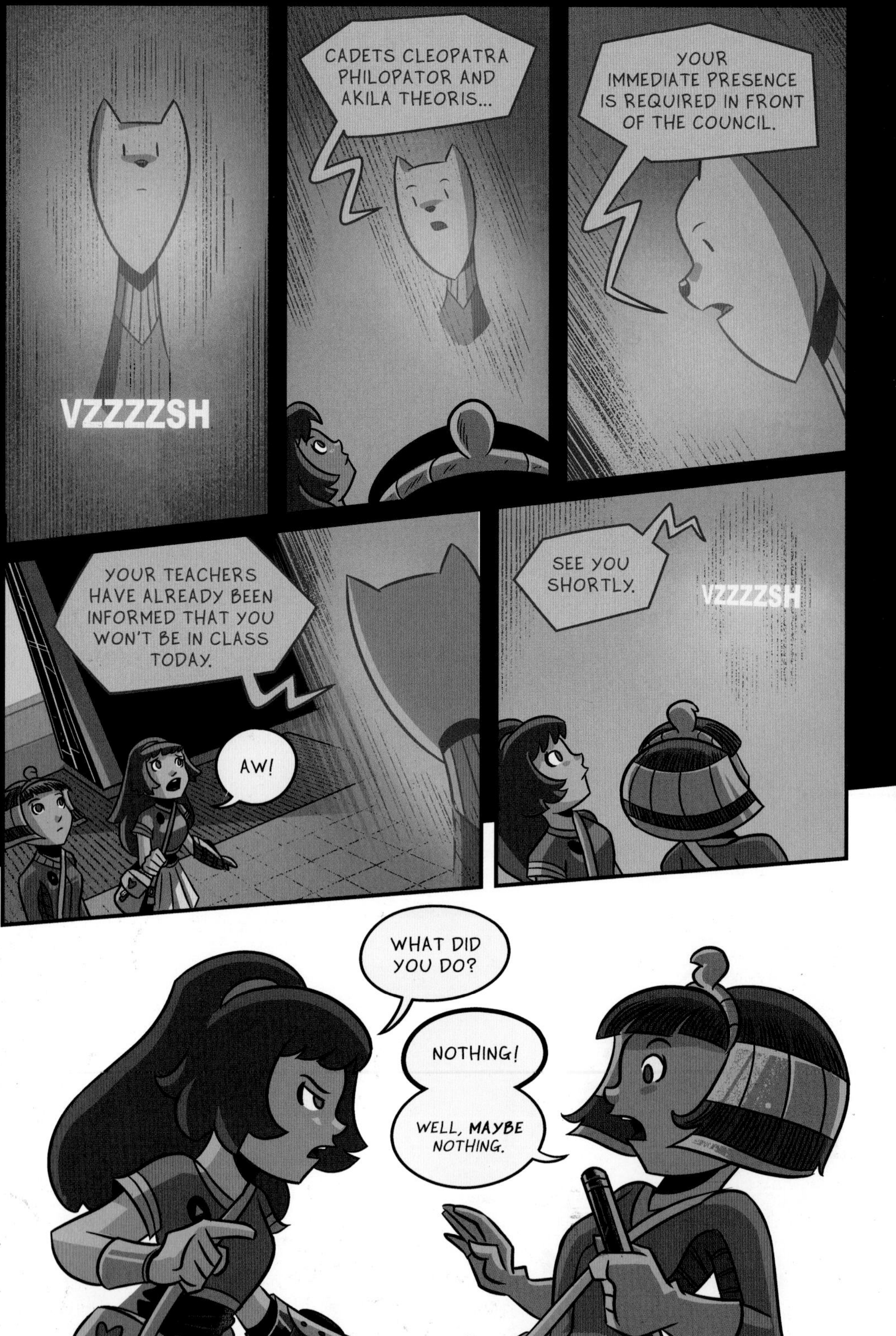
VZZZZSH
CADETS CLEOPATRA PHILOPATOR AND AKILA THEORIS...
YOUR IMMEDIATE PRESENCE IS REQUIRED IN FRONT OF THE COUNCIL.
YOUR TEACHERS HAVE ALREADY BEEN INFORMED THAT YOU WON'T BE IN CLASS TODAY.
AW!
SEE YOU SHORTLY.
VZZZZSH
WHAT DID YOU DO?
NOTHING!
WELL, **MAYBE** NOTHING.

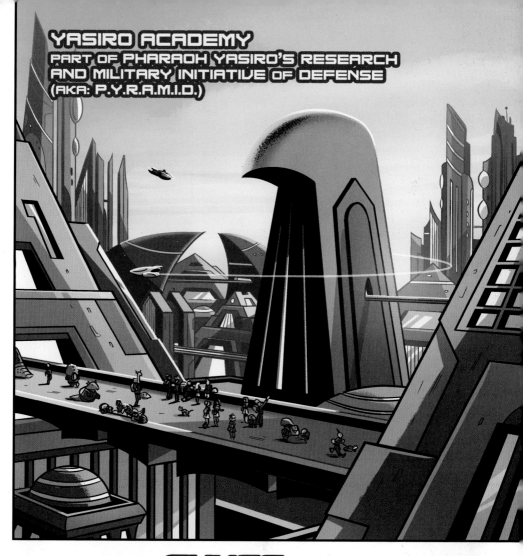

YASIRO ACADEMY
PART OF PHARAOH YASIRO'S RESEARCH
AND MILITARY INITIATIVE OF DEFENSE
(AKA: P.Y.R.A.M.I.D.)

SHUFF

OH MY
RA!

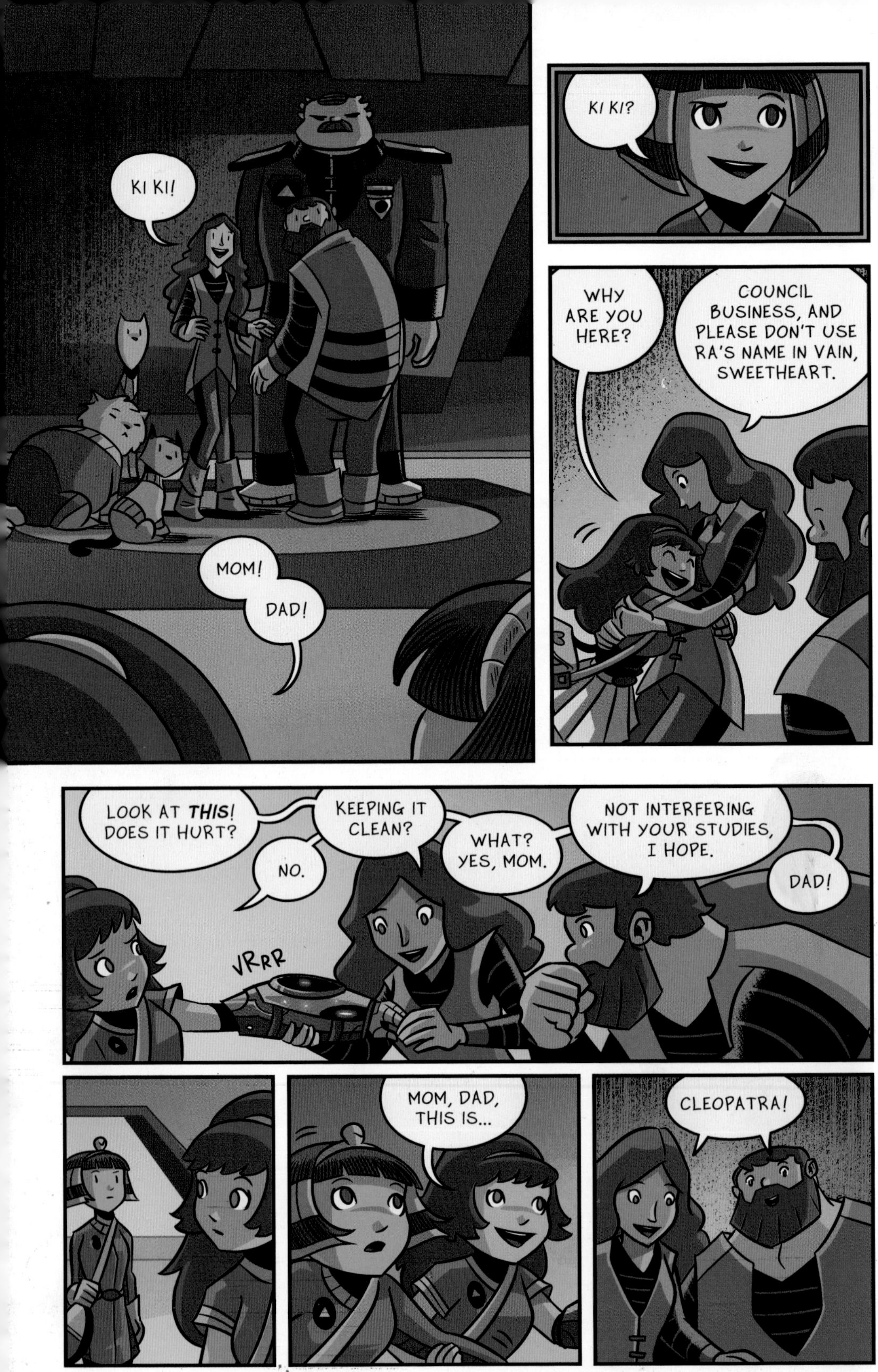
KI KI!
MOM!
DAD!
KI KI?
WHY ARE YOU HERE?
COUNCIL BUSINESS, AND PLEASE DON'T USE RA'S NAME IN VAIN, SWEETHEART.
LOOK AT THIS! DOES IT HURT?
NO.
KEEPING IT CLEAN?
WHAT? YES, MOM.
NOT INTERFERING WITH YOUR STUDIES, I HOPE.
DAD!
VRRR
MOM, DAD, THIS IS...
CLEOPATRA!

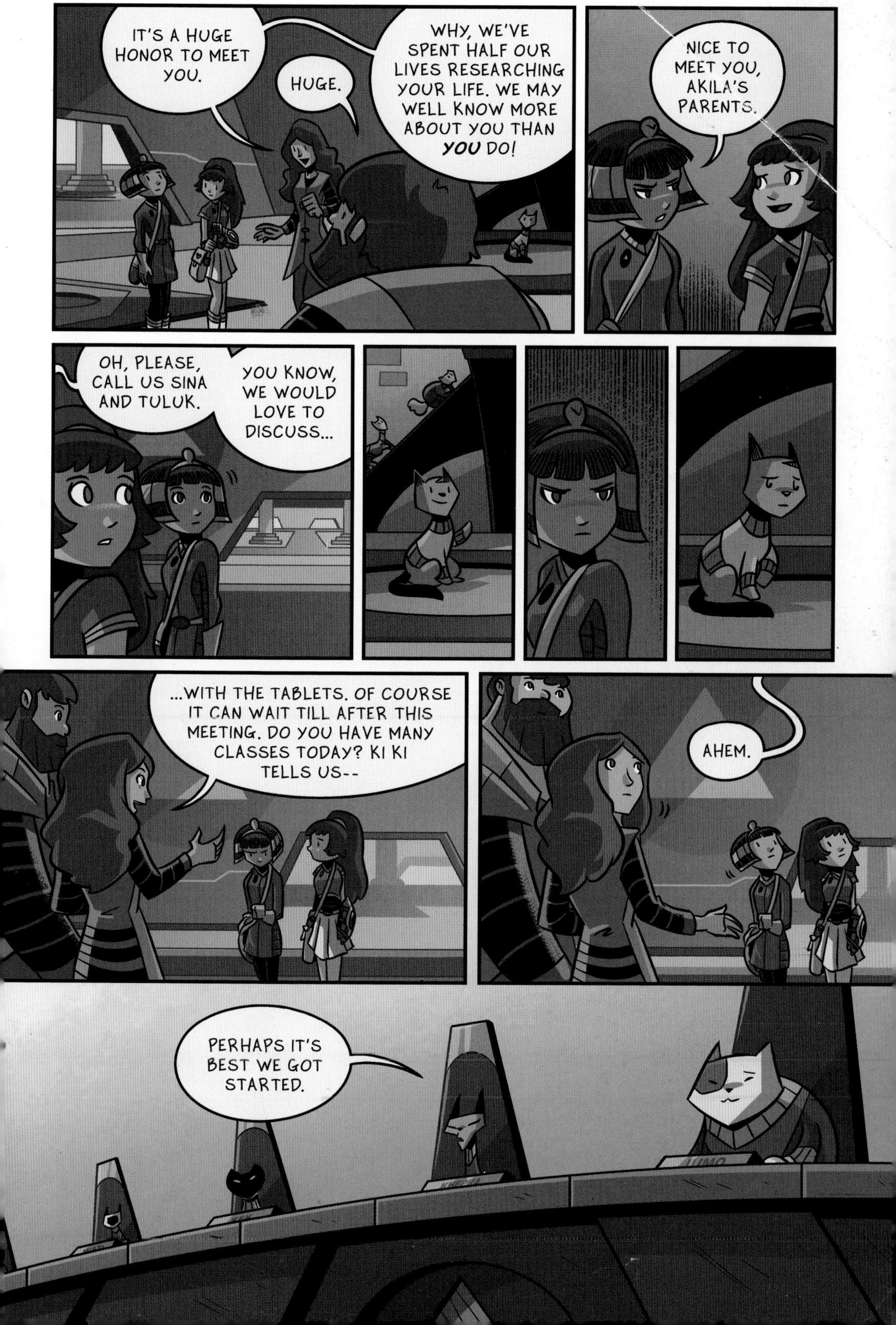
IT'S A HUGE HONOR TO MEET YOU.
HUGE.
WHY, WE'VE SPENT HALF OUR LIVES RESEARCHING YOUR LIFE. WE MAY WELL KNOW MORE ABOUT YOU THAN *YOU* DO!
NICE TO MEET YOU, AKILA'S PARENTS.
OH, PLEASE, CALL US SINA AND TULUK.
YOU KNOW, WE WOULD LOVE TO DISCUSS...
...WITH THE TABLETS. OF COURSE IT CAN WAIT TILL AFTER THIS MEETING. DO YOU HAVE MANY CLASSES TODAY? KI KI TELLS US--
AHEM.
PERHAPS IT'S BEST WE GOT STARTED.

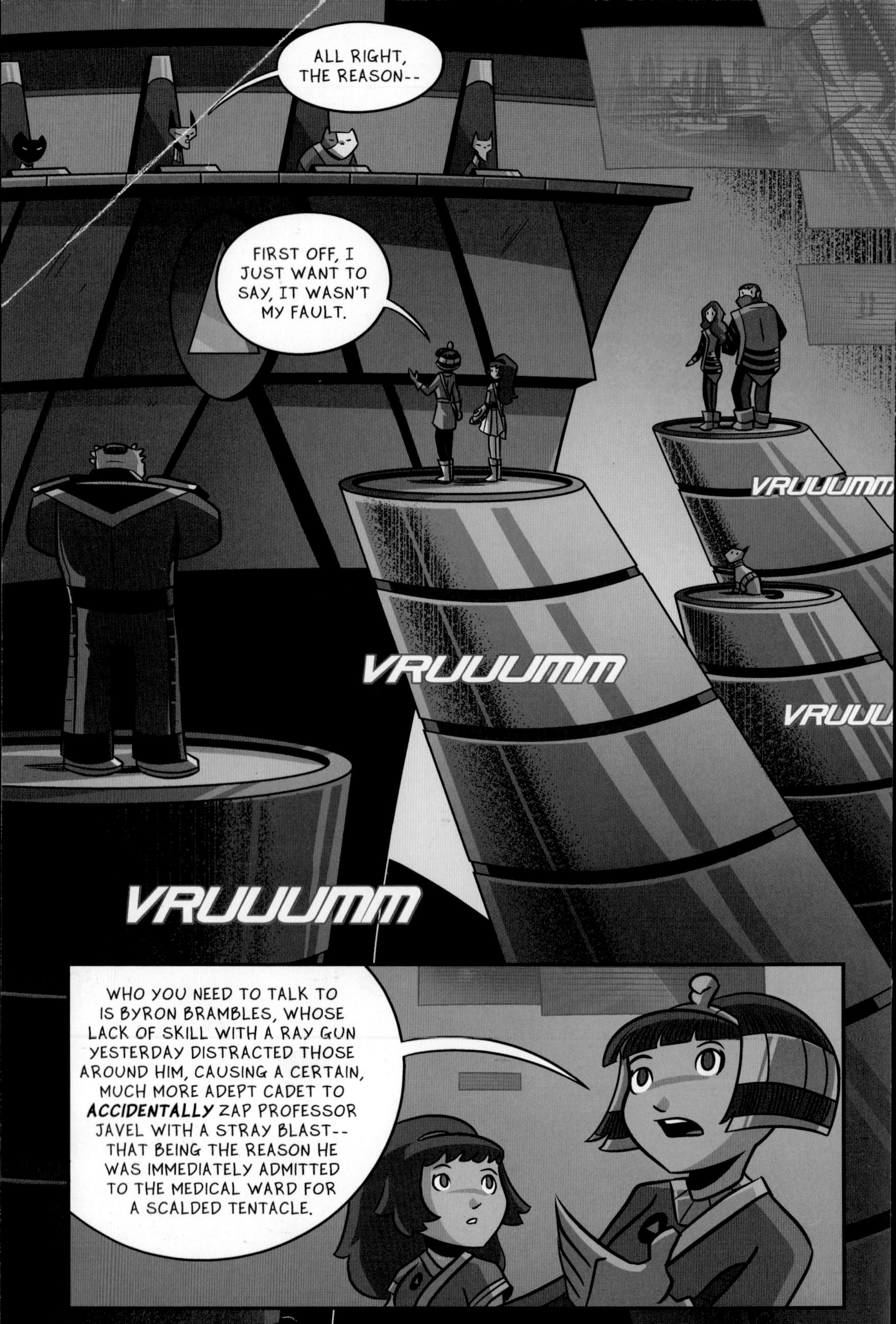
ALL RIGHT, THE REASON--
FIRST OFF, I JUST WANT TO SAY, IT WASN'T MY FAULT.
VRUUUMM
VRUUUMM
VRUUUMM
VRUUU
WHO YOU NEED TO TALK TO IS BYRON BRAMBLES, WHOSE LACK OF SKILL WITH A RAY GUN YESTERDAY DISTRACTED THOSE AROUND HIM, CAUSING A CERTAIN, MUCH MORE ADEPT CADET TO **ACCIDENTALLY** ZAP PROFESSOR JAVEL WITH A STRAY BLAST--THAT BEING THE REASON HE WAS IMMEDIATELY ADMITTED TO THE MEDICAL WARD FOR A SCALDED TENTACLE.

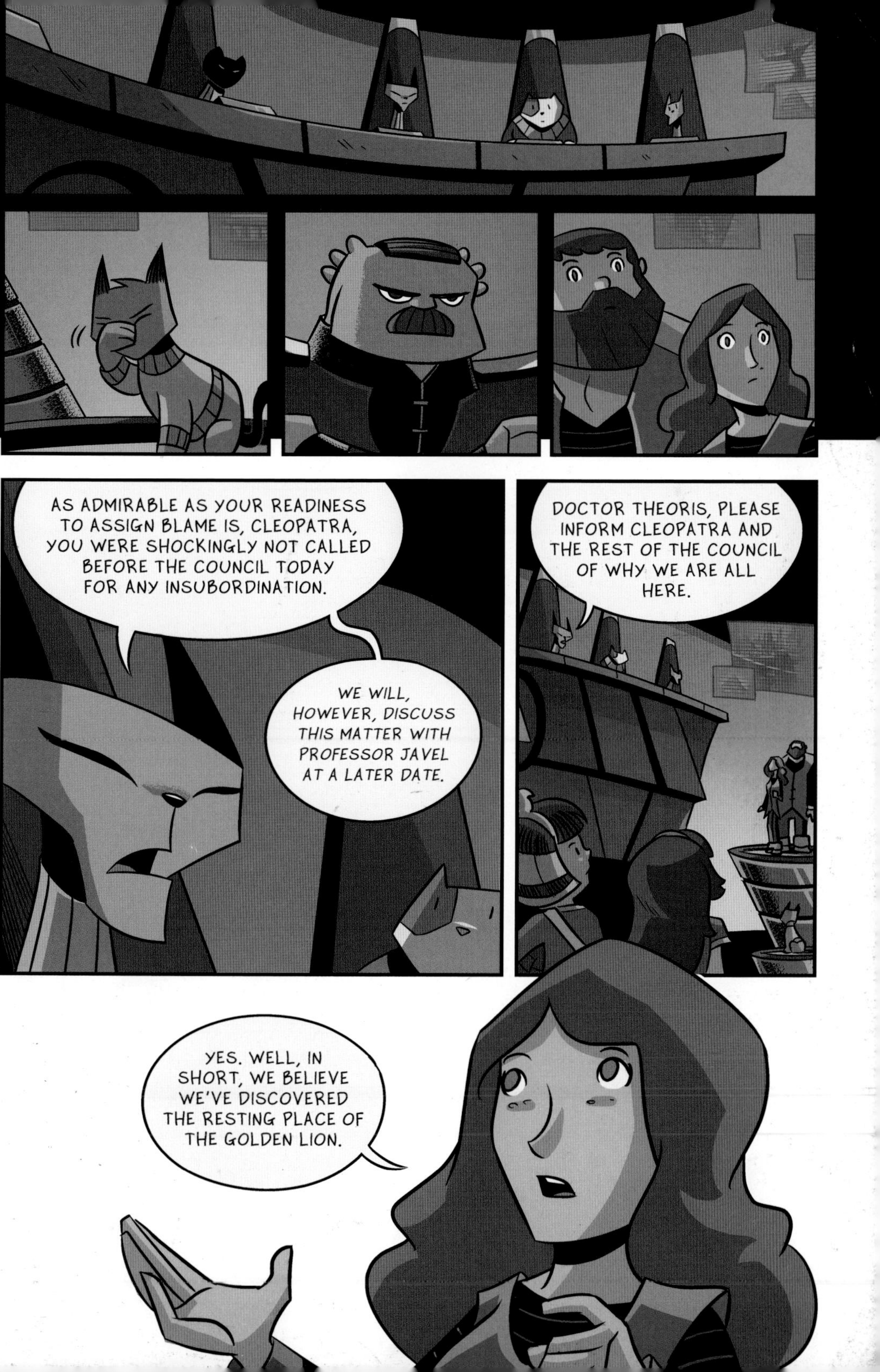

AS ADMIRABLE AS YOUR READINESS TO ASSIGN BLAME IS, CLEOPATRA, YOU WERE SHOCKINGLY NOT CALLED BEFORE THE COUNCIL TODAY FOR ANY INSUBORDINATION.
WE WILL, HOWEVER, DISCUSS THIS MATTER WITH PROFESSOR JAVEL AT A LATER DATE.
DOCTOR THEORIS, PLEASE INFORM CLEOPATRA AND THE REST OF THE COUNCIL OF WHY WE ARE ALL HERE.
YES. WELL, IN SHORT, WE BELIEVE WE'VE DISCOVERED THE RESTING PLACE OF THE GOLDEN LION.

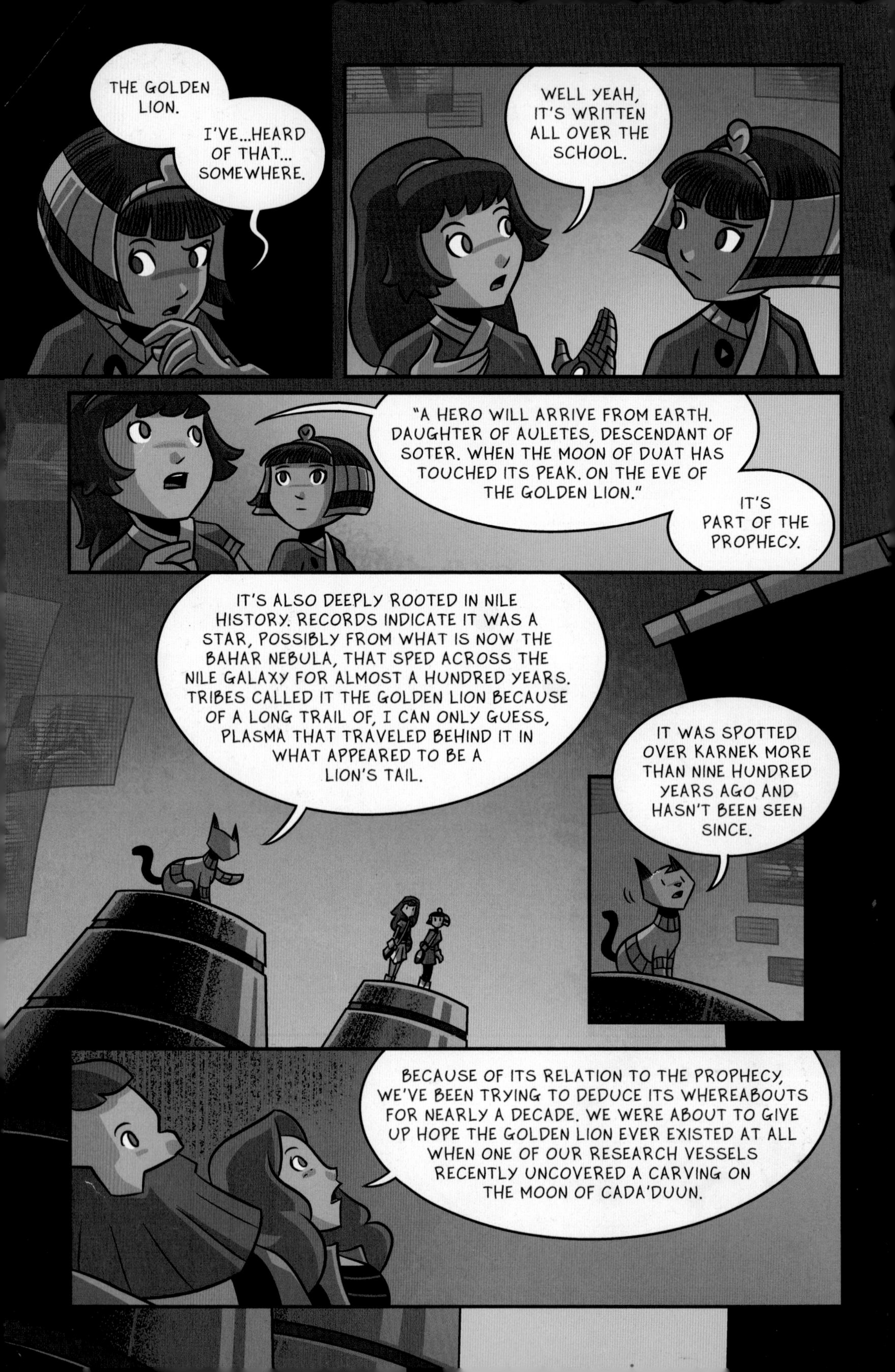

THE GOLDEN LION.
I'VE...HEARD OF THAT... SOMEWHERE.
WELL YEAH, IT'S WRITTEN ALL OVER THE SCHOOL.
"A HERO WILL ARRIVE FROM EARTH. DAUGHTER OF AULETES, DESCENDANT OF SOTER. WHEN THE MOON OF DUAT HAS TOUCHED ITS PEAK. ON THE EVE OF THE GOLDEN LION."
IT'S PART OF THE PROPHECY.
IT'S ALSO DEEPLY ROOTED IN NILE HISTORY. RECORDS INDICATE IT WAS A STAR, POSSIBLY FROM WHAT IS NOW THE BAHAR NEBULA, THAT SPED ACROSS THE NILE GALAXY FOR ALMOST A HUNDRED YEARS. TRIBES CALLED IT THE GOLDEN LION BECAUSE OF A LONG TRAIL OF, I CAN ONLY GUESS, PLASMA THAT TRAVELED BEHIND IT IN WHAT APPEARED TO BE A LION'S TAIL.
IT WAS SPOTTED OVER KARNEK MORE THAN NINE HUNDRED YEARS AGO AND HASN'T BEEN SEEN SINCE.
BECAUSE OF ITS RELATION TO THE PROPHECY, WE'VE BEEN TRYING TO DEDUCE ITS WHEREABOUTS FOR NEARLY A DECADE. WE WERE ABOUT TO GIVE UP HOPE THE GOLDEN LION EVER EXISTED AT ALL WHEN ONE OF OUR RESEARCH VESSELS RECENTLY UNCOVERED A CARVING ON THE MOON OF CADA'DUUN.

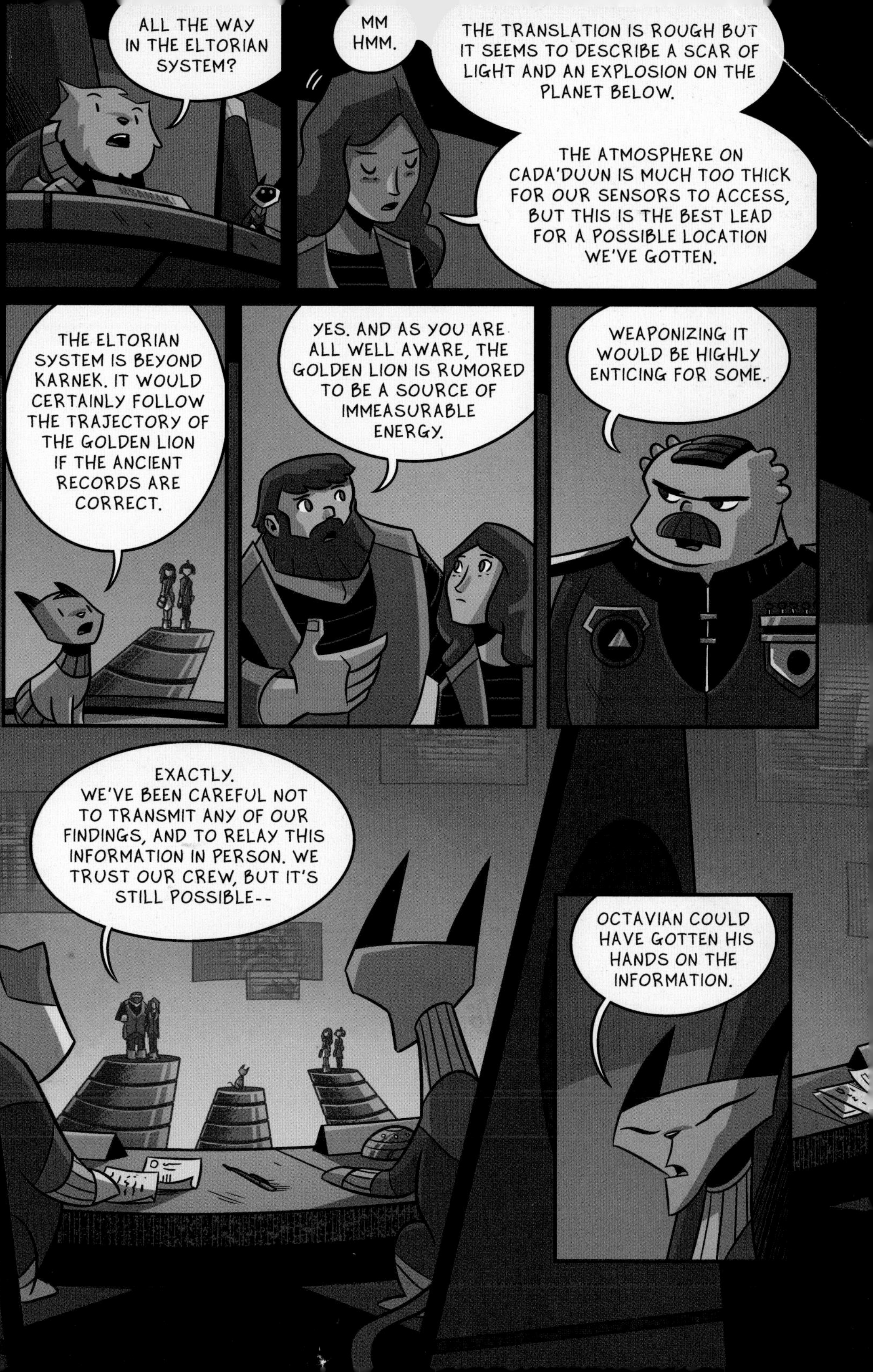
ALL THE WAY IN THE ELTORIAN SYSTEM?
MM HMM.
THE TRANSLATION IS ROUGH BUT IT SEEMS TO DESCRIBE A SCAR OF LIGHT AND AN EXPLOSION ON THE PLANET BELOW.
THE ATMOSPHERE ON CADA'DUUN IS MUCH TOO THICK FOR OUR SENSORS TO ACCESS, BUT THIS IS THE BEST LEAD FOR A POSSIBLE LOCATION WE'VE GOTTEN.
THE ELTORIAN SYSTEM IS BEYOND KARNEK. IT WOULD CERTAINLY FOLLOW THE TRAJECTORY OF THE GOLDEN LION IF THE ANCIENT RECORDS ARE CORRECT.
YES. AND AS YOU ARE ALL WELL AWARE, THE GOLDEN LION IS RUMORED TO BE A SOURCE OF IMMEASURABLE ENERGY.
WEAPONIZING IT WOULD BE HIGHLY ENTICING FOR SOME.
EXACTLY. WE'VE BEEN CAREFUL NOT TO TRANSMIT ANY OF OUR FINDINGS, AND TO RELAY THIS INFORMATION IN PERSON. WE TRUST OUR CREW, BUT IT'S STILL POSSIBLE--
OCTAVIAN COULD HAVE GOTTEN HIS HANDS ON THE INFORMATION.

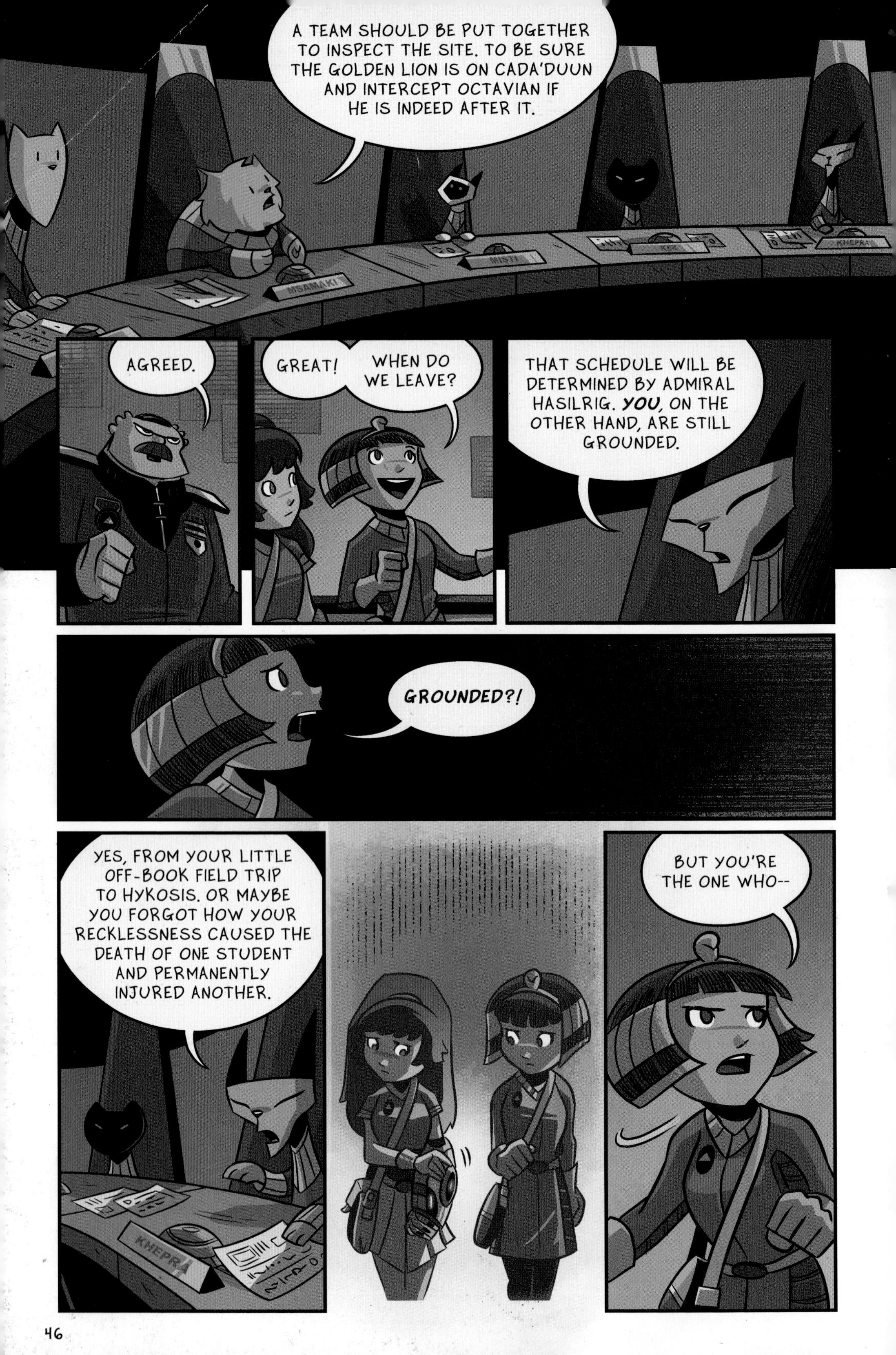
A TEAM SHOULD BE PUT TOGETHER TO INSPECT THE SITE. TO BE SURE THE GOLDEN LION IS ON CADA'DUUN AND INTERCEPT OCTAVIAN IF HE IS INDEED AFTER IT.
MSAMAKI
MISTI
KEK
KHEPRA
AGREED.
GREAT!
WHEN DO WE LEAVE?
THAT SCHEDULE WILL BE DETERMINED BY ADMIRAL HASILRIG. ***YOU,*** ON THE OTHER HAND, ARE STILL GROUNDED.
***GROUNDED?!***
YES, FROM YOUR LITTLE OFF-BOOK FIELD TRIP TO HYKOSIS. OR MAYBE YOU FORGOT HOW YOUR RECKLESSNESS CAUSED THE DEATH OF ONE STUDENT AND PERMANENTLY INJURED ANOTHER.
KHEPRA
BUT YOU'RE THE ONE WHO--

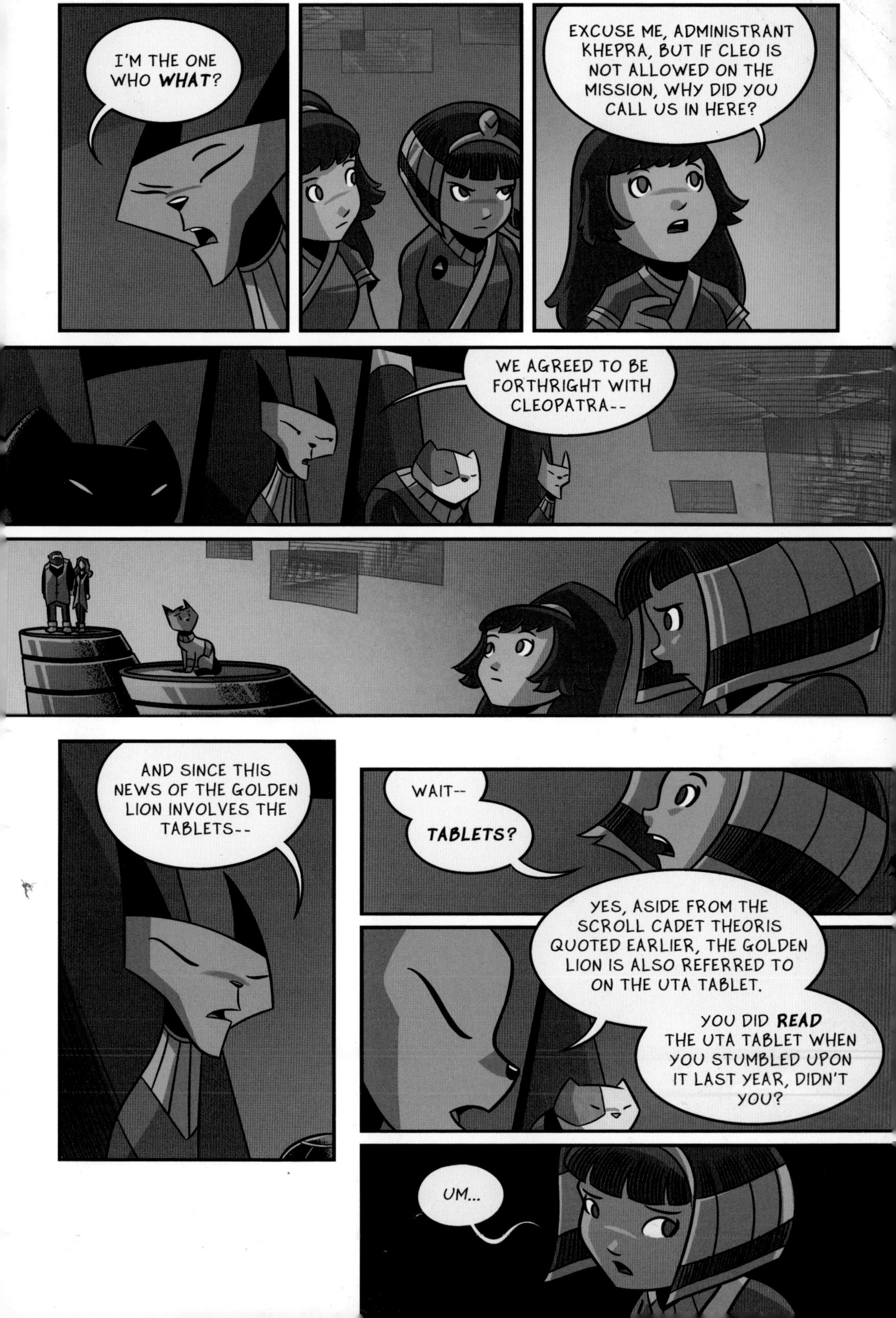
I'M THE ONE WHO WHAT?
EXCUSE ME, ADMINISTRANT KHEPRA, BUT IF CLEO IS NOT ALLOWED ON THE MISSION, WHY DID YOU CALL US IN HERE?
WE AGREED TO BE FORTHRIGHT WITH CLEOPATRA--
AND SINCE THIS NEWS OF THE GOLDEN LION INVOLVES THE TABLETS--
WAIT--
TABLETS?
YES, ASIDE FROM THE SCROLL CADET THEORIS QUOTED EARLIER, THE GOLDEN LION IS ALSO REFERRED TO ON THE UTA TABLET.
YOU DID READ THE UTA TABLET WHEN YOU STUMBLED UPON IT LAST YEAR, DIDN'T YOU?
UM...

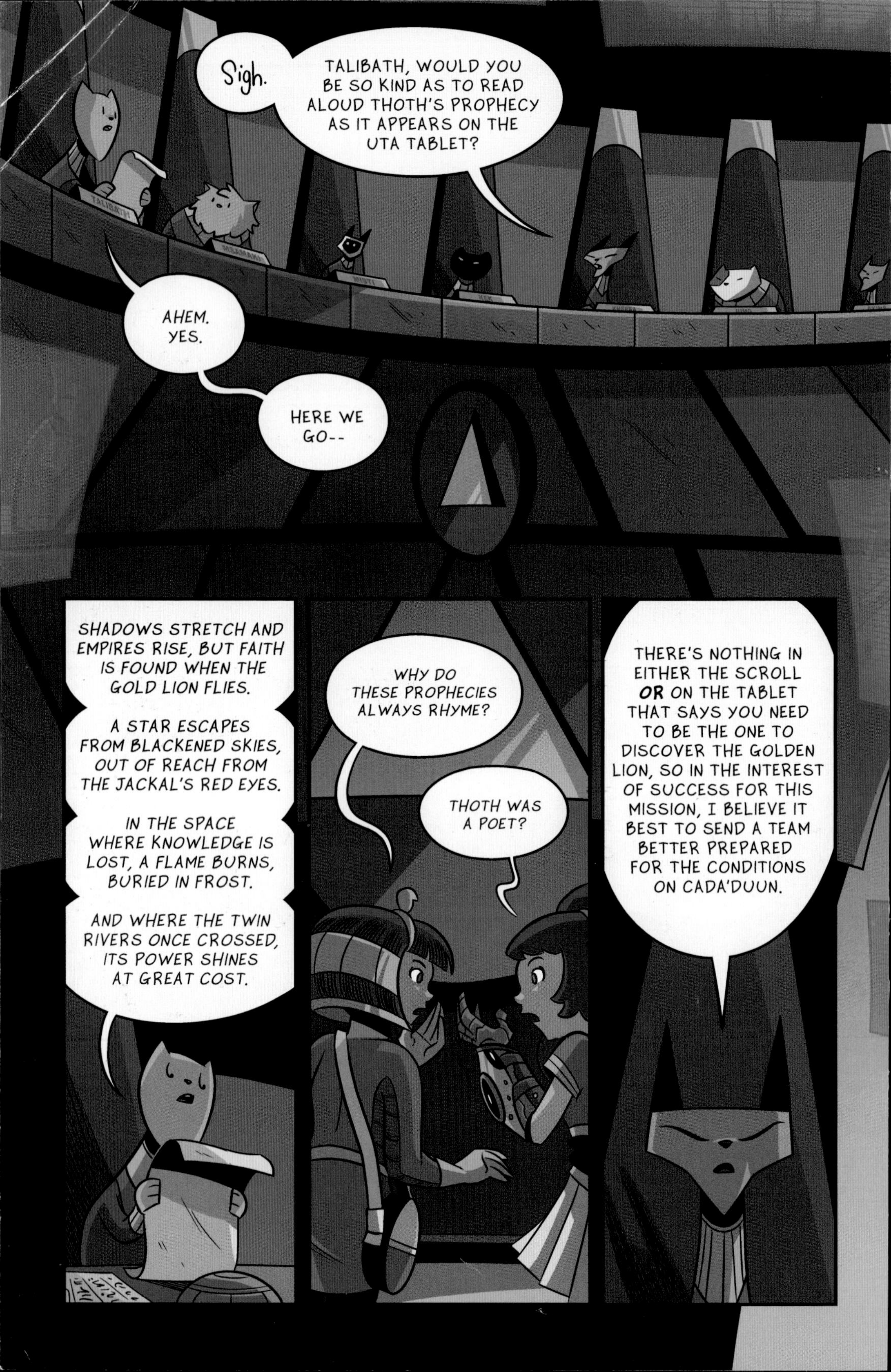
Sigh.
TALIBATH, WOULD YOU BE SO KIND AS TO READ ALOUD THOTH'S PROPHECY AS IT APPEARS ON THE UTA TABLET?
AHEM. YES.
HERE WE GO--
SHADOWS STRETCH AND EMPIRES RISE, BUT FAITH IS FOUND WHEN THE GOLD LION FLIES.
A STAR ESCAPES FROM BLACKENED SKIES, OUT OF REACH FROM THE JACKAL'S RED EYES.
IN THE SPACE WHERE KNOWLEDGE IS LOST, A FLAME BURNS, BURIED IN FROST.
AND WHERE THE TWIN RIVERS ONCE CROSSED, ITS POWER SHINES AT GREAT COST.
WHY DO THESE PROPHECIES ALWAYS RHYME?
THOTH WAS A POET?
THERE'S NOTHING IN EITHER THE SCROLL **OR** ON THE TABLET THAT SAYS YOU NEED TO BE THE ONE TO DISCOVER THE GOLDEN LION, SO IN THE INTEREST OF SUCCESS FOR THIS MISSION, I BELIEVE IT BEST TO SEND A TEAM BETTER PREPARED FOR THE CONDITIONS ON CADA'DUUN.

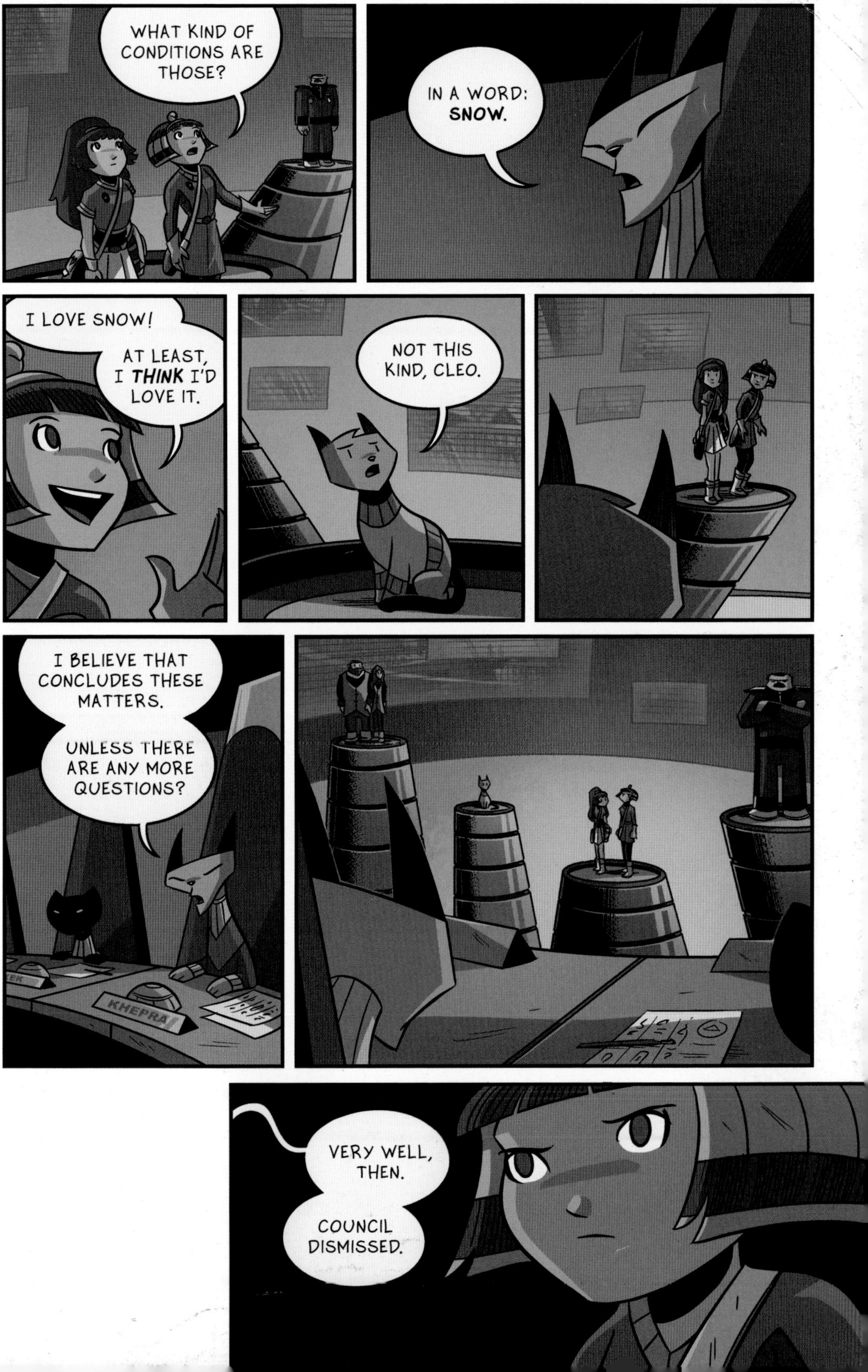
WHAT KIND OF CONDITIONS ARE THOSE?
IN A WORD: **SNOW.**
I LOVE SNOW!
AT LEAST, I **THINK** I'D LOVE IT.
NOT THIS KIND, CLEO.
I BELIEVE THAT CONCLUDES THESE MATTERS.
UNLESS THERE ARE ANY MORE QUESTIONS?
KHEPRA
VERY WELL, THEN.
COUNCIL DISMISSED.

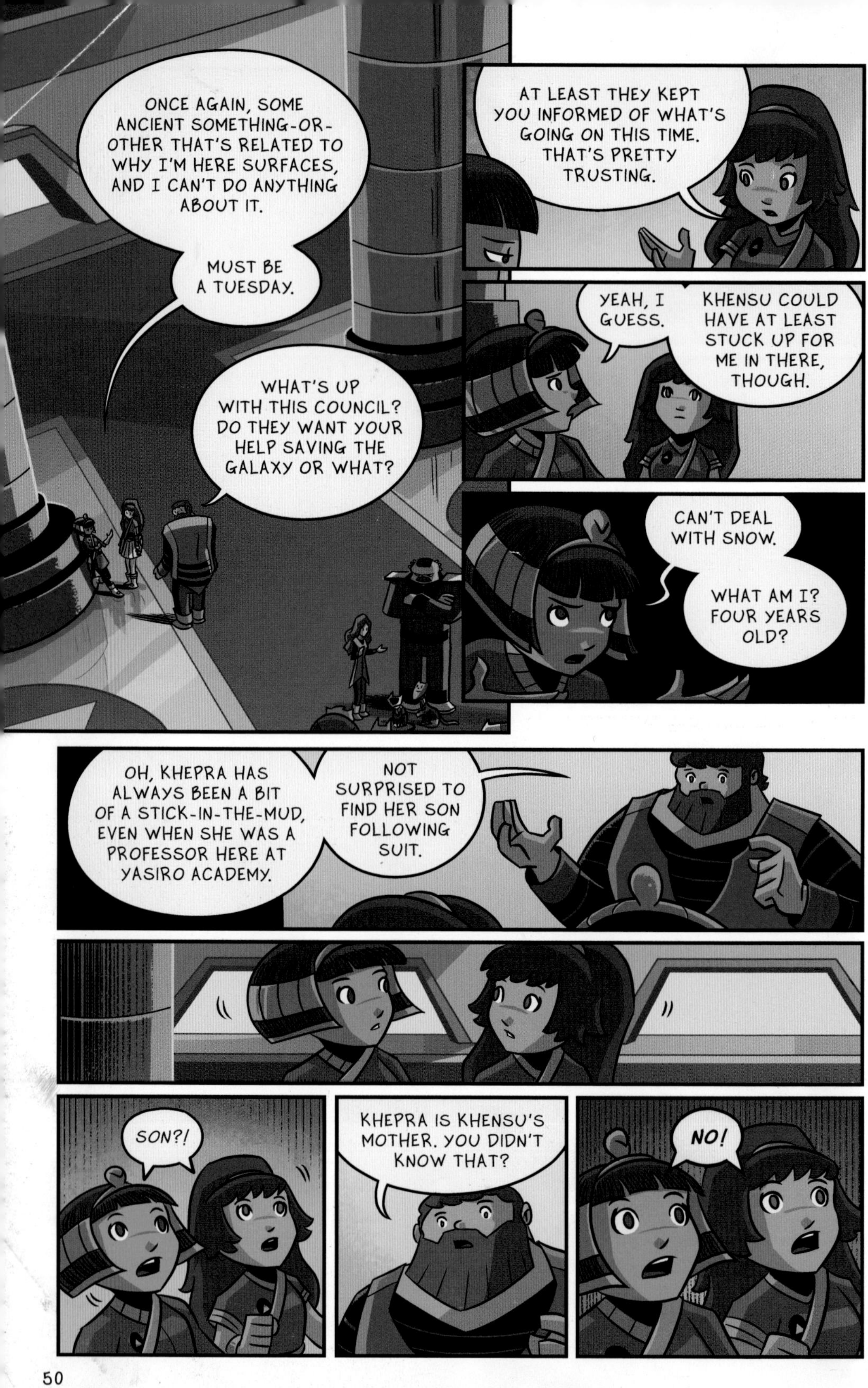
ONCE AGAIN, SOME ANCIENT SOMETHING-OR-OTHER THAT'S RELATED TO WHY I'M HERE SURFACES, AND I CAN'T DO ANYTHING ABOUT IT.
MUST BE A TUESDAY.
WHAT'S UP WITH THIS COUNCIL? DO THEY WANT YOUR HELP SAVING THE GALAXY OR WHAT?
AT LEAST THEY KEPT YOU INFORMED OF WHAT'S GOING ON THIS TIME. THAT'S PRETTY TRUSTING.
YEAH, I GUESS.
KHENSU COULD HAVE AT LEAST STUCK UP FOR ME IN THERE, THOUGH.
CAN'T DEAL WITH SNOW.
WHAT AM I? FOUR YEARS OLD?
OH, KHEPRA HAS ALWAYS BEEN A BIT OF A STICK-IN-THE-MUD, EVEN WHEN SHE WAS A PROFESSOR HERE AT YASIRO ACADEMY.
NOT SURPRISED TO FIND HER SON FOLLOWING SUIT.
SON?!
KHEPRA IS KHENSU'S MOTHER. YOU DIDN'T KNOW THAT?
NO!

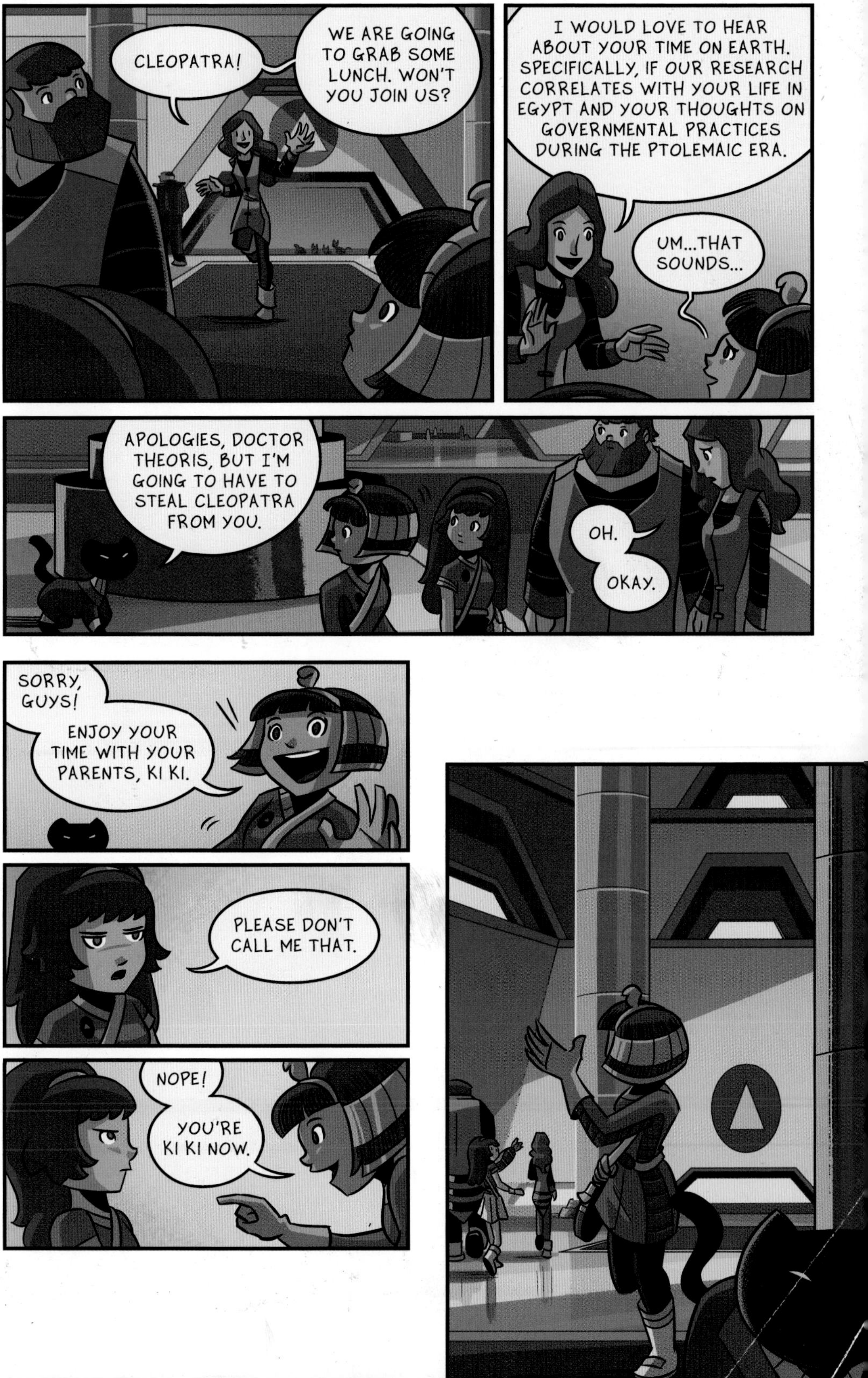
CLEOPATRA!
WE ARE GOING TO GRAB SOME LUNCH. WON'T YOU JOIN US?
I WOULD LOVE TO HEAR ABOUT YOUR TIME ON EARTH. SPECIFICALLY, IF OUR RESEARCH CORRELATES WITH YOUR LIFE IN EGYPT AND YOUR THOUGHTS ON GOVERNMENTAL PRACTICES DURING THE PTOLEMAIC ERA.
UM...THAT SOUNDS...
APOLOGIES, DOCTOR THEORIS, BUT I'M GOING TO HAVE TO STEAL CLEOPATRA FROM YOU.
OH.
OKAY.
SORRY, GUYS!
ENJOY YOUR TIME WITH YOUR PARENTS, KI KI.
PLEASE DON'T CALL ME THAT.
NOPE!
YOU'RE KI KI NOW.

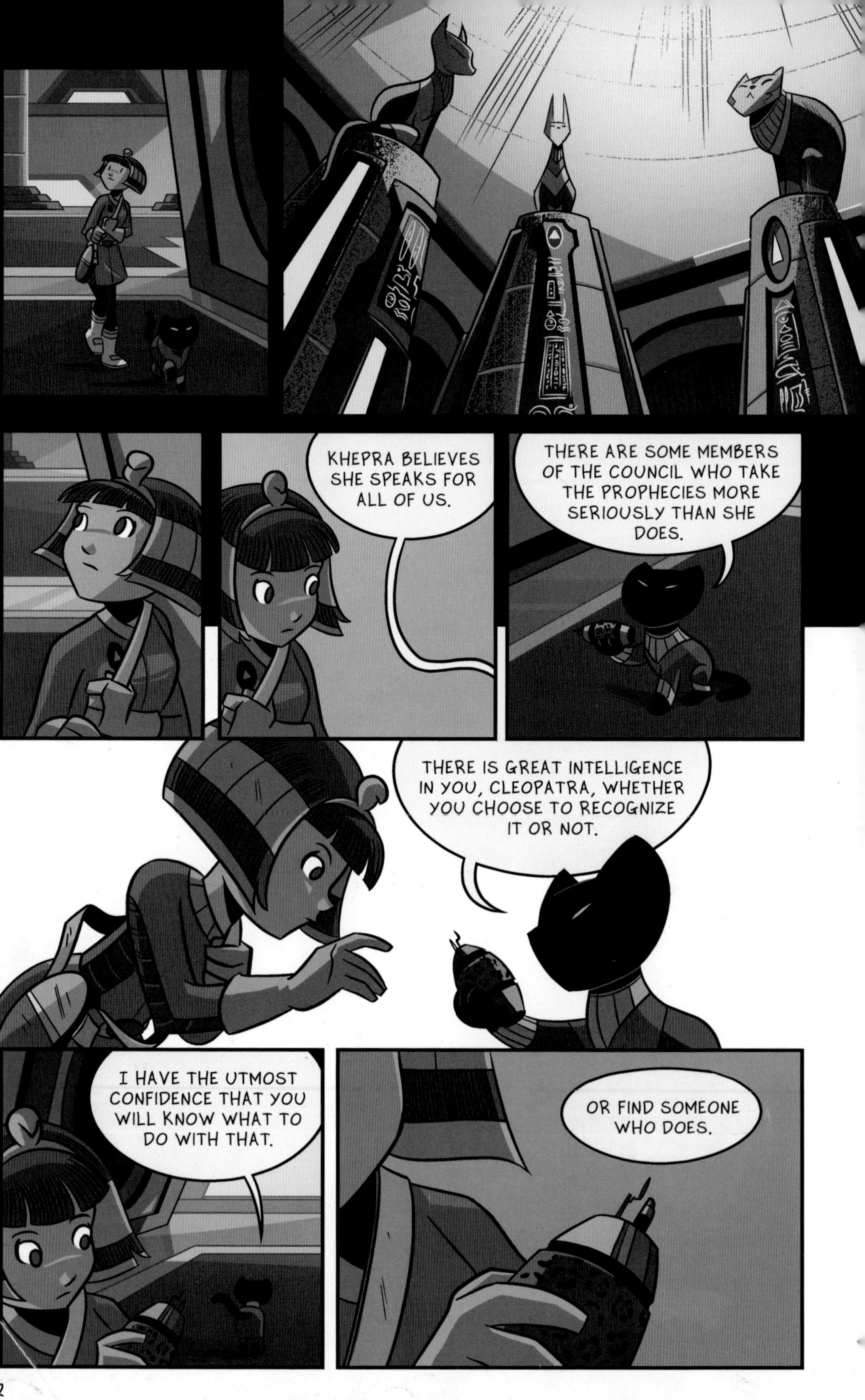
KHEPRA BELIEVES SHE SPEAKS FOR ALL OF US.
THERE ARE SOME MEMBERS OF THE COUNCIL WHO TAKE THE PROPHECIES MORE SERIOUSLY THAN SHE DOES.
THERE IS GREAT INTELLIGENCE IN YOU, CLEOPATRA, WHETHER YOU CHOOSE TO RECOGNIZE IT OR NOT.
I HAVE THE UTMOST CONFIDENCE THAT YOU WILL KNOW WHAT TO DO WITH THAT.
OR FIND SOMEONE WHO DOES.

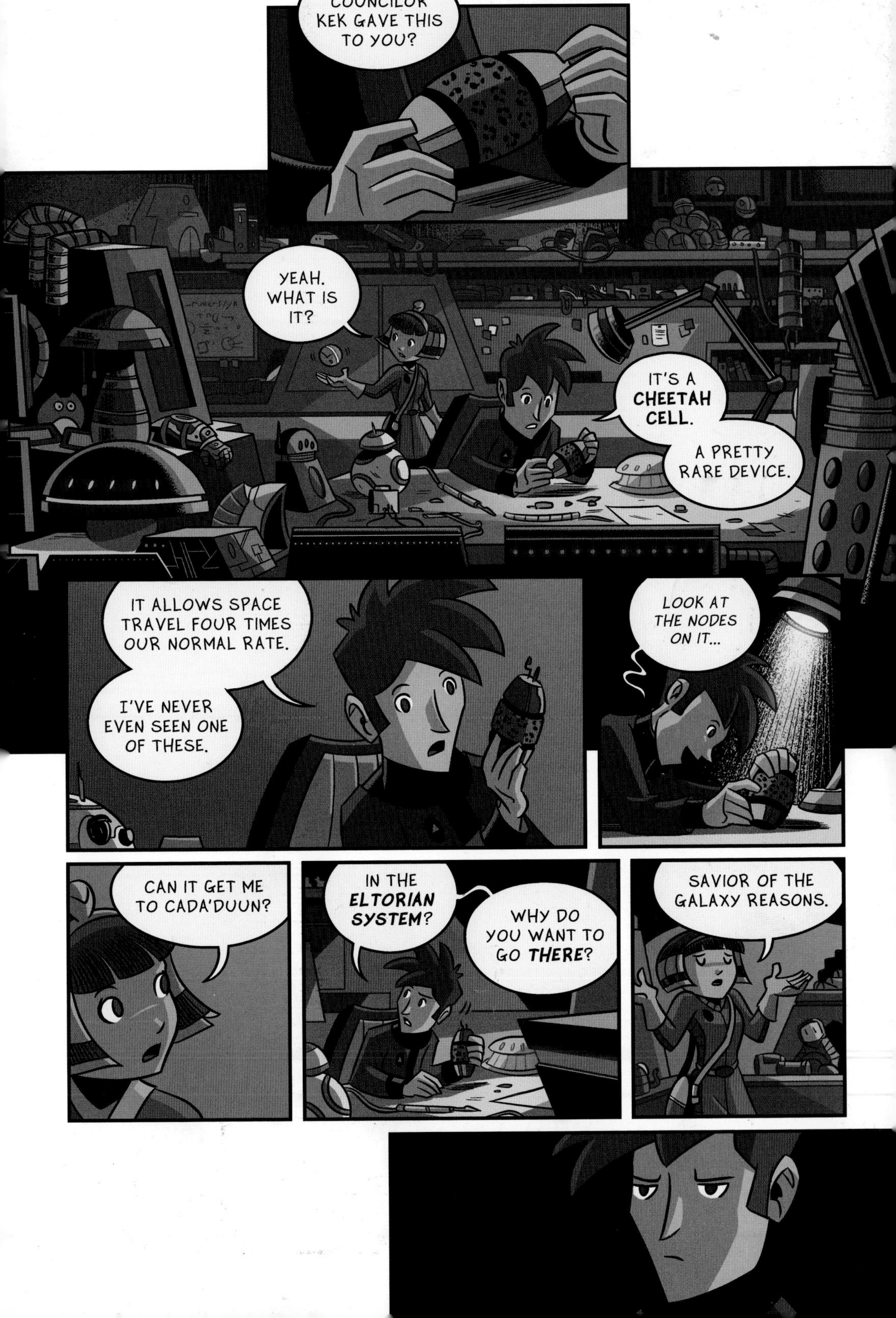
COUNCILOR KEK GAVE THIS TO YOU?
YEAH. WHAT IS IT?
IT'S A **CHEETAH CELL**.
A PRETTY RARE DEVICE.
IT ALLOWS SPACE TRAVEL FOUR TIMES OUR NORMAL RATE.
I'VE NEVER EVEN SEEN ONE OF THESE.
LOOK AT THE NODES ON IT...
CAN IT GET ME TO CADA'DUUN?
IN THE ***ELTORIAN SYSTEM***?
WHY DO YOU WANT TO GO **THERE**?
SAVIOR OF THE GALAXY REASONS.

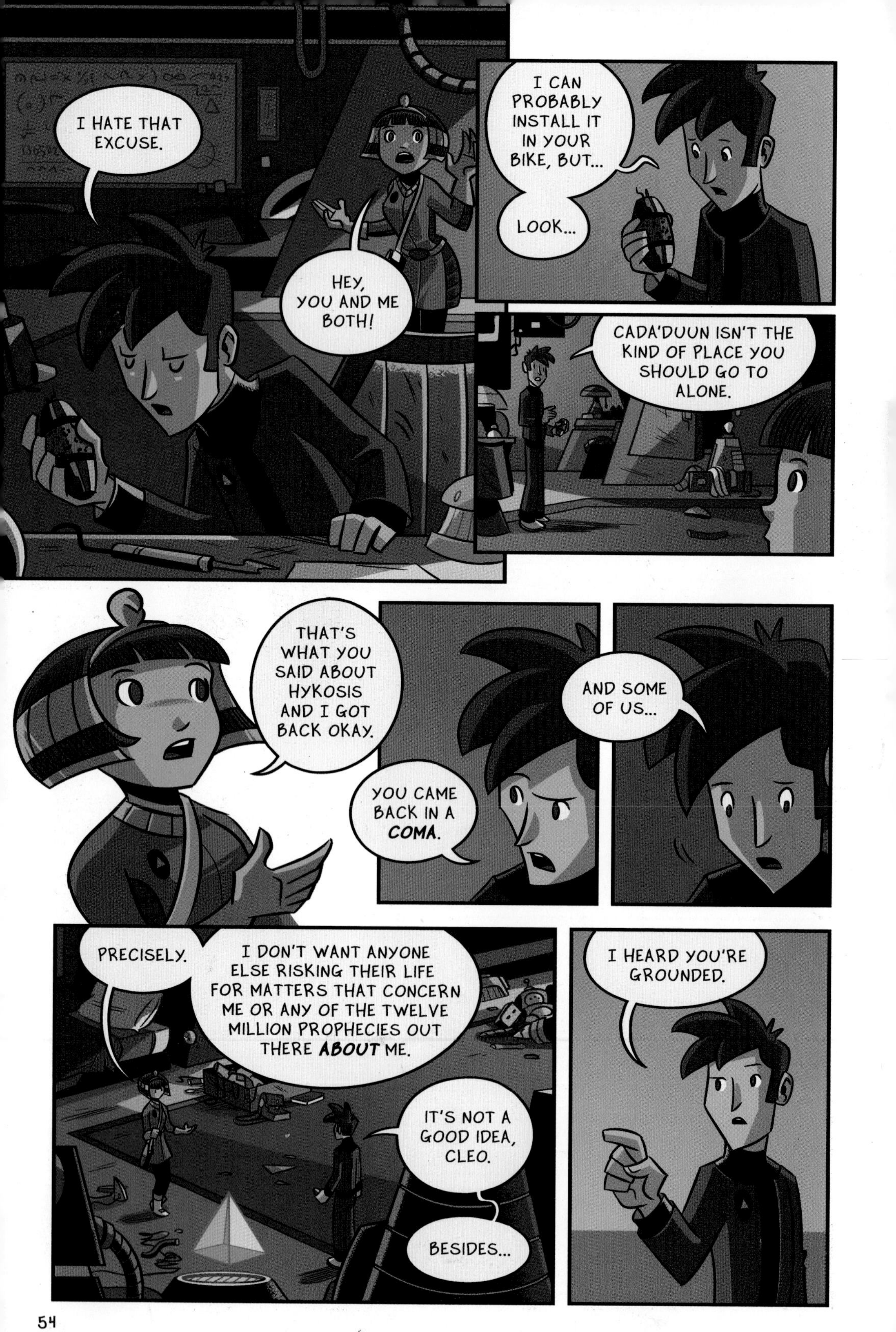
I HATE THAT EXCUSE.
HEY, YOU AND ME BOTH!
I CAN PROBABLY INSTALL IT IN YOUR BIKE, BUT...
LOOK...
CADA'DUUN ISN'T THE KIND OF PLACE YOU SHOULD GO TO ALONE.
THAT'S WHAT YOU SAID ABOUT HYKOSIS AND I GOT BACK OKAY.
YOU CAME BACK IN A COMA.
AND SOME OF US...
PRECISELY.
I DON'T WANT ANYONE ELSE RISKING THEIR LIFE FOR MATTERS THAT CONCERN ME OR ANY OF THE TWELVE MILLION PROPHECIES OUT THERE ABOUT ME.
IT'S NOT A GOOD IDEA, CLEO.
BESIDES...
I HEARD YOU'RE GROUNDED.

EH...IT'S A FLEXIBLE SORT OF GROUNDED.

C'MON, BRIAN. WHY WOULD KEK GIVE THAT TO ME IF HE DIDN'T WANT ME TO USE IT?

MAYBE THERE'S A REASON I'M SUPPOSED TO GO ALONE.

IT'S NOT JUST THAT. THE ENVIRONMENTAL CONDITIONS IN THAT SECTION OF THE GALAXY ARE INCREDIBLY HARSH.

I'M NOT SURE EVEN A *SAVIOR OF THE GALAXY* IS EQUIPPED TO HANDLE THEM.

THEN EQUIP ME.

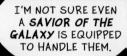

IF I DON'T HELP YOU WITH THIS, YOU'RE PROBABLY GOING TO TRY TO FIND A WAY OUT THERE ON YOUR OWN, AREN'T YOU?

PROBABLY.

AND IT'LL INVOLVE A METHOD THAT WILL MOST LIKELY GET YOU KILLED, WON'T IT?

MOST LIKELY.

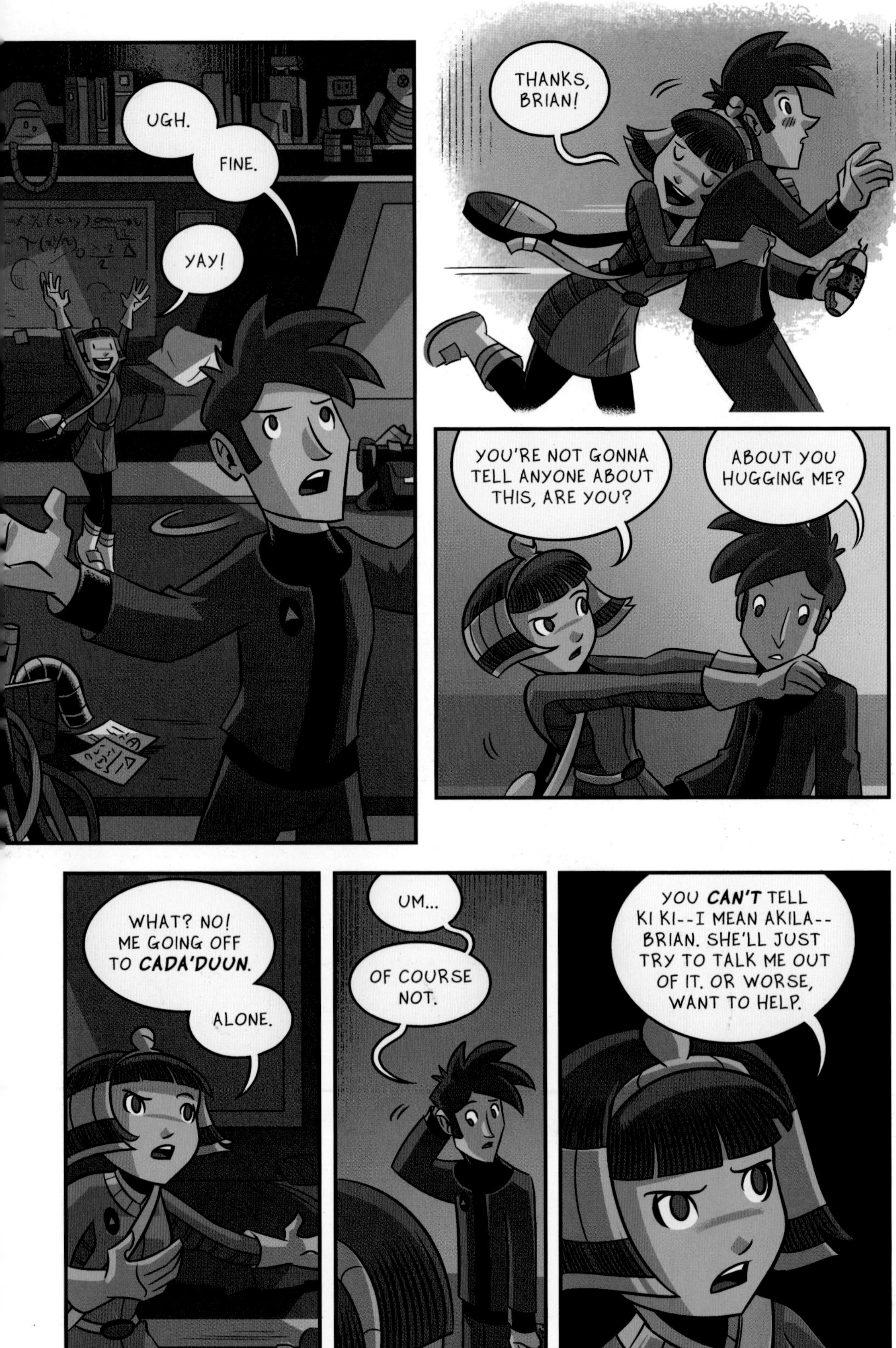
UGH.
FINE.
YAY!
THANKS, BRIAN!
YOU'RE NOT GONNA TELL ANYONE ABOUT THIS, ARE YOU?
ABOUT YOU HUGGING ME?
WHAT? NO! ME GOING OFF TO **CADA'DUUN**.
ALONE.
UM...
OF COURSE NOT.
YOU **CAN'T** TELL KI KI--I MEAN AKILA--BRIAN. SHE'LL JUST TRY TO TALK ME OUT OF IT. OR WORSE, WANT TO HELP.

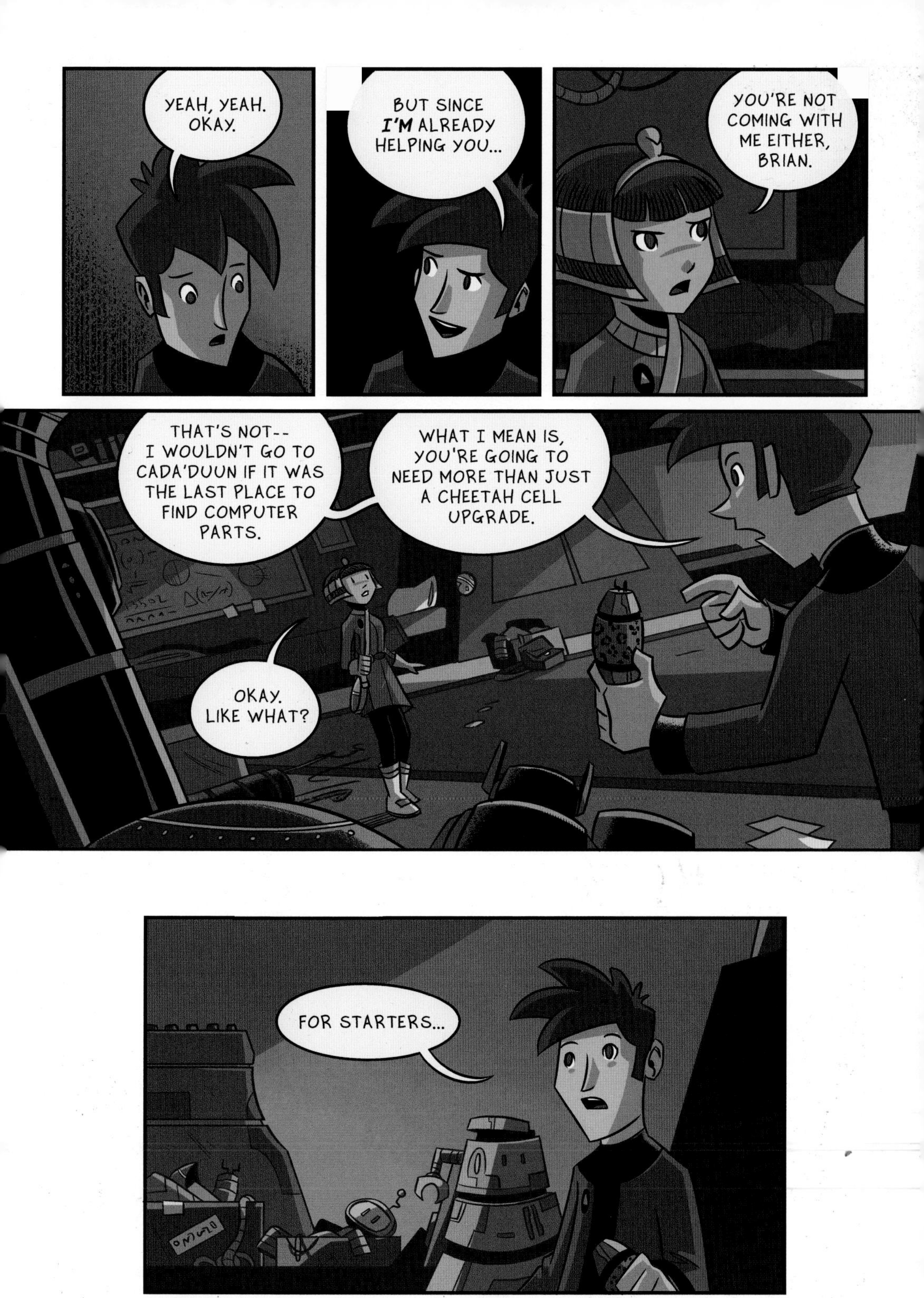
YEAH, YEAH. OKAY.
BUT SINCE I'M ALREADY HELPING YOU...
YOU'RE NOT COMING WITH ME EITHER, BRIAN.
THAT'S NOT-- I WOULDN'T GO TO CADA'DUUN IF IT WAS THE LAST PLACE TO FIND COMPUTER PARTS.
WHAT I MEAN IS, YOU'RE GOING TO NEED MORE THAN JUST A CHEETAH CELL UPGRADE.
OKAY. LIKE WHAT?
FOR STARTERS...

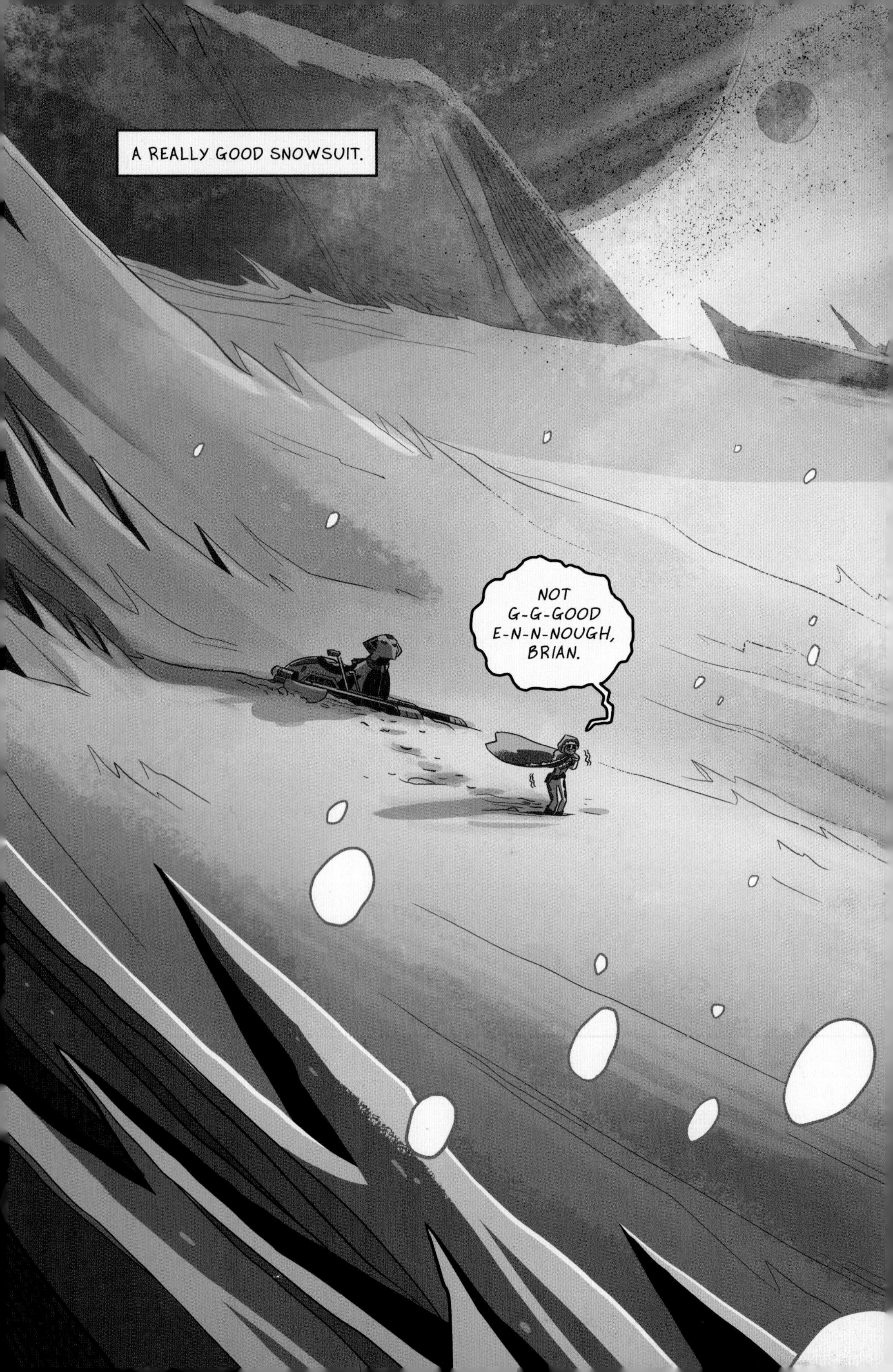
A REALLY GOOD SNOWSUIT.
NOT G-G-GOOD E-N-N-NOUGH, BRIAN.

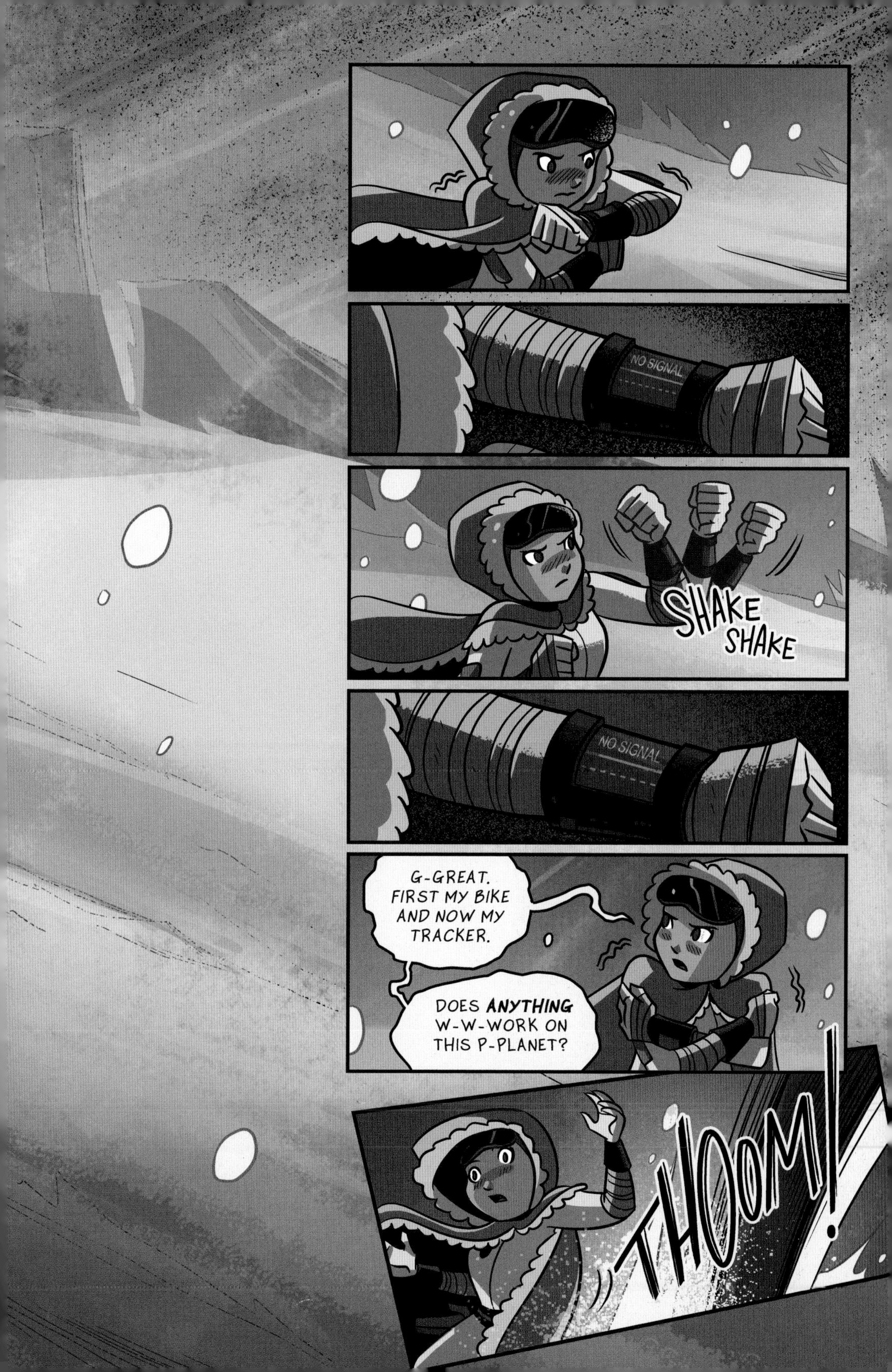
NO SIGNAL
SHAKE SHAKE
NO SIGNAL
G-GREAT. FIRST MY BIKE AND NOW MY TRACKER.
DOES **ANYTHING** W-W-WORK ON THIS P-PLANET?
THOOM!

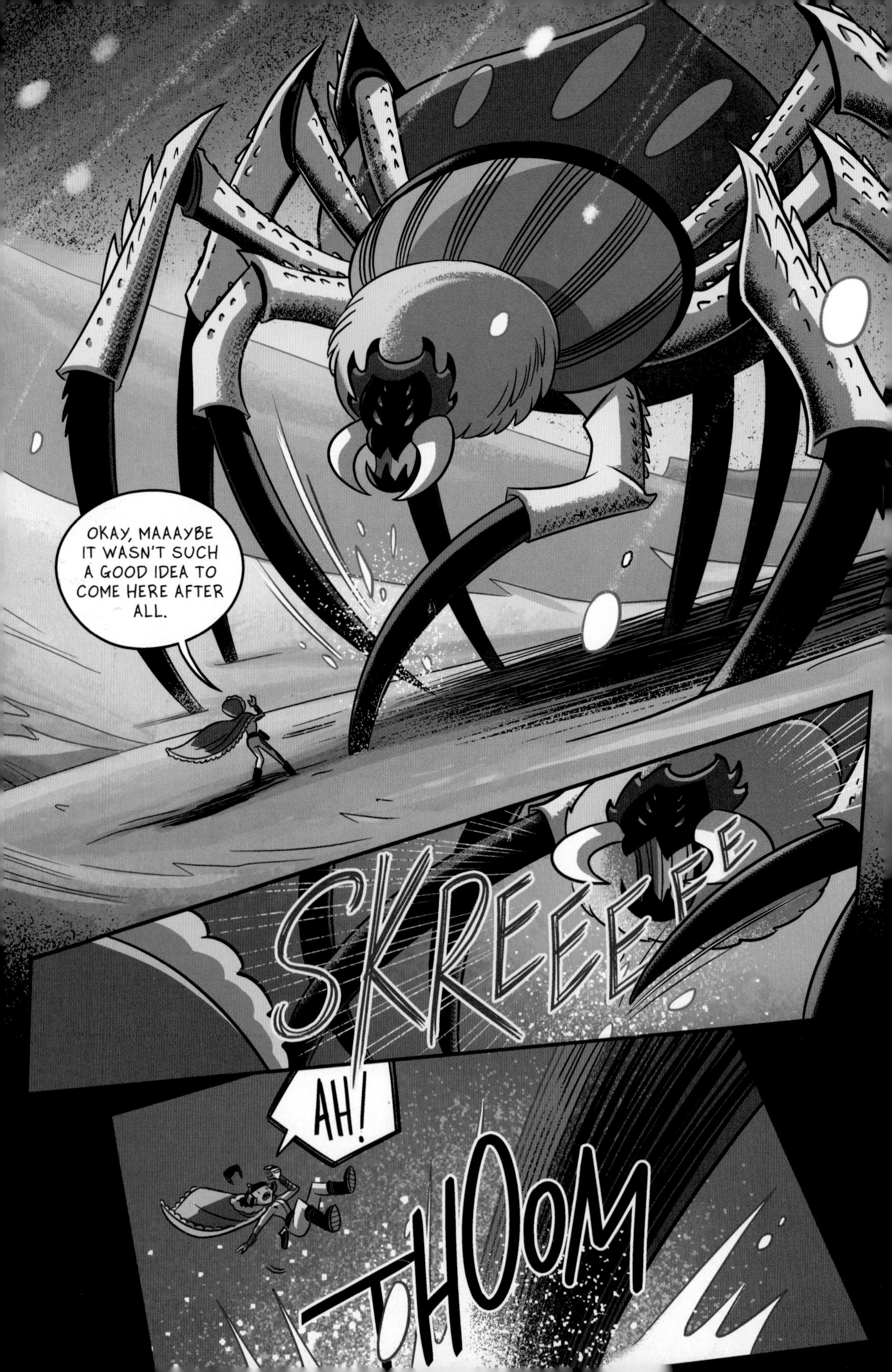
OKAY, MAAAYBE IT WASN'T SUCH A GOOD IDEA TO COME HERE AFTER ALL.
SKREEEEE
AH!
THOOM

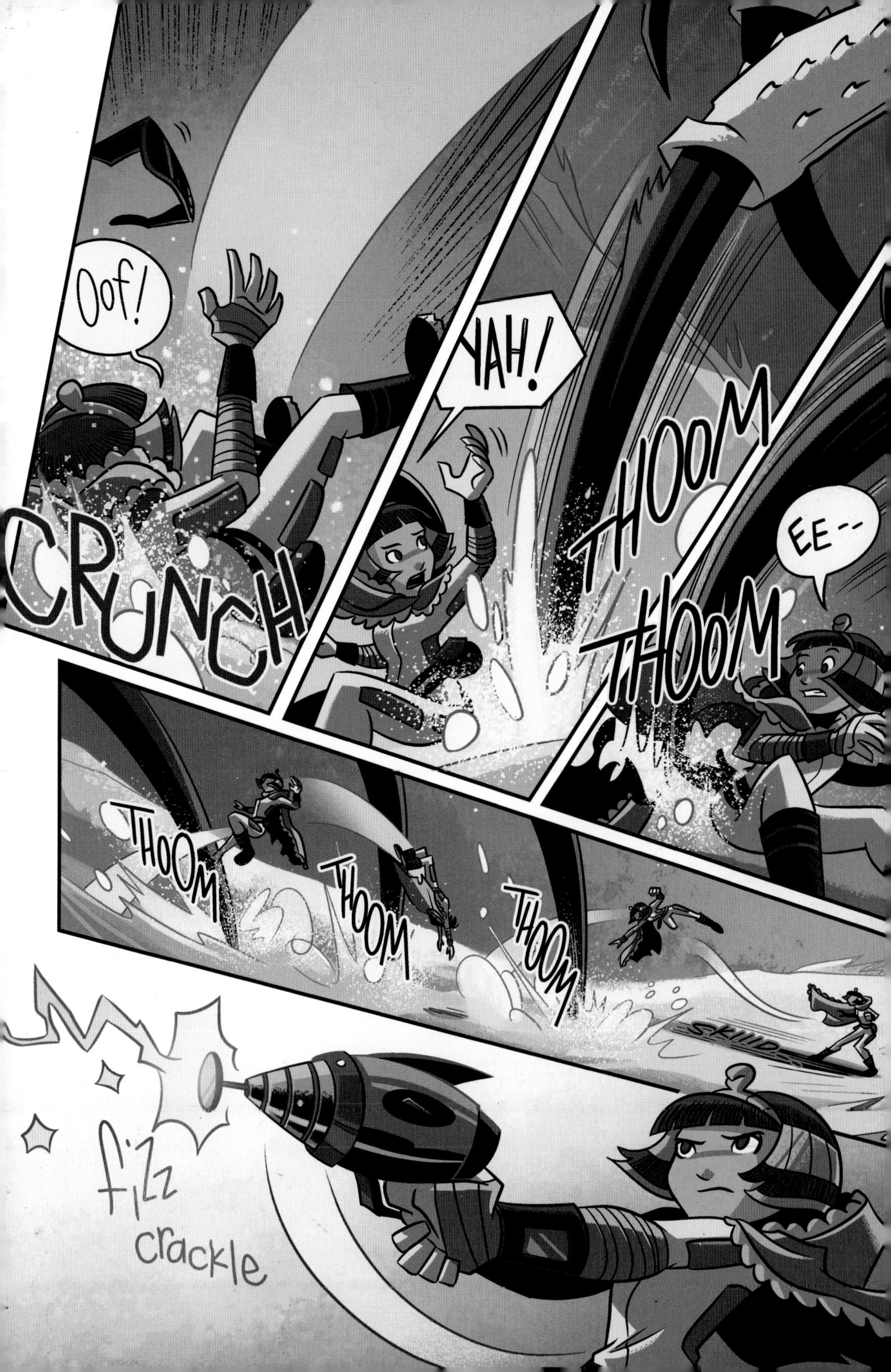
Oof!
CRUNCH
YAH!
THOOM
THOOM
EE--
THOOM
THOOM
THOOM
SKIIID
fizz
crackle

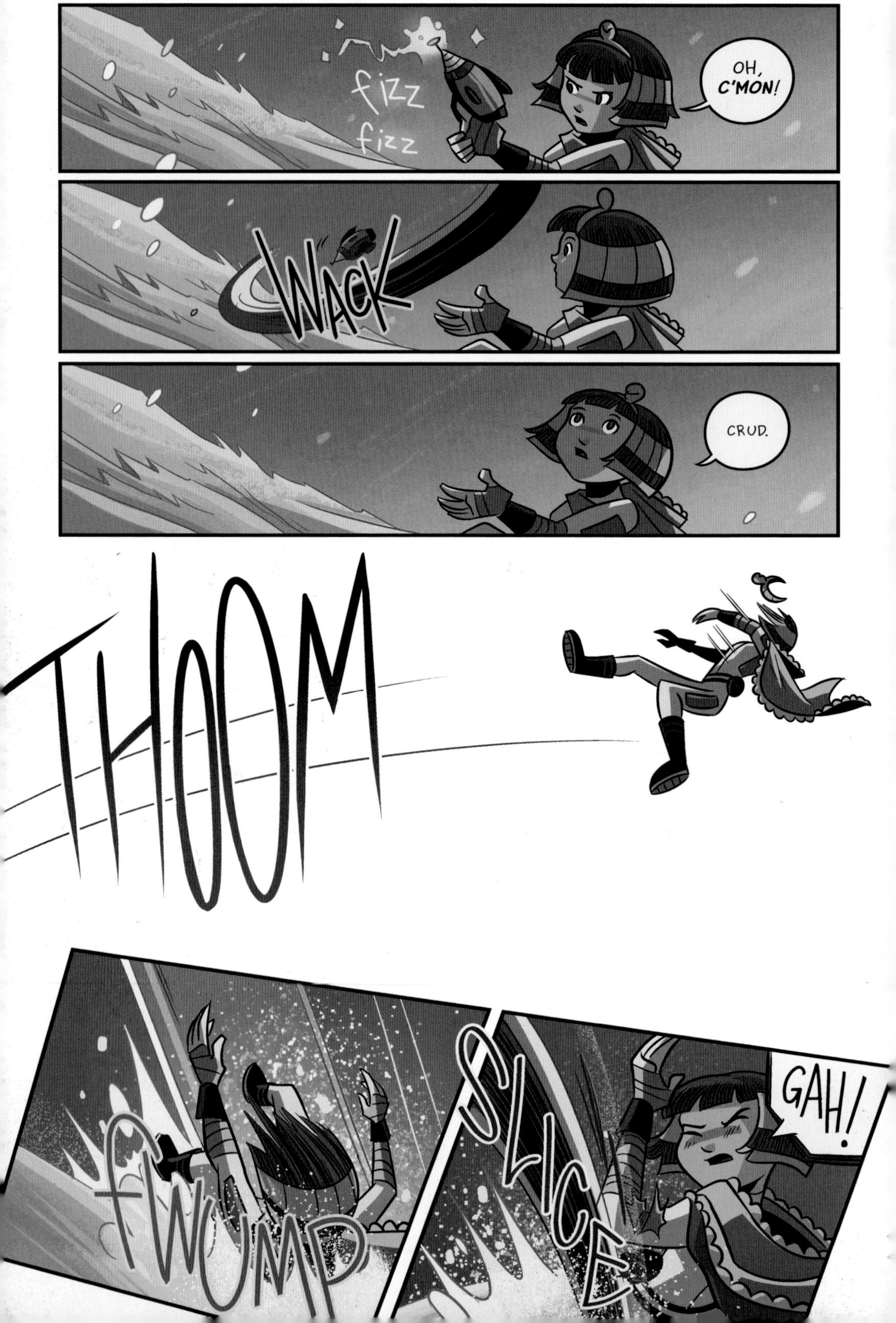
fizz
fizz
OH, C'MON!
WACK
CRUD.
THOOM
FWUMP
SLICE
GAH!

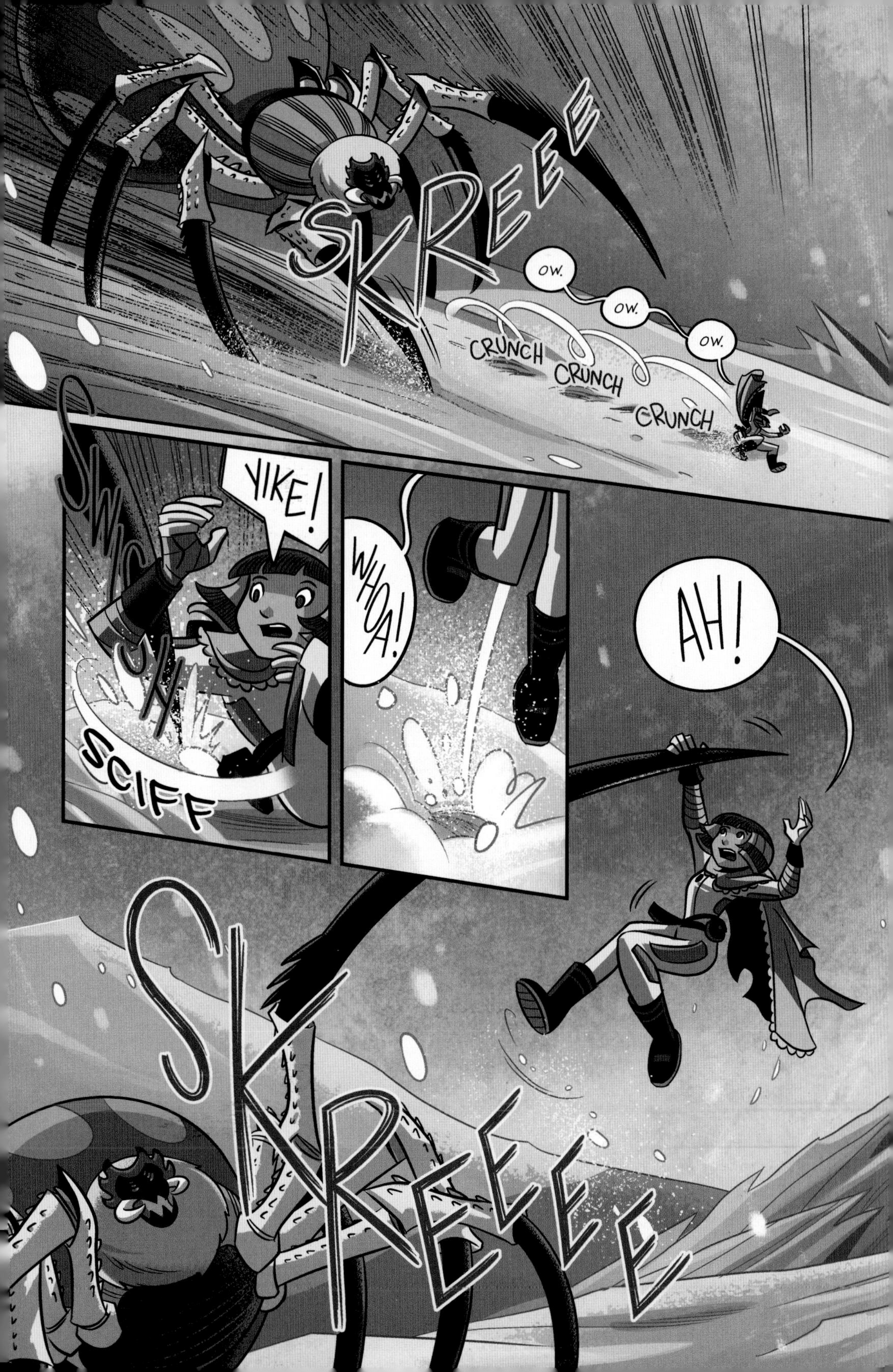
SKREEE
OW.
OW.
OW.
CRUNCH
CRUNCH
CRUNCH
SWISHHH
YIKE!
SCIFF
WHOA!
AH!
SKREEEE

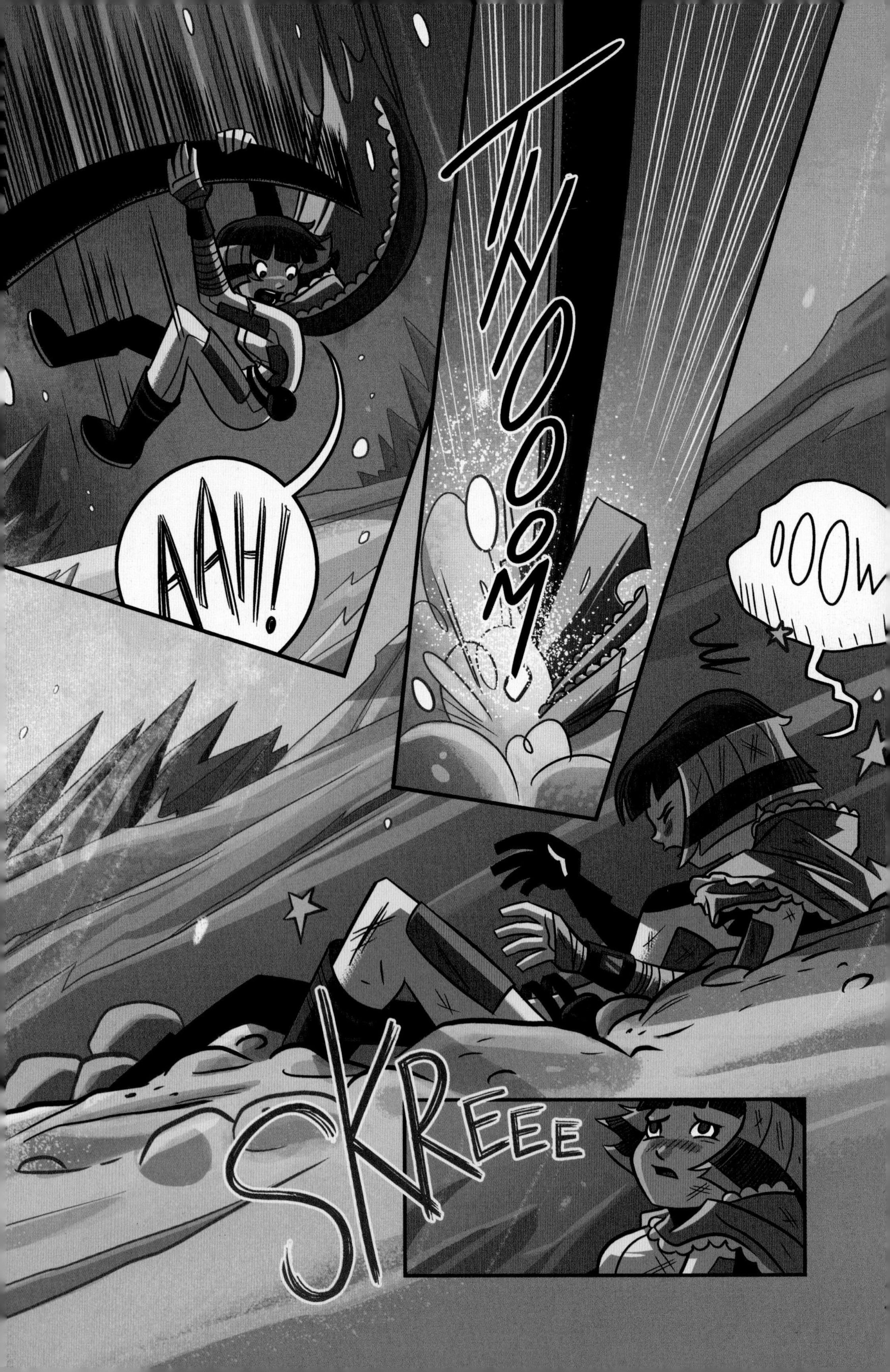
AAH!
THOOOOM
OOOW
SKREEE

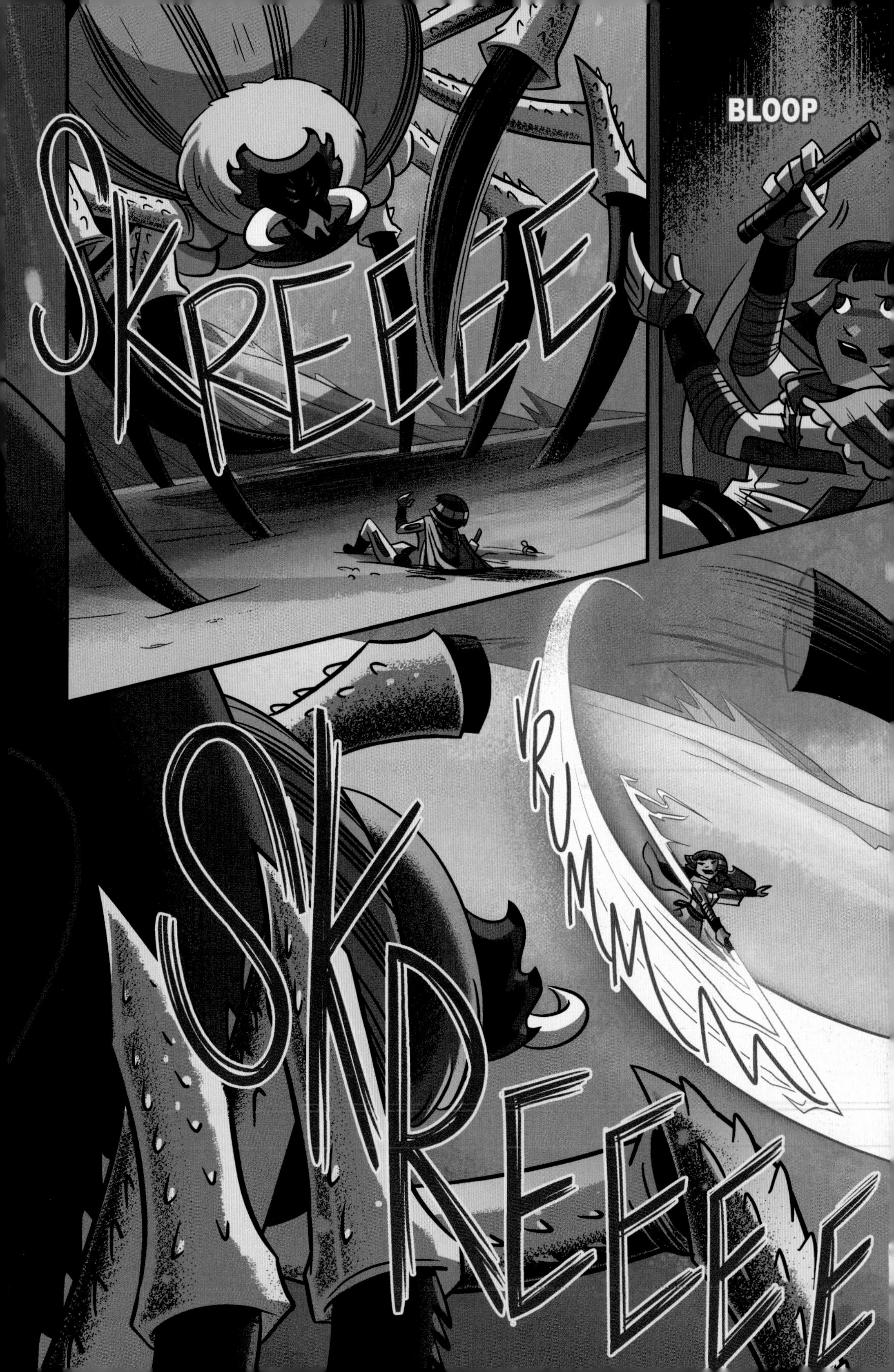
SKREEEEE
BLOOP
VRUMMMM
SKREEEEE

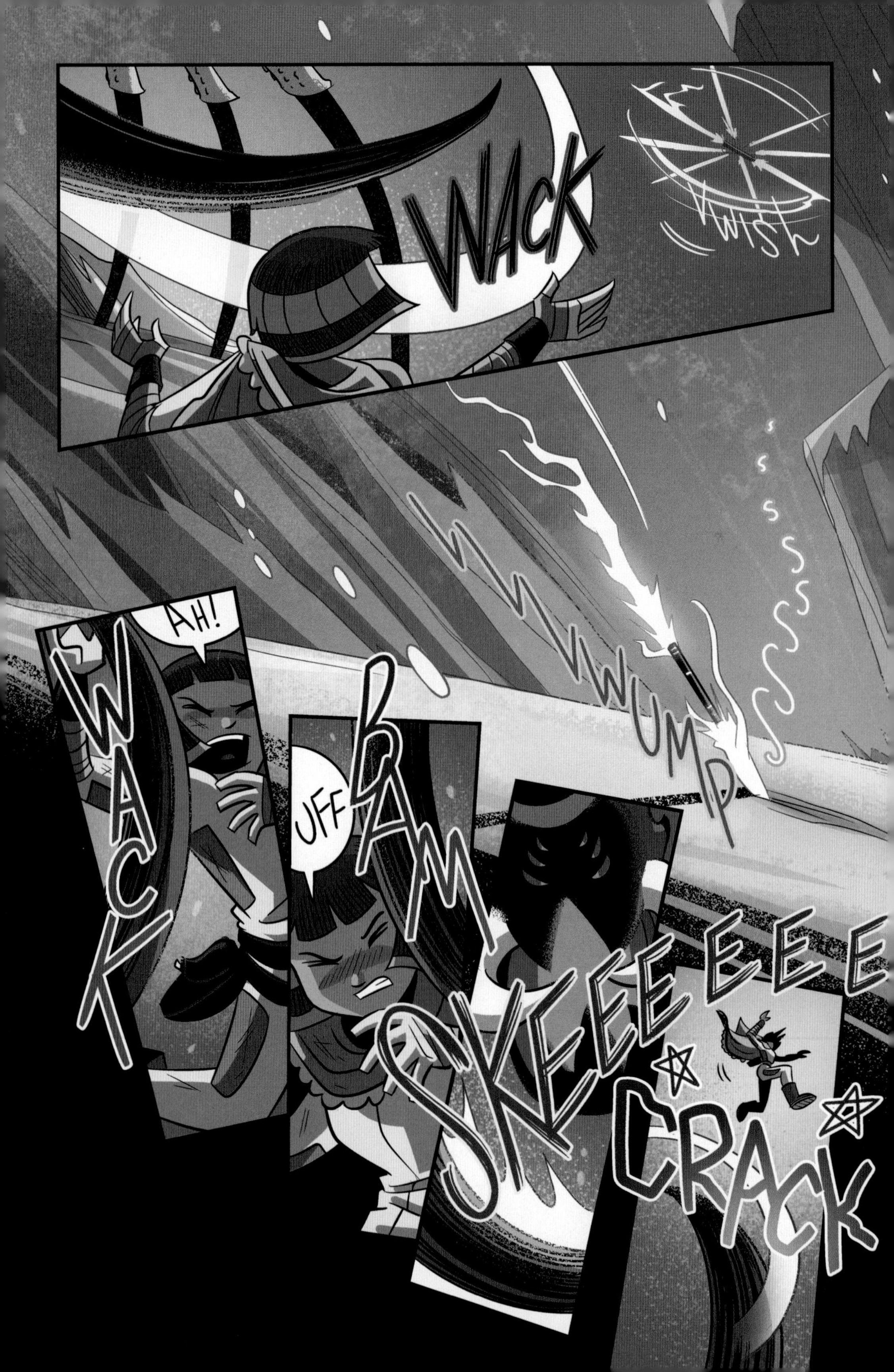
WACK
VWISH
VVVVVWUMP
SSSSSS
AH!
WACK
UFF
BAM
SKEEEEEEE
CRACK

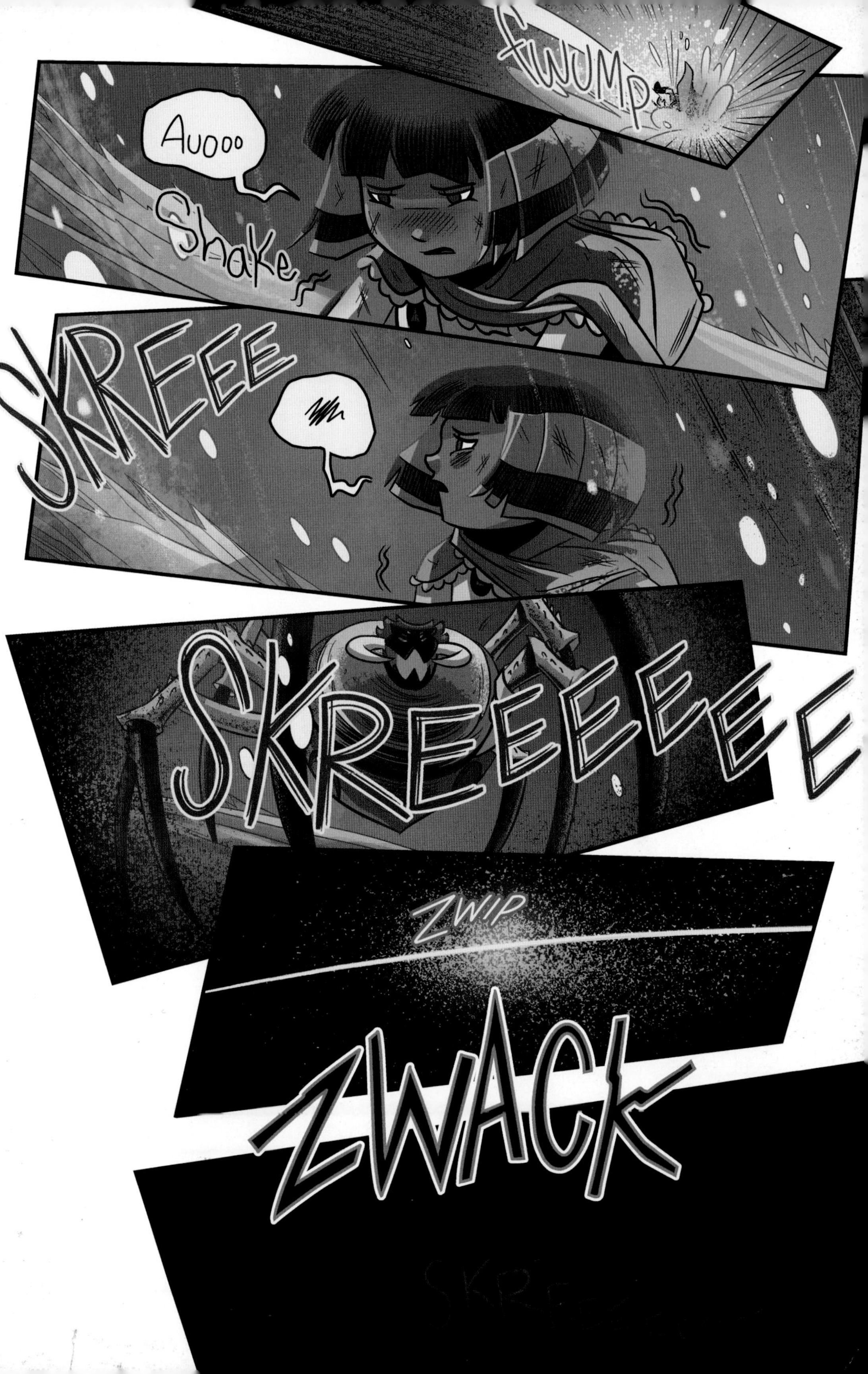
fWUMp
Auooo
Shake
SKREEE
SKREEEEEEE
ZWIP
ZWACK

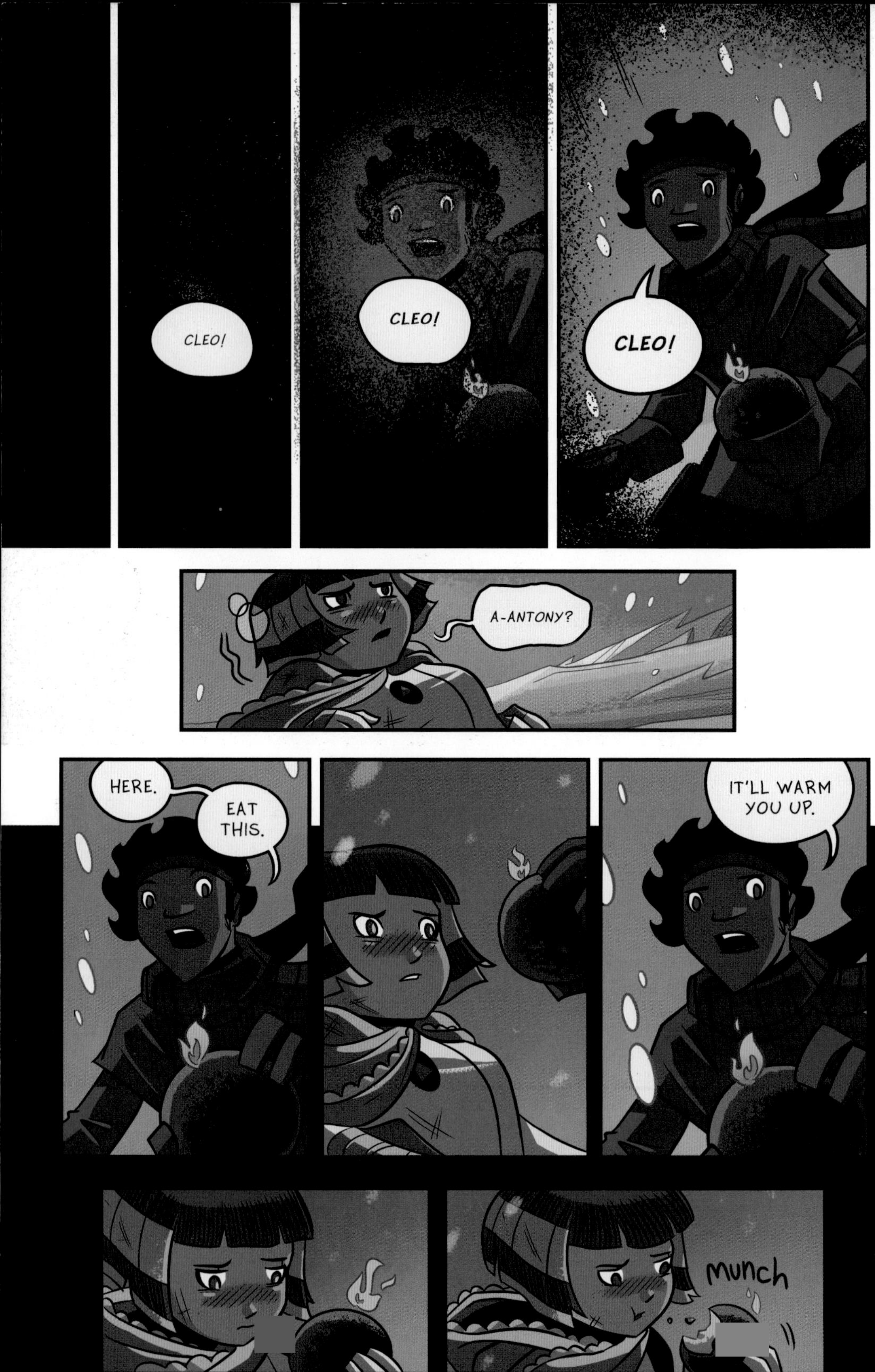
CLEO!
CLEO!
CLEO!
A-ANTONY?
HERE.
EAT THIS.
IT'LL WARM YOU UP.
Munch

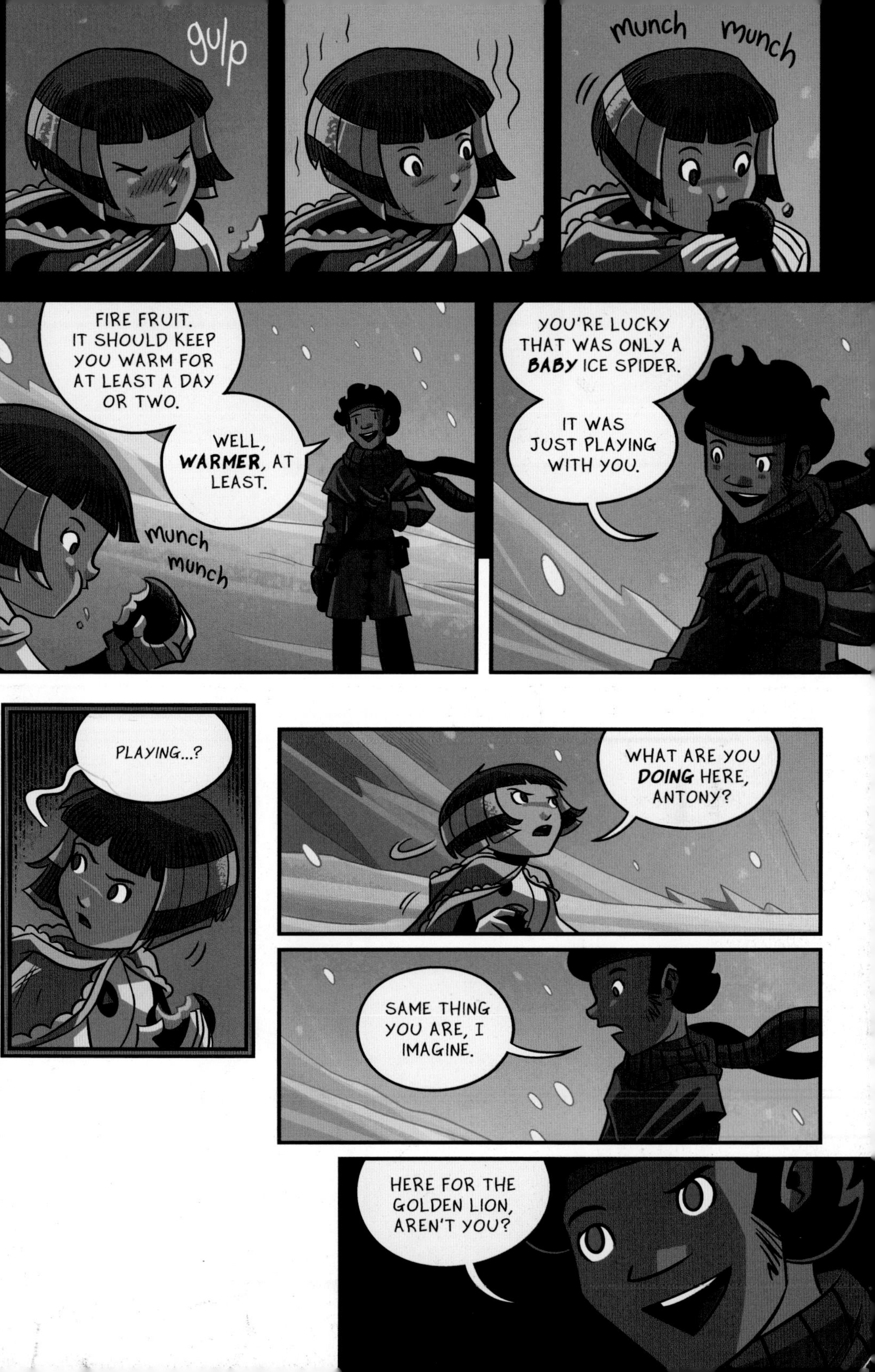
gulp
munch munch
FIRE FRUIT. IT SHOULD KEEP YOU WARM FOR AT LEAST A DAY OR TWO.
WELL, **WARMER**, AT LEAST.
munch munch
YOU'RE LUCKY THAT WAS ONLY A ***BABY*** ICE SPIDER.
IT WAS JUST PLAYING WITH YOU.
PLAYING...?
WHAT ARE YOU ***DOING*** HERE, ANTONY?
SAME THING YOU ARE, I IMAGINE.
HERE FOR THE GOLDEN LION, AREN'T YOU?

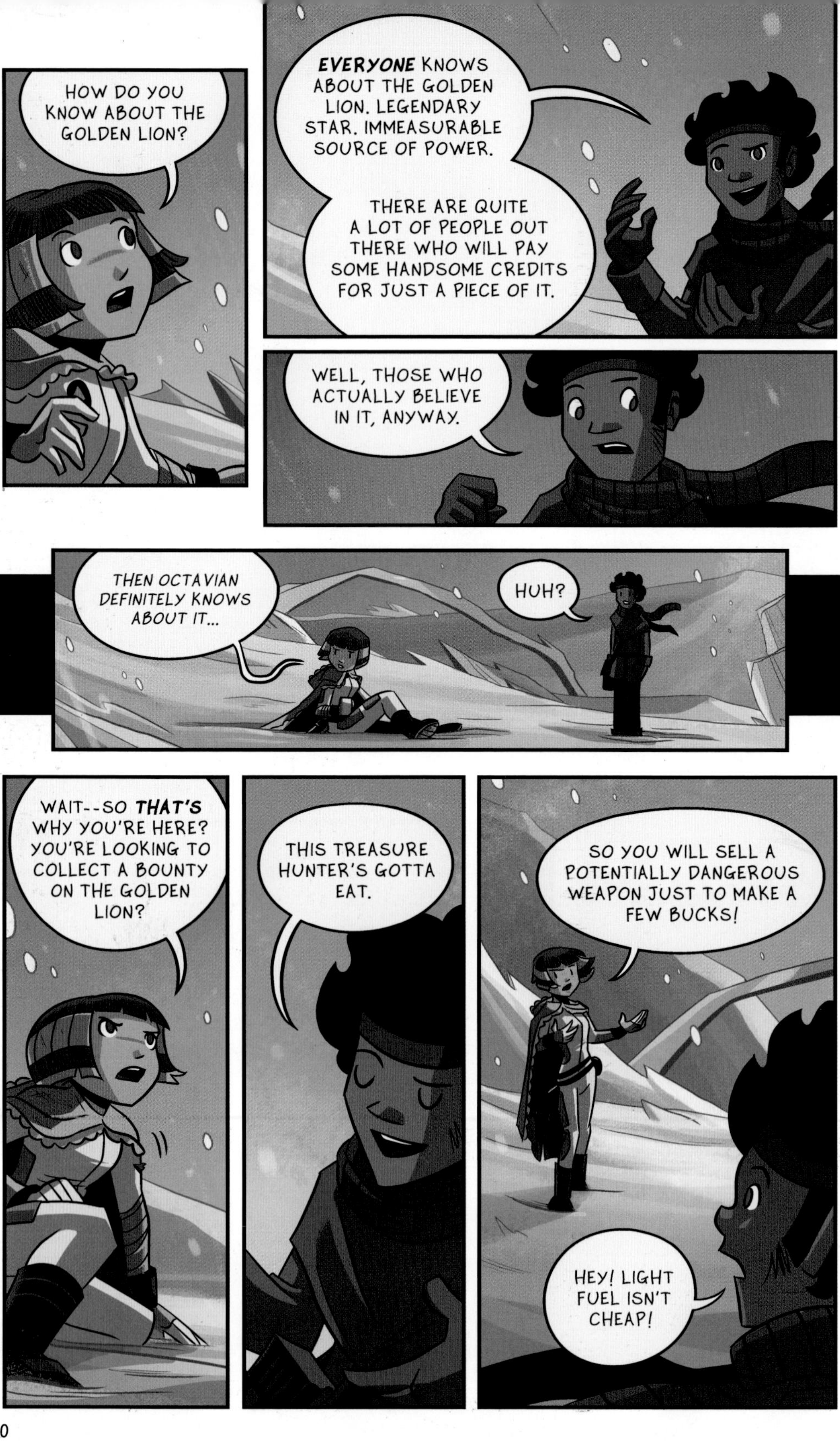
HOW DO YOU KNOW ABOUT THE GOLDEN LION?
EVERYONE KNOWS ABOUT THE GOLDEN LION. LEGENDARY STAR. IMMEASURABLE SOURCE OF POWER.
THERE ARE QUITE A LOT OF PEOPLE OUT THERE WHO WILL PAY SOME HANDSOME CREDITS FOR JUST A PIECE OF IT.
WELL, THOSE WHO ACTUALLY BELIEVE IN IT, ANYWAY.
THEN OCTAVIAN DEFINITELY KNOWS ABOUT IT...
HUH?
WAIT--SO THAT'S WHY YOU'RE HERE? YOU'RE LOOKING TO COLLECT A BOUNTY ON THE GOLDEN LION?
THIS TREASURE HUNTER'S GOTTA EAT.
SO YOU WILL SELL A POTENTIALLY DANGEROUS WEAPON JUST TO MAKE A FEW BUCKS!
HEY! LIGHT FUEL ISN'T CHEAP!

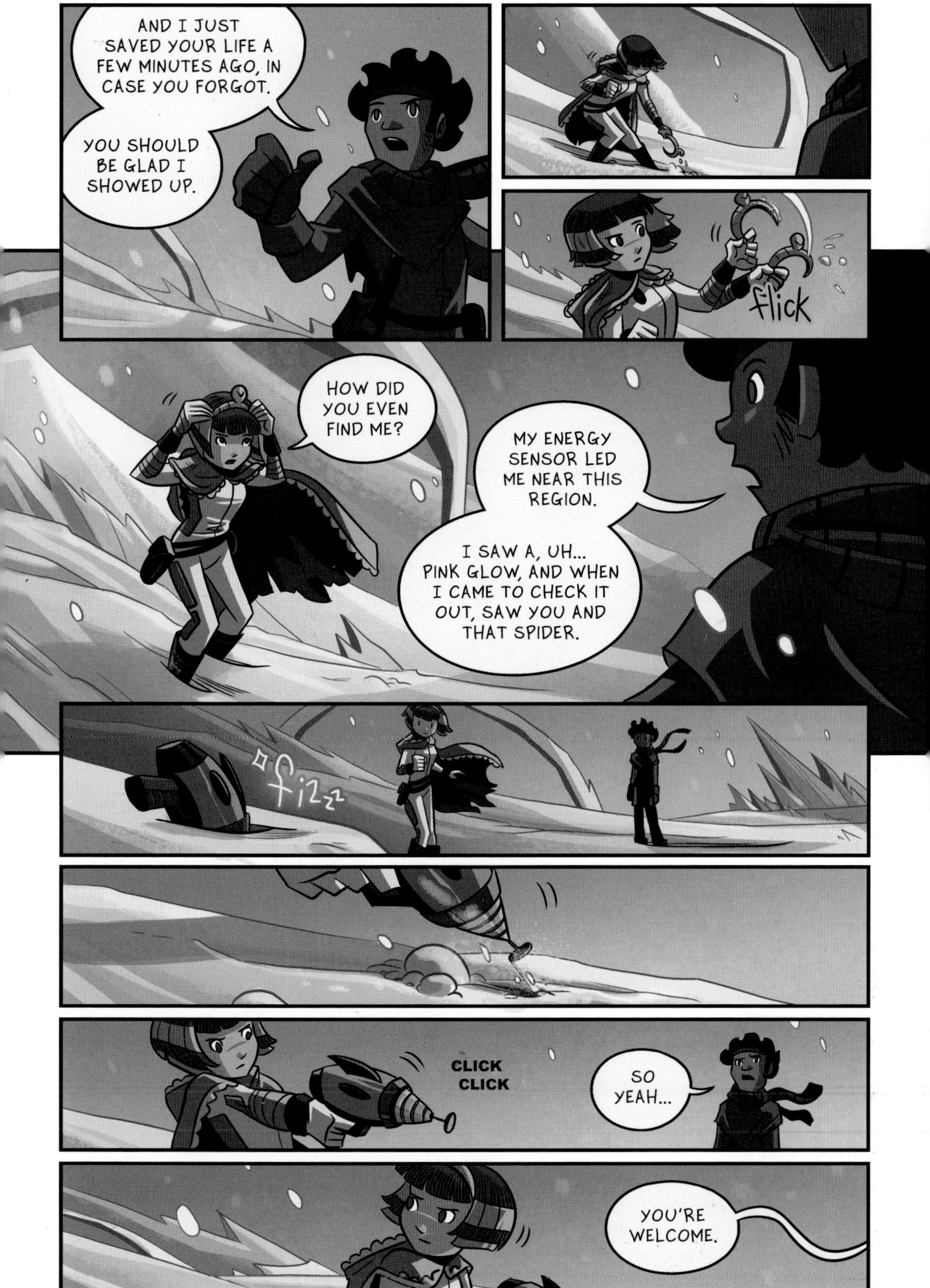
AND I JUST SAVED YOUR LIFE A FEW MINUTES AGO, IN CASE YOU FORGOT.
YOU SHOULD BE GLAD I SHOWED UP.
flick
HOW DID YOU EVEN FIND ME?
MY ENERGY SENSOR LED ME NEAR THIS REGION.
I SAW A, UH... PINK GLOW, AND WHEN I CAME TO CHECK IT OUT, SAW YOU AND THAT SPIDER.
fizzz
CLICK CLICK
SO YEAH...
YOU'RE WELCOME.

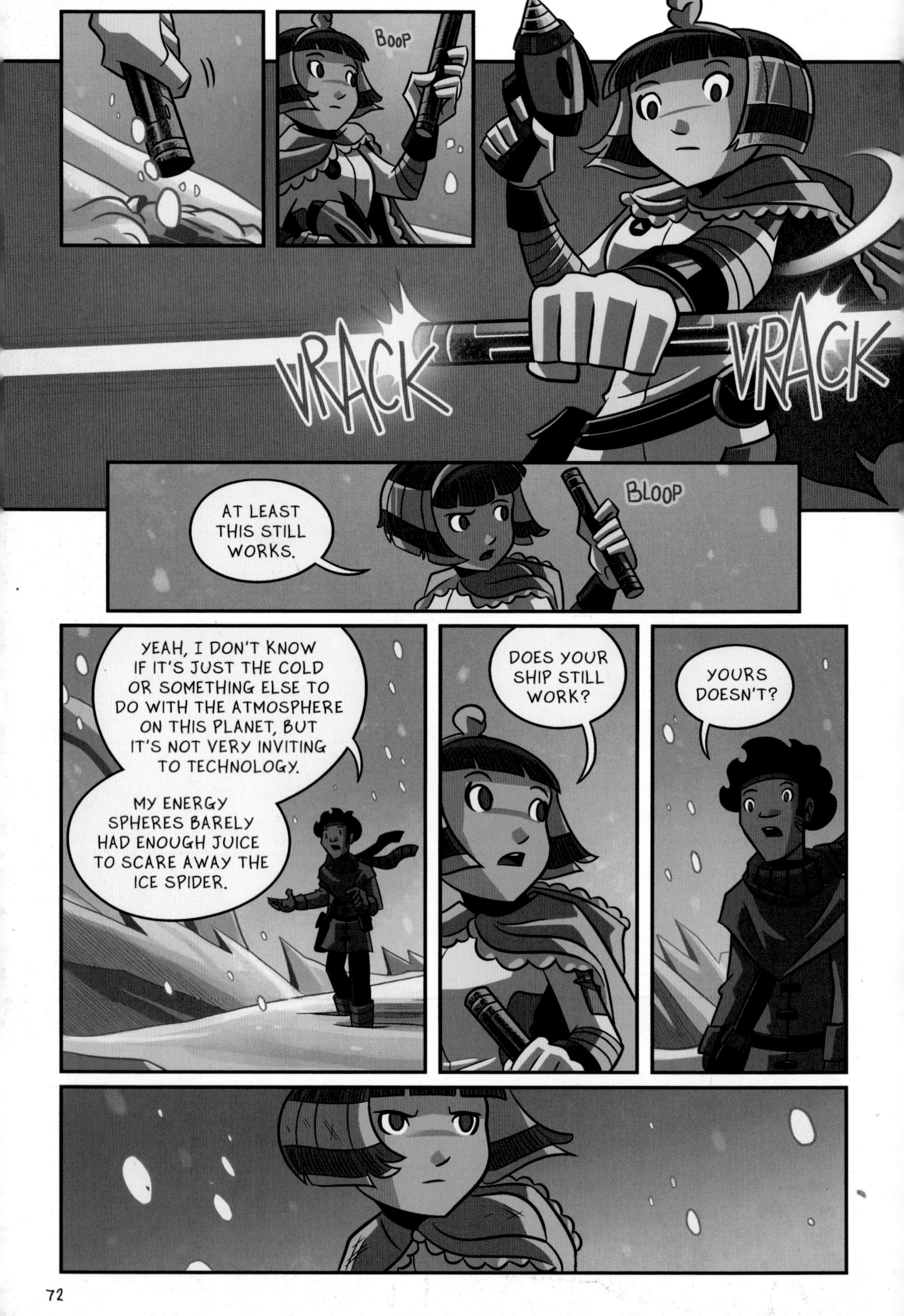
BOOP
VRACK
VRACK
BLOOP
AT LEAST THIS STILL WORKS.
YEAH, I DON'T KNOW IF IT'S JUST THE COLD OR SOMETHING ELSE TO DO WITH THE ATMOSPHERE ON THIS PLANET, BUT IT'S NOT VERY INVITING TO TECHNOLOGY.
MY ENERGY SPHERES BARELY HAD ENOUGH JUICE TO SCARE AWAY THE ICE SPIDER.
DOES YOUR SHIP STILL WORK?
YOURS DOESN'T?

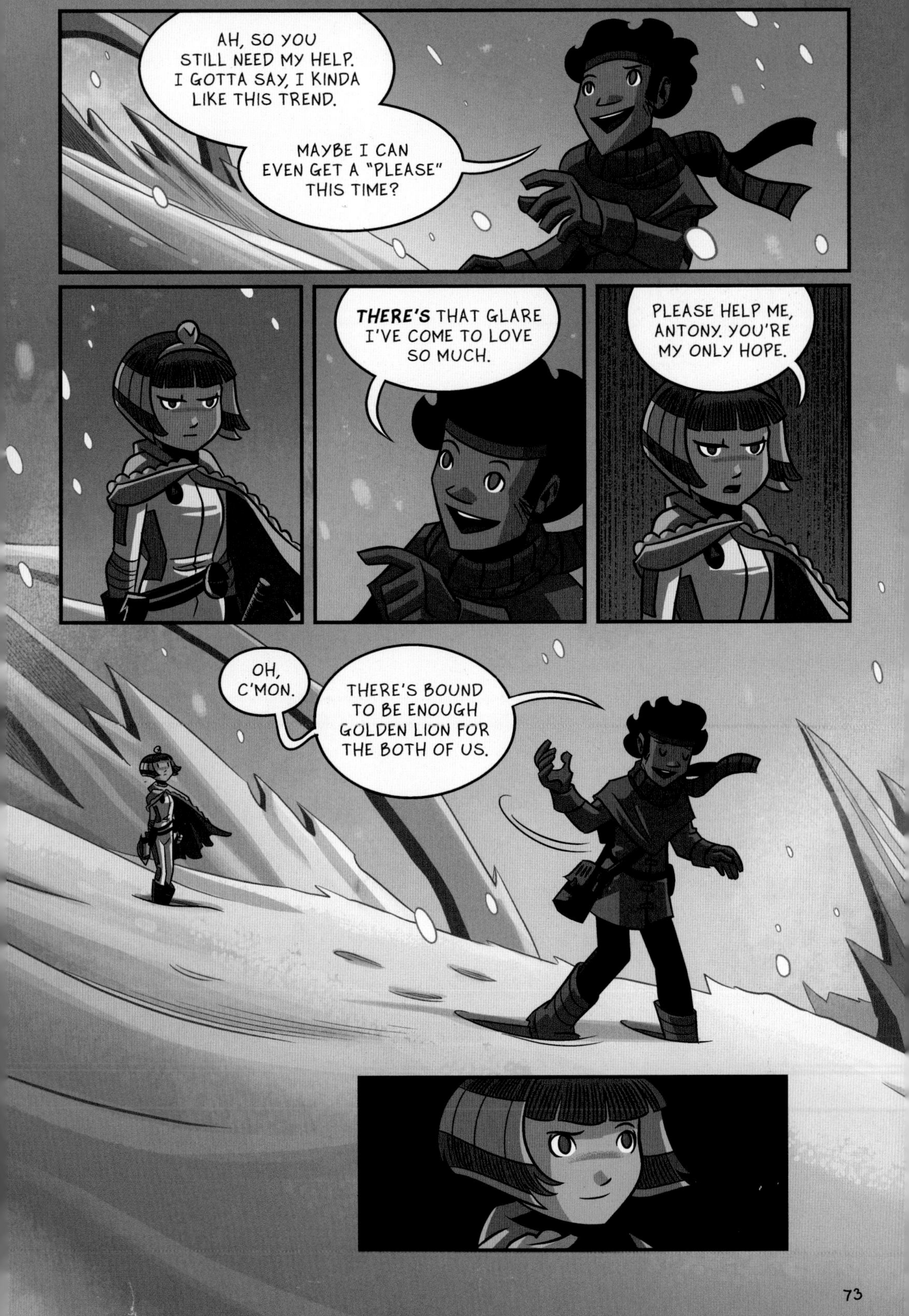
AH, SO YOU STILL NEED MY HELP. I GOTTA SAY, I KINDA LIKE THIS TREND.
MAYBE I CAN EVEN GET A "PLEASE" THIS TIME?
**THERE'S** THAT GLARE I'VE COME TO LOVE SO MUCH.
PLEASE HELP ME, ANTONY. YOU'RE MY ONLY HOPE.
OH, C'MON.
THERE'S BOUND TO BE ENOUGH GOLDEN LION FOR THE BOTH OF US.

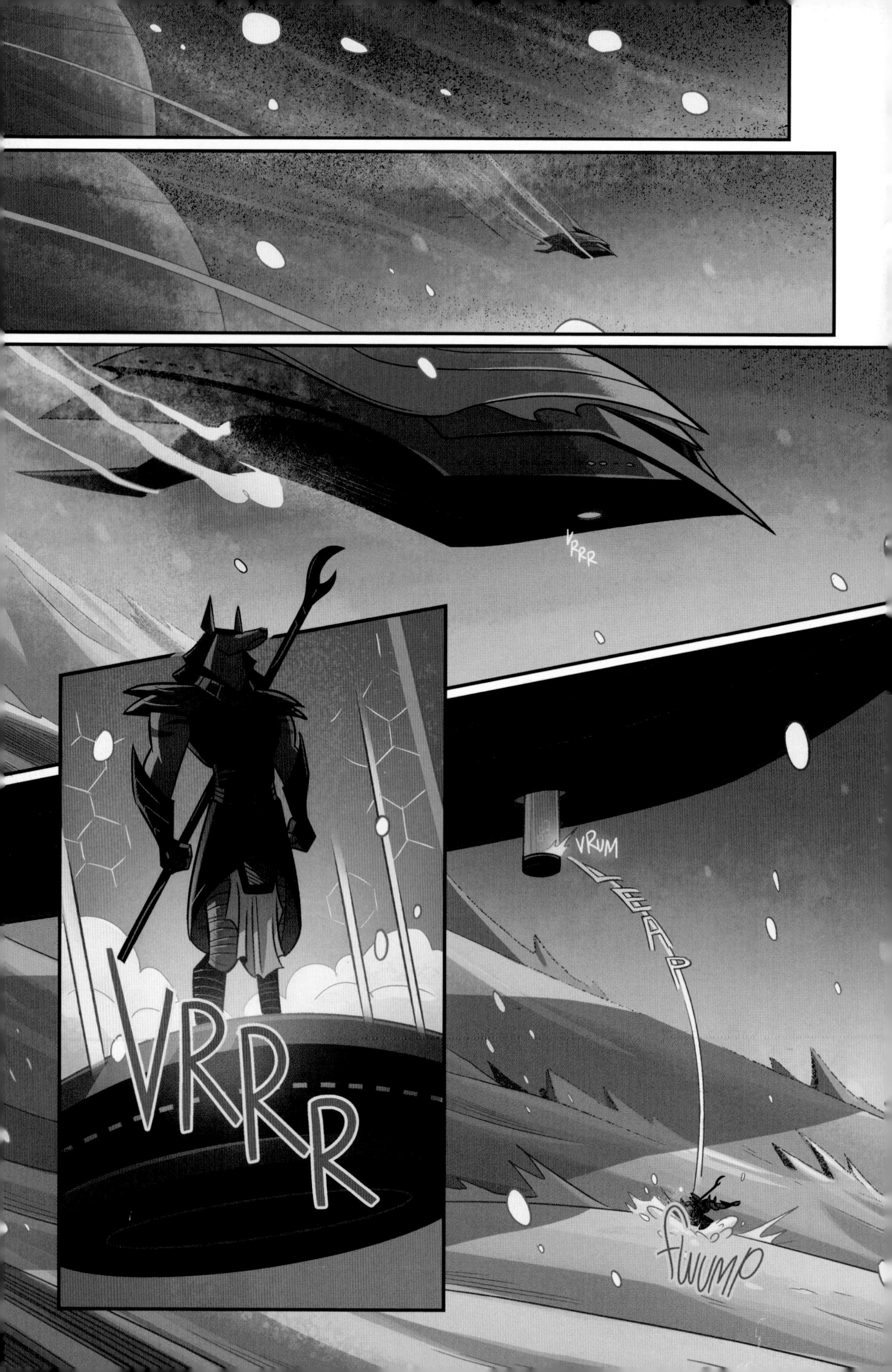
VRRR
VRRR
VRUM
LEAP
FWUMP

sniff

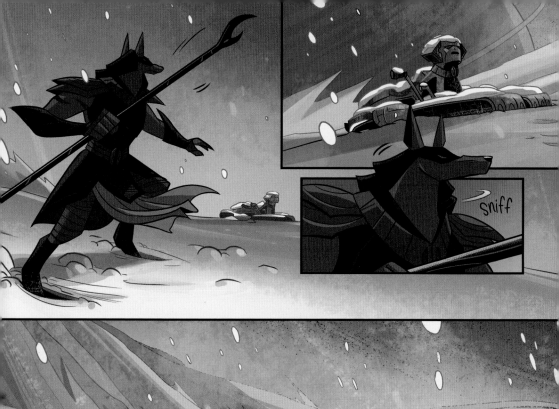

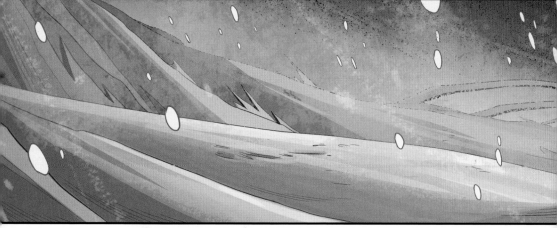

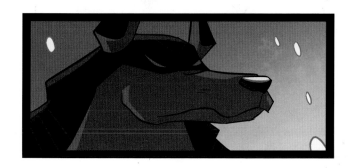

# CHAPTER TWO

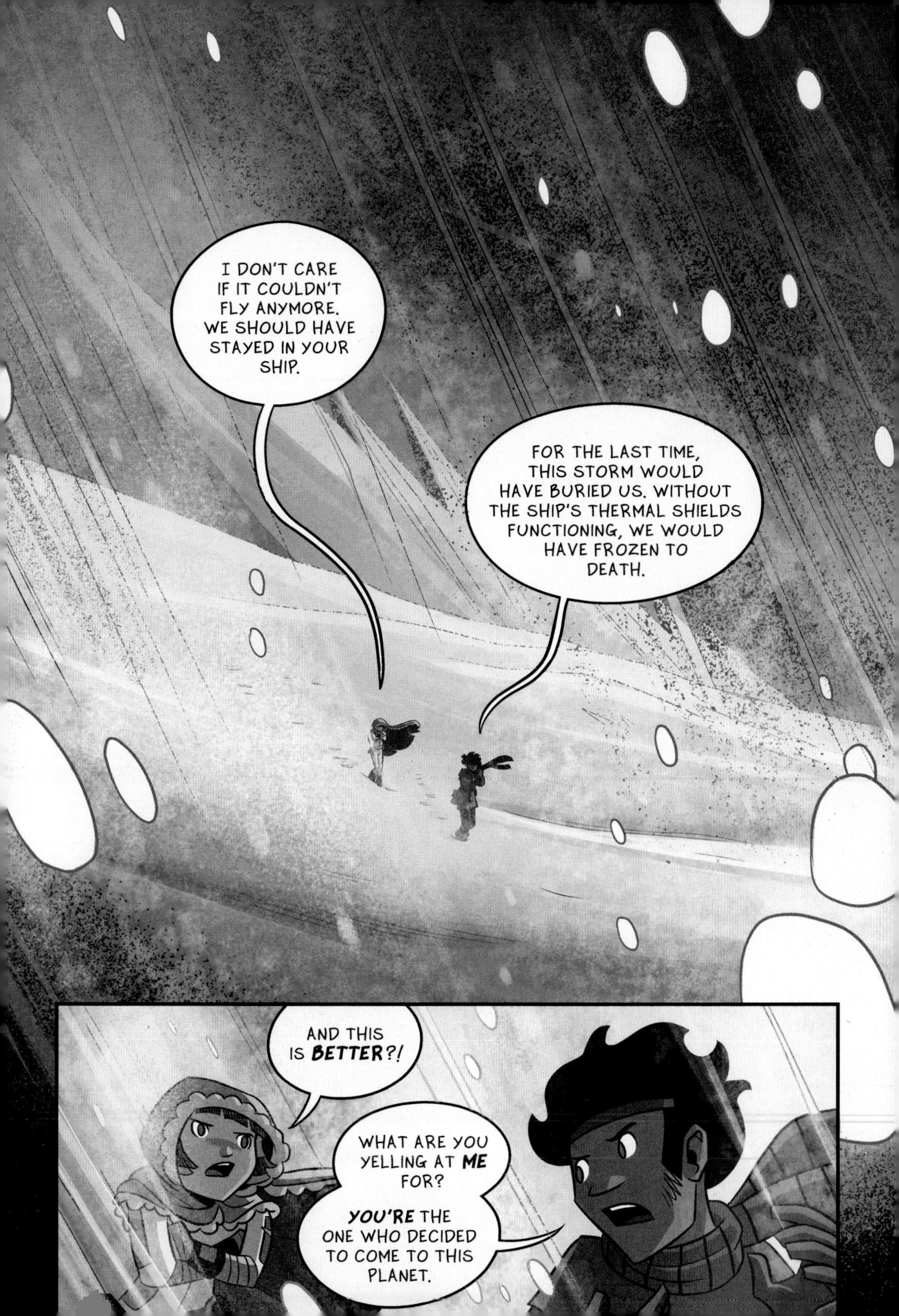
I DON'T CARE IF IT COULDN'T FLY ANYMORE. WE SHOULD HAVE STAYED IN YOUR SHIP.
FOR THE LAST TIME, THIS STORM WOULD HAVE BURIED US. WITHOUT THE SHIP'S THERMAL SHIELDS FUNCTIONING, WE WOULD HAVE FROZEN TO DEATH.
AND THIS IS **BETTER**?!
WHAT ARE YOU YELLING AT **ME** FOR?
***YOU'RE*** THE ONE WHO DECIDED TO COME TO THIS PLANET.

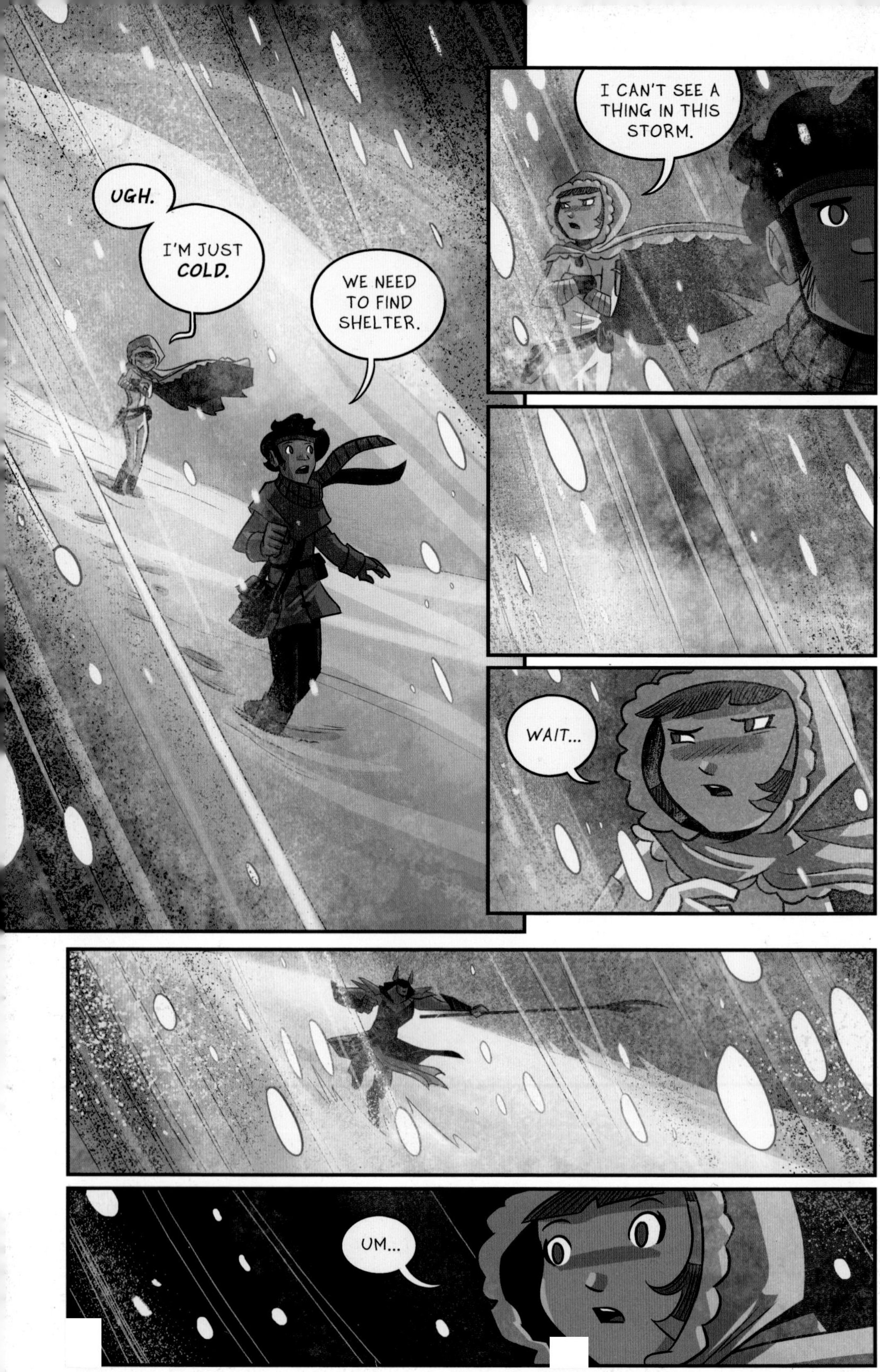
UGH.
I'M JUST COLD.
WE NEED TO FIND SHELTER.
I CAN'T SEE A THING IN THIS STORM.
WAIT...
UM...

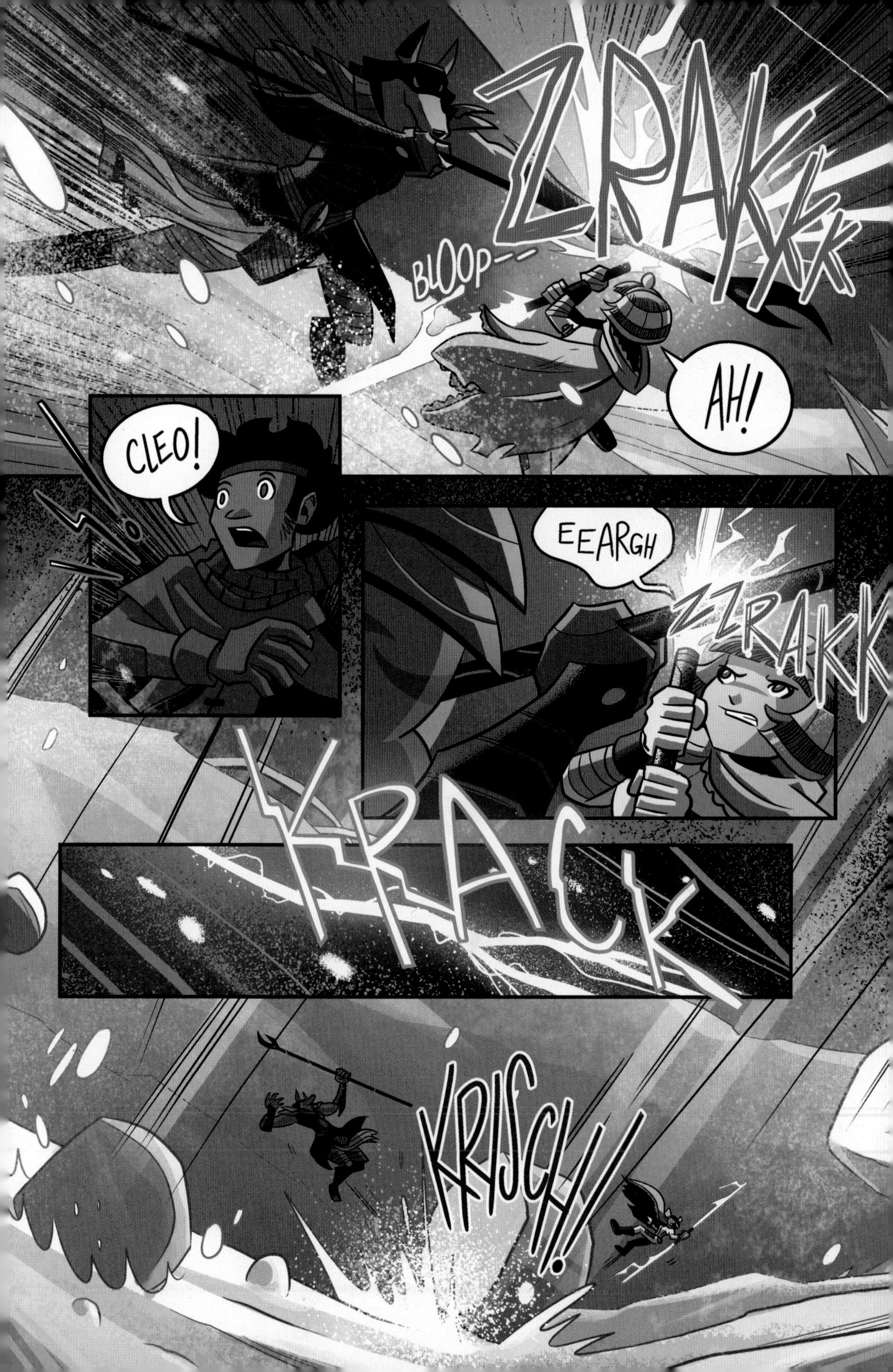
ZRAKKKK
BLOOP---
AH!
CLEO!
EEARGH
ZZRAKK
KRACK
KRISCH!!

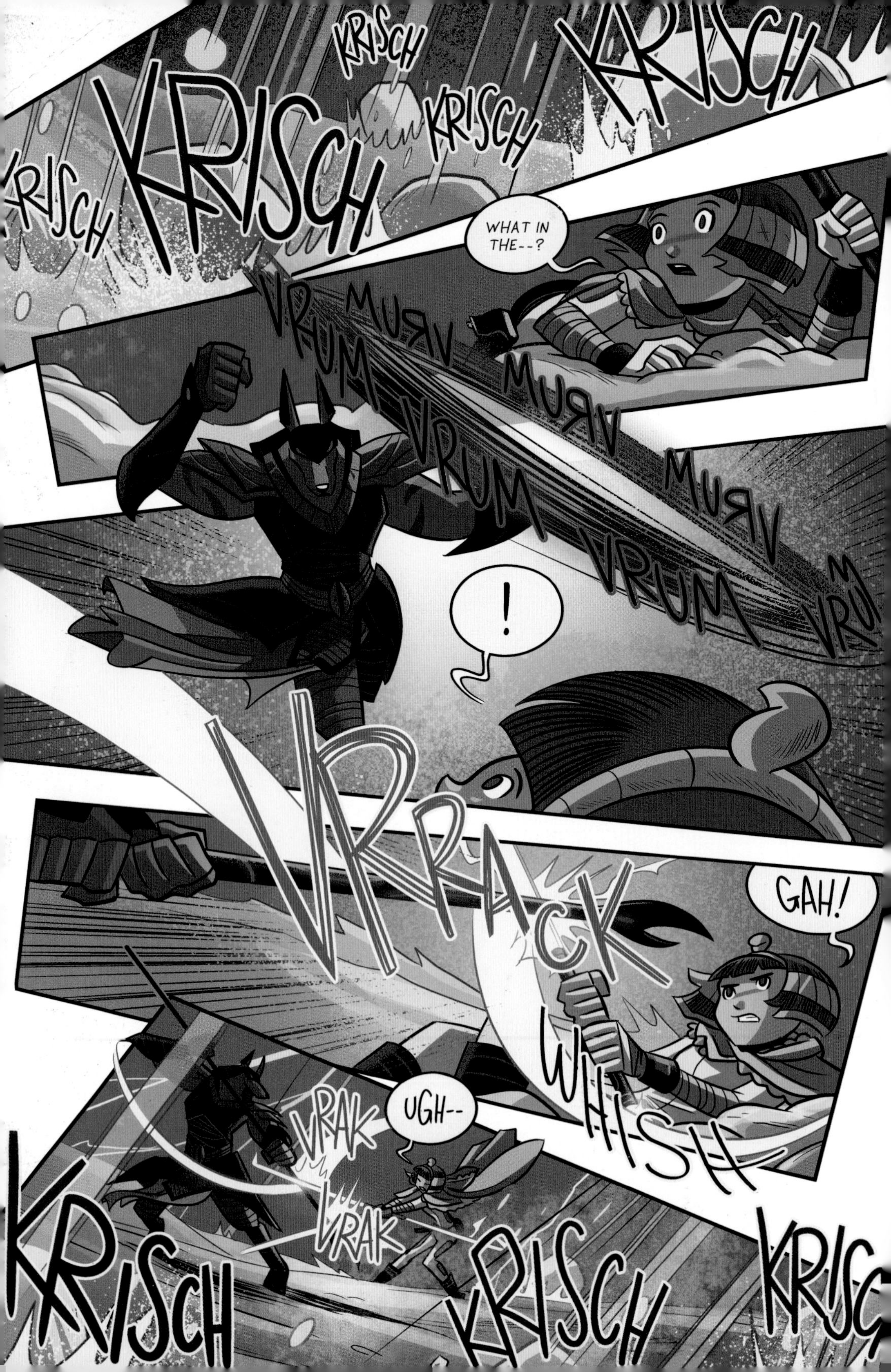
KRISCH
KRISCH
KRISCH
KRISCH
KRISCH
WHAT IN THE--?
VRUM VRUM VRUM VRUM VRUM VRUM VRUM VRUM
!
VRRACK
GAH!
WHISH
VRAK
UGH--
VRAK
KRISCH
KRISCH
KRISCH

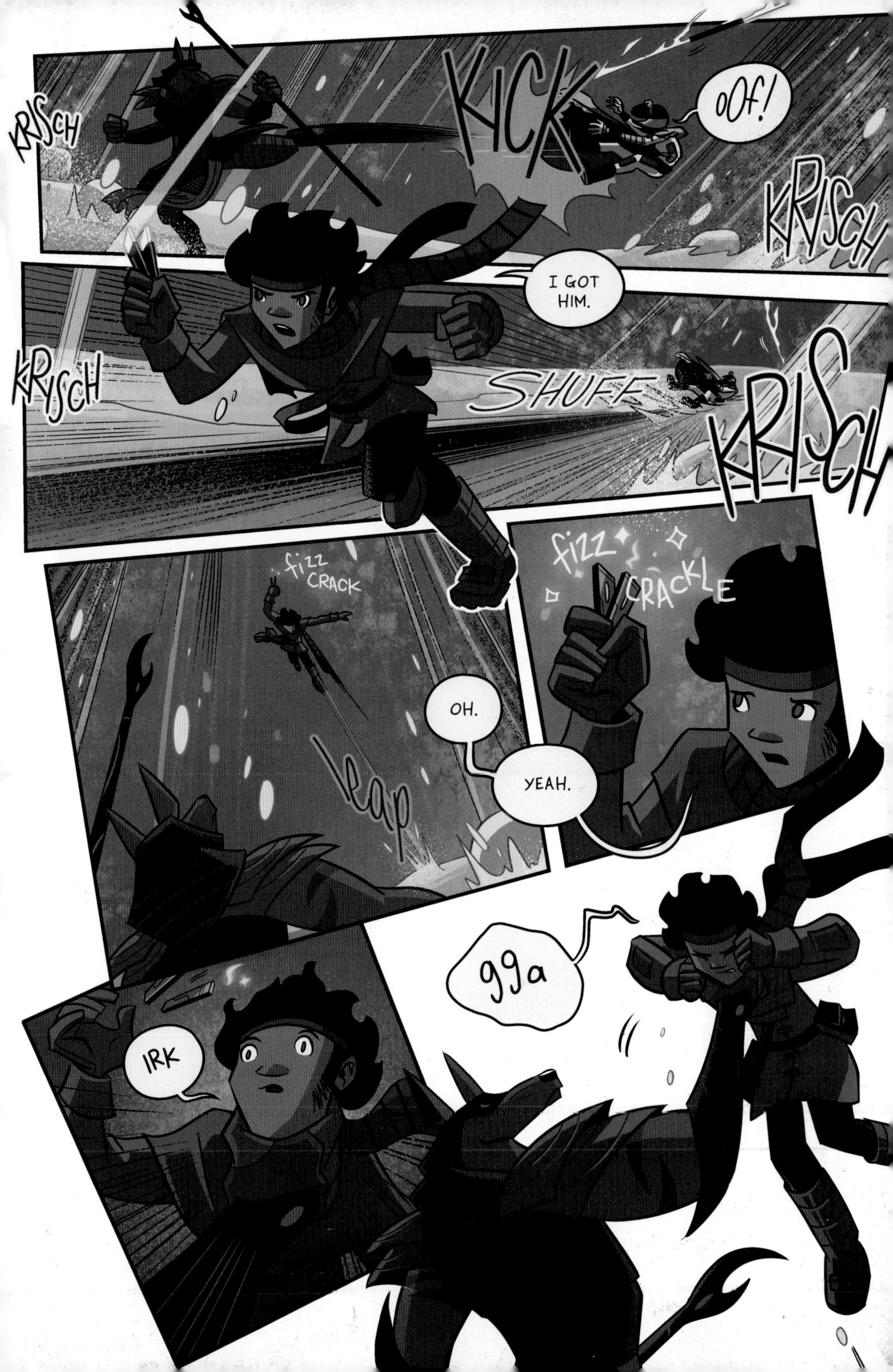

KRISCH
KICK
oOf!
KRISCH
I GOT HIM.
KRISCH
SHUFF
KRISCH
fizz CRACK
leap
fizz CRACKLE
OH.
YEAH.
gga
IRK

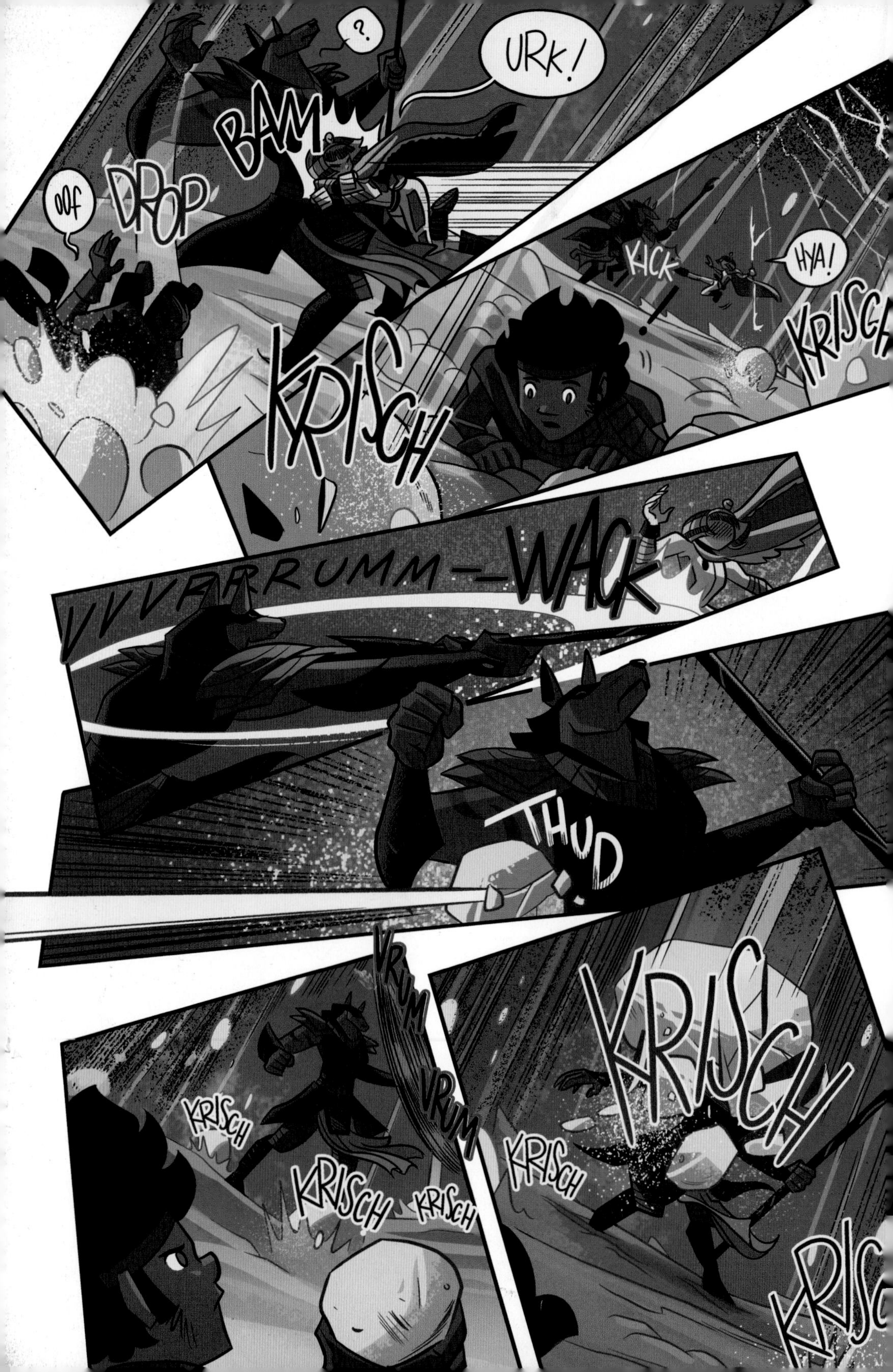
?
URK!
BAM
OOF
DROP
KRISCH
KICK
HYA!
KRISCH
VVVVRRRUMM--WACK
THUD
VRUM
VRUM
KRISCH
KRISCH
KRISCH
KRISCH
KRISCH
KRISCH

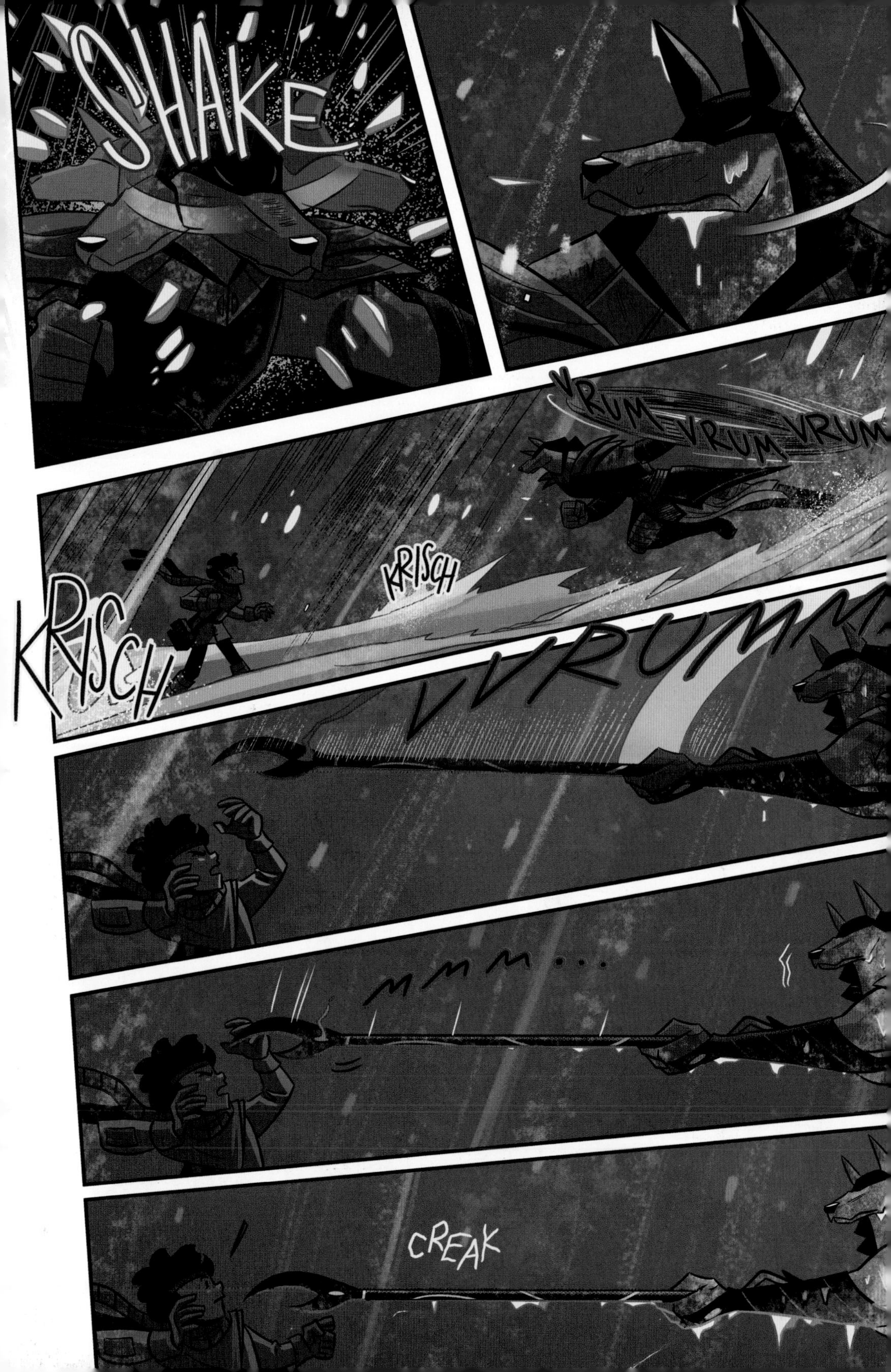
SHAKE
VRUM VRUM VRUM
KRISCH
KRISCH
VVRUMM
MMM...
CREAK

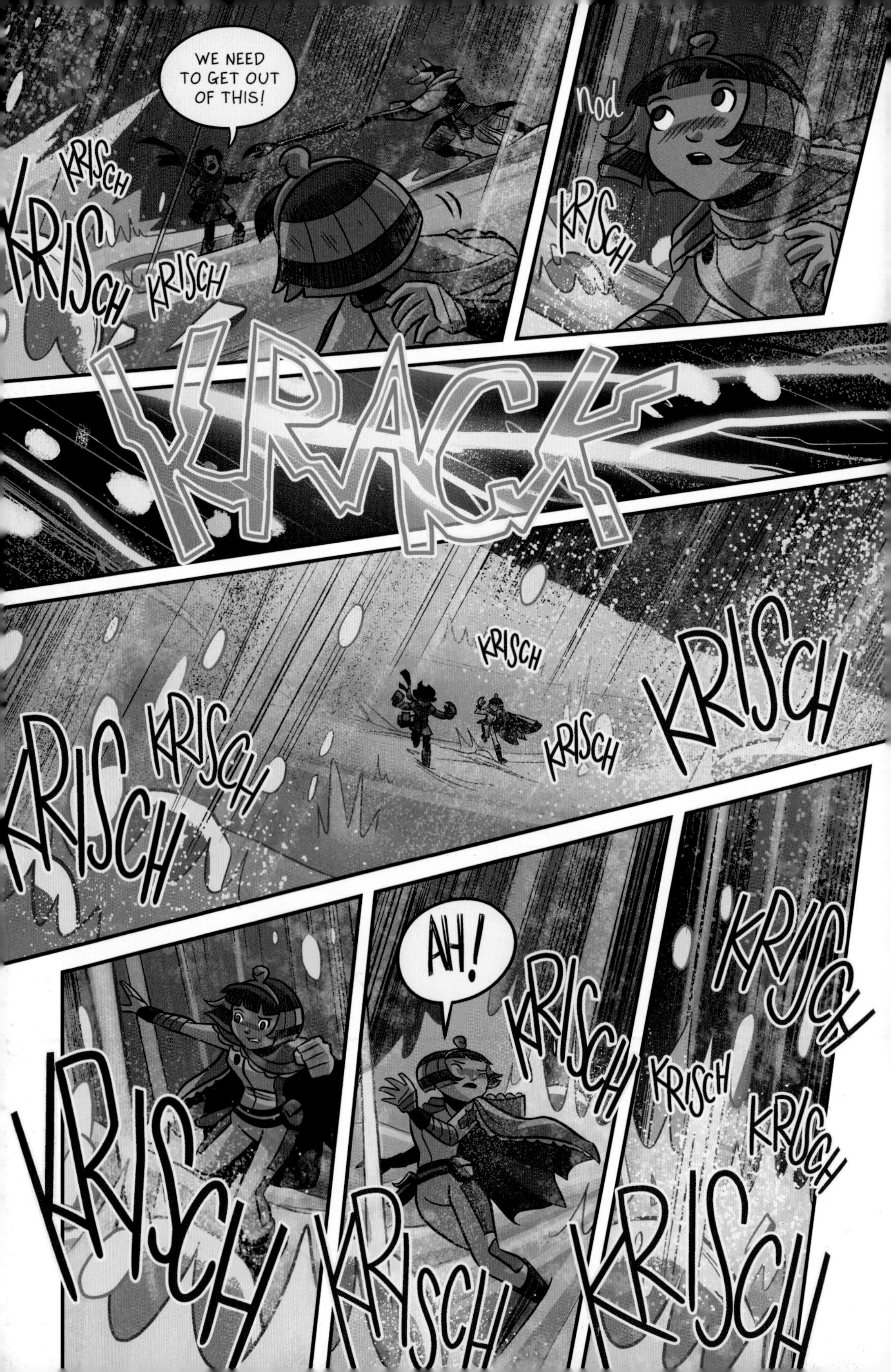
WE NEED TO GET OUT OF THIS!
KRISCH
KRISCH
KRISCH
nod
KRISCH
KRACK
KRISCH
KRISCH
KRISCH
KRISCH
KRISCH
KRISCH
AH!
KRISCH
KRISCH
KRISCH
KRUSCH
KRISCH
KRISCH
KRISCH

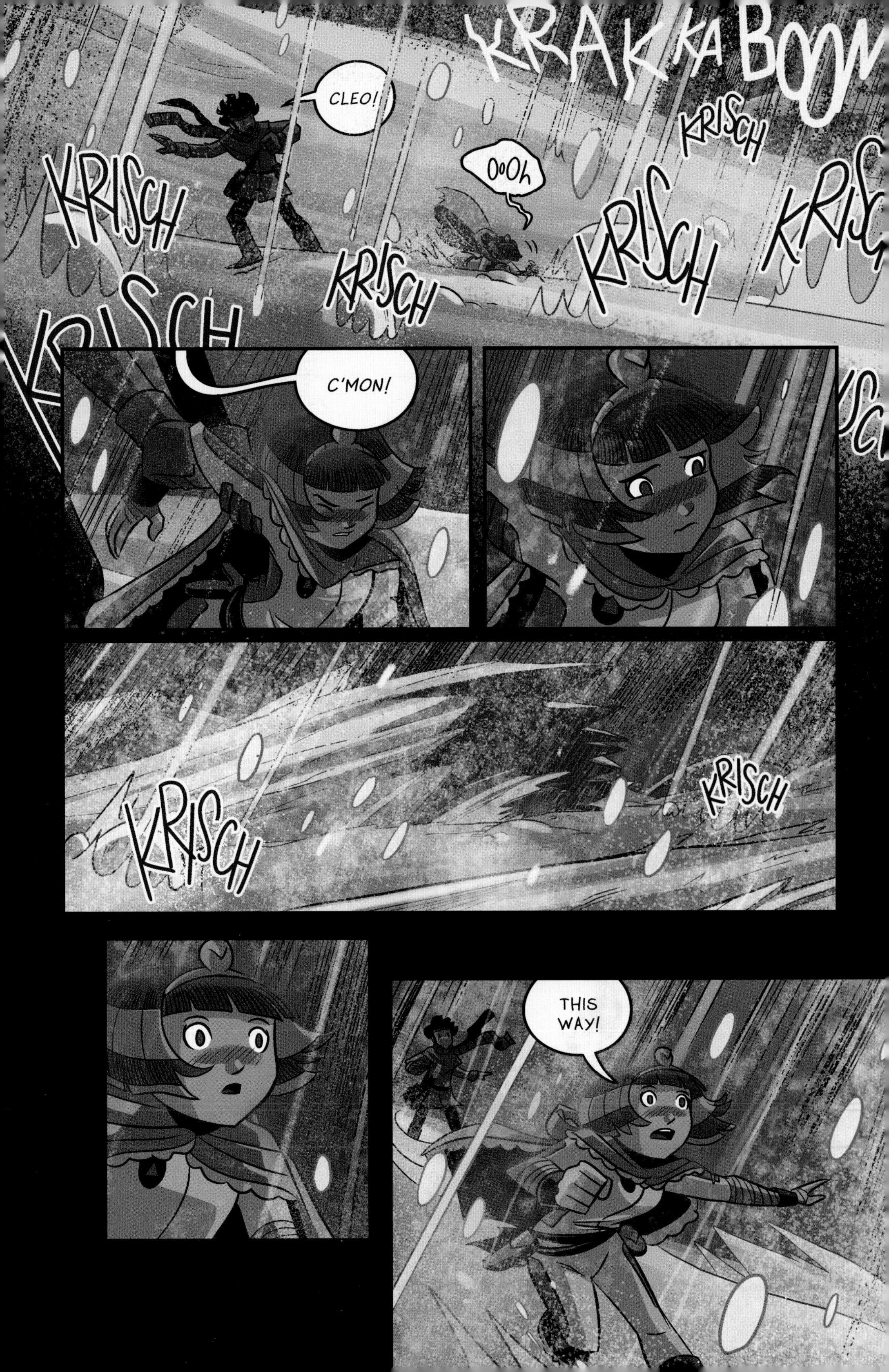
KRAK KA BOOM
CLEO!
OoOh
KRISCH
KRISCH
KRISCH
KRISCH
KRISCH
KRISCH
C'MON!
KRISCH
KRISCH
THIS WAY!

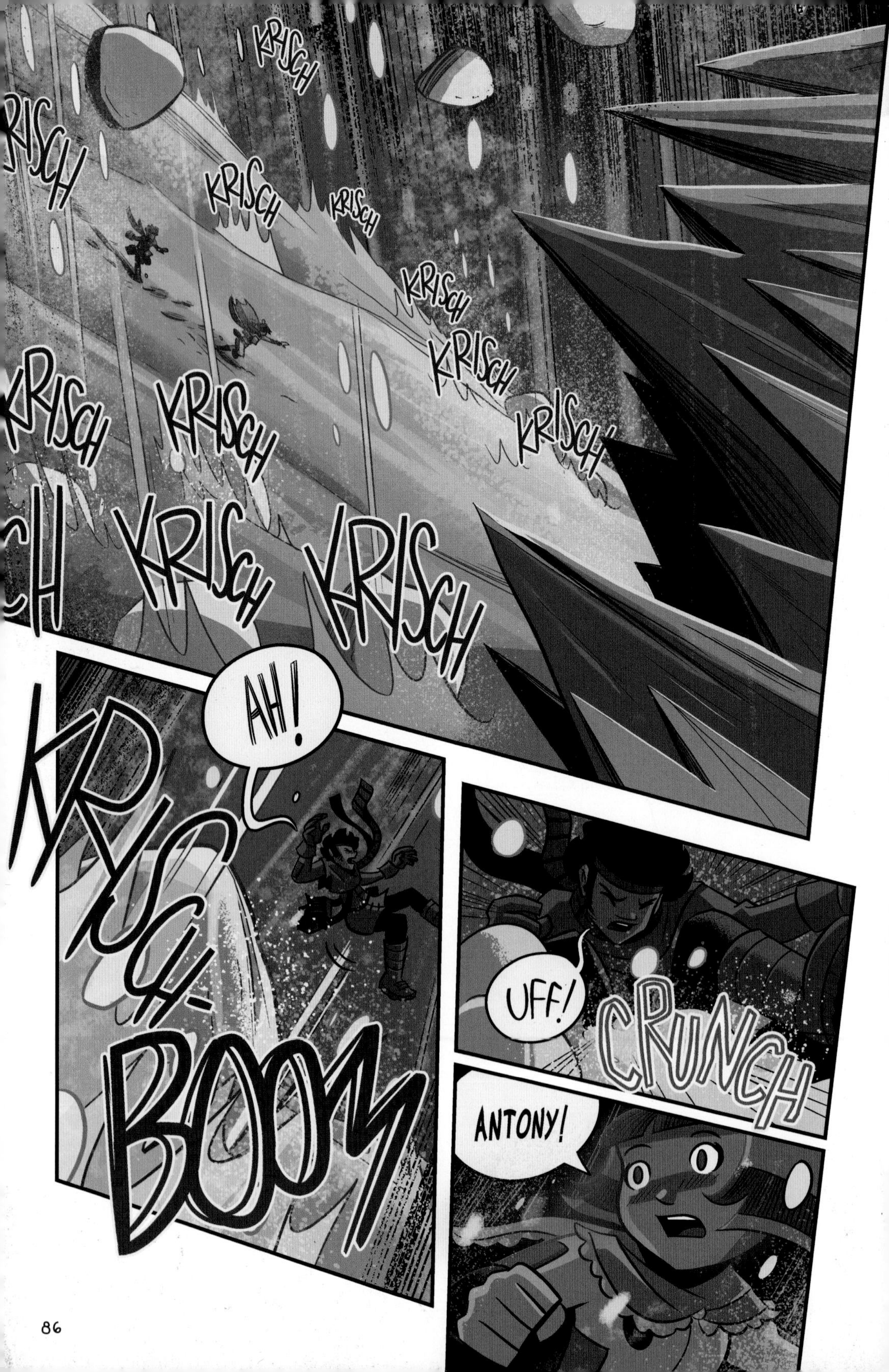
KRISCH
KRISCH
KRISCH
KRISCH
KRISCH
KRISCH
KRISCH
KRISCH
KRISCH
CH
KRISCH
KRISCH
AH!
KRISCH-BOOM
UFF!
CRUNCH
ANTONY!

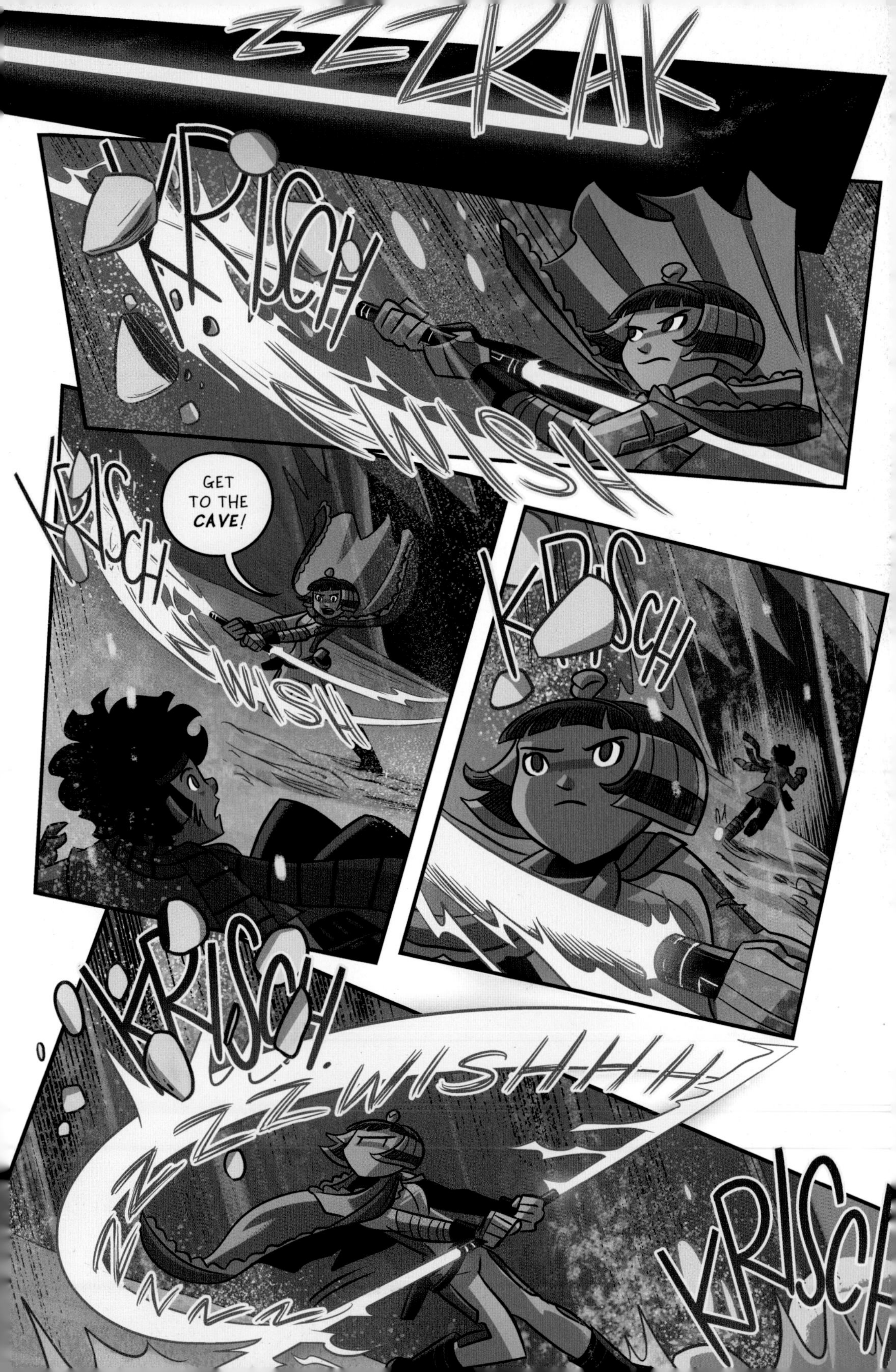
ZZZKAK
KRISCH
ZWISH
KRISCH
GET TO THE CAVE!
ZWISH
KRISCH
KRISCH
ZZZWISHHH
KRISCH

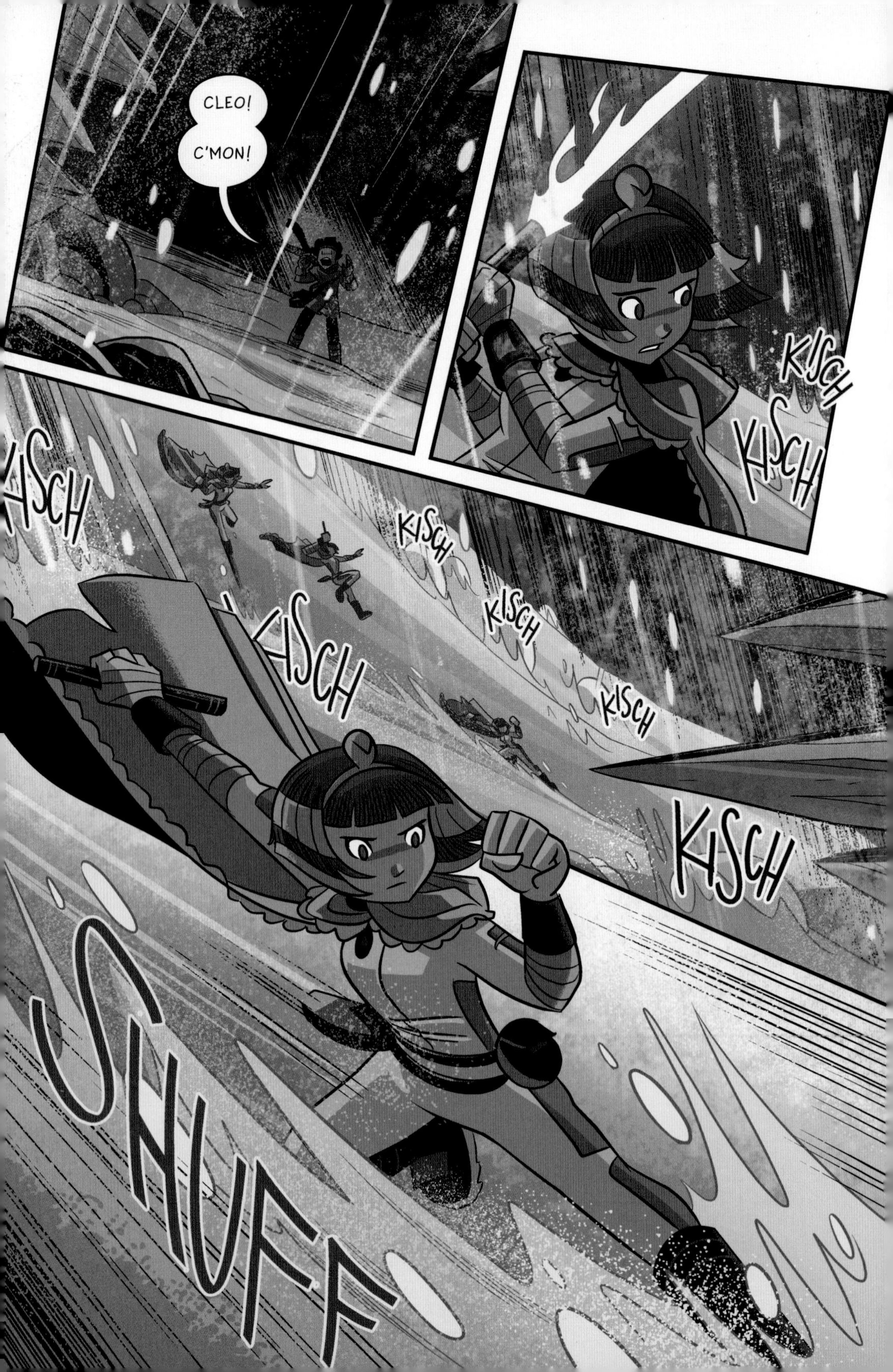
CLEO!
C'MON!
KISCH
KISCH
KISCH
KISCH
KISCH
KISCH
KISCH
KISCH
SHUFF

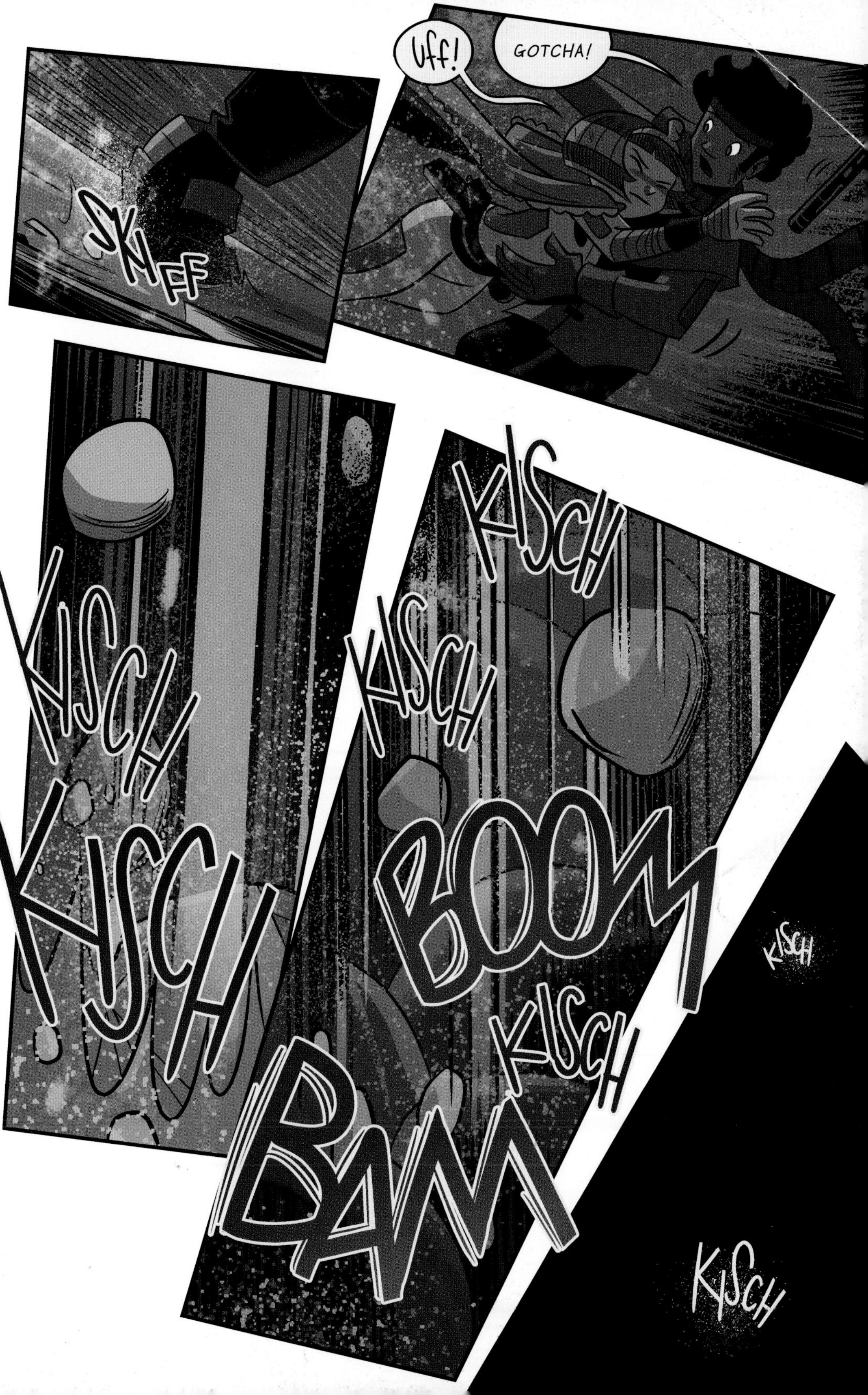
SKIFF
Uff!
GOTCHA!
KISCH
KISCH
KISCH
KISCH
BOOM
KISCH
BAM
KISCH
KISCH

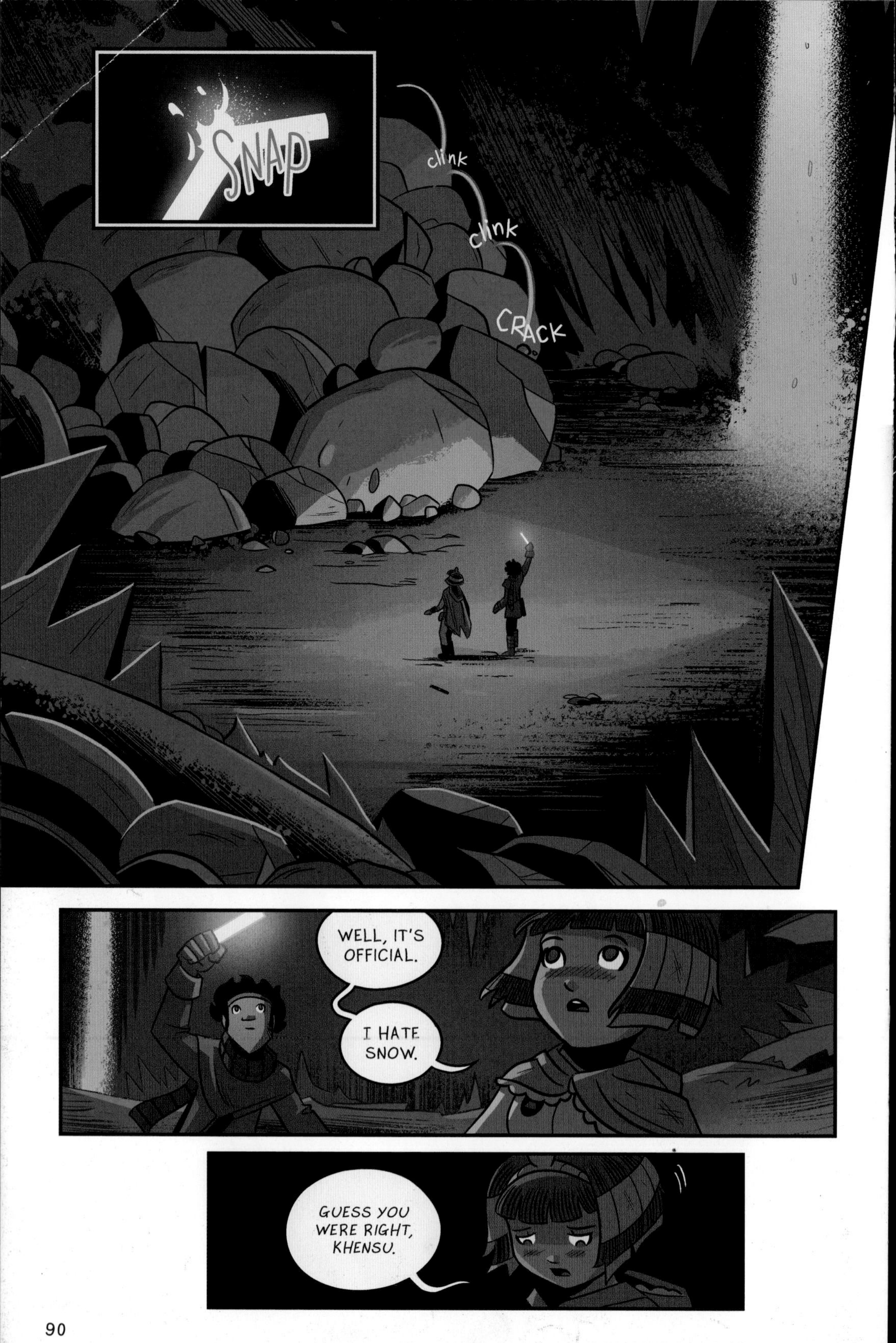
SNAP
clink
clink
CRACK
WELL, IT'S OFFICIAL.
I HATE SNOW.
GUESS YOU WERE RIGHT, KHENSU.

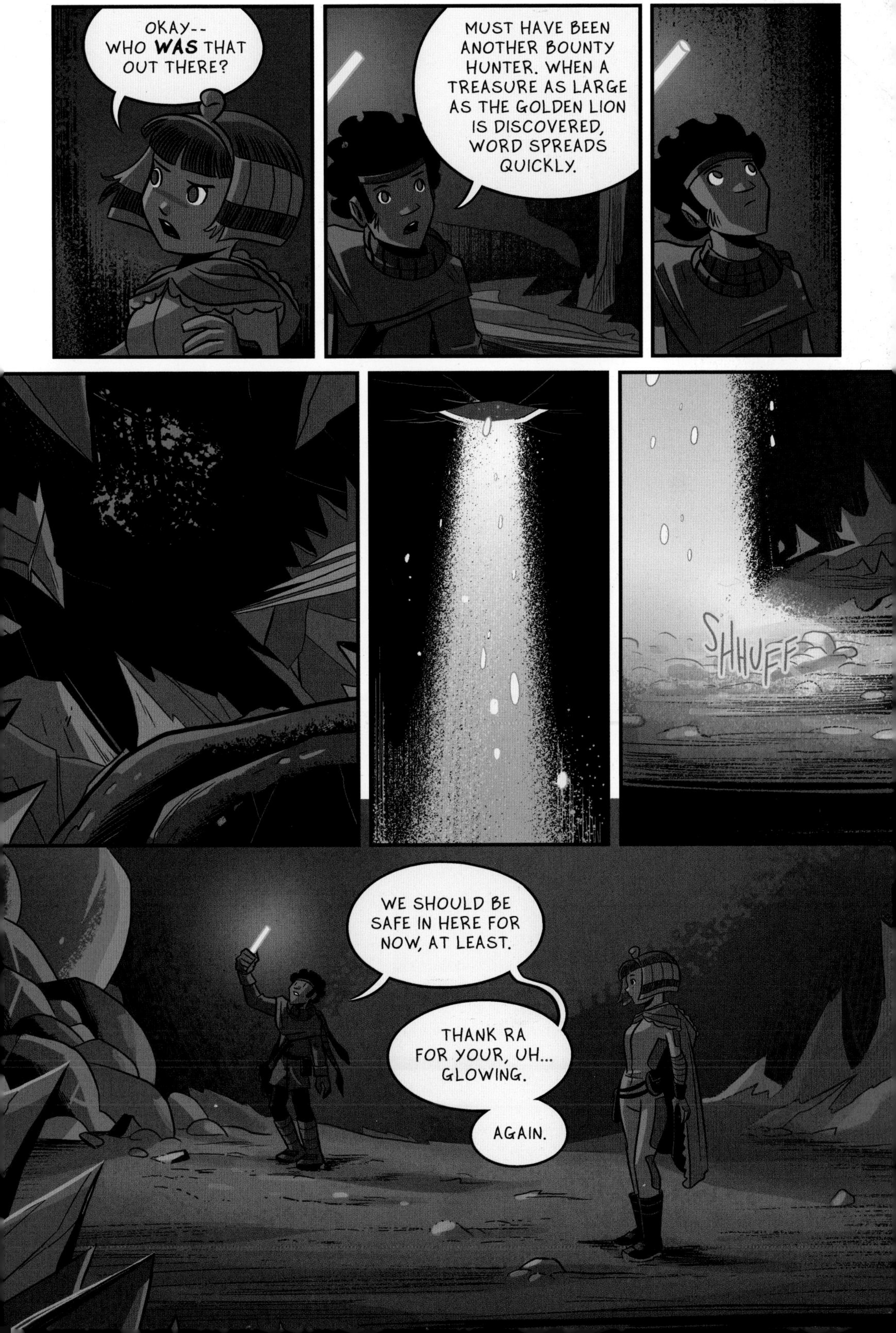
OKAY-- WHO WAS THAT OUT THERE?
MUST HAVE BEEN ANOTHER BOUNTY HUNTER. WHEN A TREASURE AS LARGE AS THE GOLDEN LION IS DISCOVERED, WORD SPREADS QUICKLY.
SHHUFF
WE SHOULD BE SAFE IN HERE FOR NOW, AT LEAST.
THANK RA FOR YOUR, UH... GLOWING.
AGAIN.

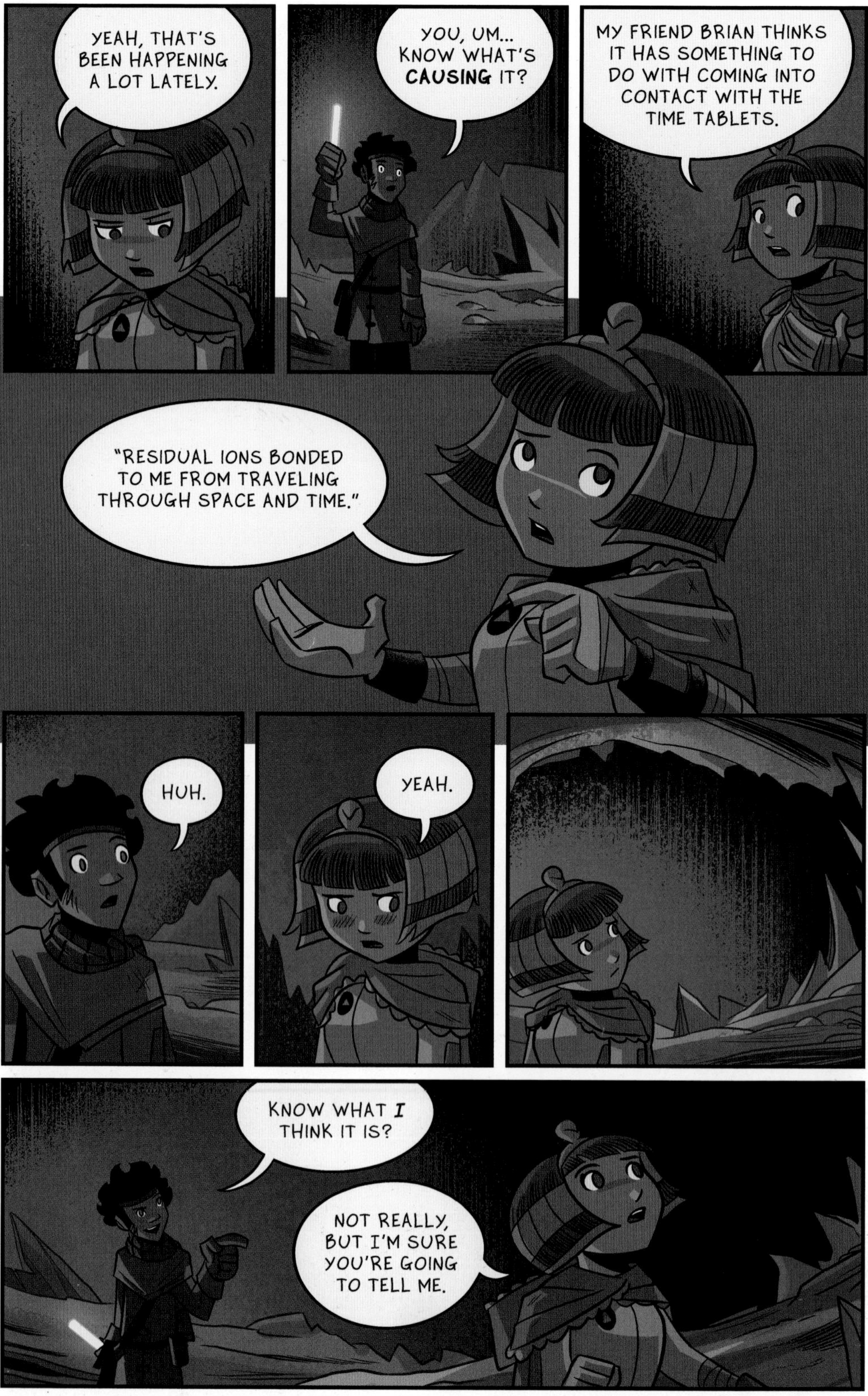
YEAH, THAT'S BEEN HAPPENING A LOT LATELY.
YOU, UM... KNOW WHAT'S **CAUSING** IT?
MY FRIEND BRIAN THINKS IT HAS SOMETHING TO DO WITH COMING INTO CONTACT WITH THE TIME TABLETS.
"RESIDUAL IONS BONDED TO ME FROM TRAVELING THROUGH SPACE AND TIME."
HUH.
YEAH.
KNOW WHAT *I* THINK IT IS?
NOT REALLY, BUT I'M SURE YOU'RE GOING TO TELL ME.

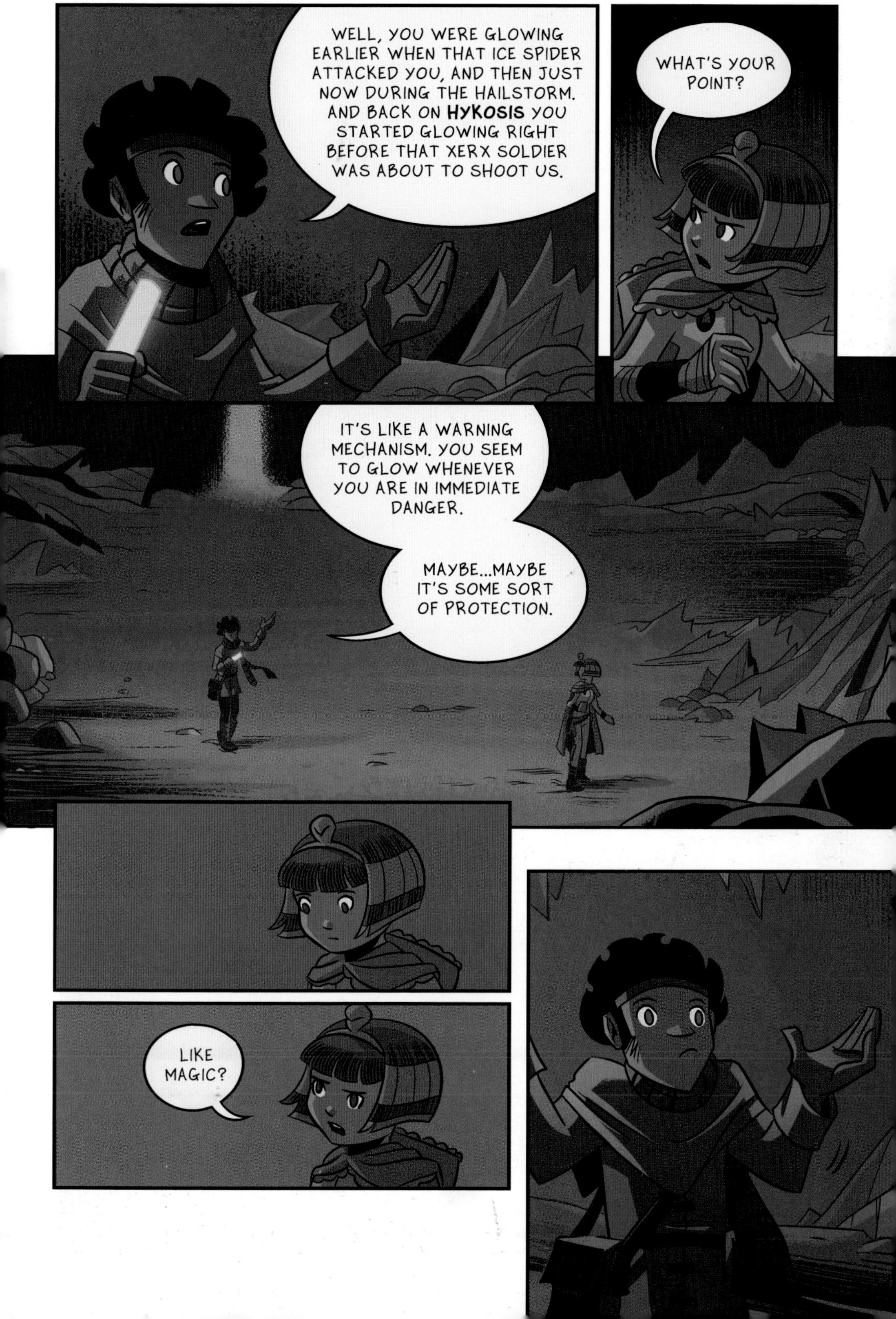
WELL, YOU WERE GLOWING EARLIER WHEN THAT ICE SPIDER ATTACKED YOU, AND THEN JUST NOW DURING THE HAILSTORM. AND BACK ON HYKOSIS YOU STARTED GLOWING RIGHT BEFORE THAT XERX SOLDIER WAS ABOUT TO SHOOT US.
WHAT'S YOUR POINT?
IT'S LIKE A WARNING MECHANISM. YOU SEEM TO GLOW WHENEVER YOU ARE IN IMMEDIATE DANGER.
MAYBE...MAYBE IT'S SOME SORT OF PROTECTION.
LIKE MAGIC?

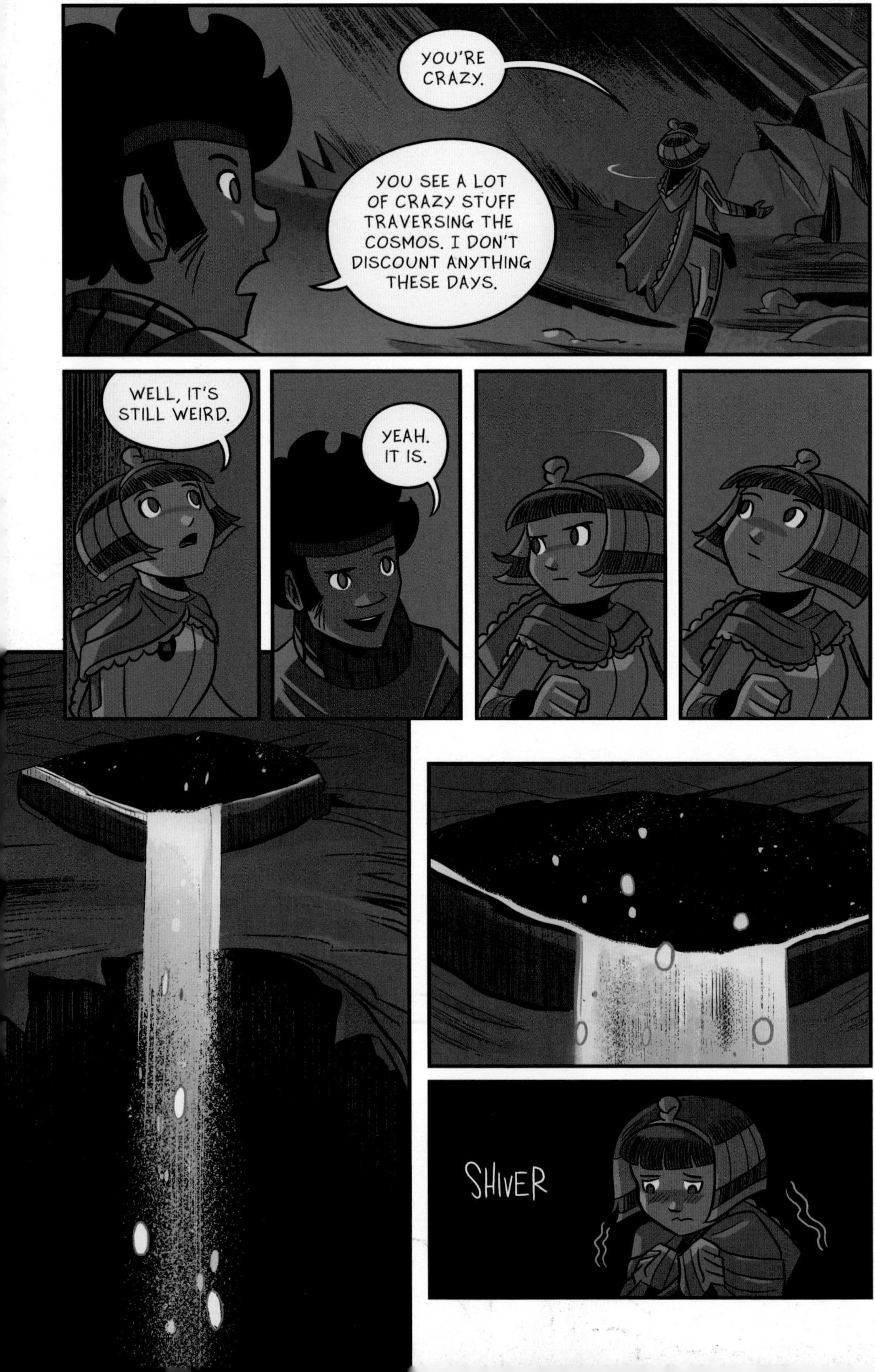
YOU'RE CRAZY.
YOU SEE A LOT OF CRAZY STUFF TRAVERSING THE COSMOS. I DON'T DISCOUNT ANYTHING THESE DAYS.
WELL, IT'S STILL WEIRD.
YEAH. IT IS.
SHIVER

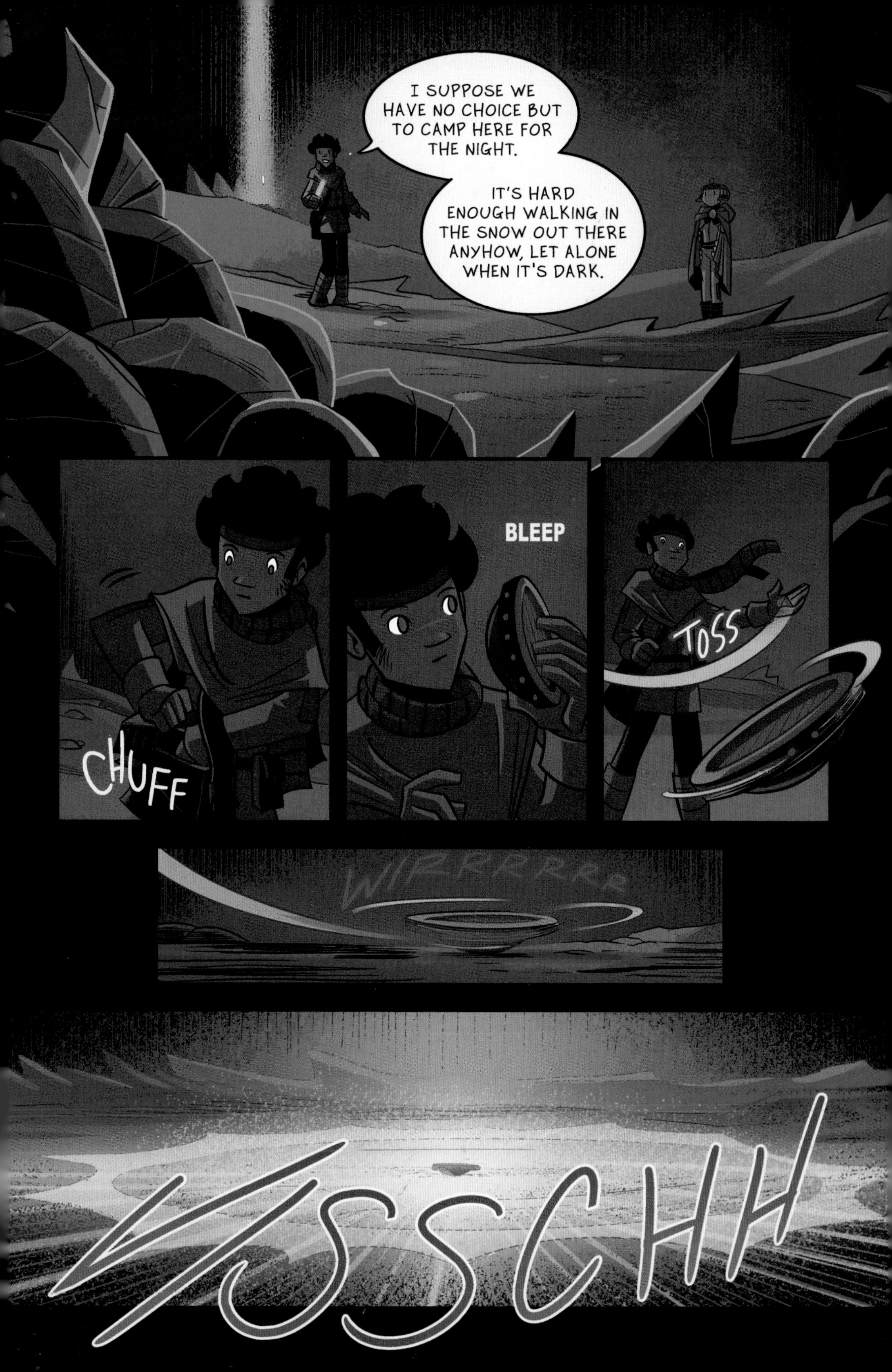
I SUPPOSE WE HAVE NO CHOICE BUT TO CAMP HERE FOR THE NIGHT.
IT'S HARD ENOUGH WALKING IN THE SNOW OUT THERE ANYHOW, LET ALONE WHEN IT'S DARK.
CHUFF
BLEEP
TOSS
WIRRRRRR
VSSCHH

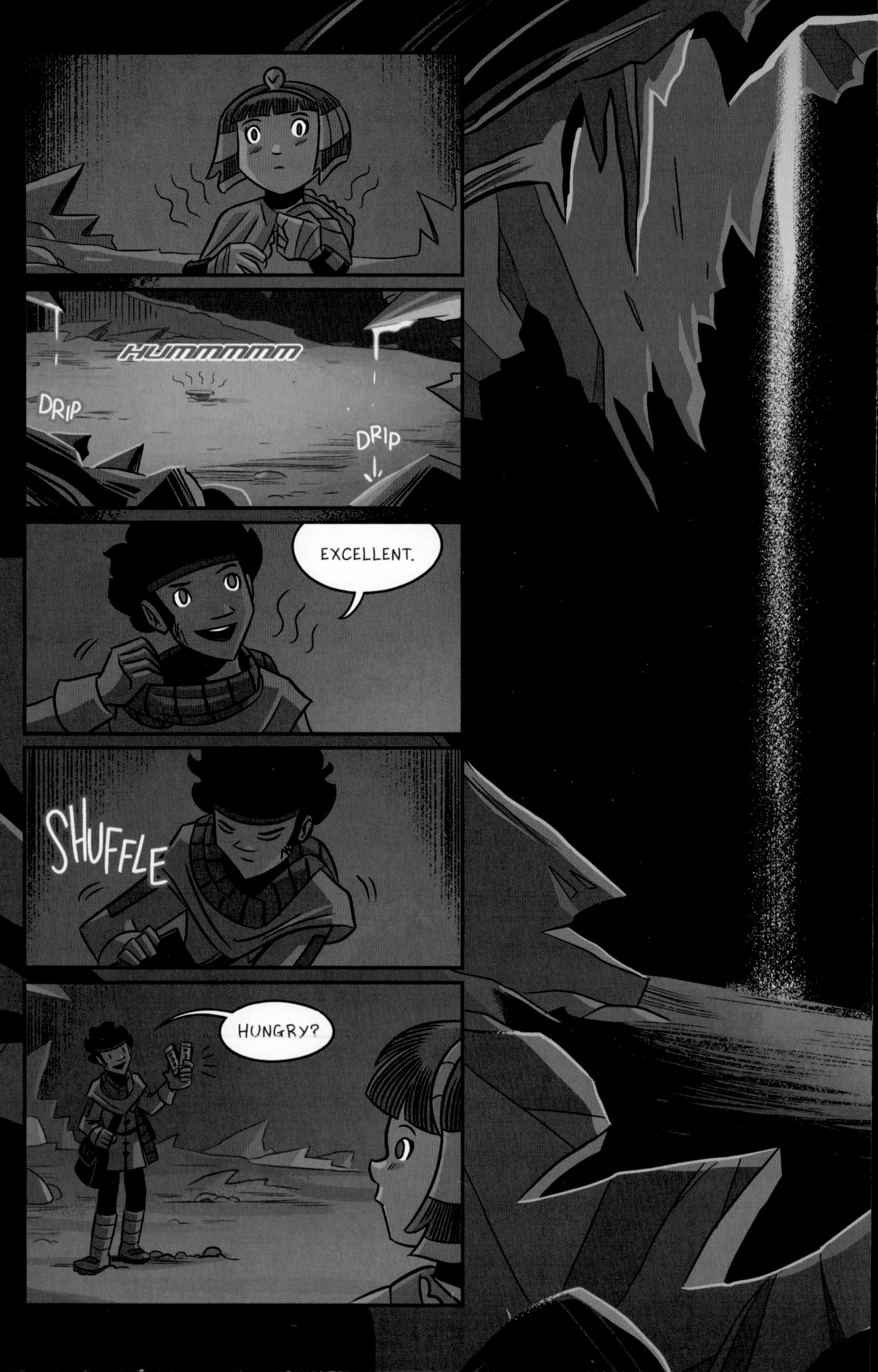
HUMMMMMM
DRIP
DRIP
EXCELLENT.
SHUFFLE
HUNGRY?

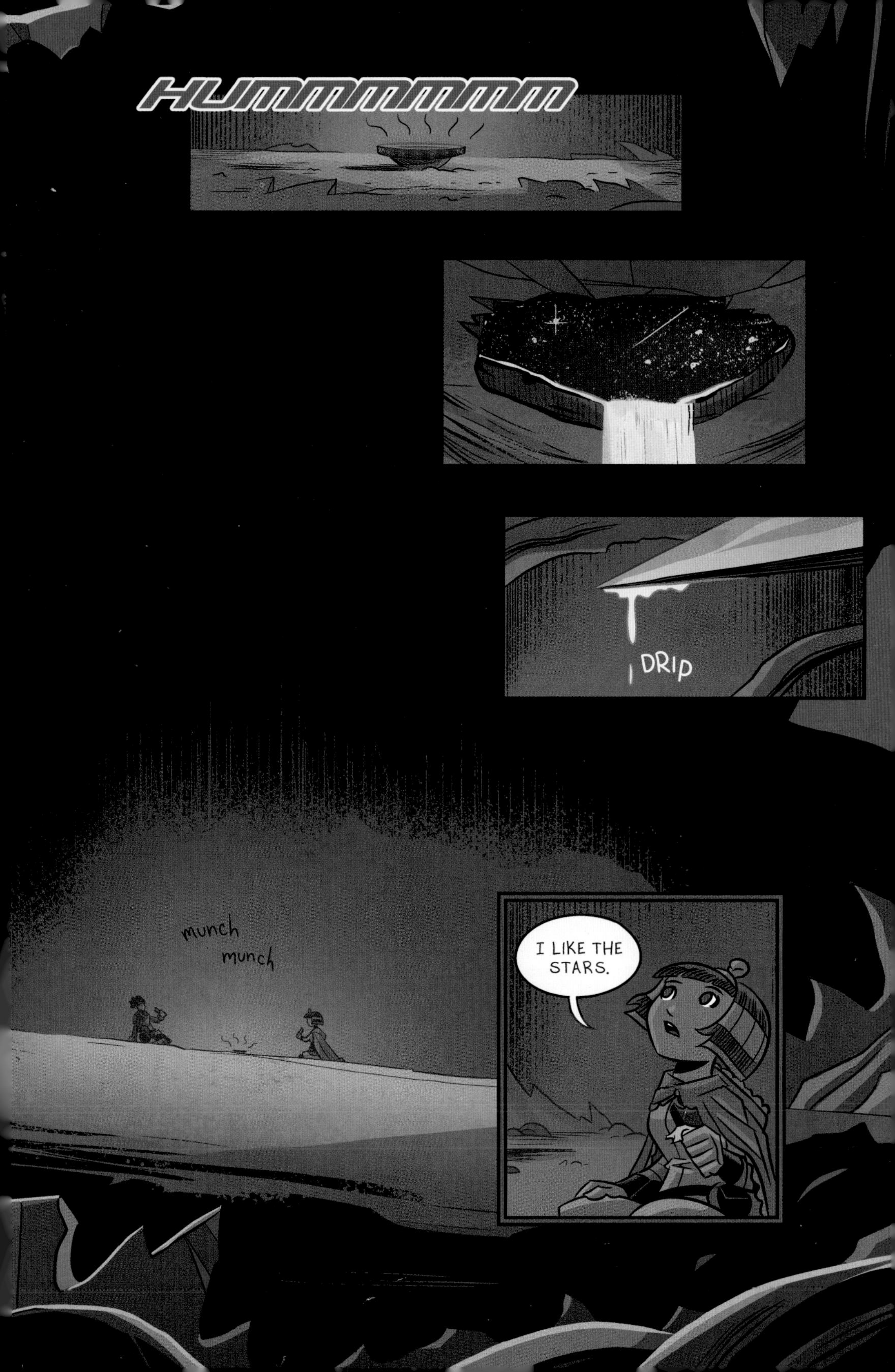
HUMMMMMM
DRIP
munch
munch
I LIKE THE STARS.

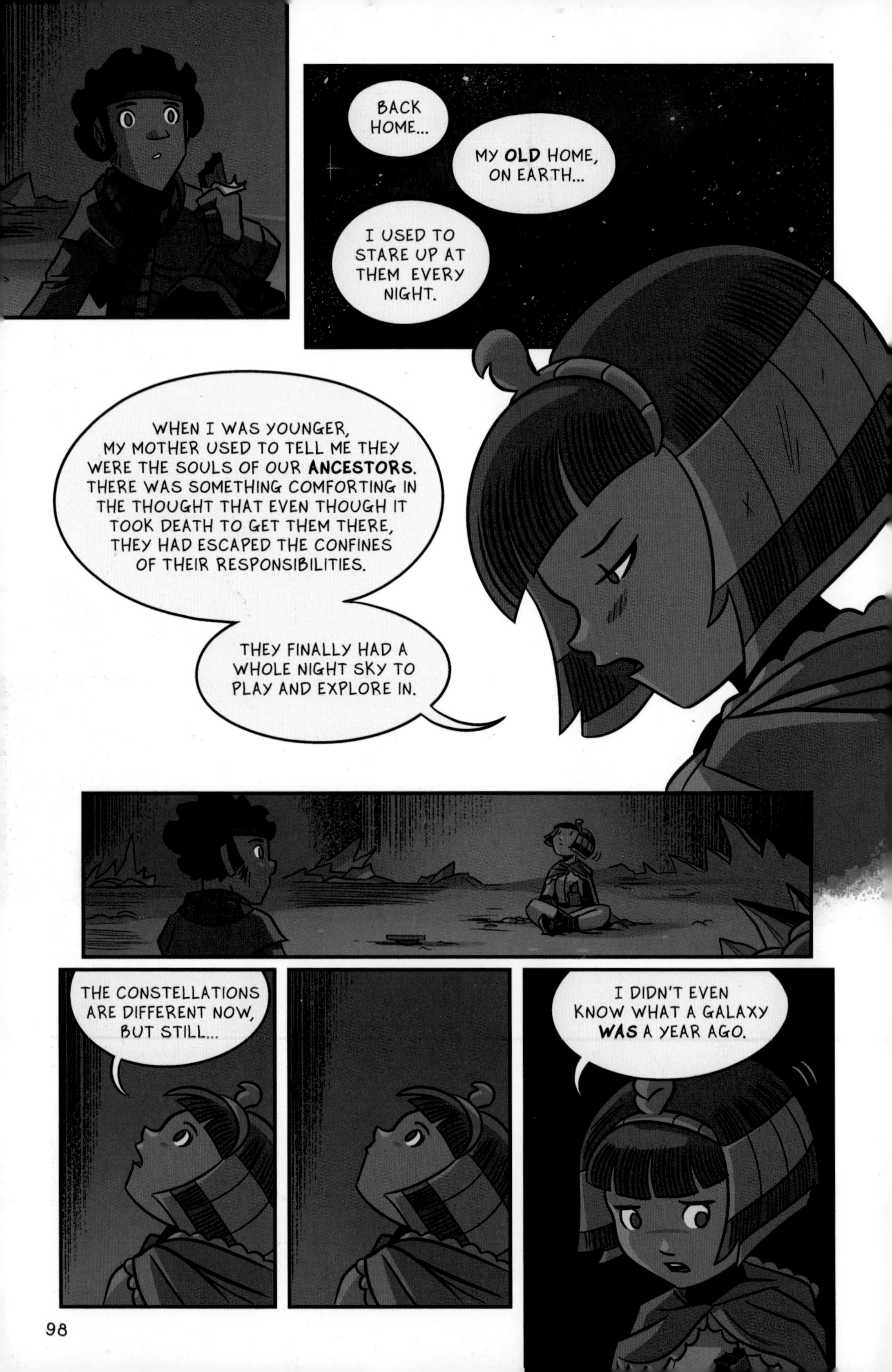
BACK HOME...
MY **OLD** HOME, ON EARTH...
I USED TO STARE UP AT THEM EVERY NIGHT.
WHEN I WAS YOUNGER, MY MOTHER USED TO TELL ME THEY WERE THE SOULS OF OUR **ANCESTORS**. THERE WAS SOMETHING COMFORTING IN THE THOUGHT THAT EVEN THOUGH IT TOOK DEATH TO GET THEM THERE, THEY HAD ESCAPED THE CONFINES OF THEIR RESPONSIBILITIES.
THEY FINALLY HAD A WHOLE NIGHT SKY TO PLAY AND EXPLORE IN.
THE CONSTELLATIONS ARE DIFFERENT NOW, BUT STILL...
I DIDN'T EVEN KNOW WHAT A GALAXY **WAS** A YEAR AGO.

AM I GLOWING AGAIN?

NO, NO!

IT'S JUST--

toss

IF YOU'RE SO DOWN ON BEING RESPONSIBLE, WHY DO YOU STILL WEAR THAT CROWN?

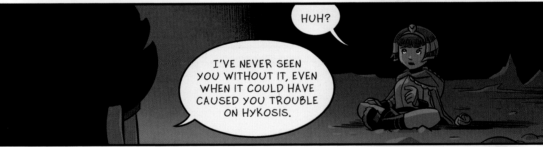

HUH?

I'VE NEVER SEEN YOU WITHOUT IT, EVEN WHEN IT COULD HAVE CAUSED YOU TROUBLE ON HYKOSIS.

I DUNNO.

IT'S A FAMILY HEIRLOOM.

IT'S...ALL I HAVE LEFT.

99

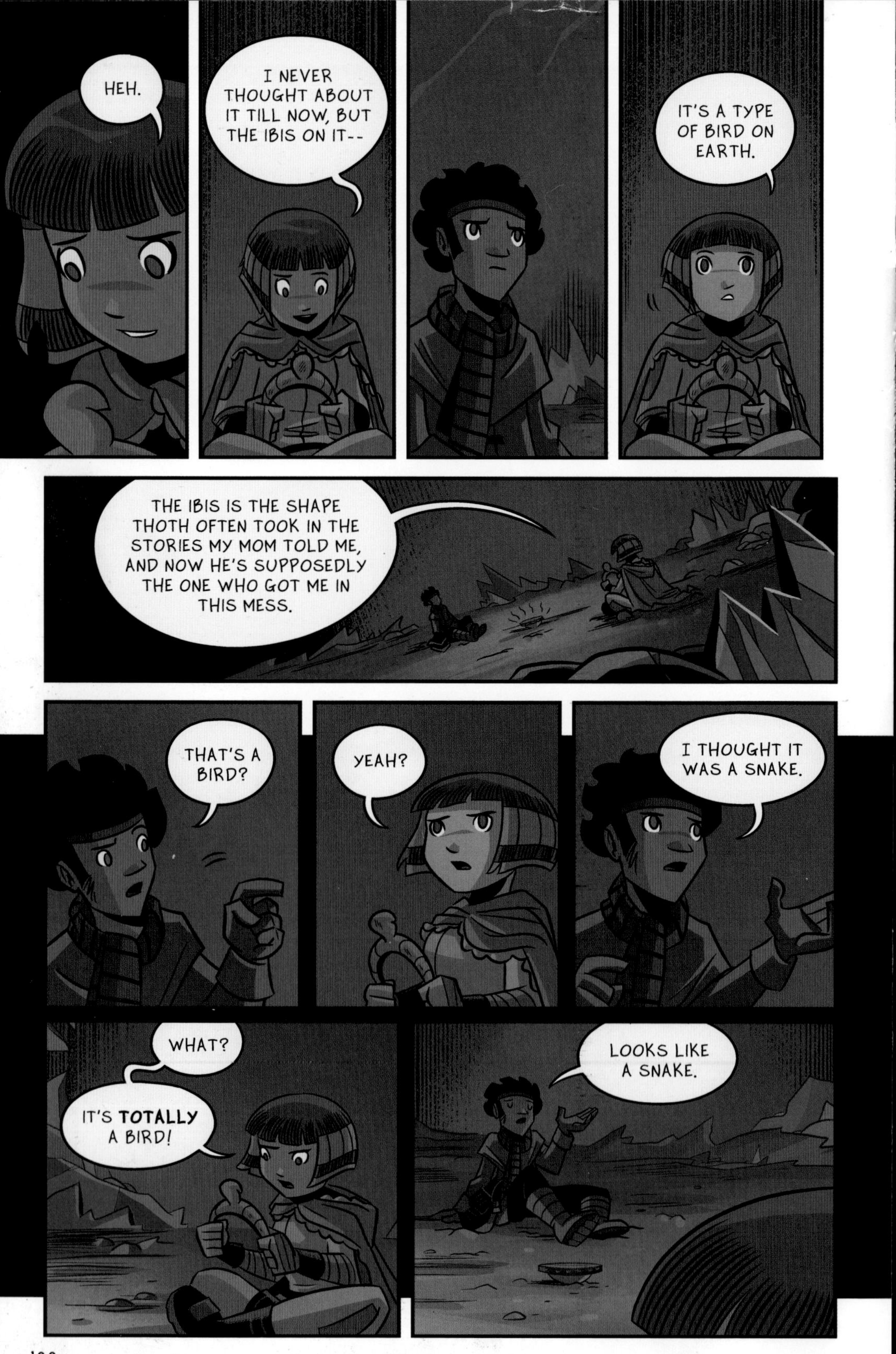
HEH.
I NEVER THOUGHT ABOUT IT TILL NOW, BUT THE IBIS ON IT--
IT'S A TYPE OF BIRD ON EARTH.
THE IBIS IS THE SHAPE THOTH OFTEN TOOK IN THE STORIES MY MOM TOLD ME, AND NOW HE'S SUPPOSEDLY THE ONE WHO GOT ME IN THIS MESS.
THAT'S A BIRD?
YEAH?
I THOUGHT IT WAS A SNAKE.
WHAT?
IT'S **TOTALLY** A BIRD!
LOOKS LIKE A SNAKE.

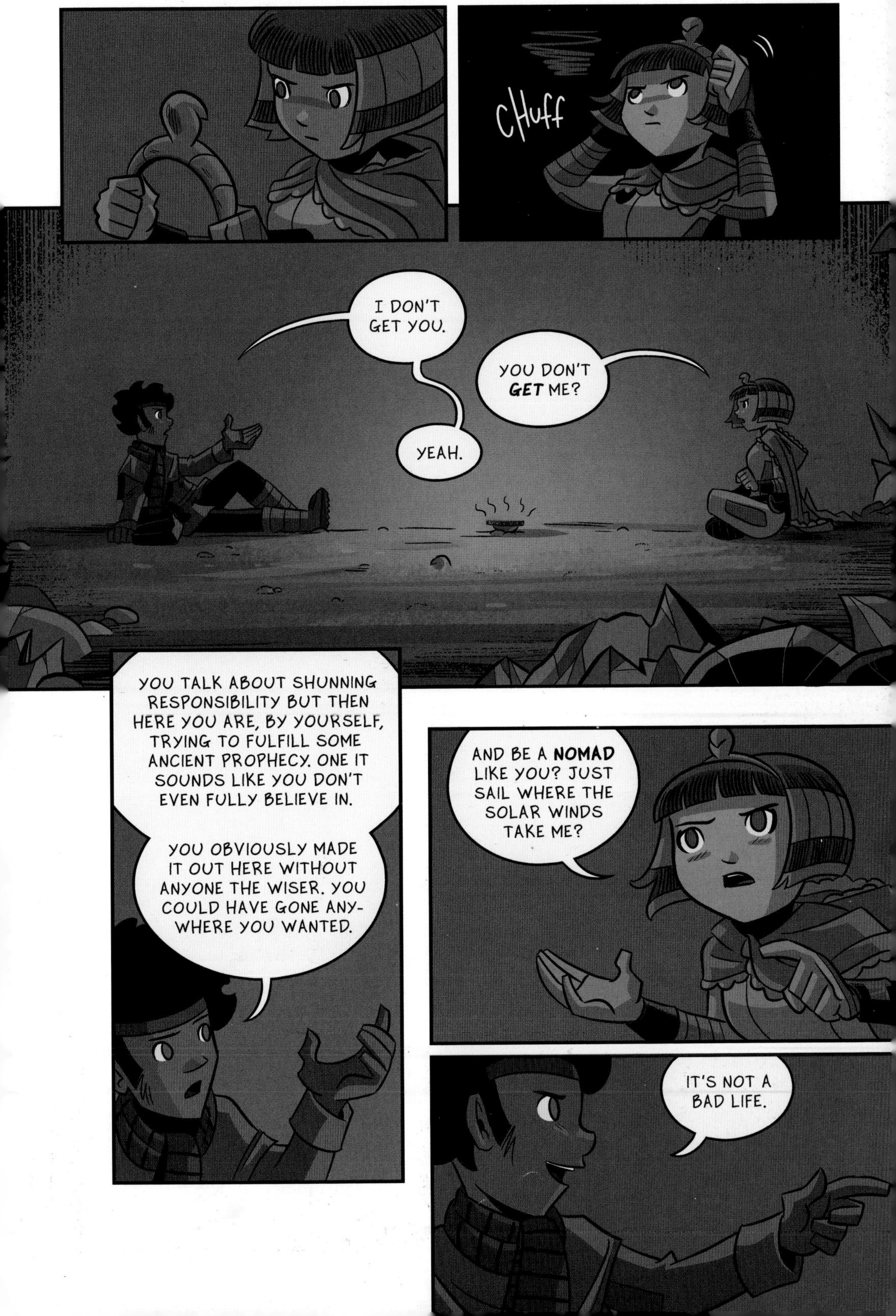
CHuff
I DON'T GET YOU.
YOU DON'T GET ME?
YEAH.
YOU TALK ABOUT SHUNNING RESPONSIBILITY BUT THEN HERE YOU ARE, BY YOURSELF, TRYING TO FULFILL SOME ANCIENT PROPHECY. ONE IT SOUNDS LIKE YOU DON'T EVEN FULLY BELIEVE IN.
YOU OBVIOUSLY MADE IT OUT HERE WITHOUT ANYONE THE WISER. YOU COULD HAVE GONE ANY-WHERE YOU WANTED.
AND BE A **NOMAD** LIKE YOU? JUST SAIL WHERE THE SOLAR WINDS TAKE ME?
IT'S NOT A BAD LIFE.

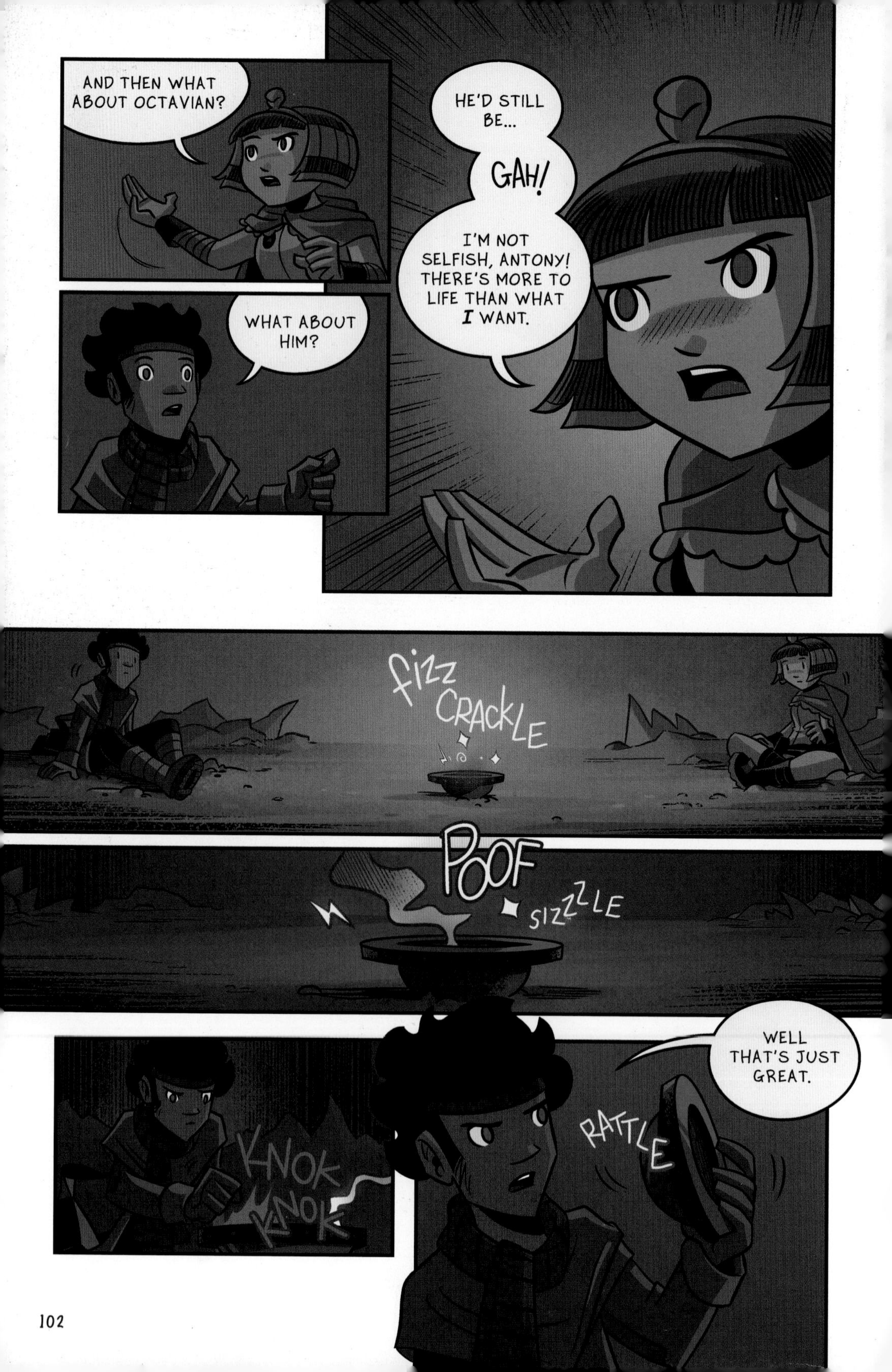
AND THEN WHAT ABOUT OCTAVIAN?
WHAT ABOUT HIM?
HE'D STILL BE...
GAH!
I'M NOT SELFISH, ANTONY! THERE'S MORE TO LIFE THAN WHAT I WANT.
fizz
CRACKLE
POOF
SIZZZLE
KNOK
KNOK
WELL THAT'S JUST GREAT.
RATTLE

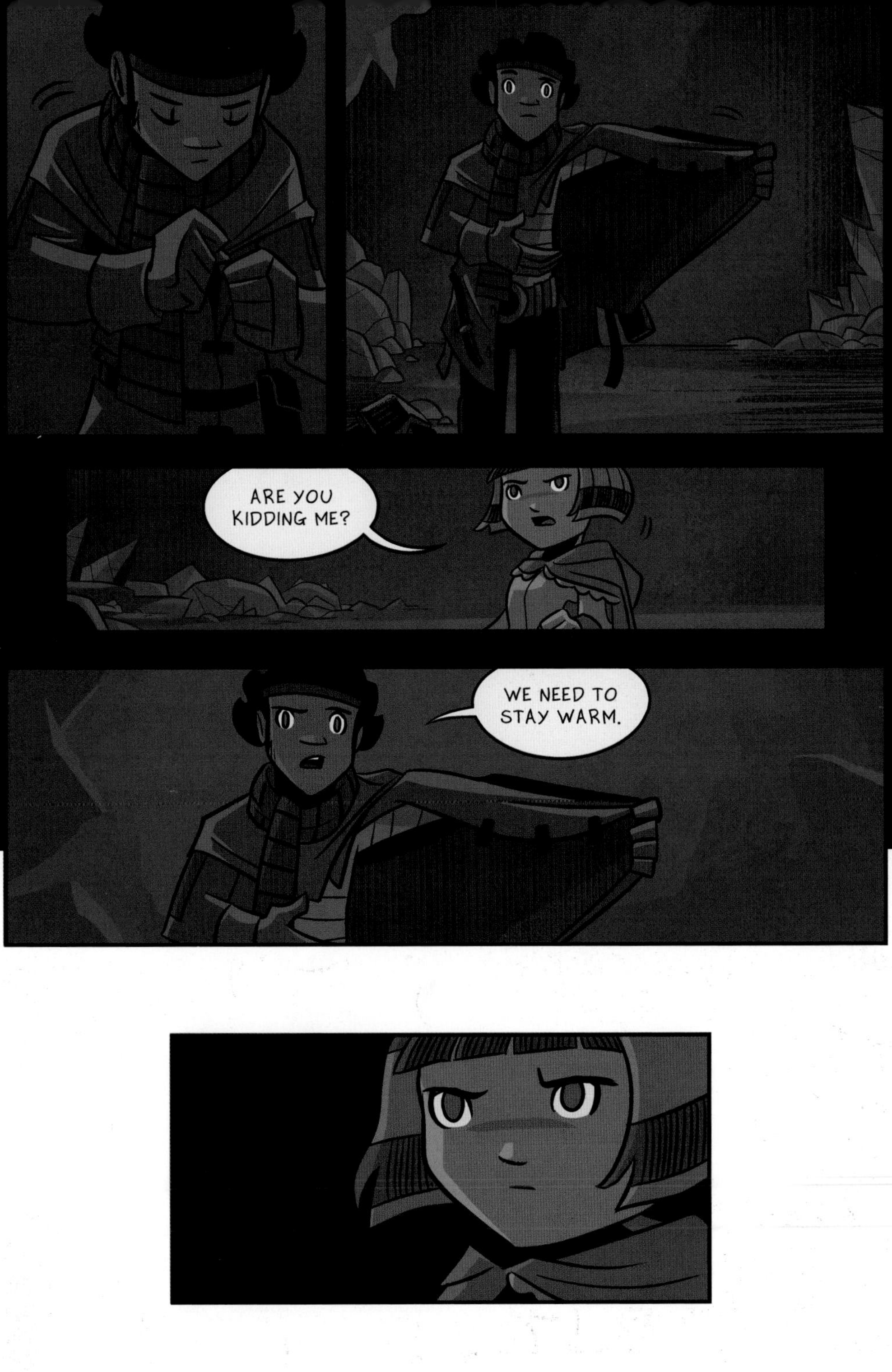
ARE YOU KIDDING ME?
WE NEED TO STAY WARM.

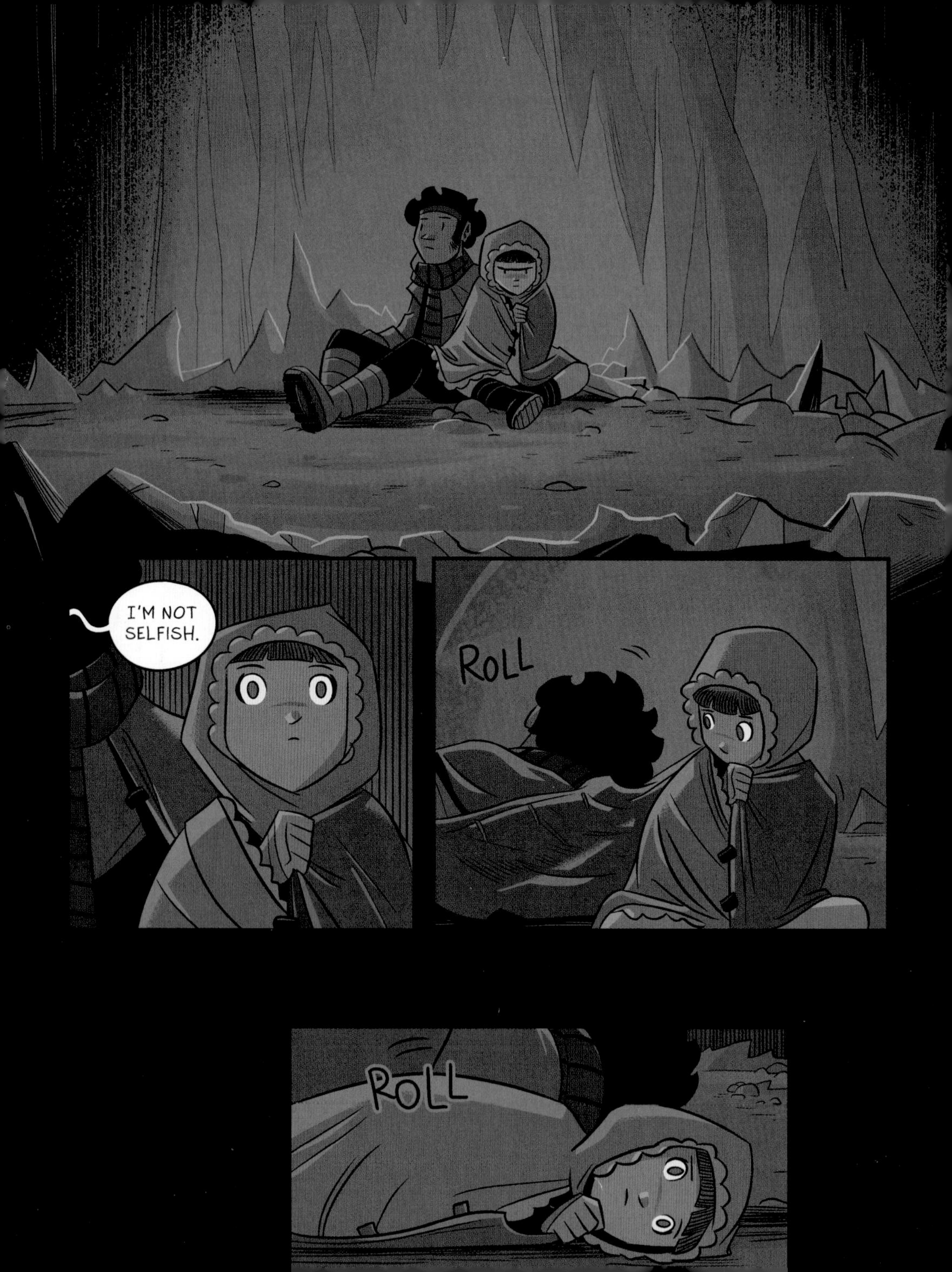

I'M NOT SELFISH.
ROLL
ROLL

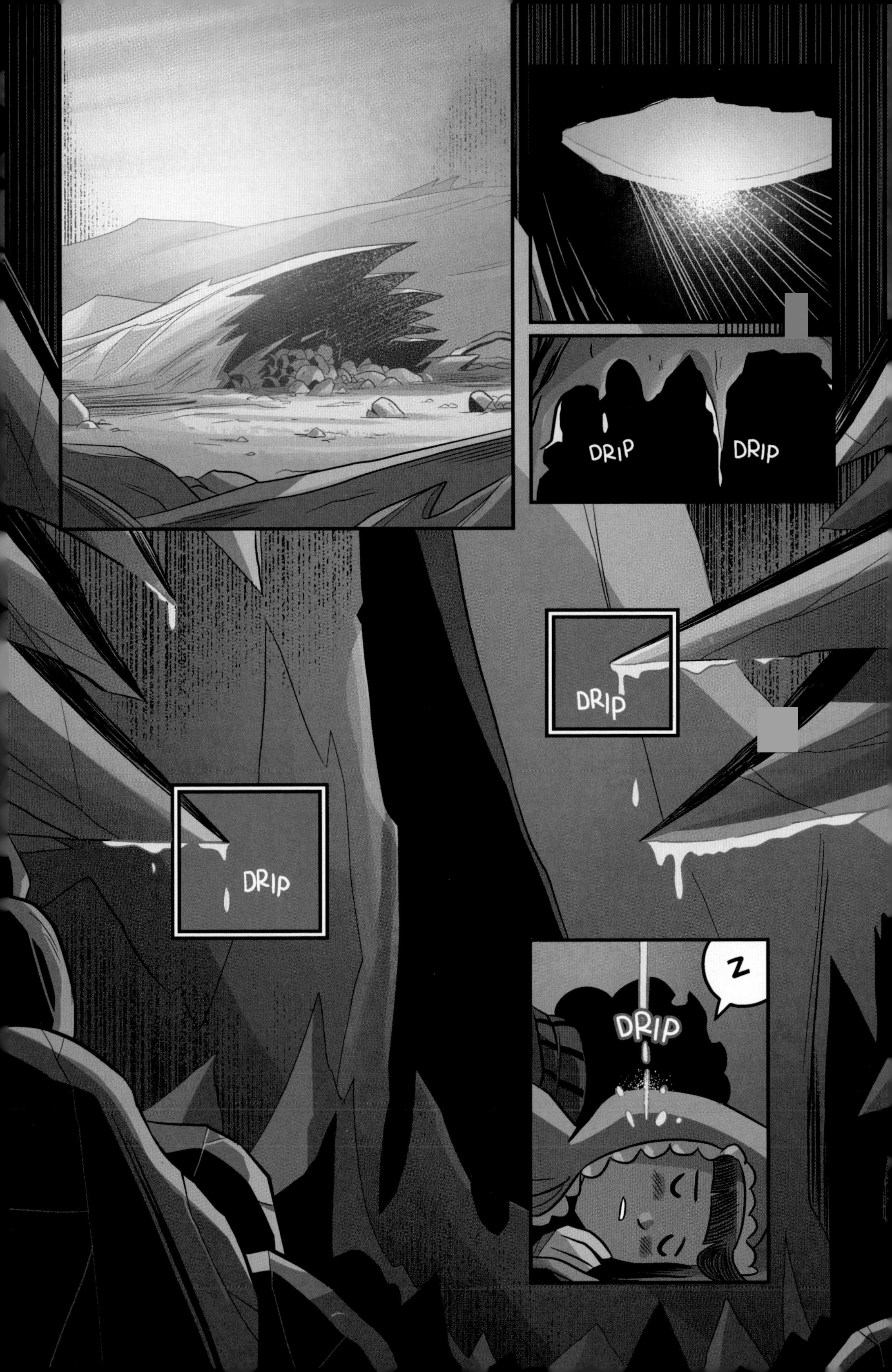
DRIP
DRIP
DRIP
DRIP
Z
DRIP

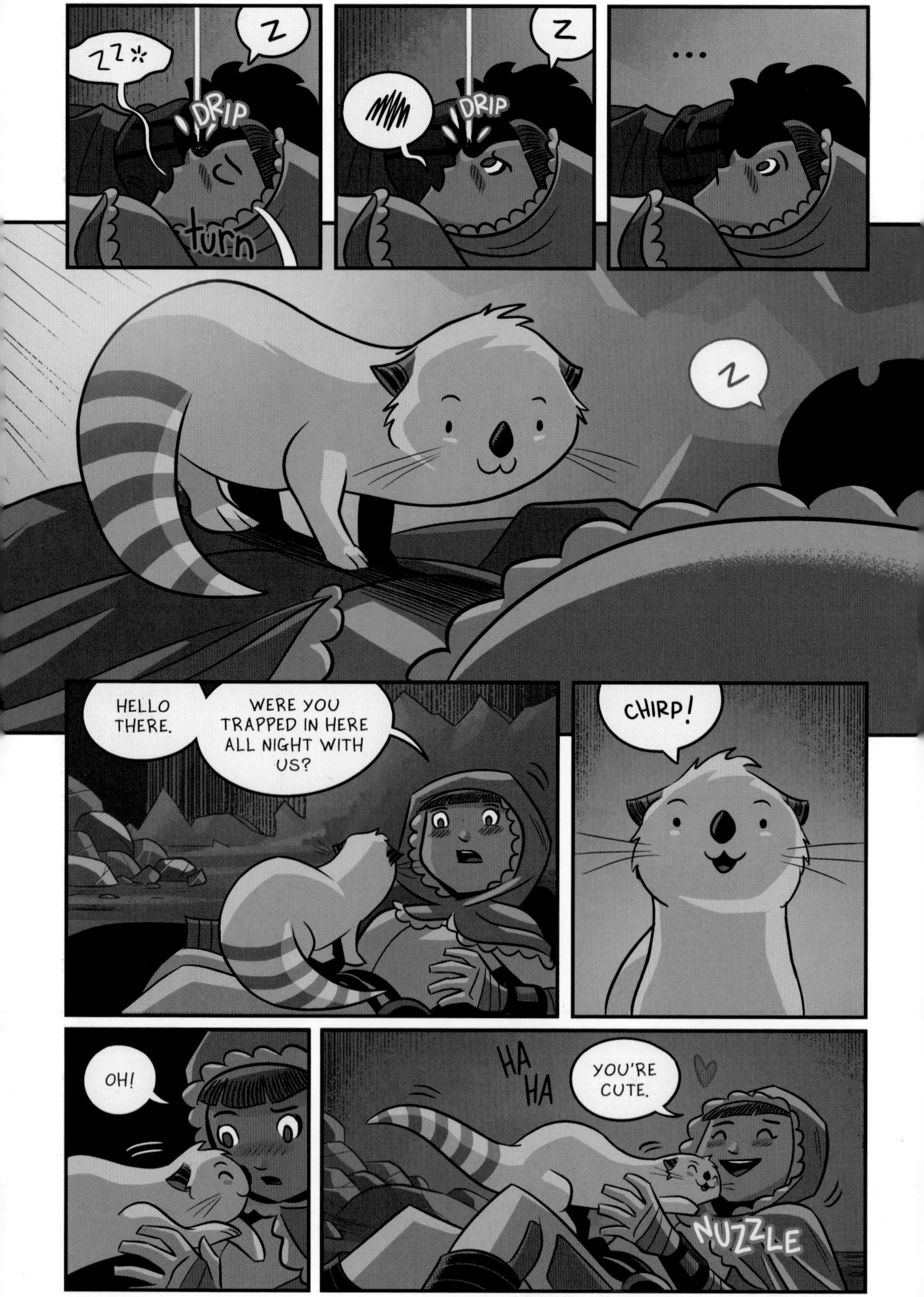

ZZ*
Z
DRIP
turn
MM
Z
DRIP
...
Z
HELLO THERE.
WERE YOU TRAPPED IN HERE ALL NIGHT WITH US?
CHIRP!
OH!
HA HA
YOU'RE CUTE.
NUZZLE

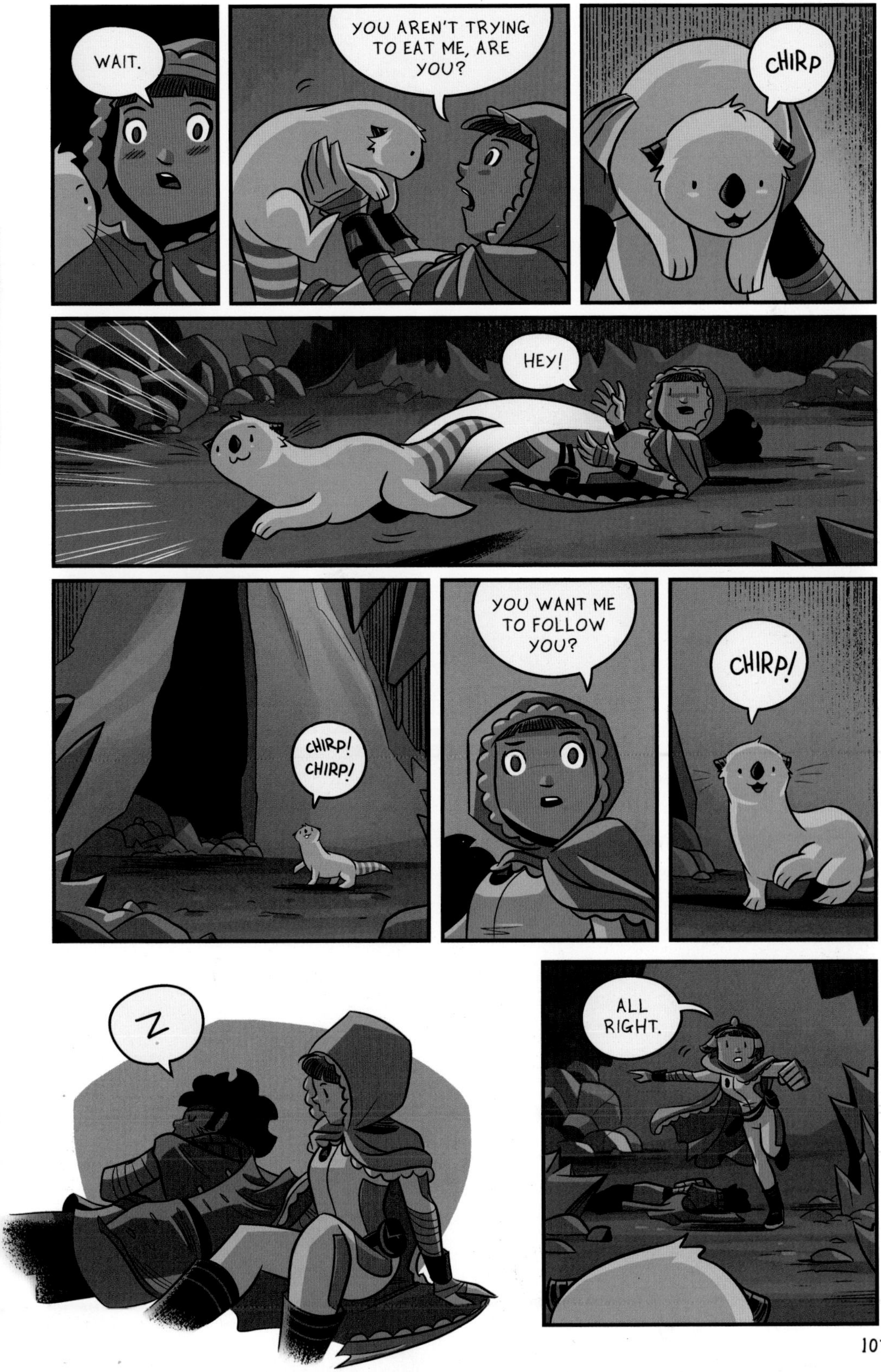
WAIT.
YOU AREN'T TRYING TO EAT ME, ARE YOU?
CHIRP
HEY!
CHIRP! CHIRP!
YOU WANT ME TO FOLLOW YOU?
CHIRP!
Z
ALL RIGHT.

GREAT.

PLEASE DON'T TELL ME I'M IN YET ANOTHER TOMB.

IS THIS A WAY OUT?

NOTHING GOOD EVER HAPPENS TO ME IN TOMBS.

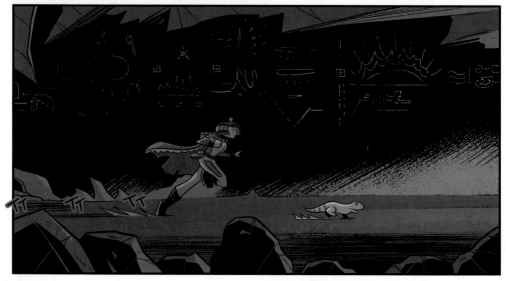

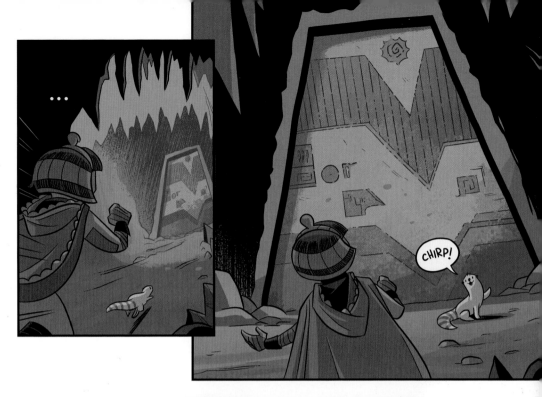

CHIRP!

YUP.

IT'S A TOMB.

THERE YOU--

WHOA.

HOW'D YOU KNOW THIS WAS HERE?

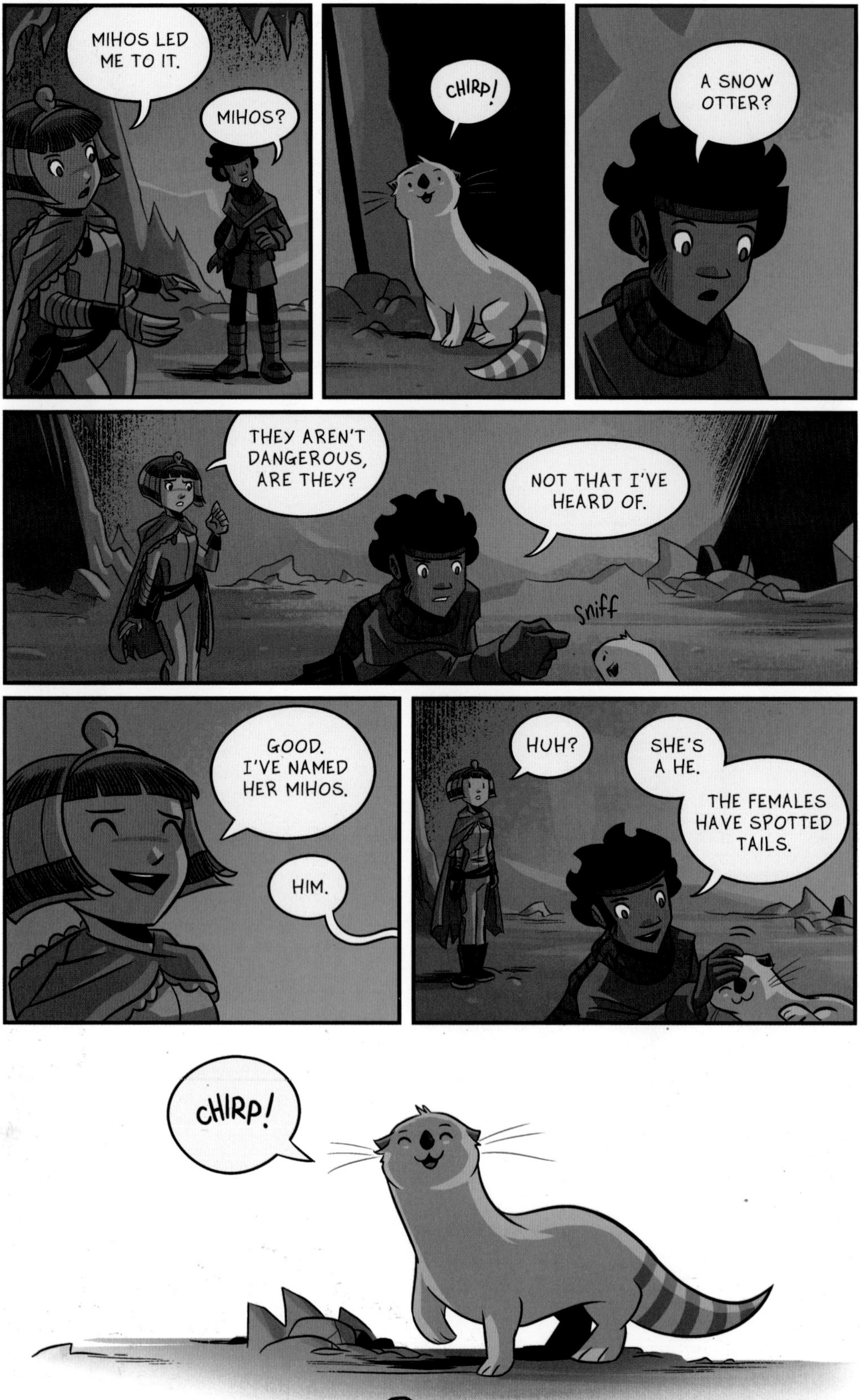
MIHOS LED ME TO IT.
MIHOS?
CHIRP!
A SNOW OTTER?
THEY AREN'T DANGEROUS, ARE THEY?
NOT THAT I'VE HEARD OF.
Sniff
GOOD. I'VE NAMED HER MIHOS.
HIM.
HUH?
SHE'S A HE.
THE FEMALES HAVE SPOTTED TAILS.
CHIRP!

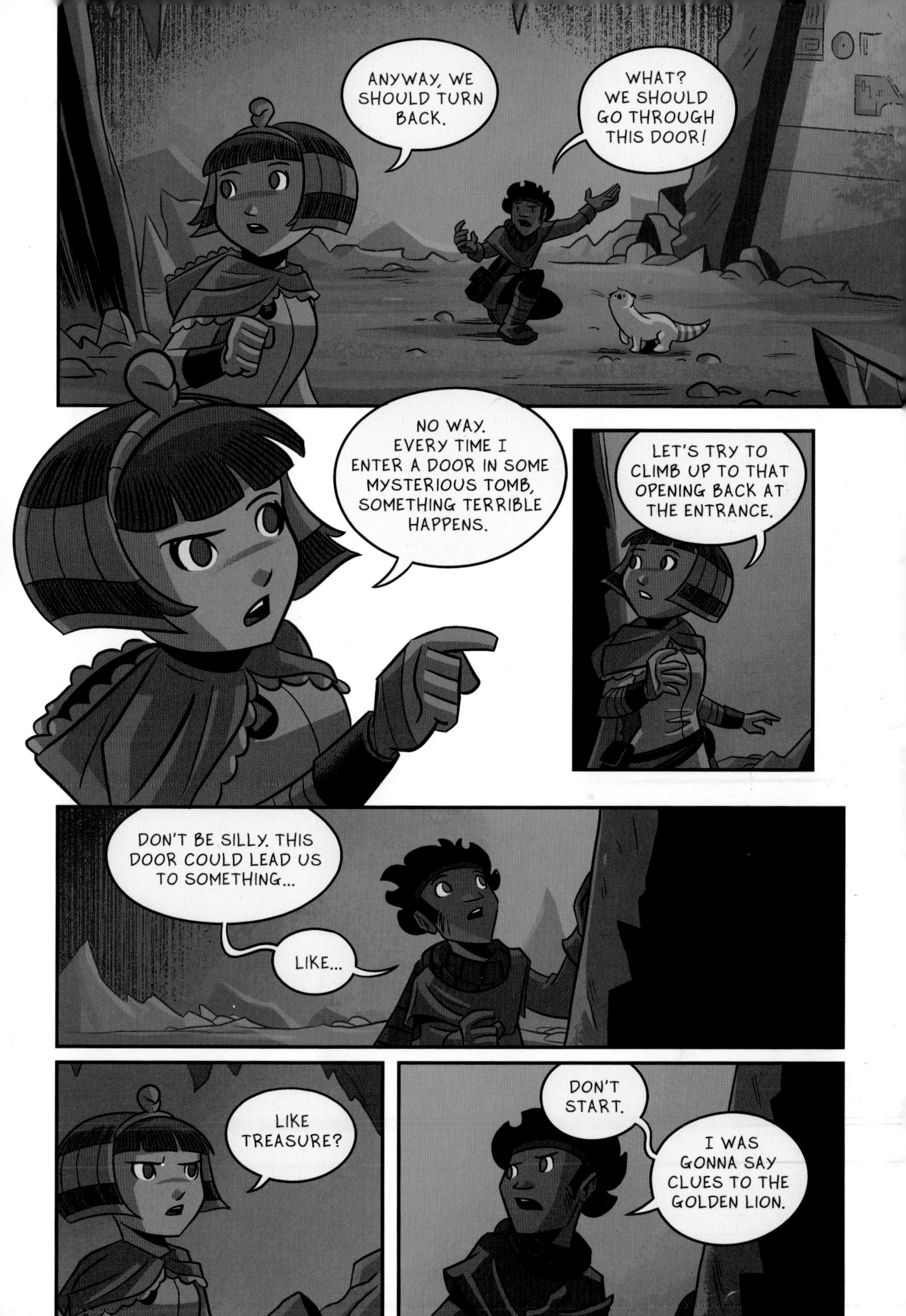
ANYWAY, WE SHOULD TURN BACK.
WHAT? WE SHOULD GO THROUGH THIS DOOR!
NO WAY. EVERY TIME I ENTER A DOOR IN SOME MYSTERIOUS TOMB, SOMETHING TERRIBLE HAPPENS.
LET'S TRY TO CLIMB UP TO THAT OPENING BACK AT THE ENTRANCE.
DON'T BE SILLY. THIS DOOR COULD LEAD US TO SOMETHING...
LIKE...
LIKE TREASURE?
DON'T START.
I WAS GONNA SAY CLUES TO THE GOLDEN LION.

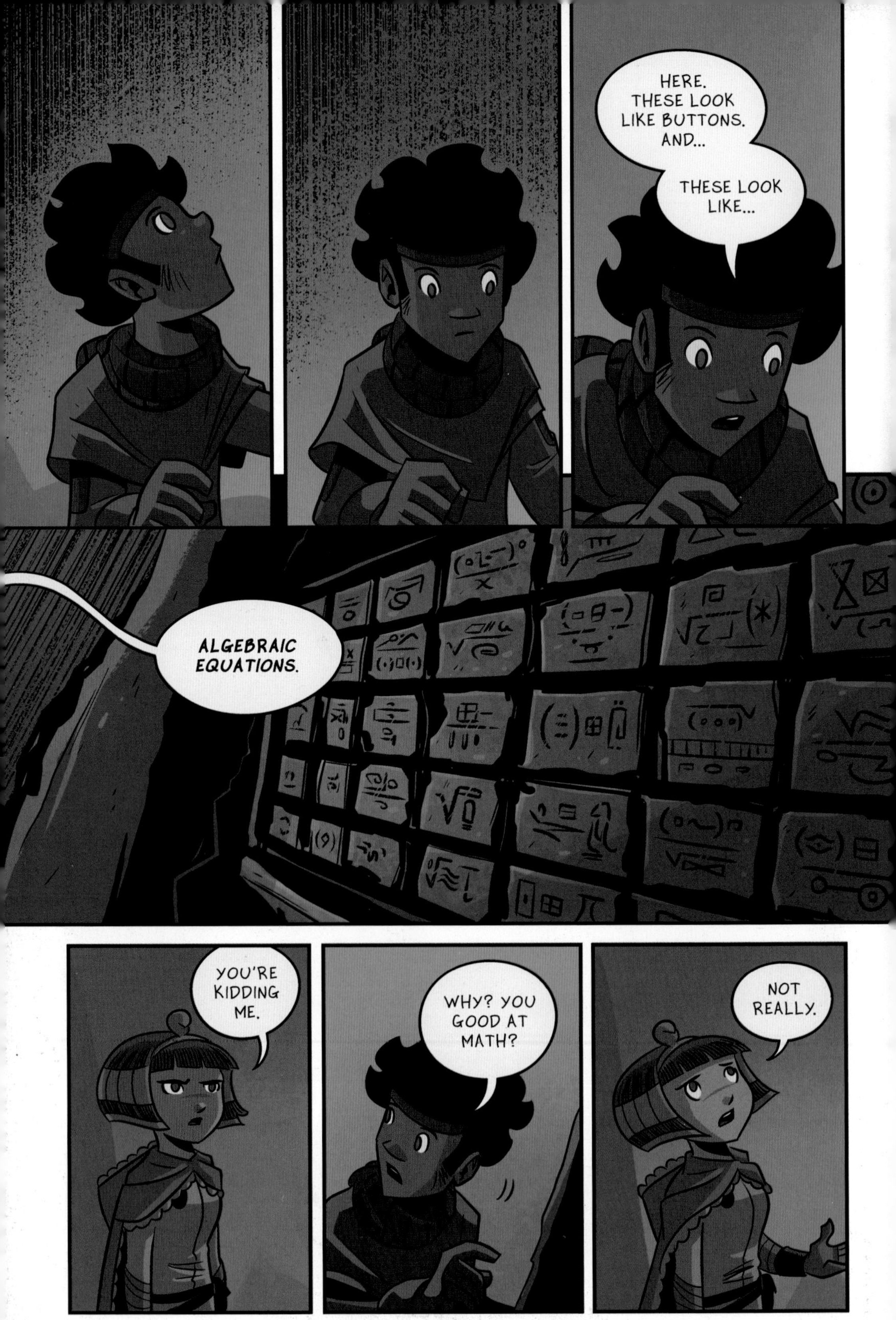
HERE. THESE LOOK LIKE BUTTONS. AND...
THESE LOOK LIKE...
ALGEBRAIC EQUATIONS.
YOU'RE KIDDING ME.
WHY? YOU GOOD AT MATH?
NOT REALLY.

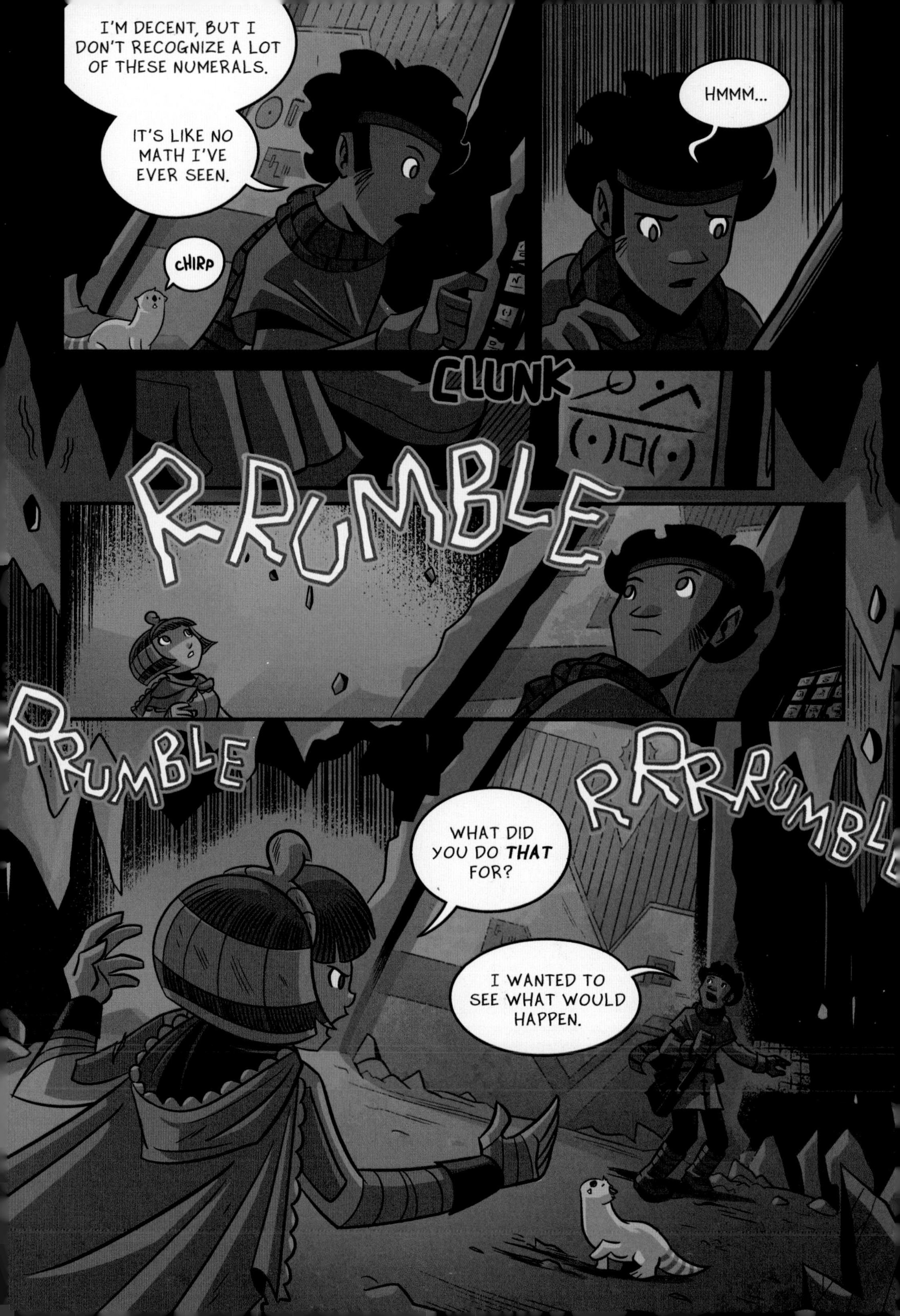
I'M DECENT, BUT I DON'T RECOGNIZE A LOT OF THESE NUMERALS.
IT'S LIKE NO MATH I'VE EVER SEEN.
CHIRP
HMMM...
CLUNK
RRUMBLE
RRUMBLE
RRRRUMBLE
WHAT DID YOU DO **THAT** FOR?
I WANTED TO SEE WHAT WOULD HAPPEN.

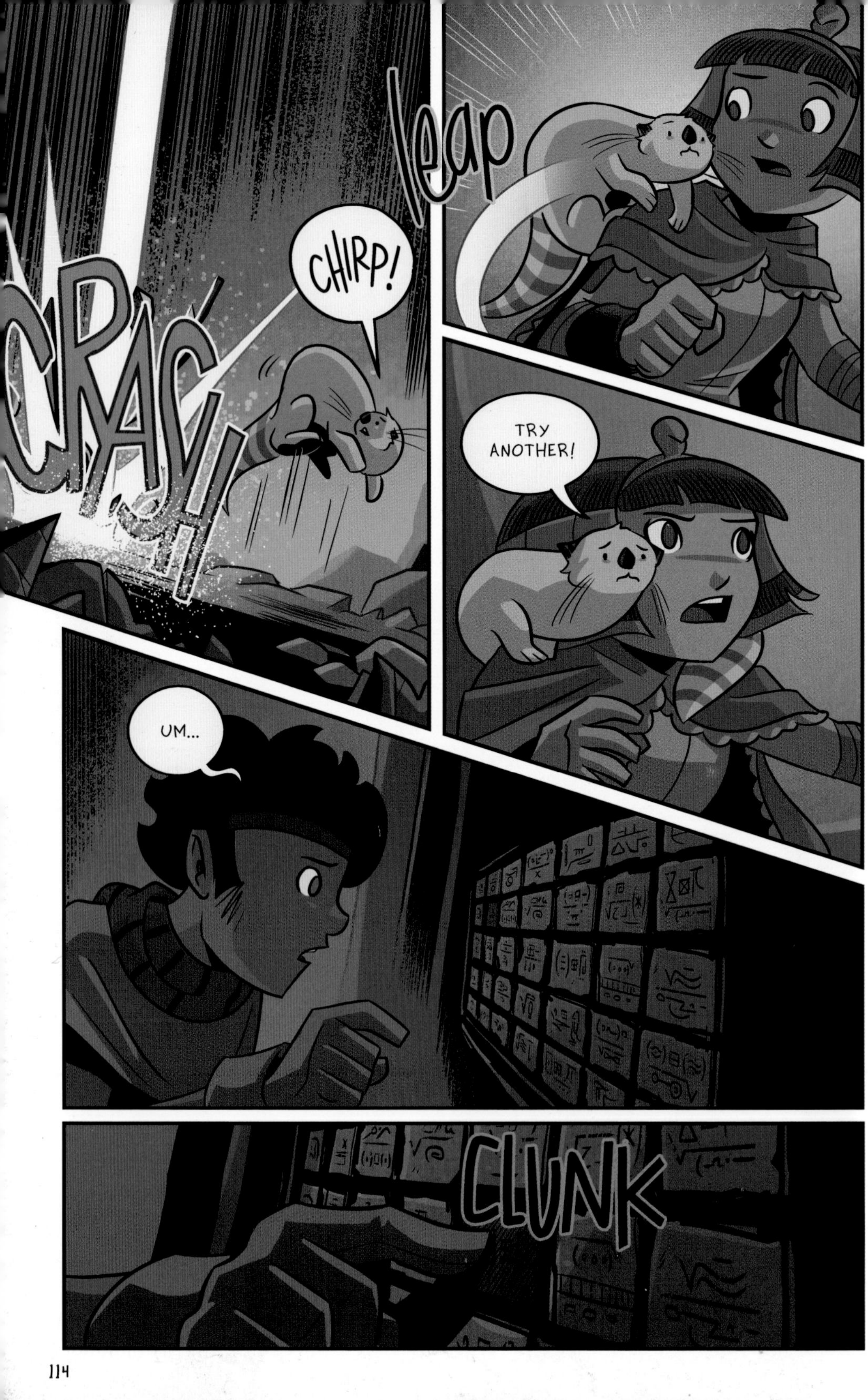

CRASH!
CHIRP!
leap
TRY ANOTHER!
UM...
CLUNK

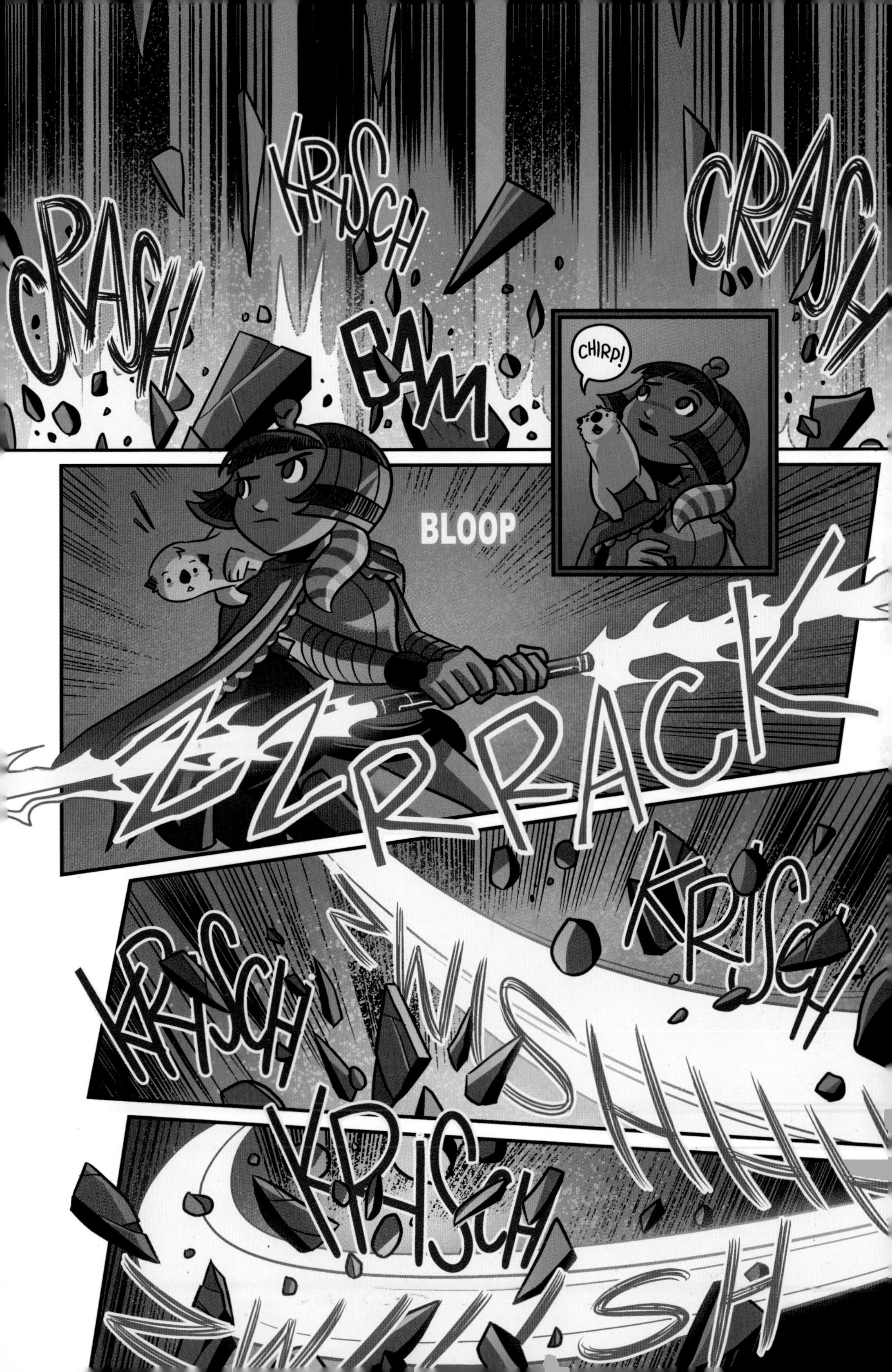
CRASH
KRISCH
BAM
CRASH
CHIRP!
BLOOP
ZZRRACK
KRISCH
KRISCH
WSHHHH
KRISCH
WSHHH

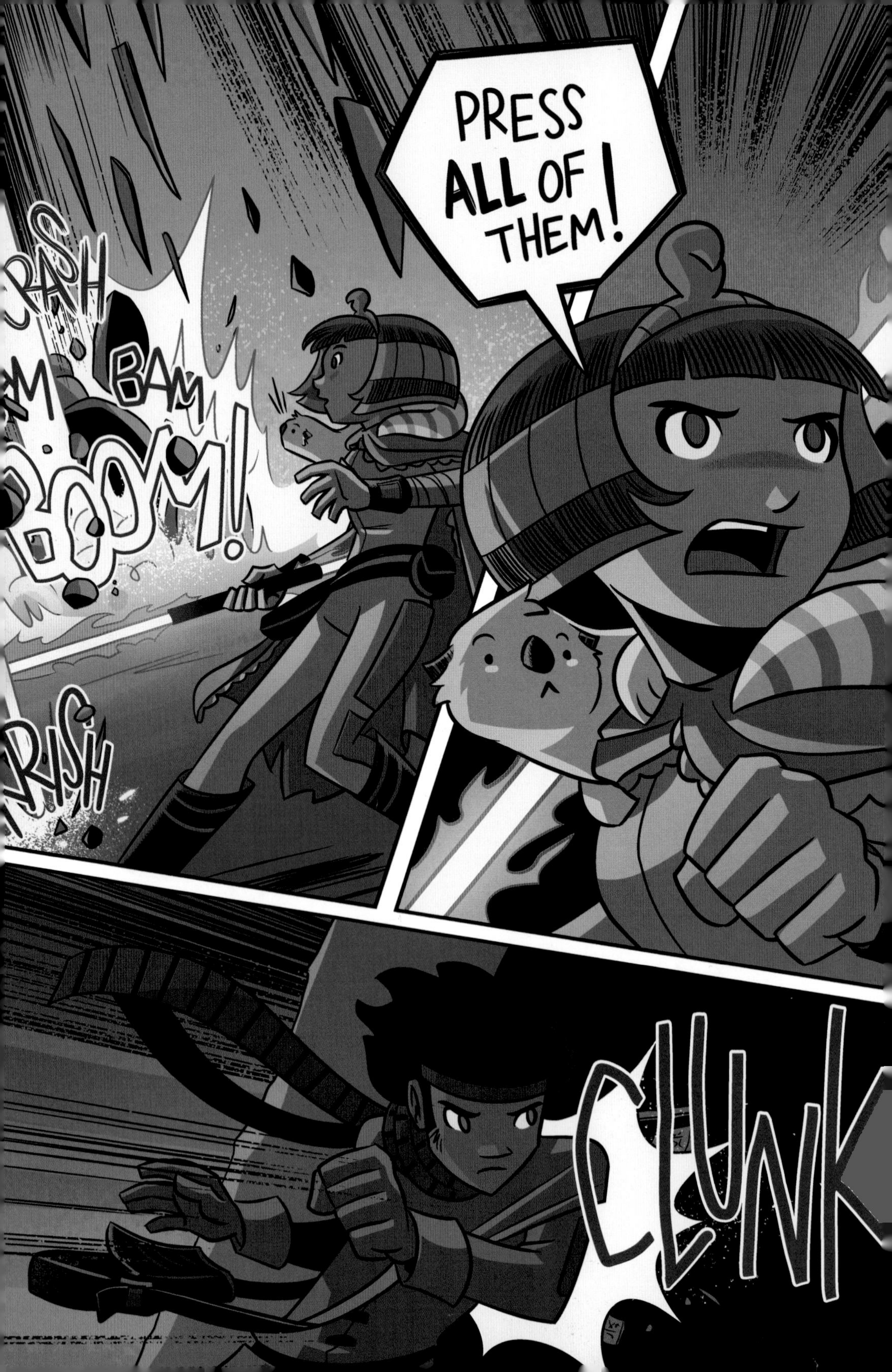
BAM
BOOM!
PRESS ALL OF THEM!
CLUNK

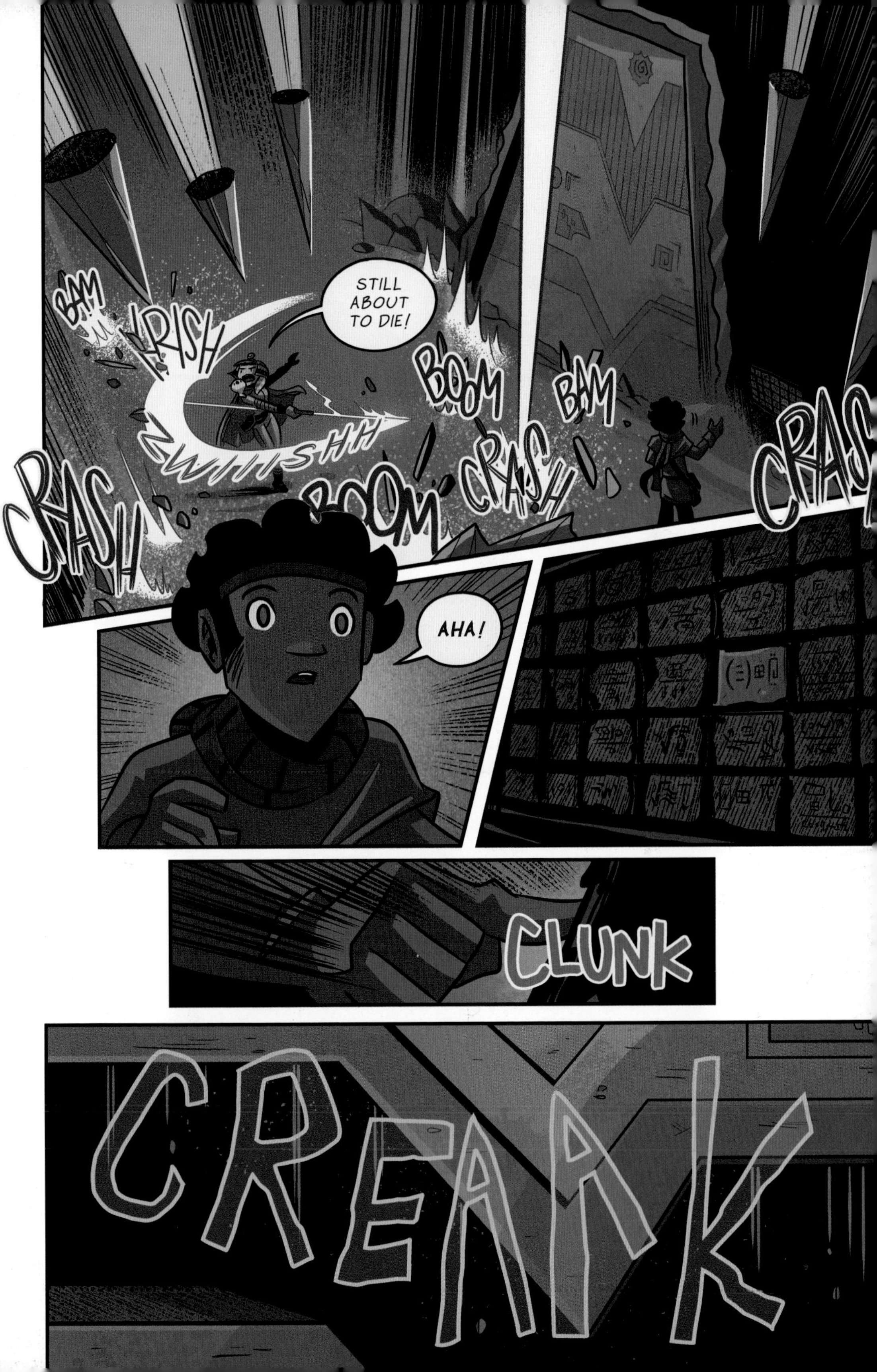

BAM
KRISH
STILL ABOUT TO DIE!
ZWIIISHH
BOOM
BAM
CRASH
BOOM
CRASH
CRASH
AHA!
CLUNK
CREAAK

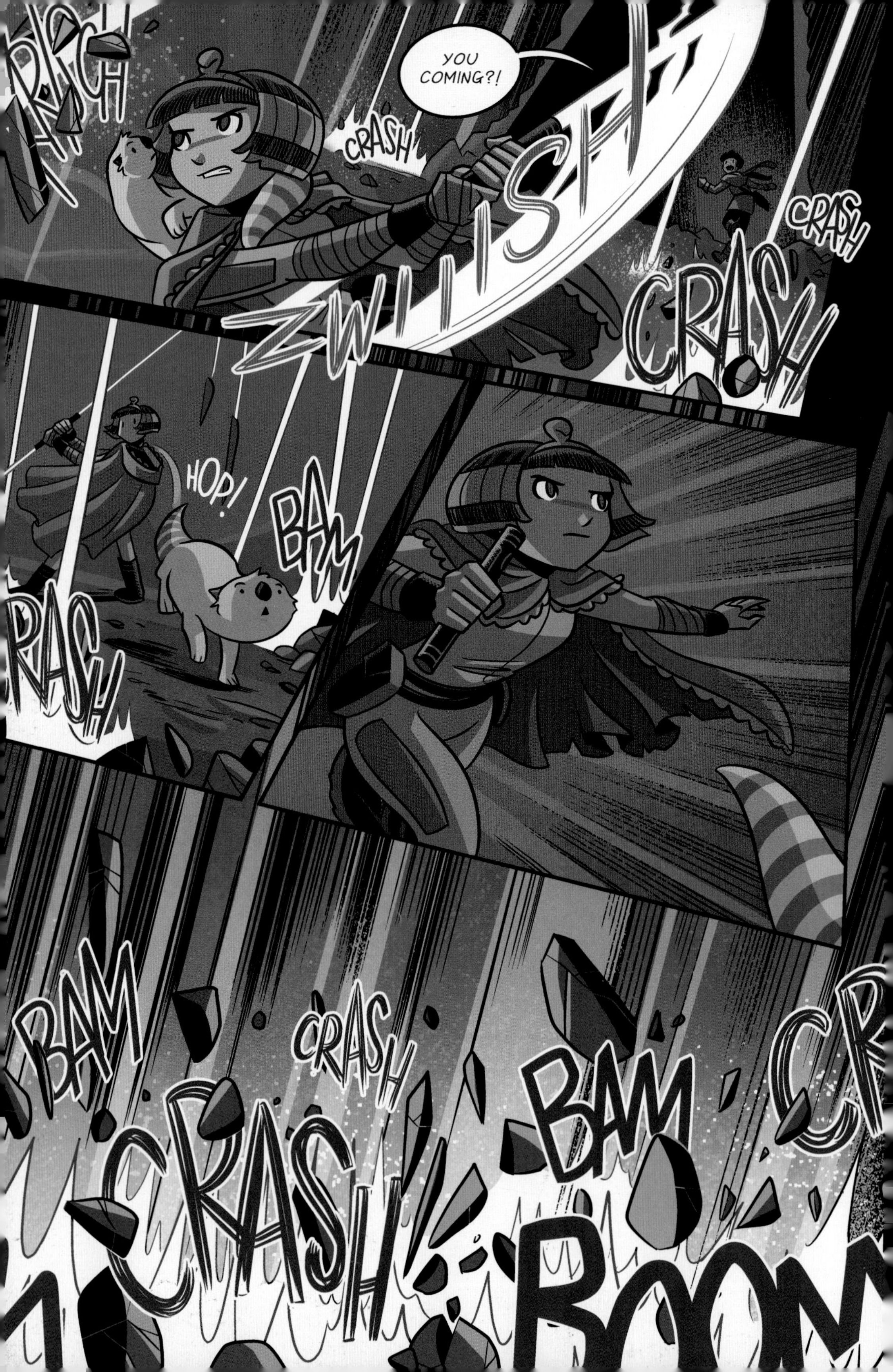
KRRSCH
YOU COMING?!
CRASH
ZWIIISSH
CRASH
CRASH
HOP!
BAM
CRASH
BAM
CRASH
BAM
CRASH
CR
BOOM

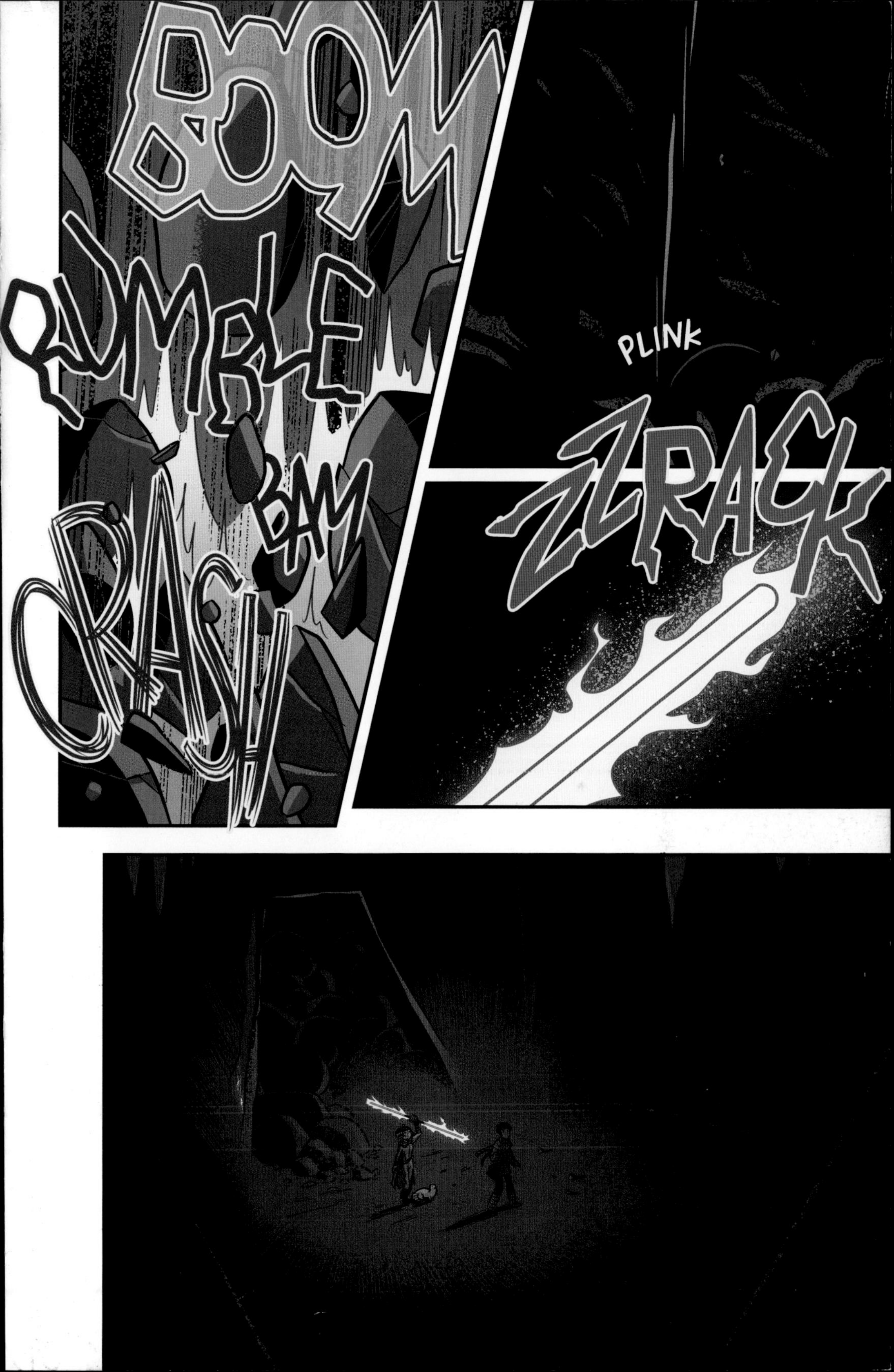
BOOM
RUMBLE
BAM
CRASH
PLINK
ZZRACK

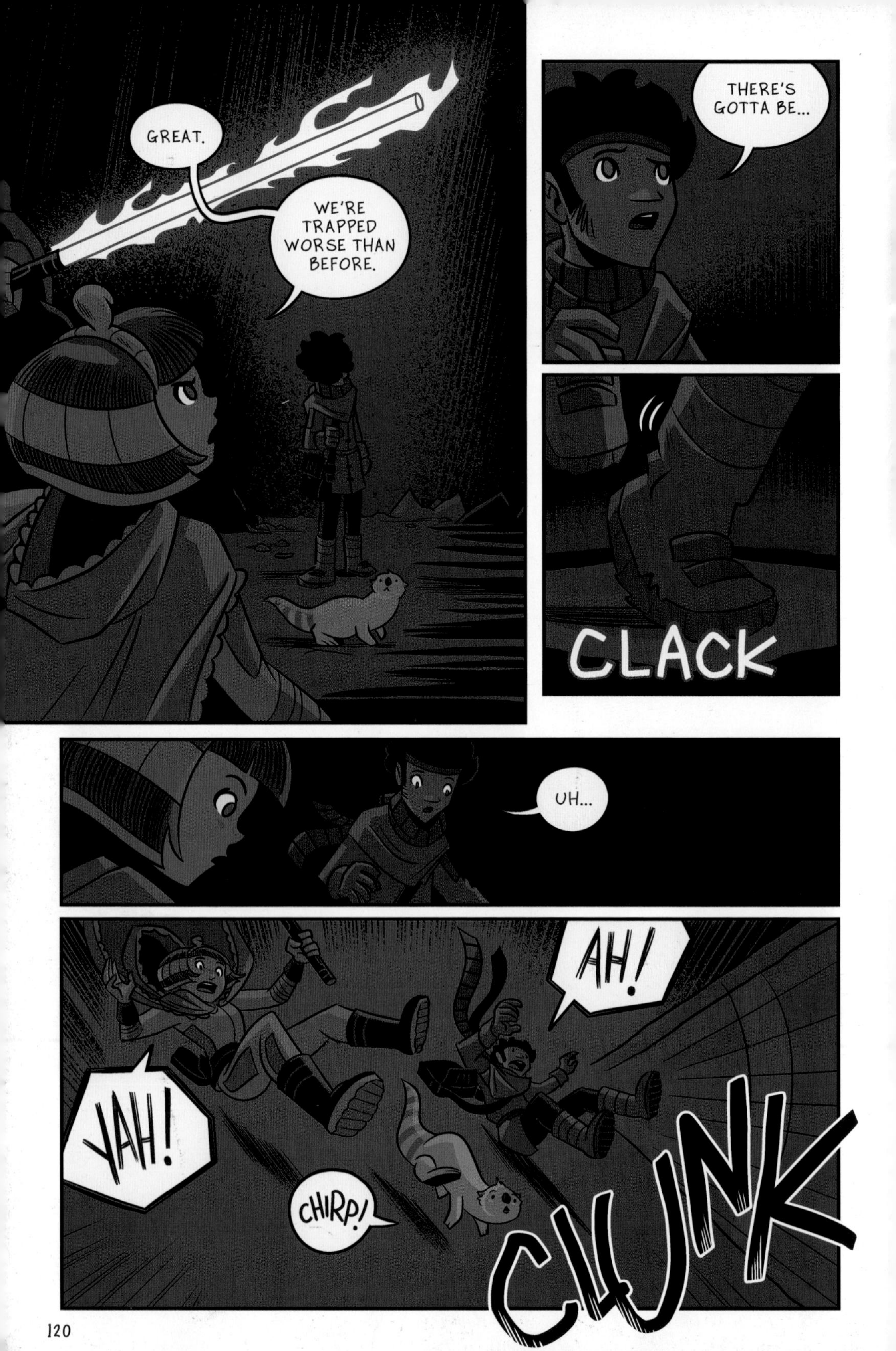
GREAT.
WE'RE TRAPPED WORSE THAN BEFORE.
THERE'S GOTTA BE...
CLACK
UH...
AH!
YAH!
CHIRP!
CLUNK

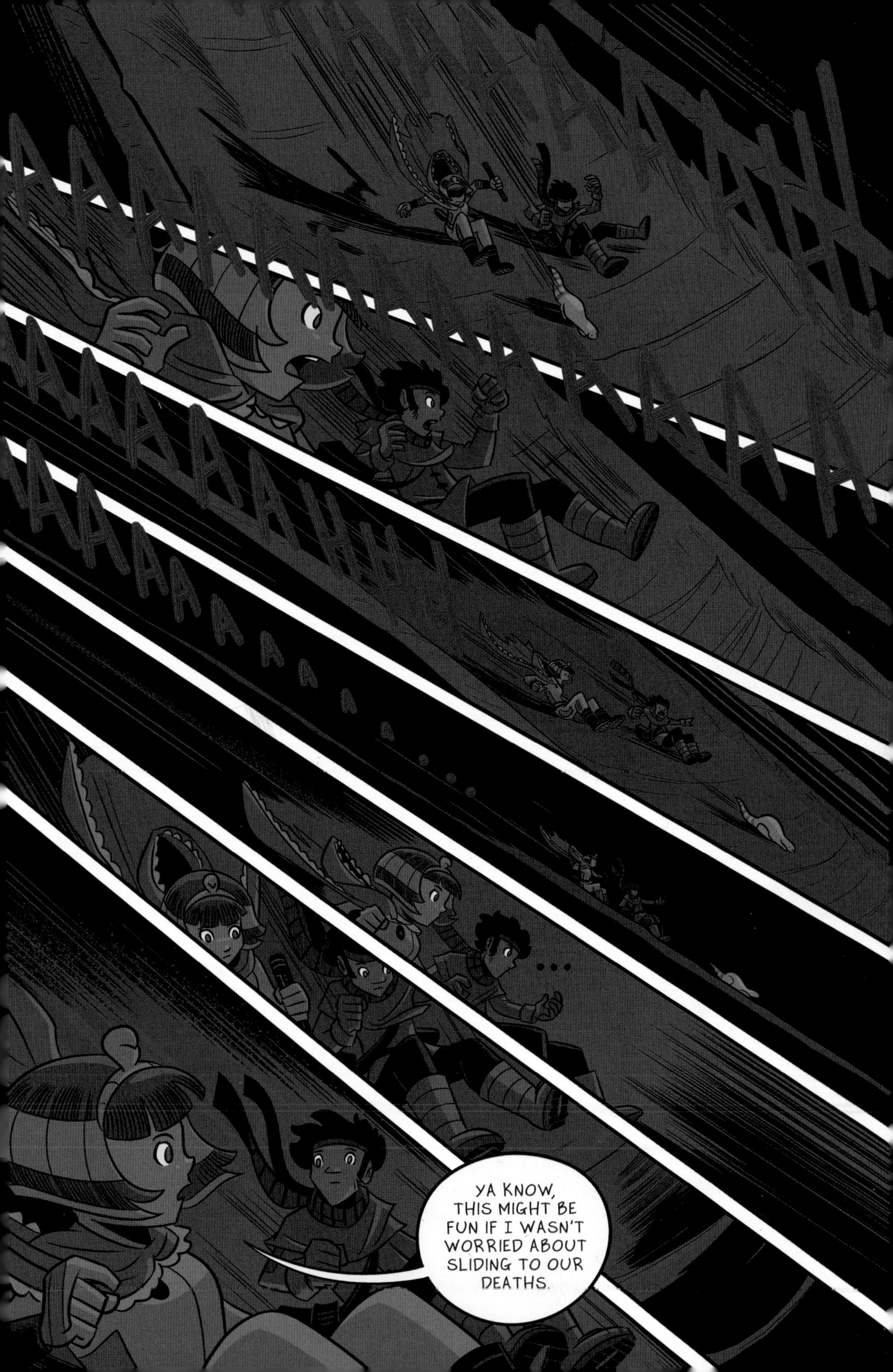

...
YA KNOW, THIS MIGHT BE FUN IF I WASN'T WORRIED ABOUT SLIDING TO OUR DEATHS.

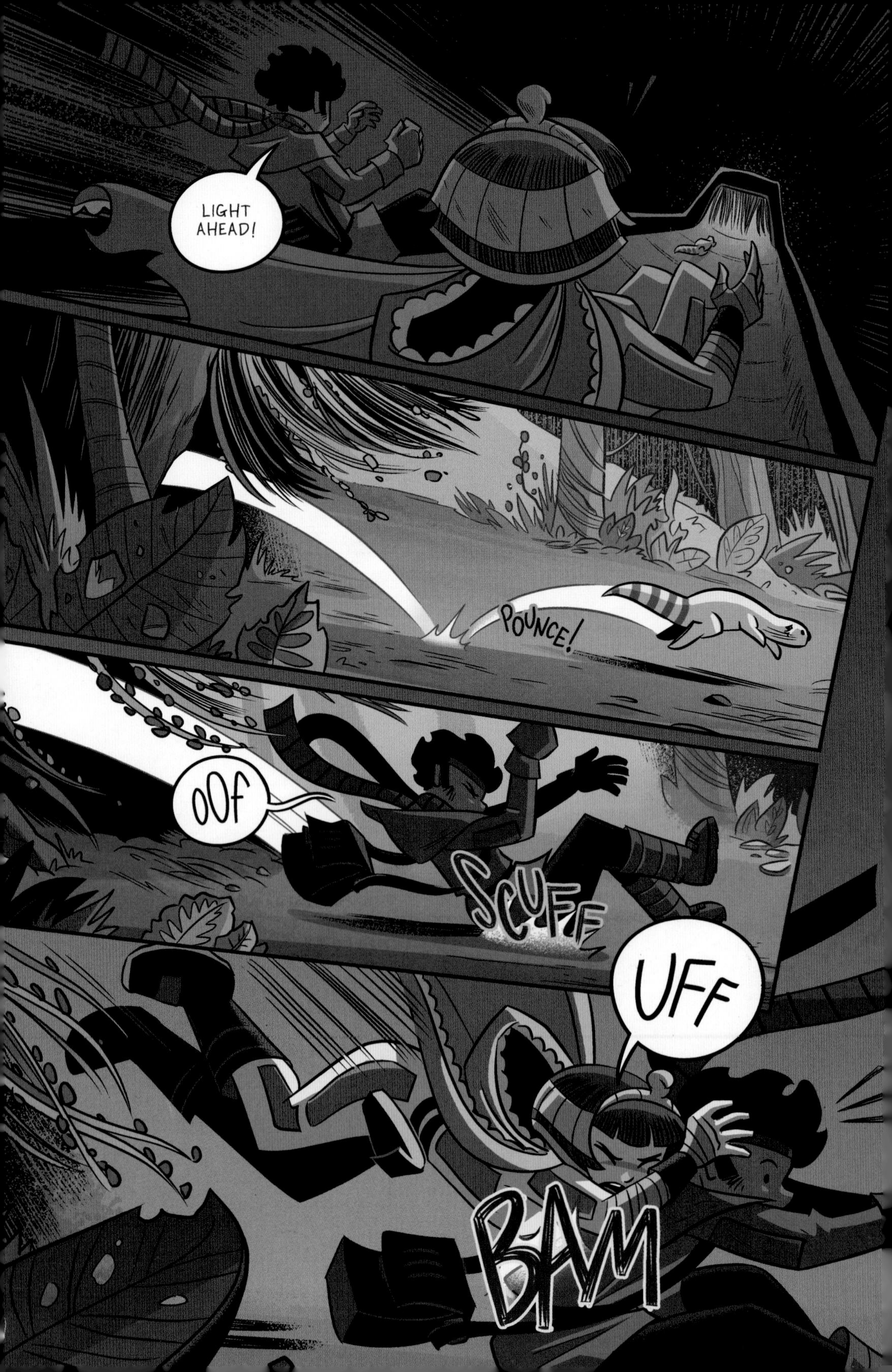
LIGHT AHEAD!
POUNCE!
OOF
SCUFF
UFF
BAM

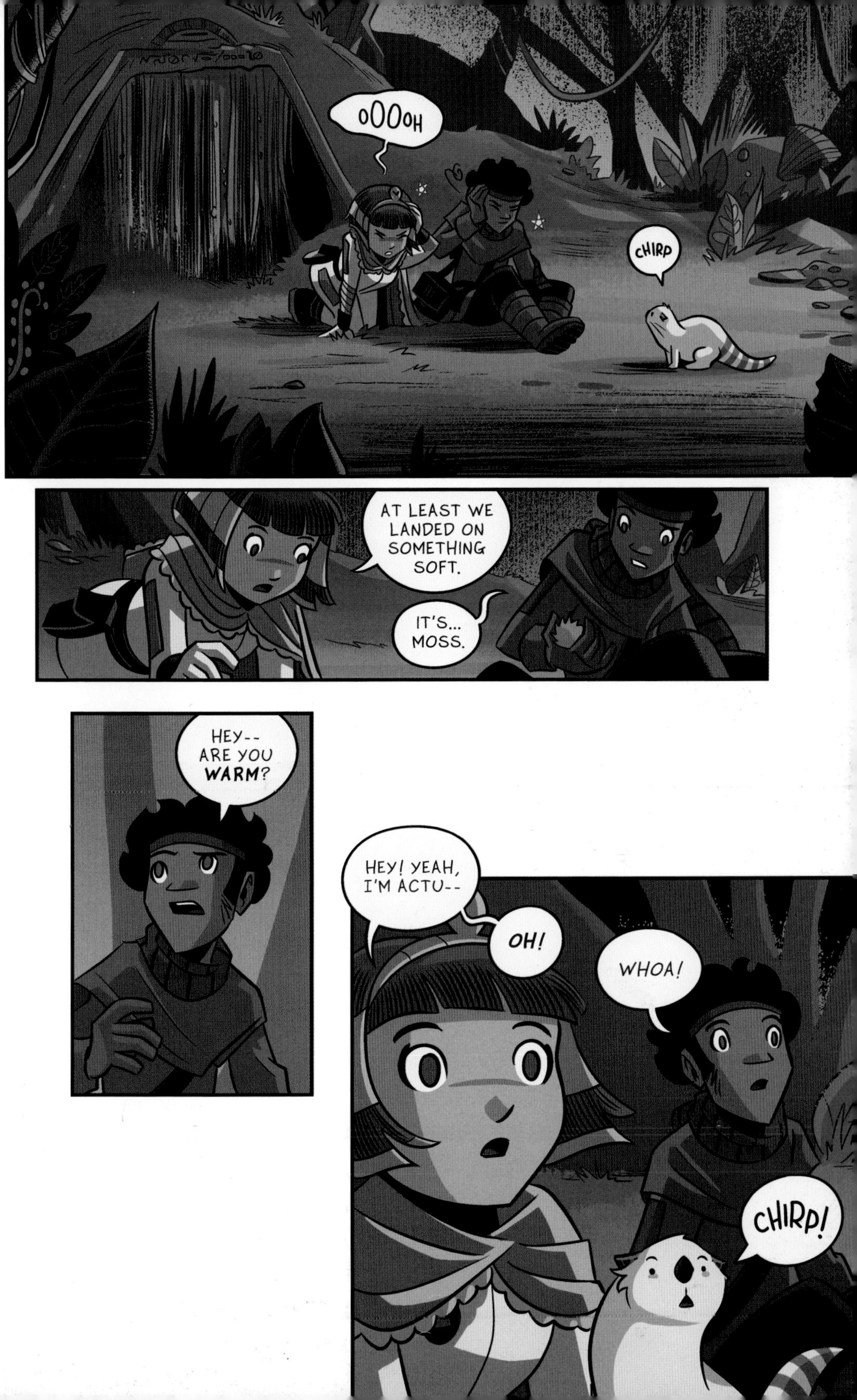

OOOOH
CHIRP
AT LEAST WE LANDED ON SOMETHING SOFT.
IT'S... MOSS.
HEY-- ARE YOU **WARM**?
HEY! YEAH, I'M ACTU--
OH!
WHOA!
CHIRP!

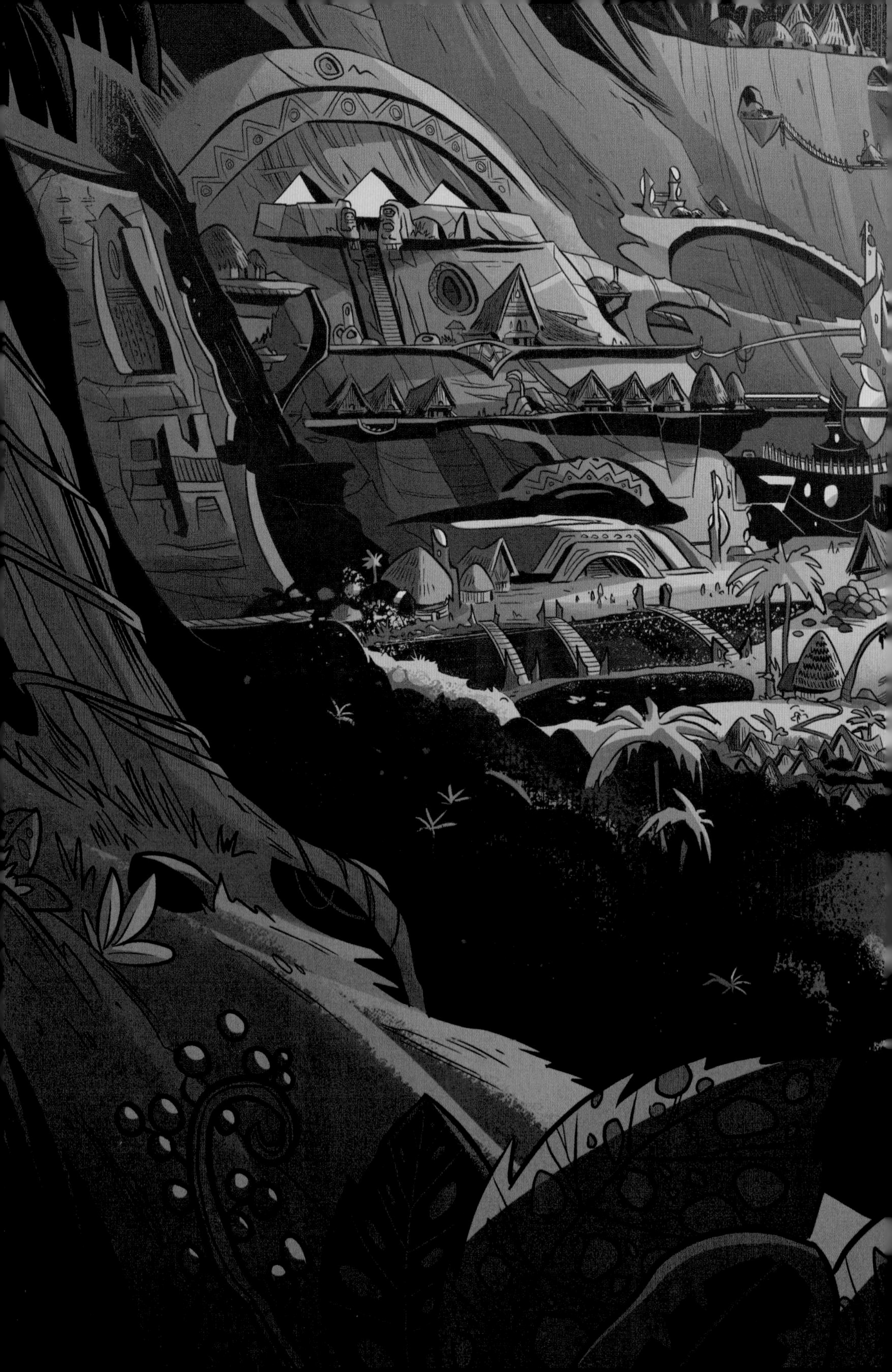

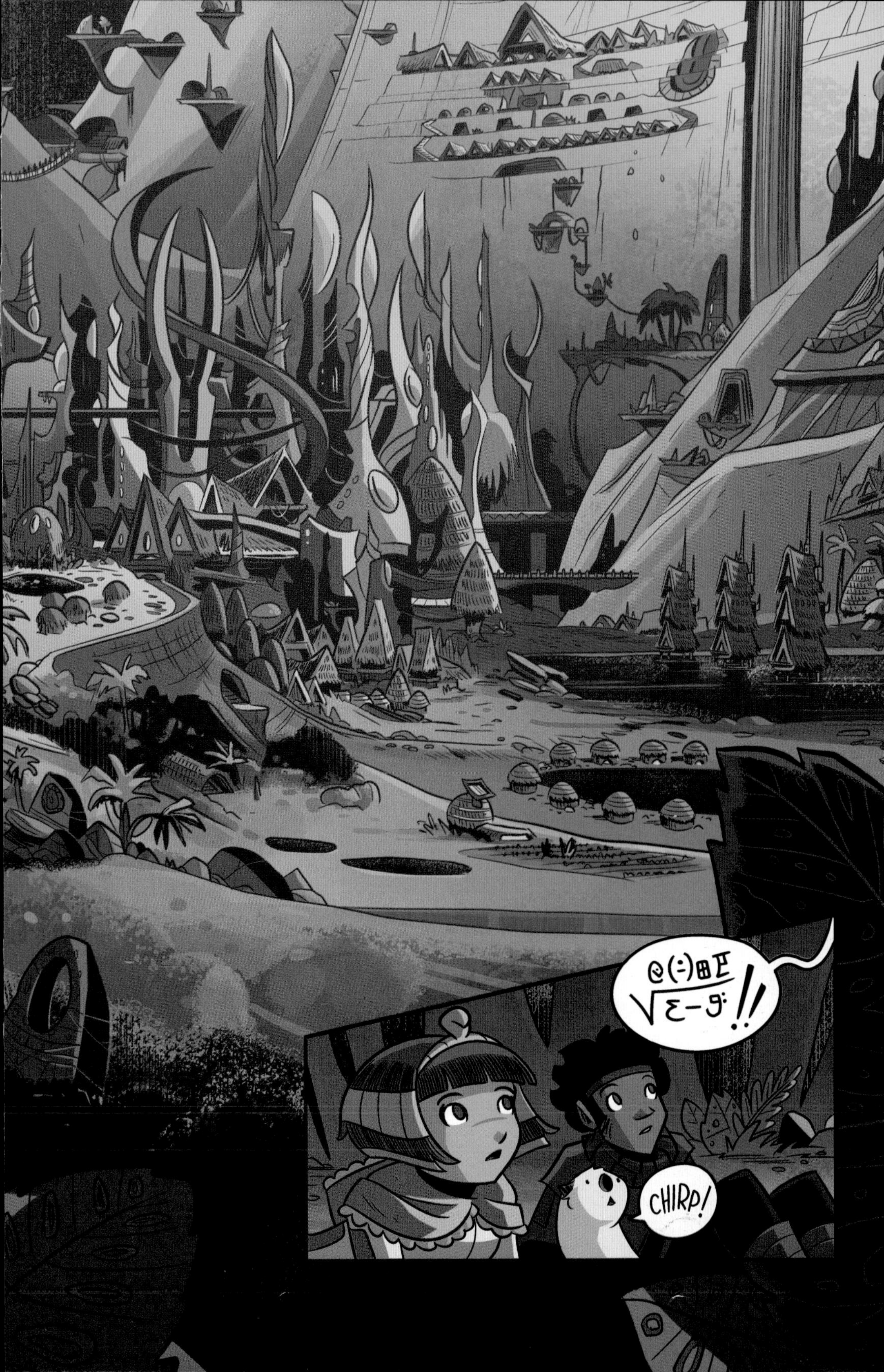
CHIRP!

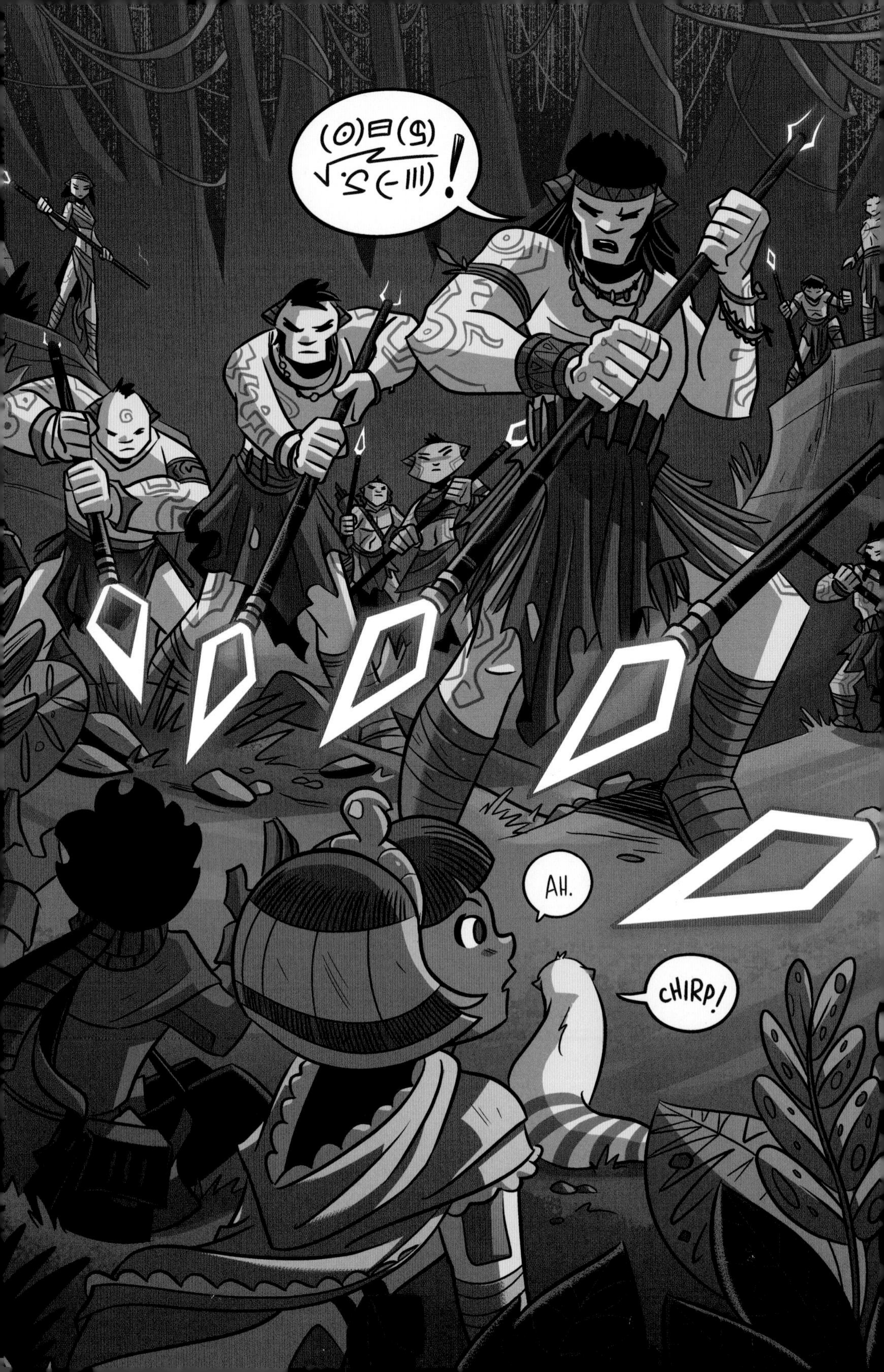
AH.
CHIRP!

# CHAPTER THREE

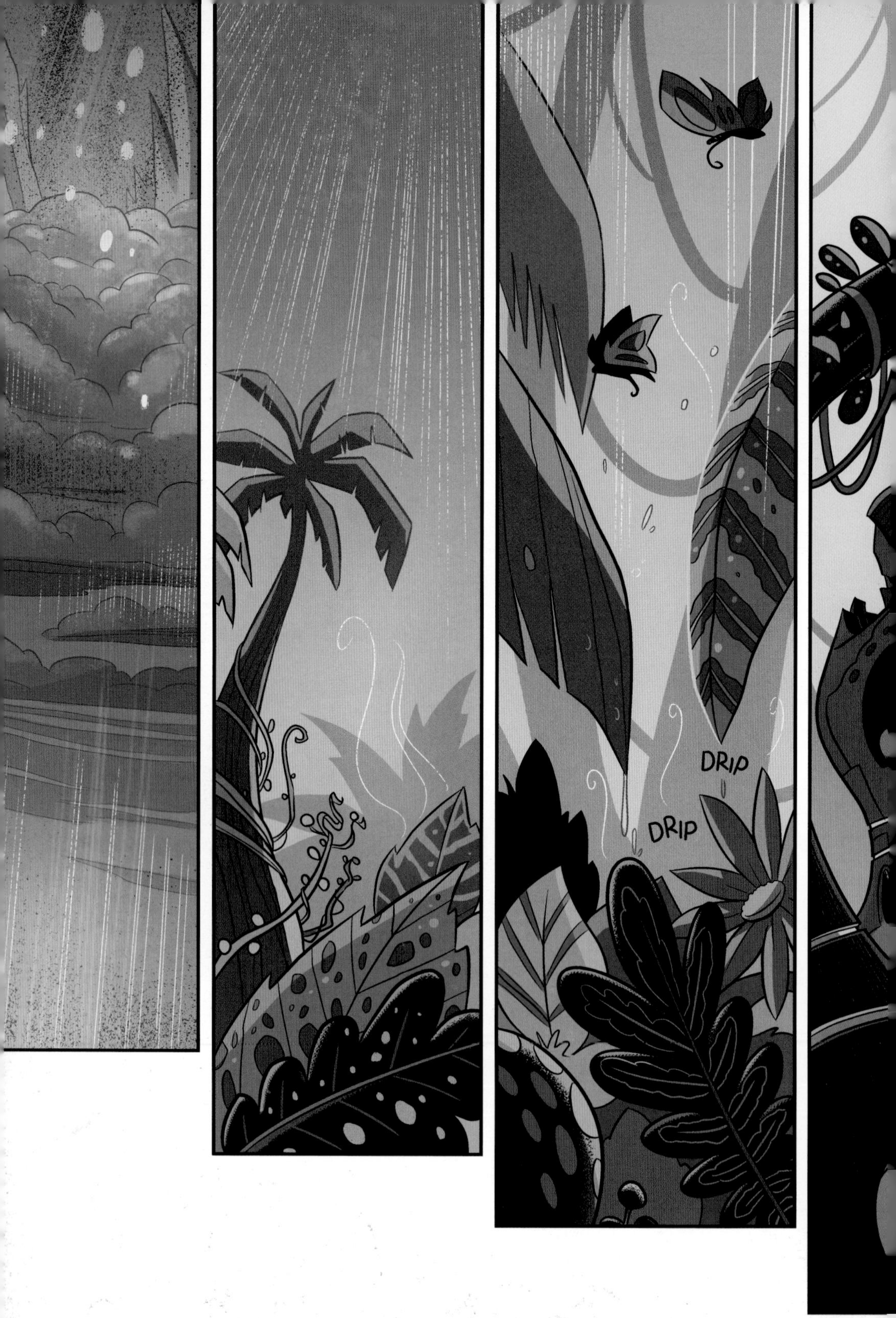
DRIP
DRIP

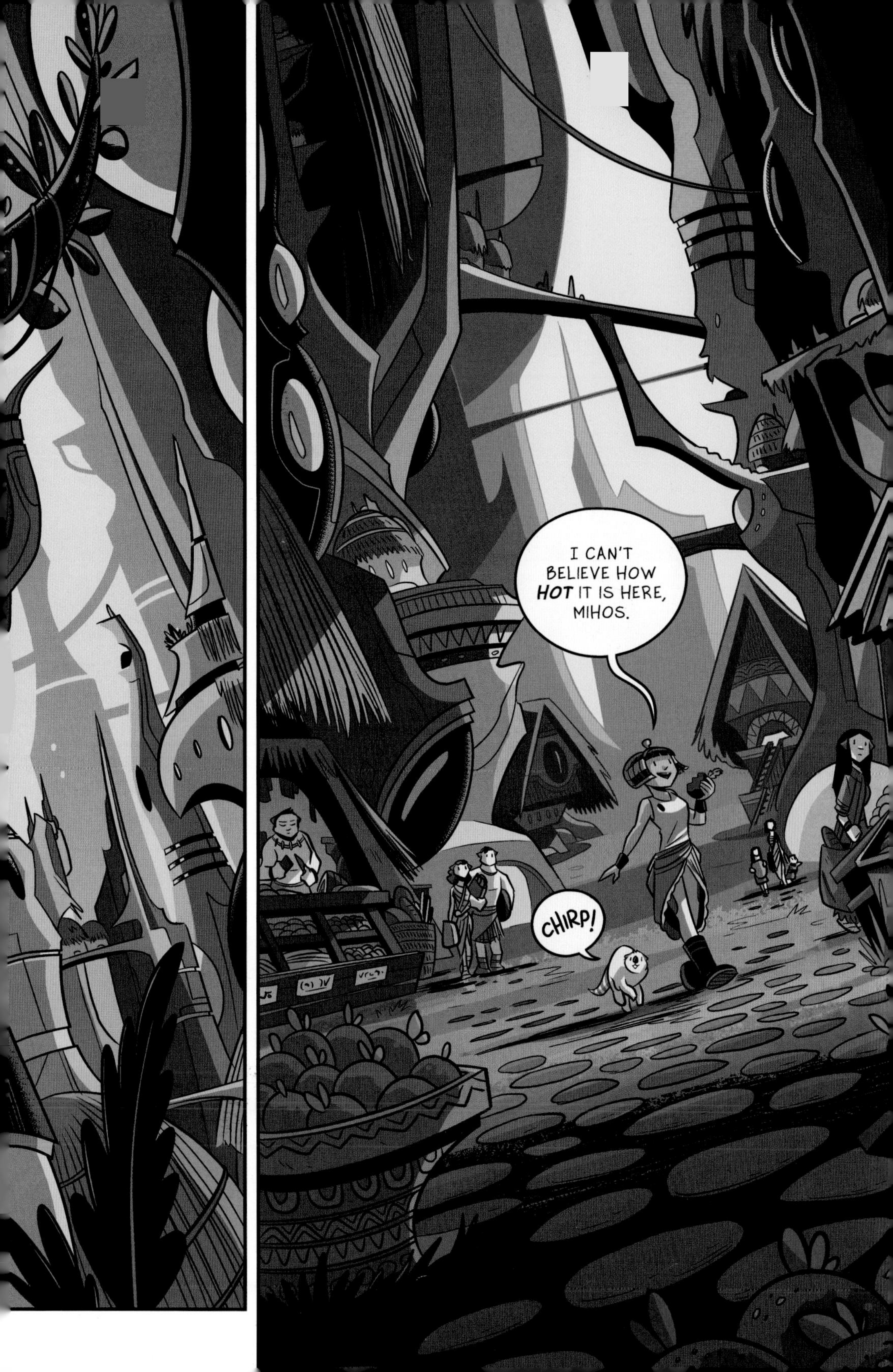
I CAN'T BELIEVE HOW HOT IT IS HERE, MIHOS.
CHIRP!

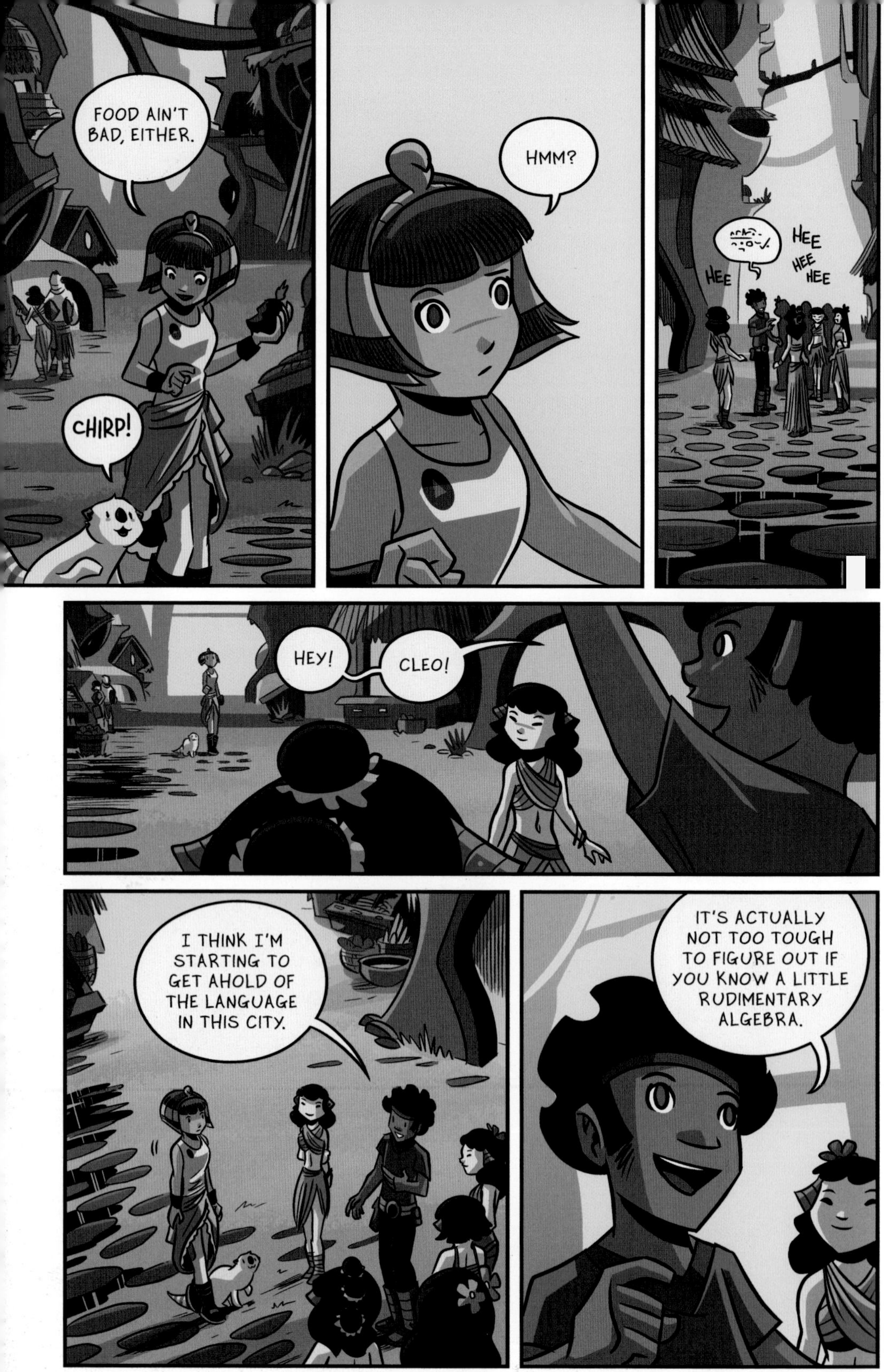
FOOD AIN'T BAD, EITHER.
CHIRP!
HMM?
HEE
HEE
HEE HEE
HEY!
CLEO!
I THINK I'M STARTING TO GET AHOLD OF THE LANGUAGE IN THIS CITY.
IT'S ACTUALLY NOT TOO TOUGH TO FIGURE OUT IF YOU KNOW A LITTLE RUDIMENTARY ALGEBRA.

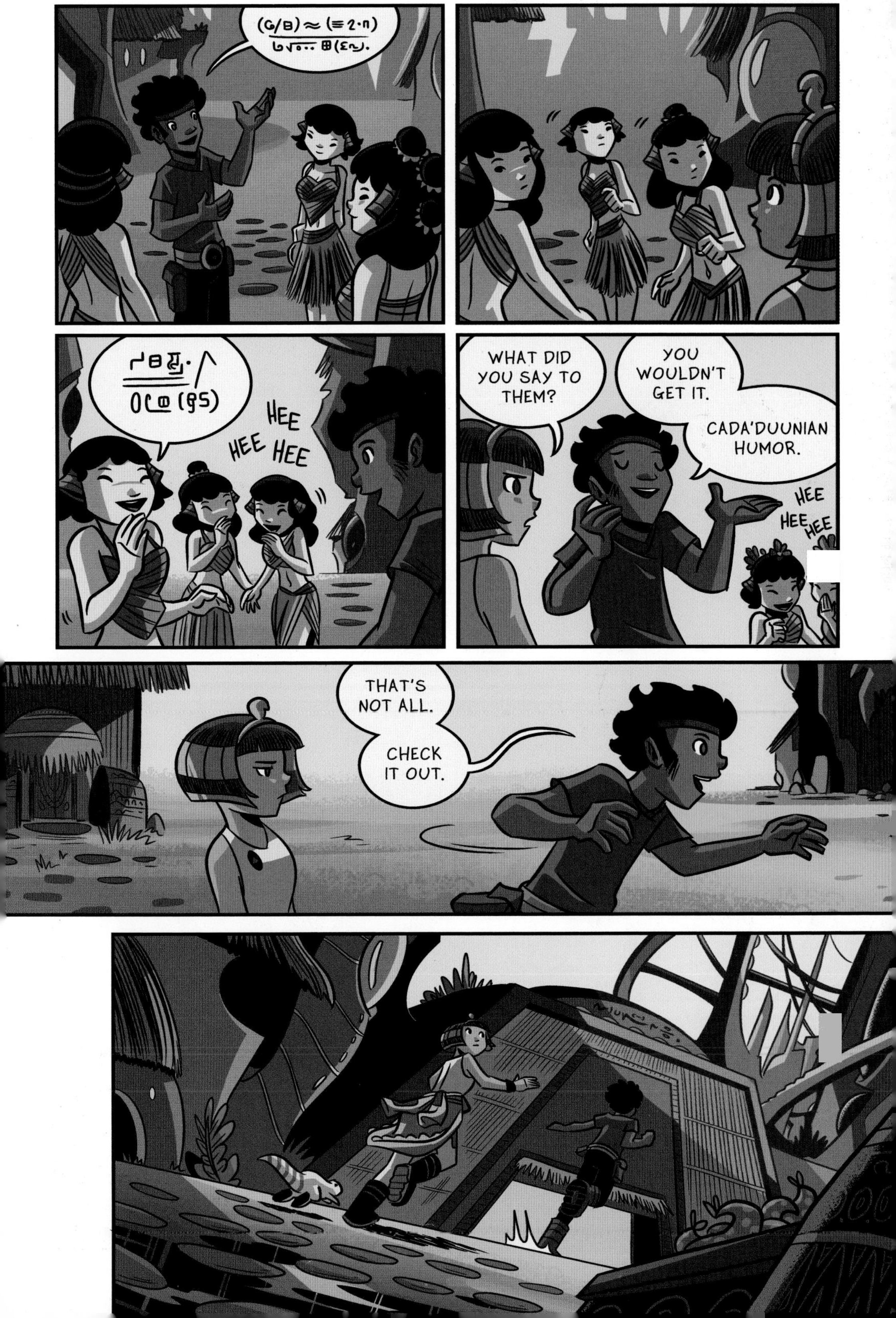
HEE
HEE HEE
WHAT DID YOU SAY TO THEM?
YOU WOULDN'T GET IT.
CADA'DUUNIAN HUMOR.
HEE
HEE HEE
THAT'S NOT ALL.
CHECK IT OUT.

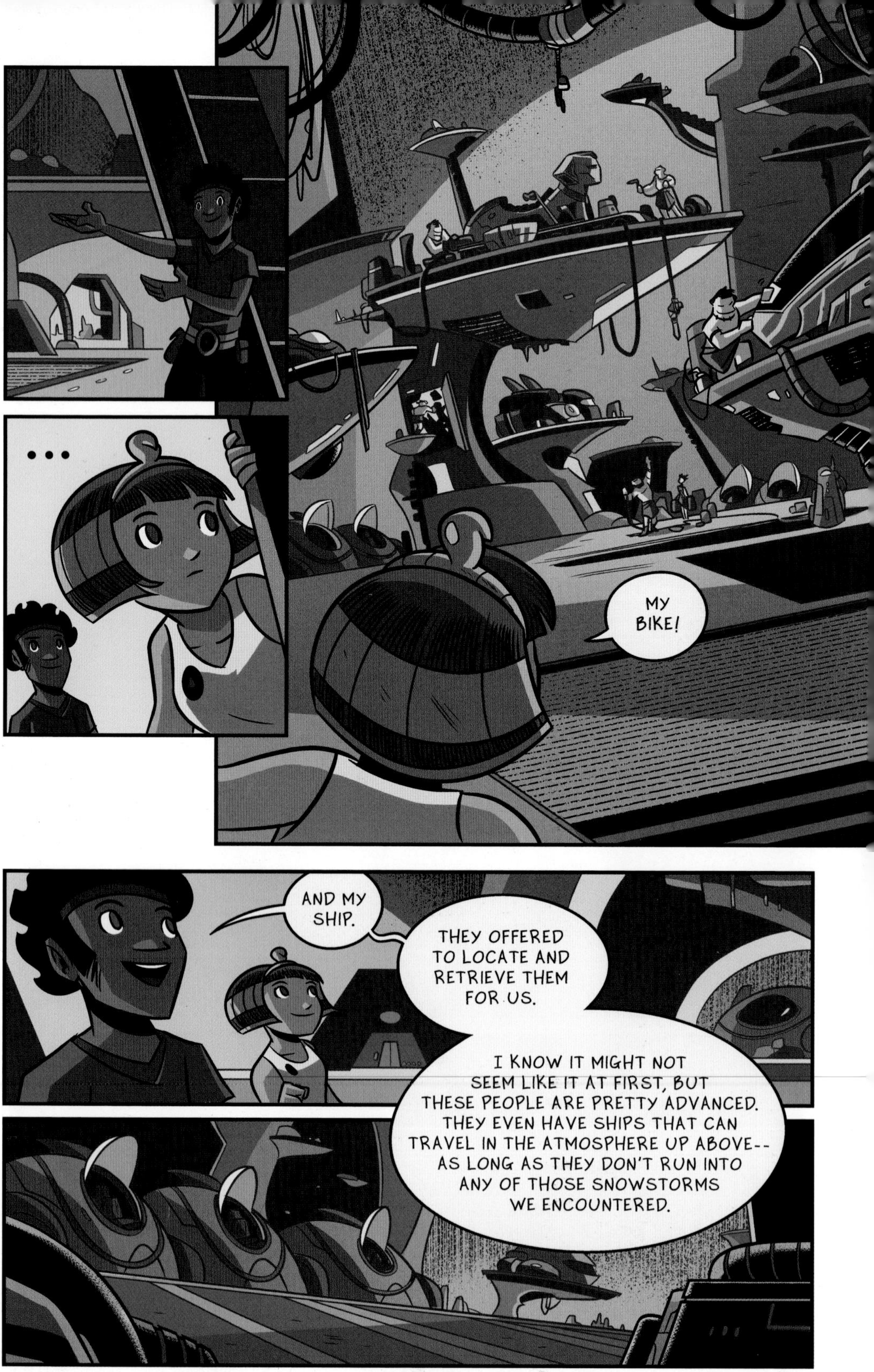
...
MY BIKE!
AND MY SHIP.
THEY OFFERED TO LOCATE AND RETRIEVE THEM FOR US.
I KNOW IT MIGHT NOT SEEM LIKE IT AT FIRST, BUT THESE PEOPLE ARE PRETTY ADVANCED. THEY EVEN HAVE SHIPS THAT CAN TRAVEL IN THE ATMOSPHERE UP ABOVE-- AS LONG AS THEY DON'T RUN INTO ANY OF THOSE SNOWSTORMS WE ENCOUNTERED.

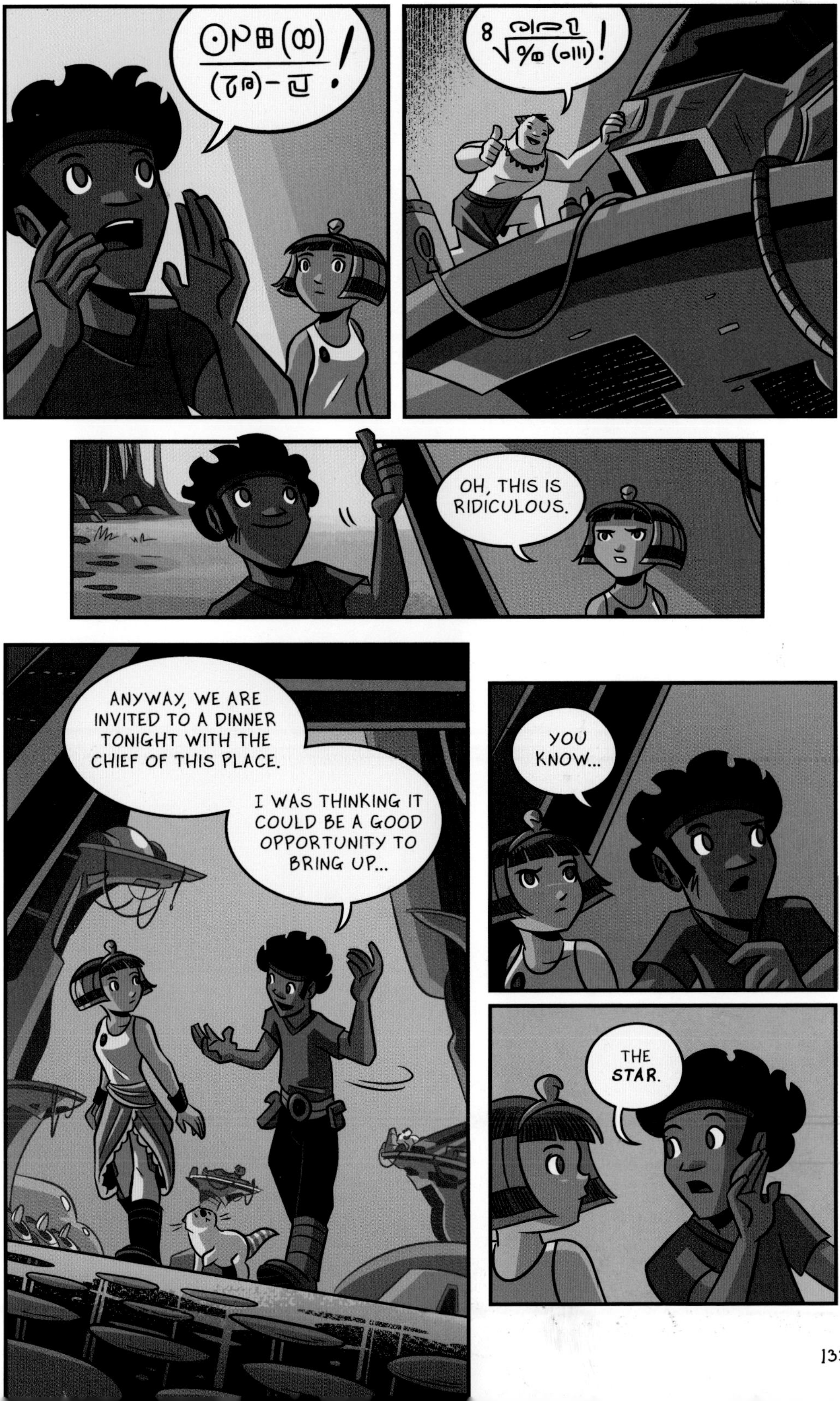
OH, THIS IS RIDICULOUS.
ANYWAY, WE ARE INVITED TO A DINNER TONIGHT WITH THE CHIEF OF THIS PLACE.
I WAS THINKING IT COULD BE A GOOD OPPORTUNITY TO BRING UP...
YOU KNOW...
THE STAR.

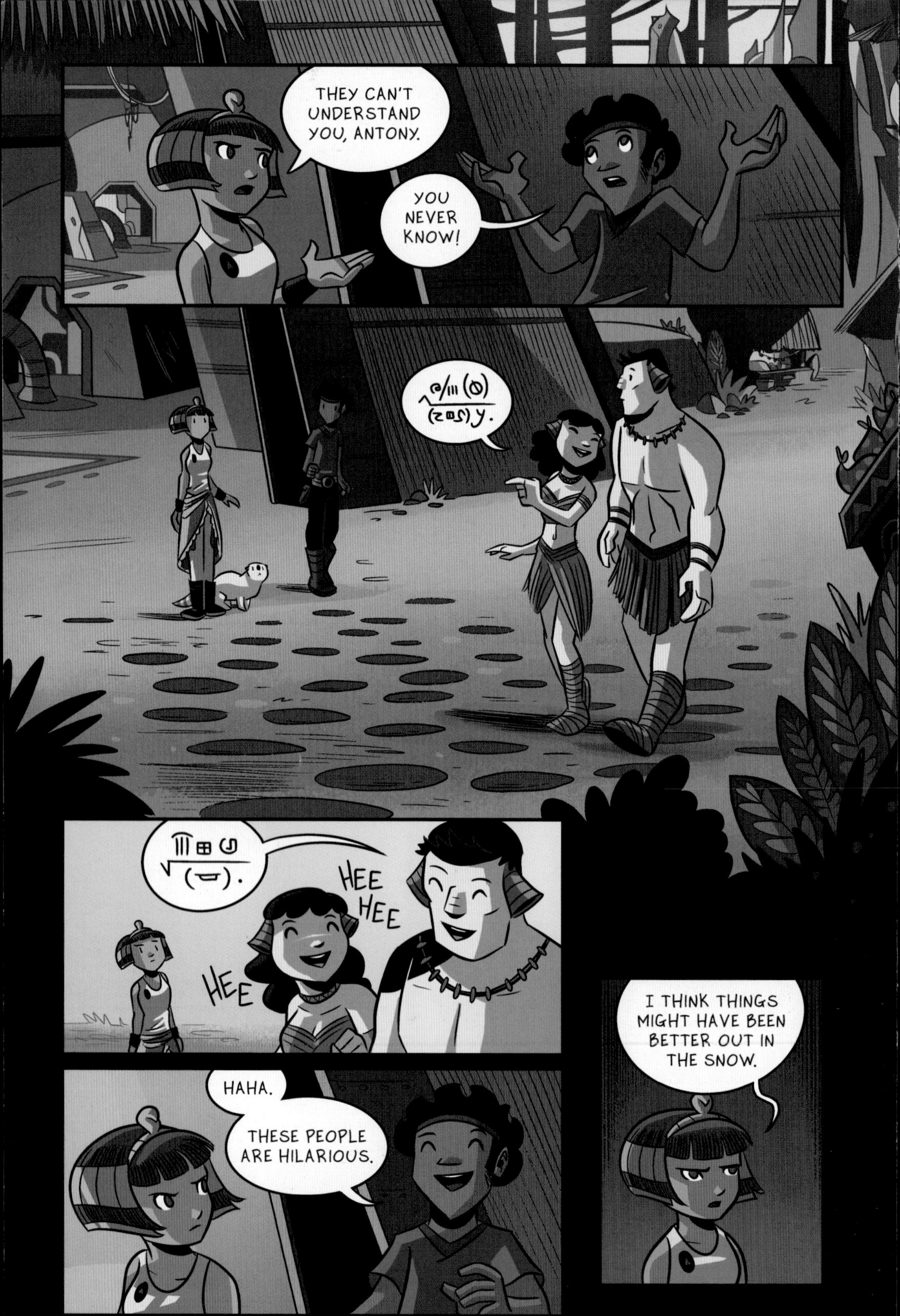
THEY CAN'T UNDERSTAND YOU, ANTONY.
YOU NEVER KNOW!
HEE HEE
HEE
HAHA.
THESE PEOPLE ARE HILARIOUS.
I THINK THINGS MIGHT HAVE BEEN BETTER OUT IN THE SNOW.

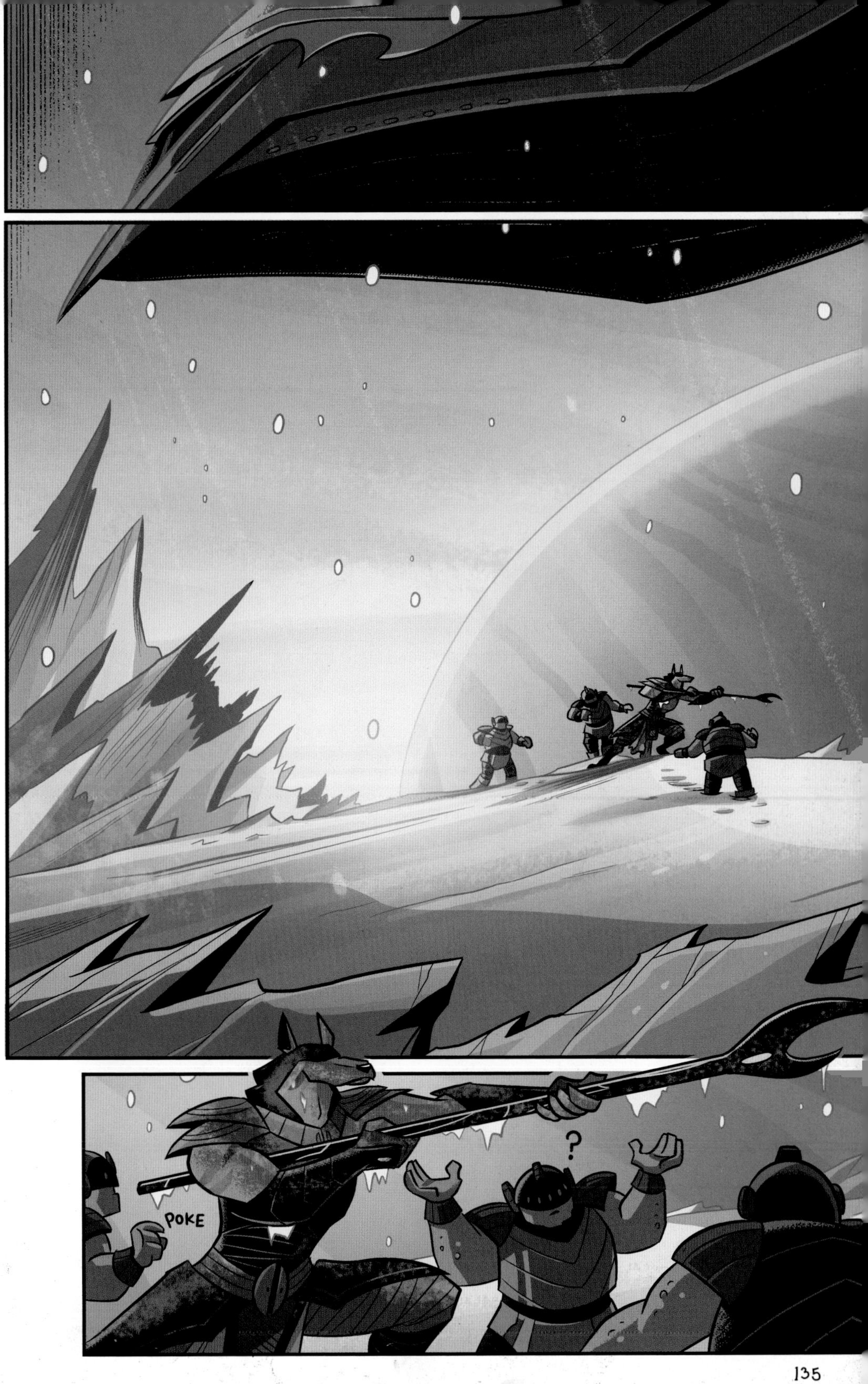
?
POKE

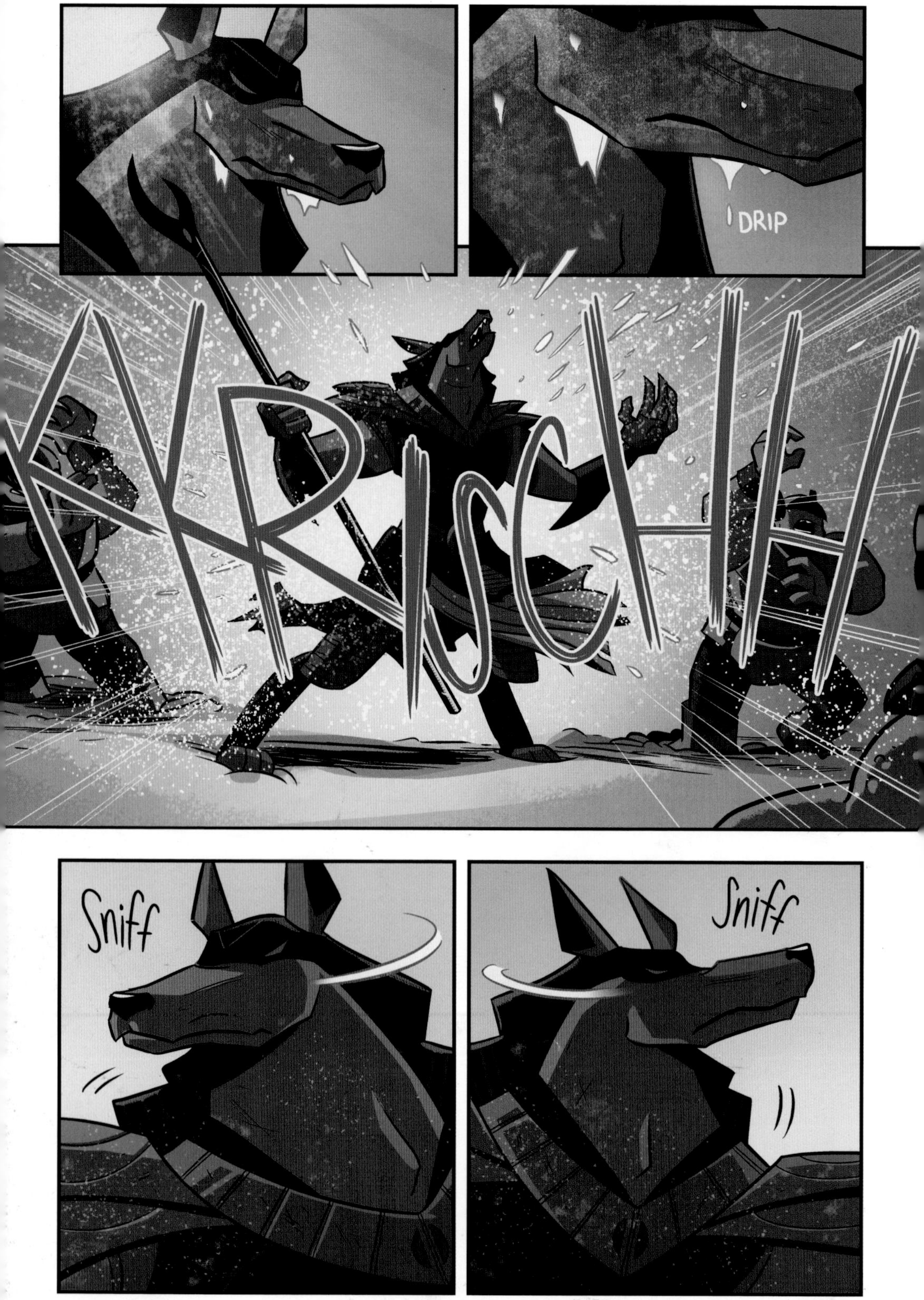
DRIP
KKRISCHH
Sniff
Sniff

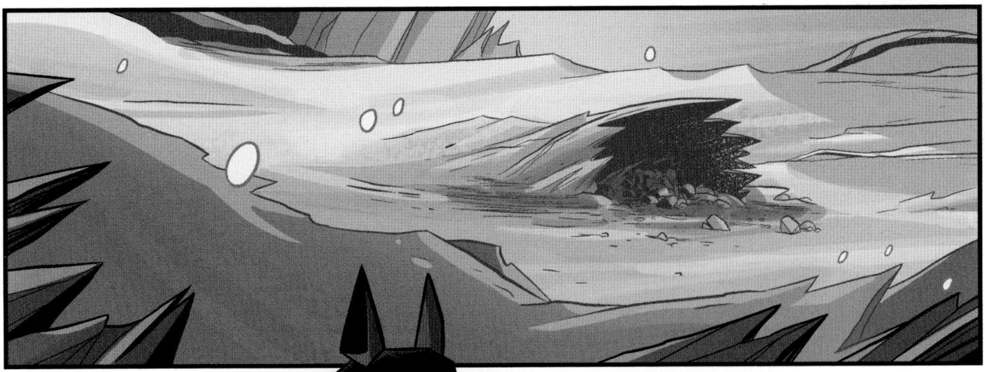

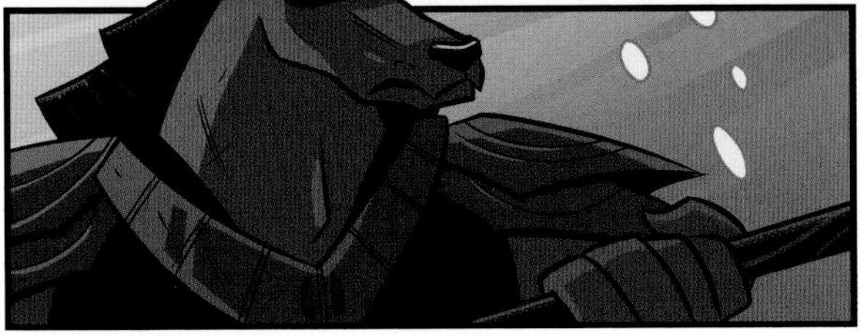

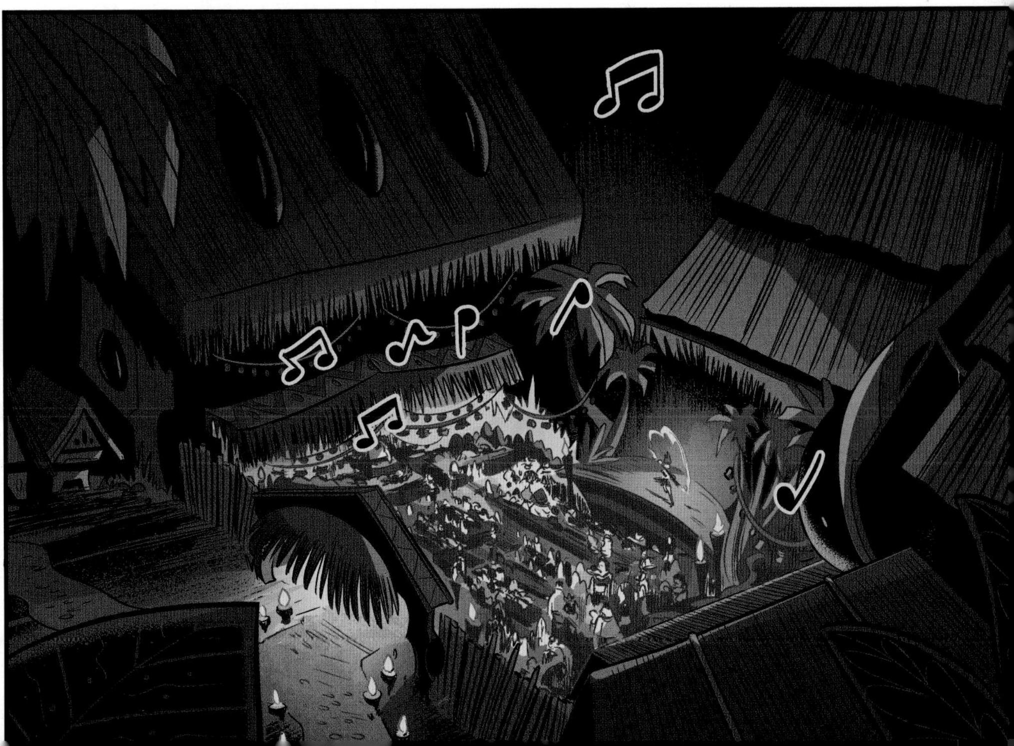

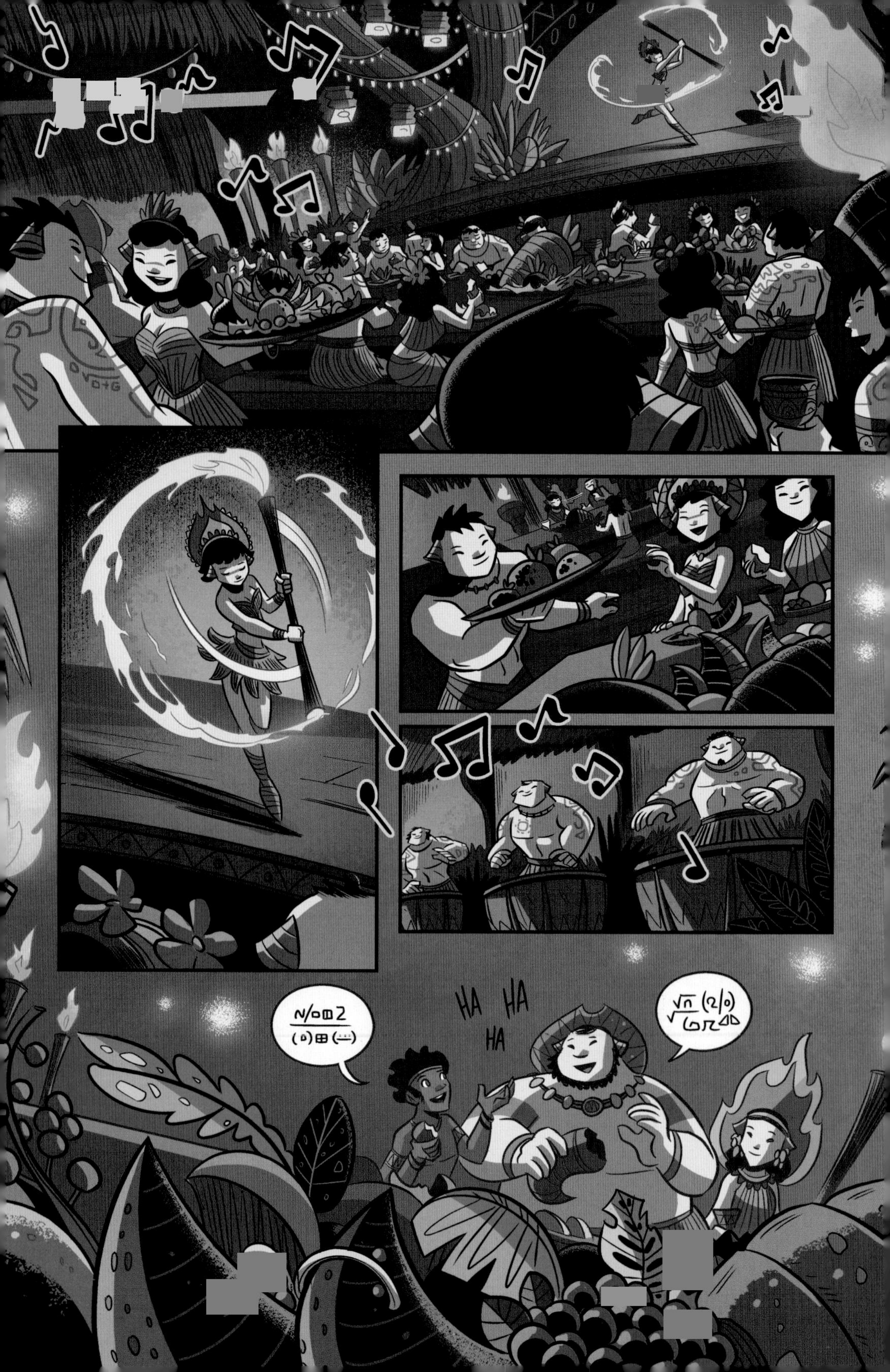
HA HA
HA

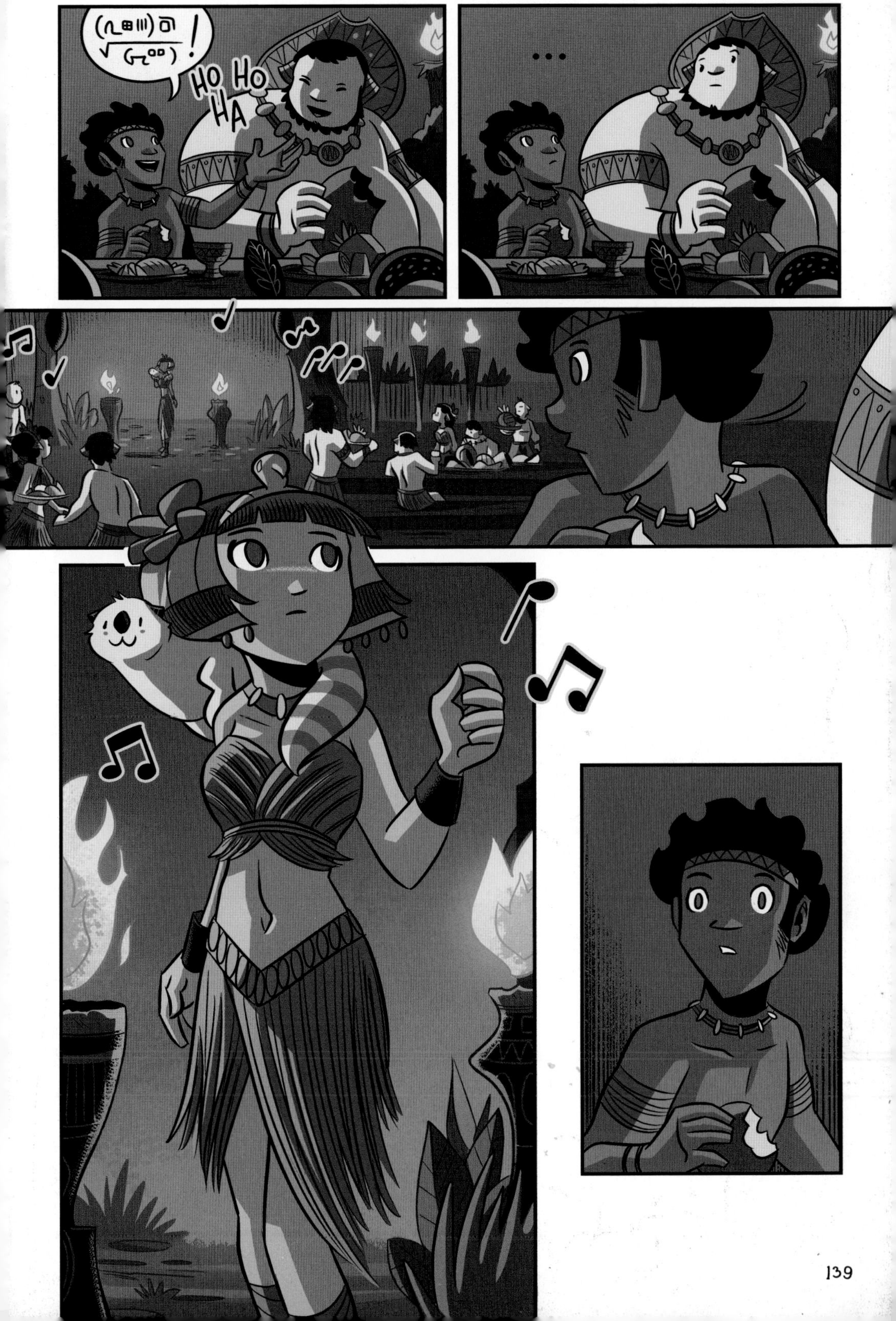
HO HO HA
...

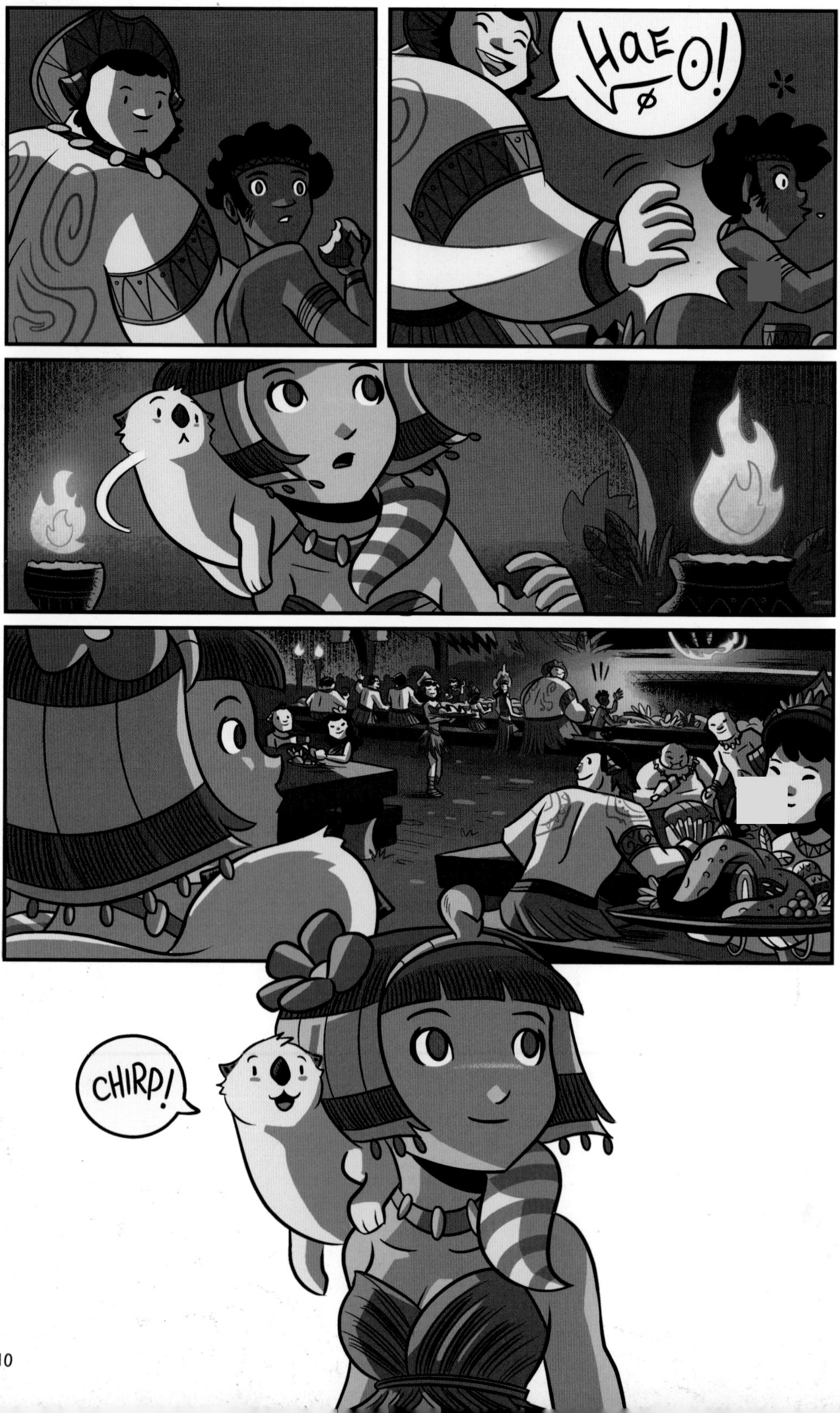
HAEØO!
CHIRP!

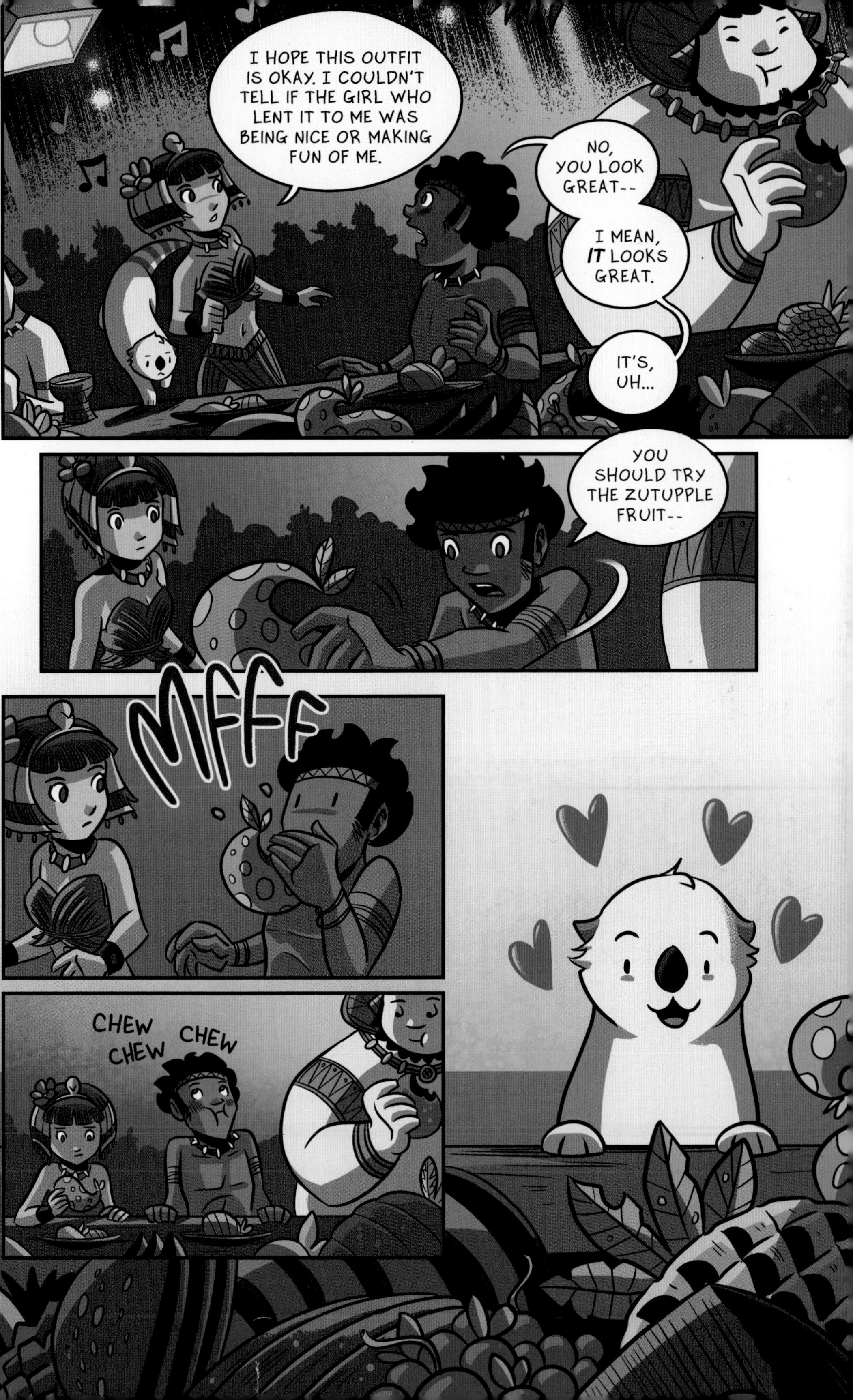
I HOPE THIS OUTFIT IS OKAY. I COULDN'T TELL IF THE GIRL WHO LENT IT TO ME WAS BEING NICE OR MAKING FUN OF ME.
NO, YOU LOOK GREAT--
I MEAN, IT LOOKS GREAT.
IT'S, UH...
YOU SHOULD TRY THE ZUTUPPLE FRUIT--
MFFF
CHEW CHEW
CHEW

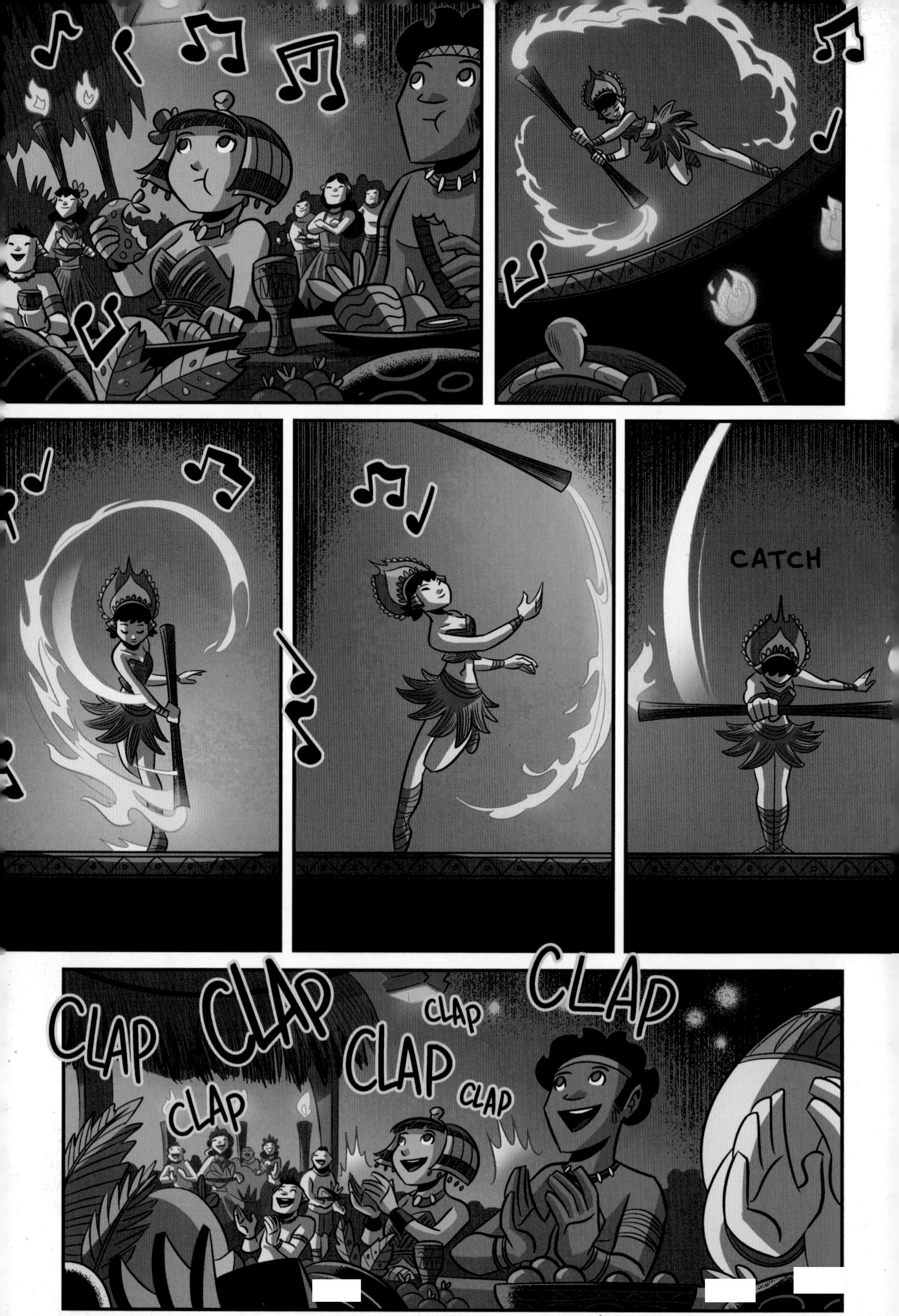
CATCH
CLAP
CLAP
CLAP
CLAP
CLAP
CLAP
CLAP

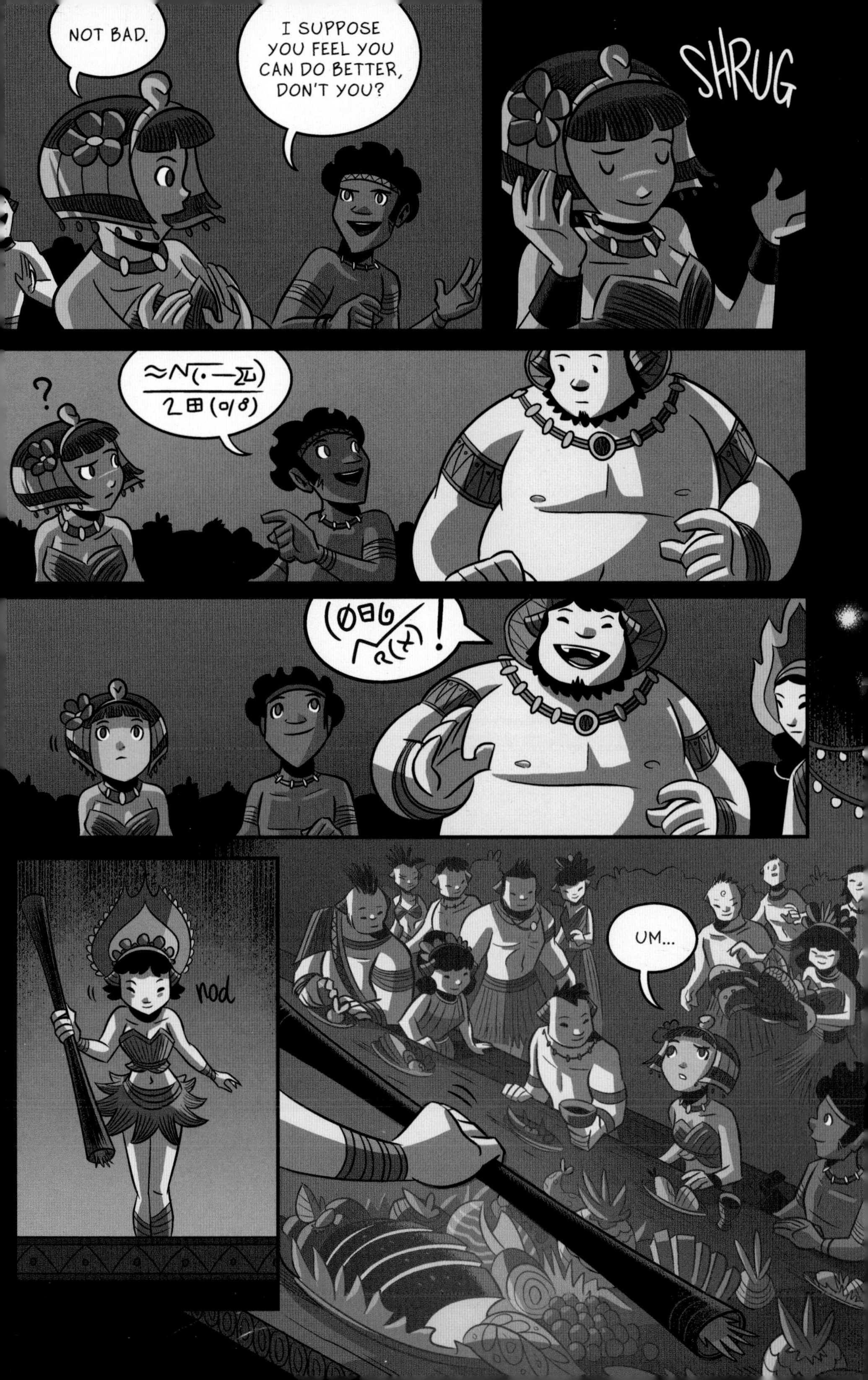
NOT BAD.
I SUPPOSE YOU FEEL YOU CAN DO BETTER, DON'T YOU?
SHRUG
?
nod
UM...

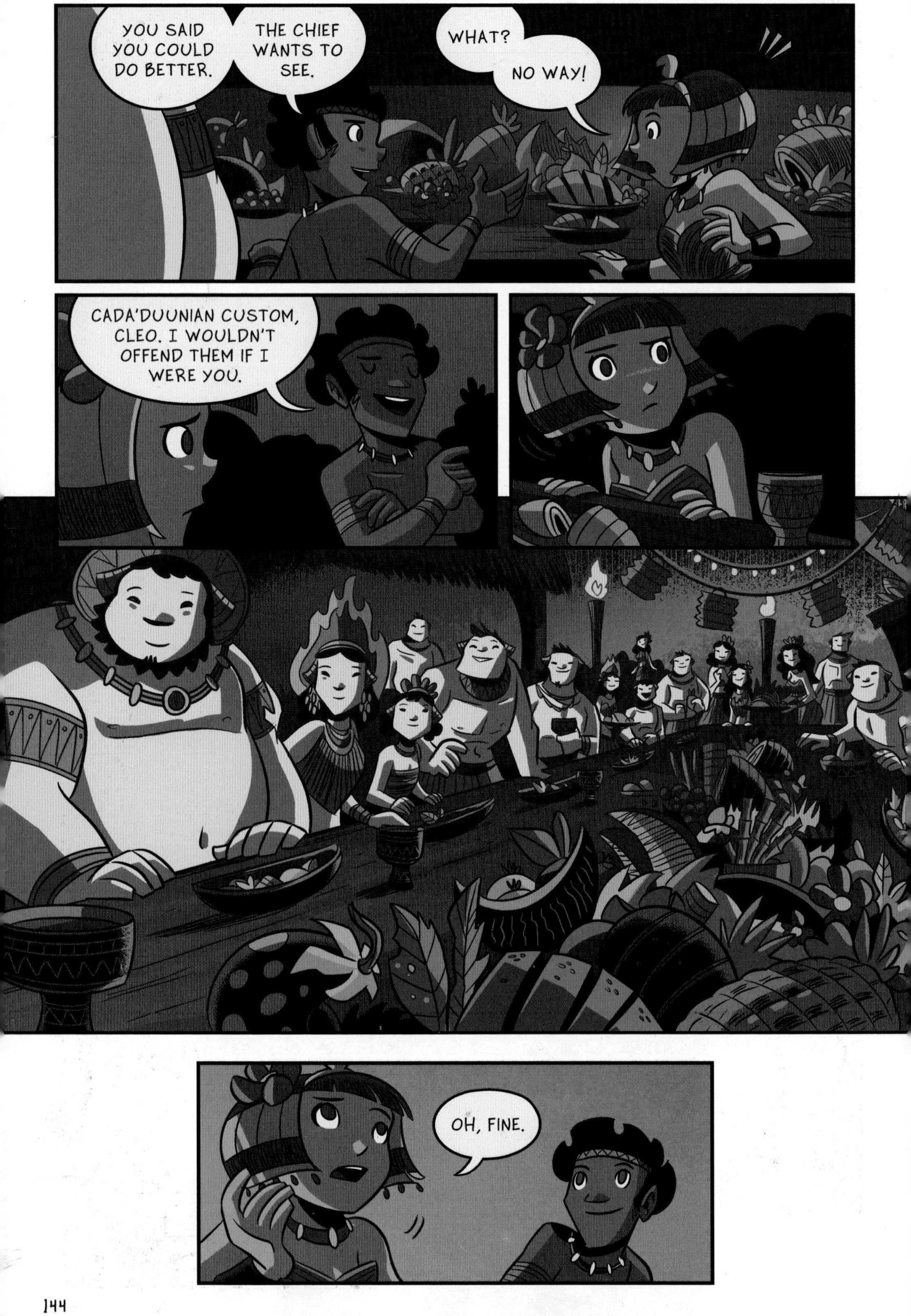
YOU SAID YOU COULD DO BETTER.
THE CHIEF WANTS TO SEE.
WHAT?
NO WAY!
CADA'DUUNIAN CUSTOM, CLEO. I WOULDN'T OFFEND THEM IF I WERE YOU.
OH, FINE.

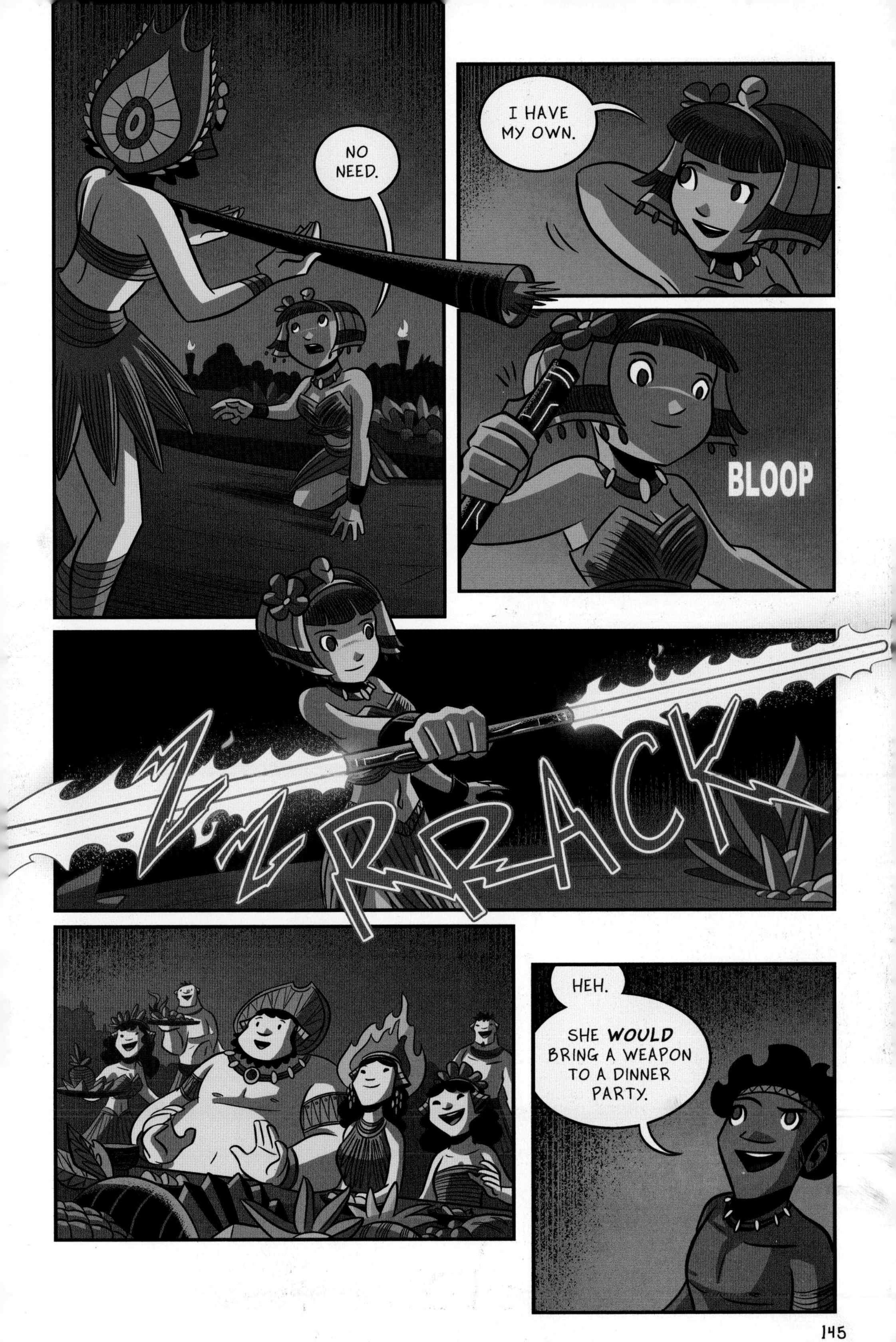
NO NEED.
I HAVE MY OWN.
BLOOP
ZZRRACK
HEH.
SHE **WOULD** BRING A WEAPON TO A DINNER PARTY.

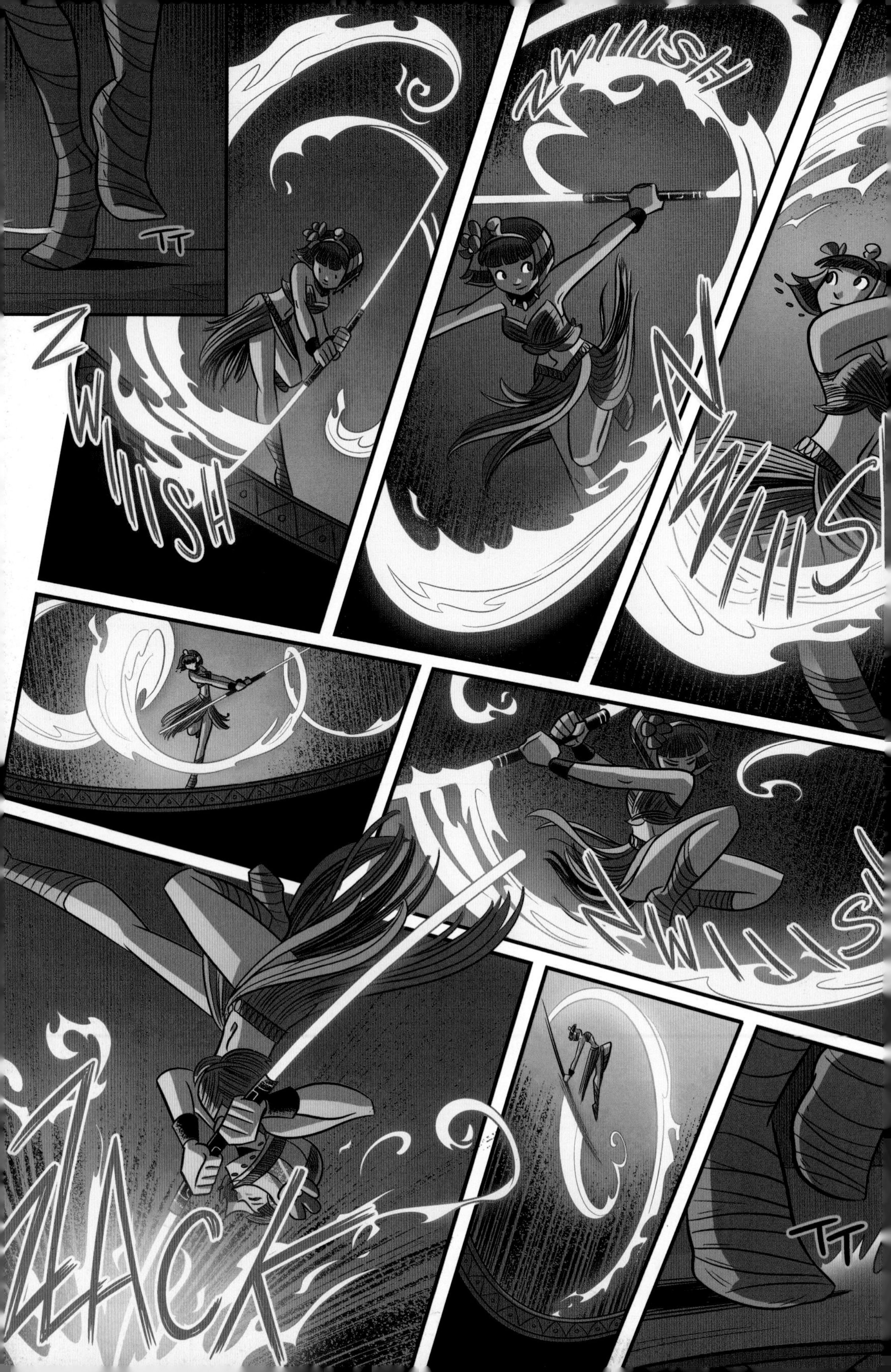
TT
ZWIIISH
ZWIIISH
ZWIIISH
ZWIIISH
ZZACK
TT

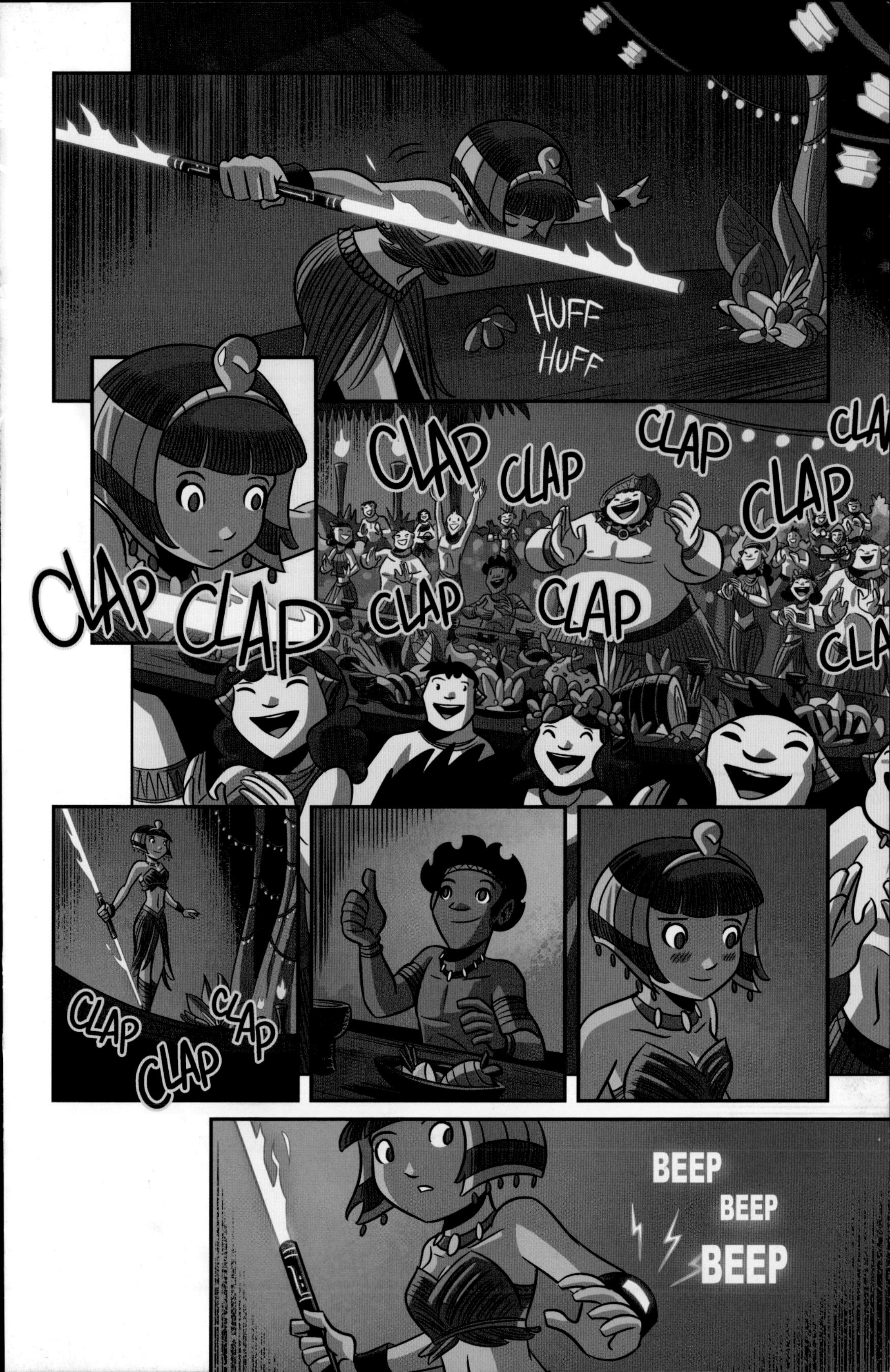
HUFF
HUFF
CLAP
CLAP
CLAP
CLAP
CLAP
CLAP
CLAP
CLAP
CLAP
CLAP
CLAP
BEEP
BEEP
BEEP

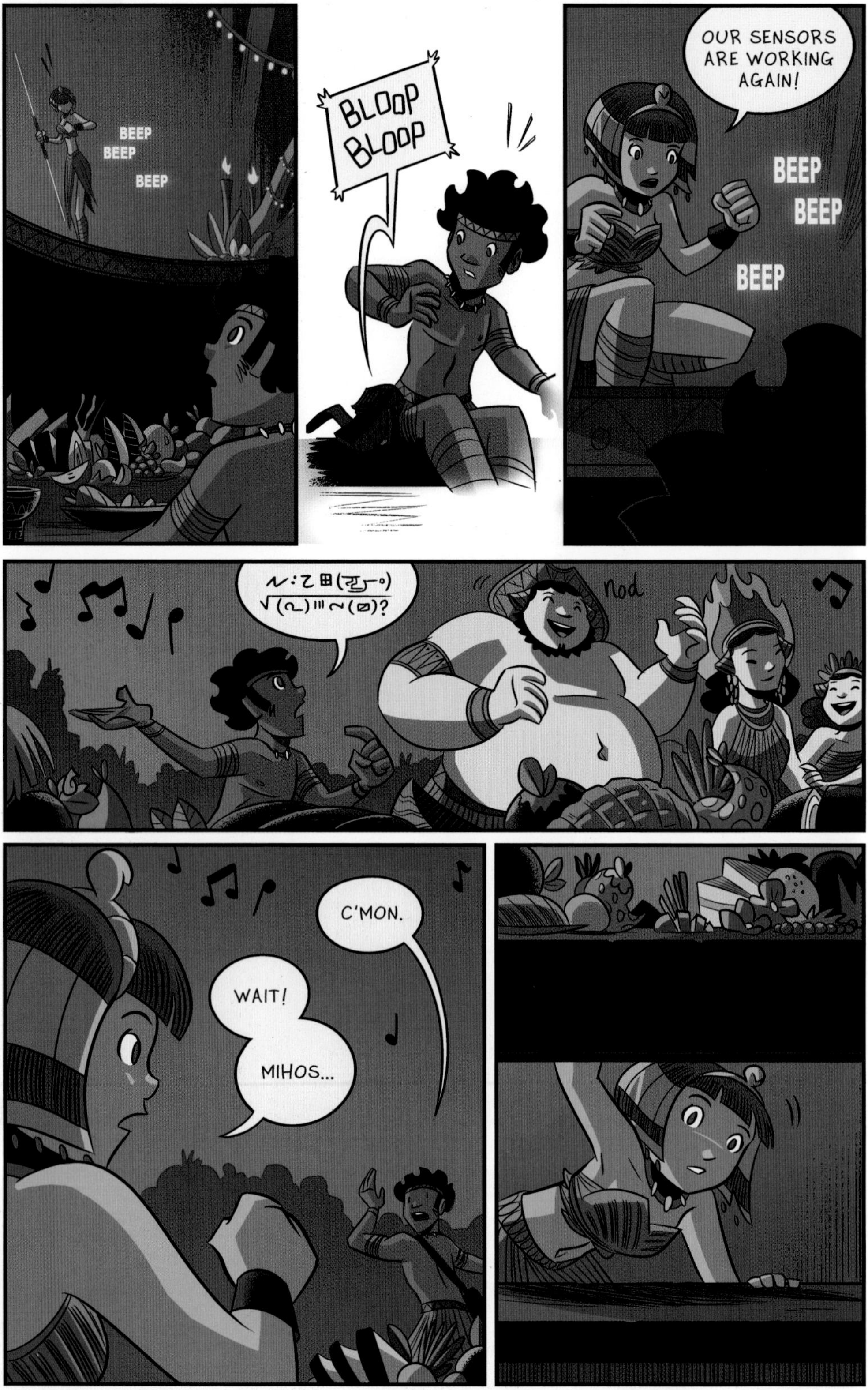
BEEP
BEEP
BEEP
BLOOP BLOOP
OUR SENSORS ARE WORKING AGAIN!
BEEP
BEEP
BEEP
nod
C'MON.
WAIT!
MIHOS...

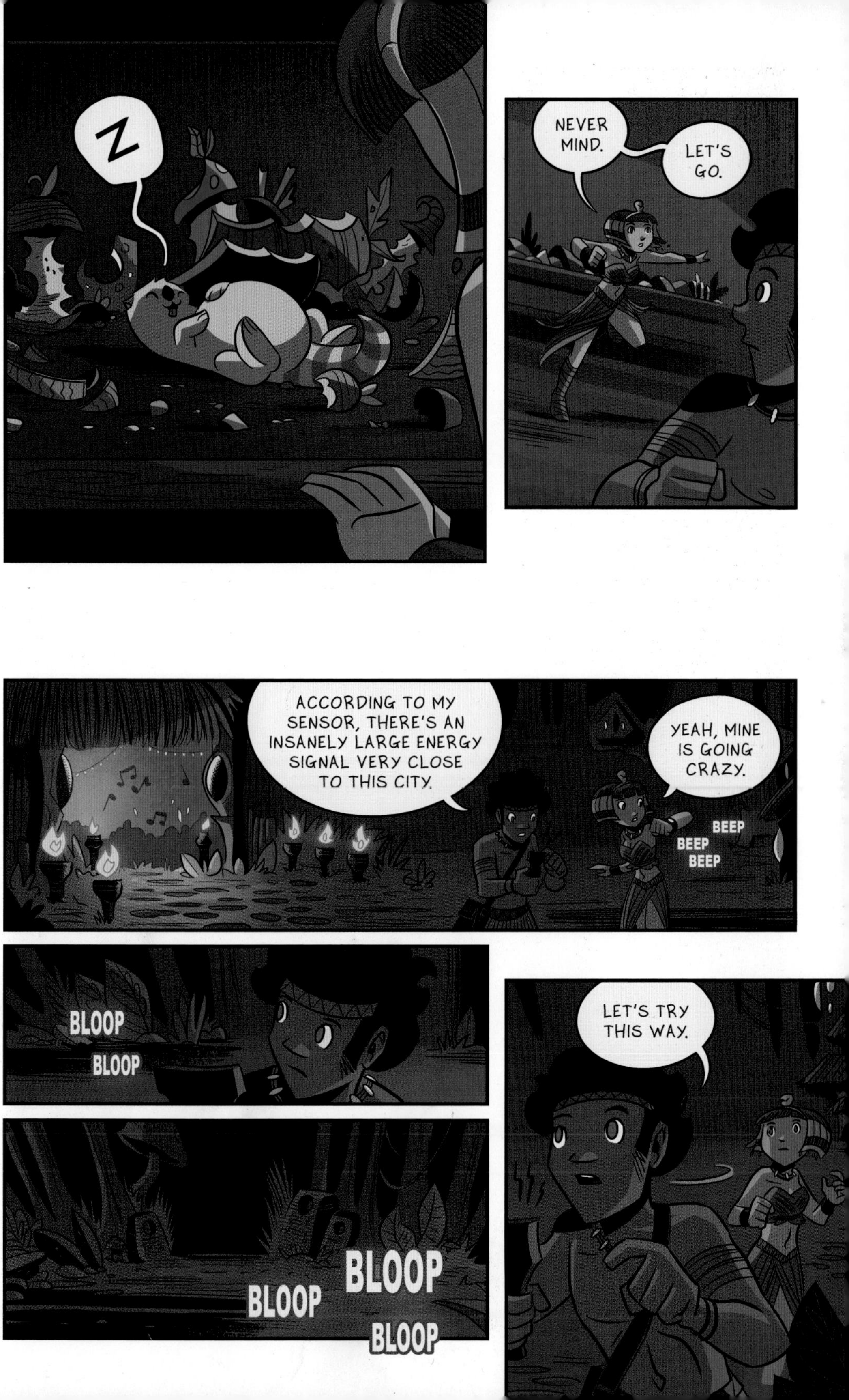
Z
NEVER MIND.
LET'S GO.
ACCORDING TO MY SENSOR, THERE'S AN INSANELY LARGE ENERGY SIGNAL VERY CLOSE TO THIS CITY.
YEAH, MINE IS GOING CRAZY.
BEEP
BEEP
BEEP
BLOOP
BLOOP
BLOOP
BLOOP
BLOOP
LET'S TRY THIS WAY.

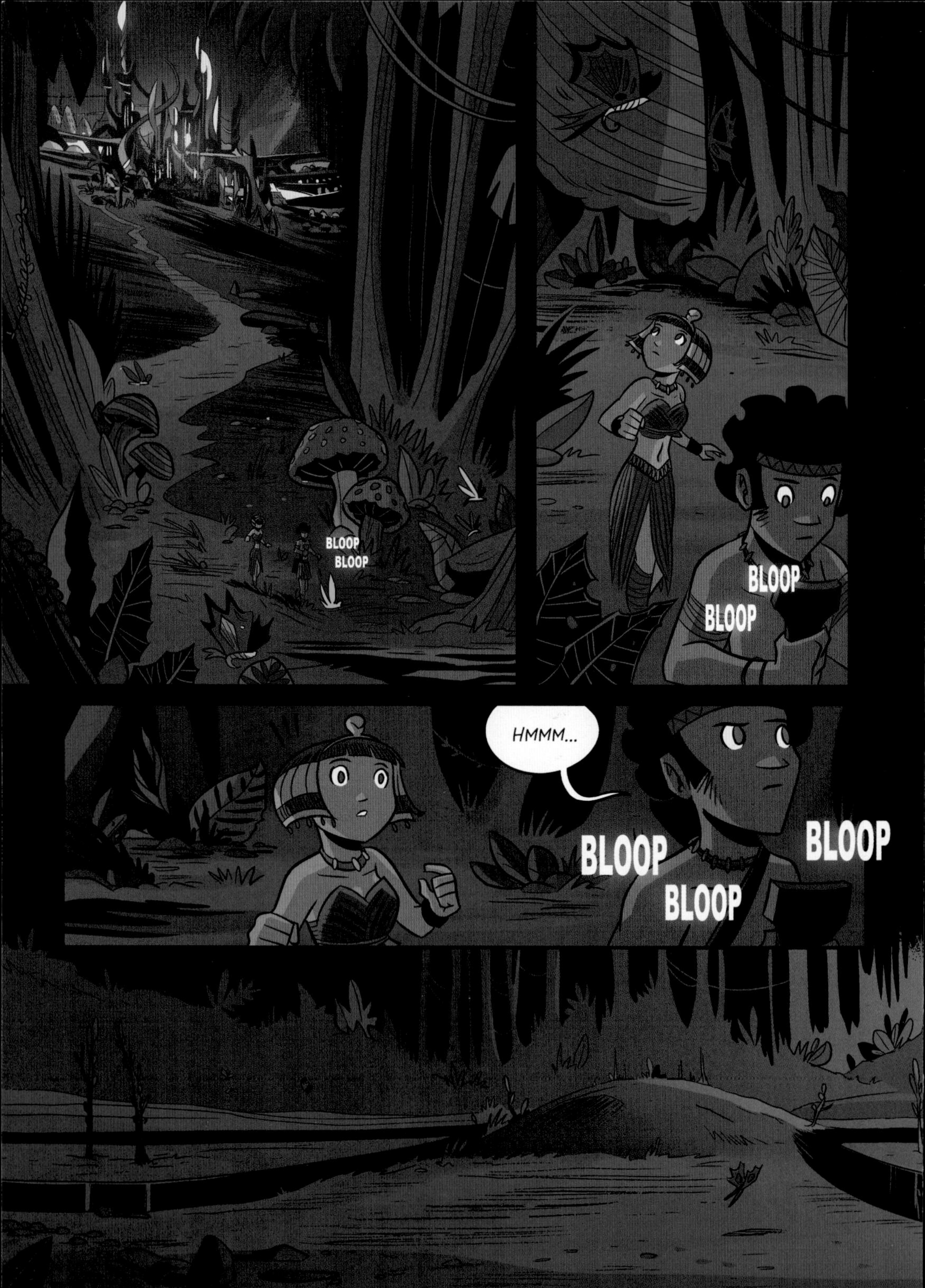
BLOOP
BLOOP
BLOOP
BLOOP
HMMM...
BLOOP
BLOOP
BLOOP

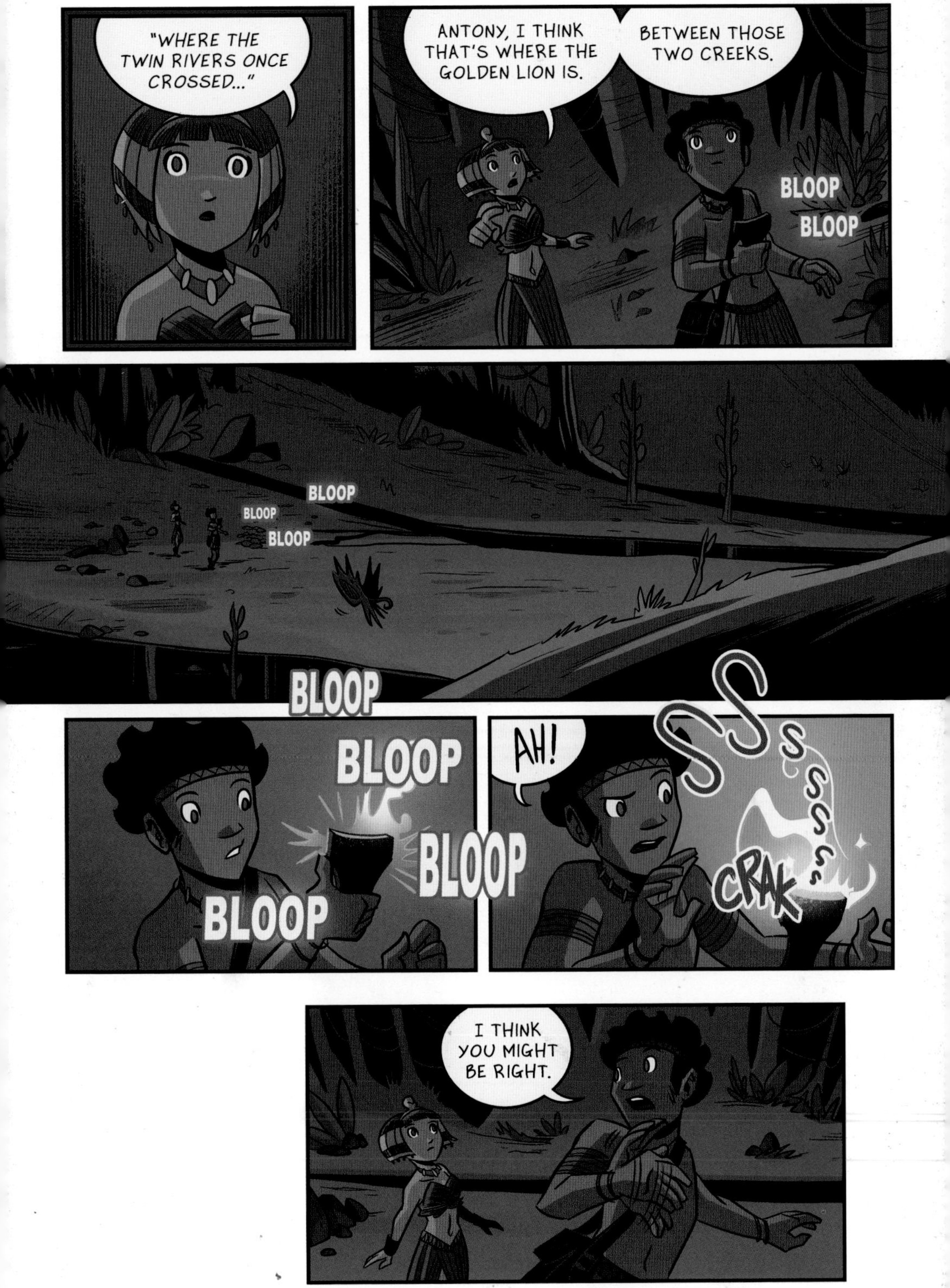
"WHERE THE TWIN RIVERS ONCE CROSSED..."
ANTONY, I THINK THAT'S WHERE THE GOLDEN LION IS.
BETWEEN THOSE TWO CREEKS.
BLOOP
BLOOP
BLOOP
BLOOP
BLOOP
BLOOP
BLOOP
BLOOP
BLOOP
AH!
SSSSSS...
CRAK
I THINK YOU MIGHT BE RIGHT.

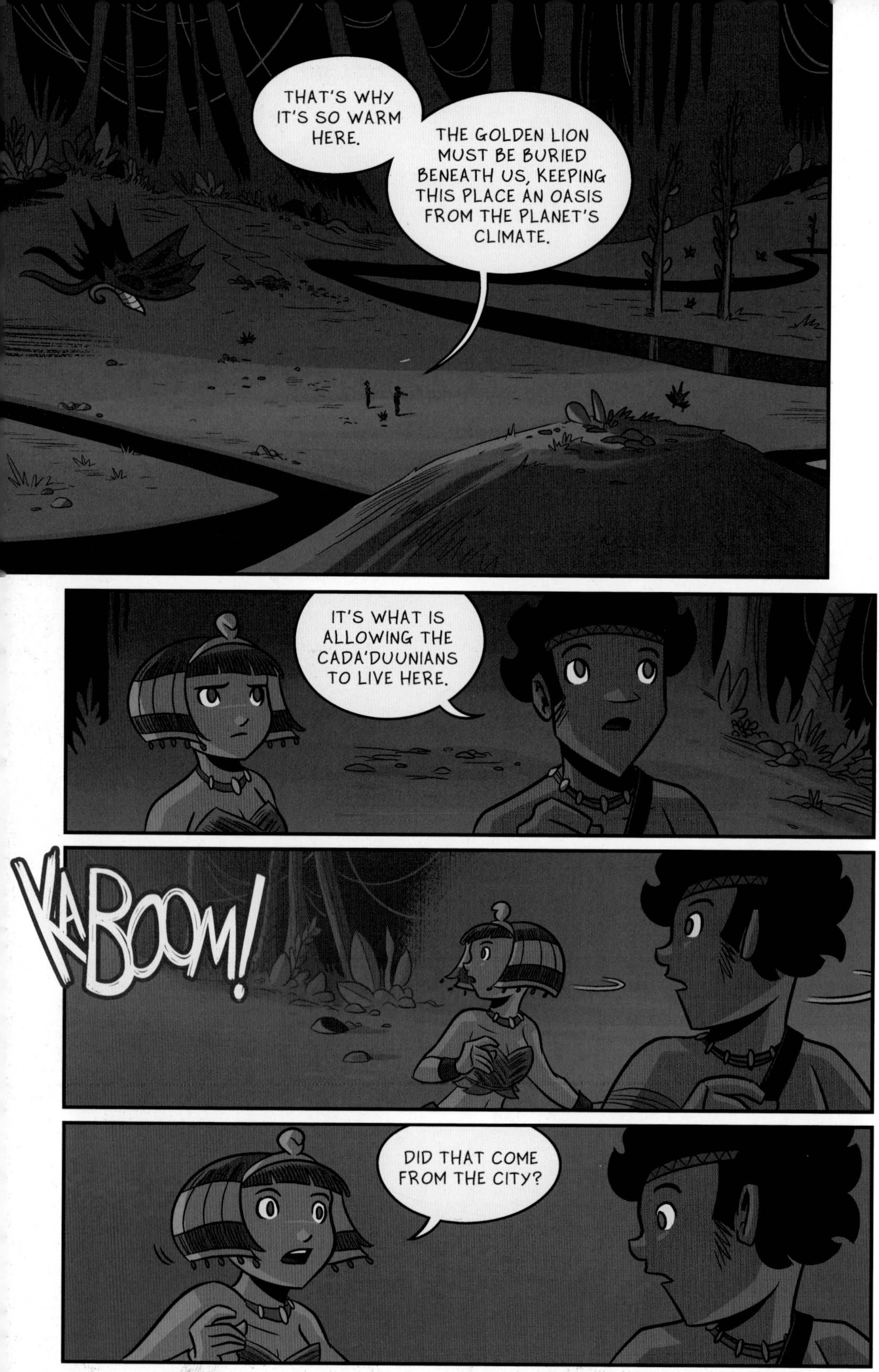
THAT'S WHY IT'S SO WARM HERE.
THE GOLDEN LION MUST BE BURIED BENEATH US, KEEPING THIS PLACE AN OASIS FROM THE PLANET'S CLIMATE.
IT'S WHAT IS ALLOWING THE CADA'DUUNIANS TO LIVE HERE.
KABOOM!
DID THAT COME FROM THE CITY?

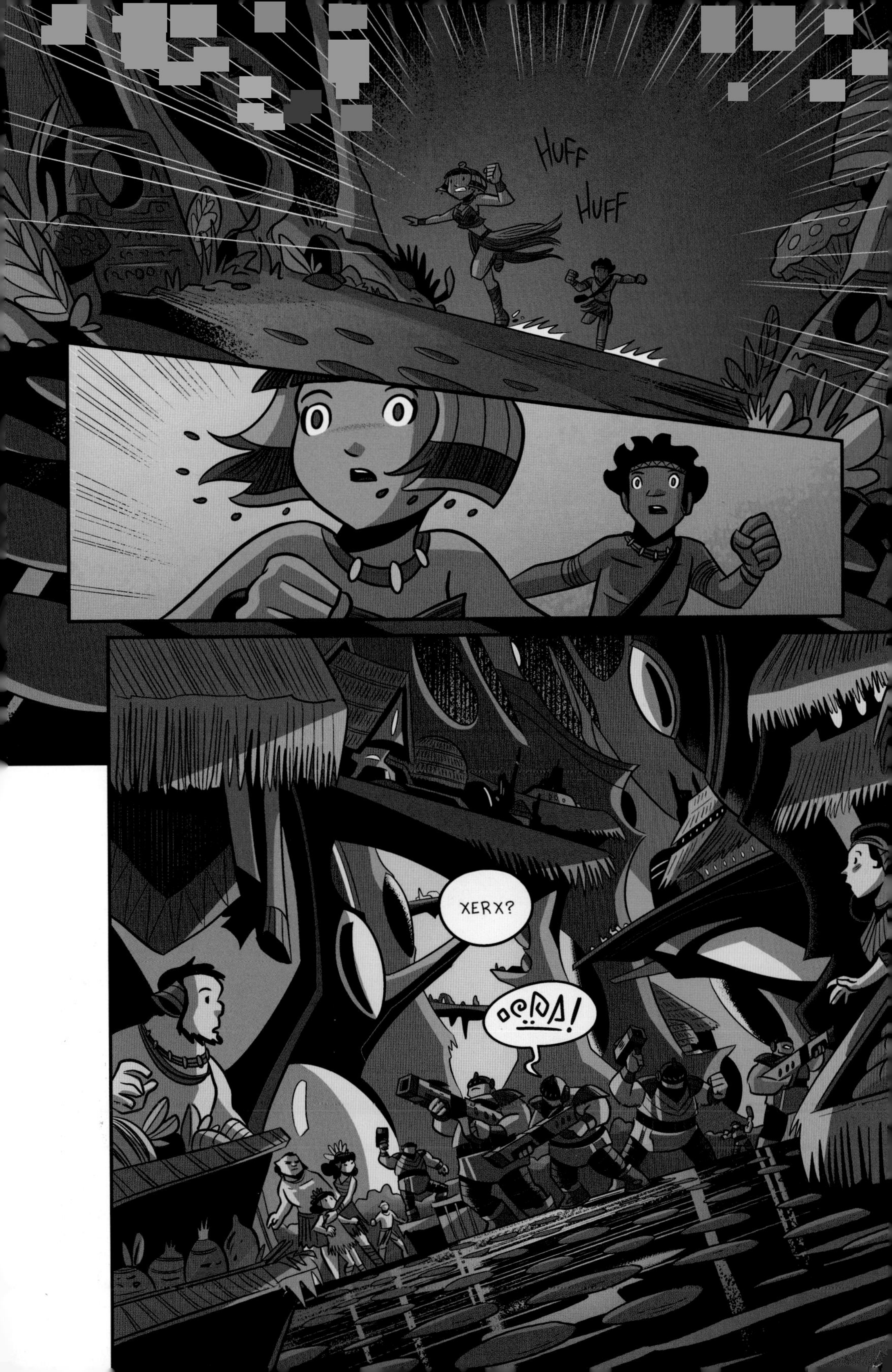
HUFF
HUFF
XERX?

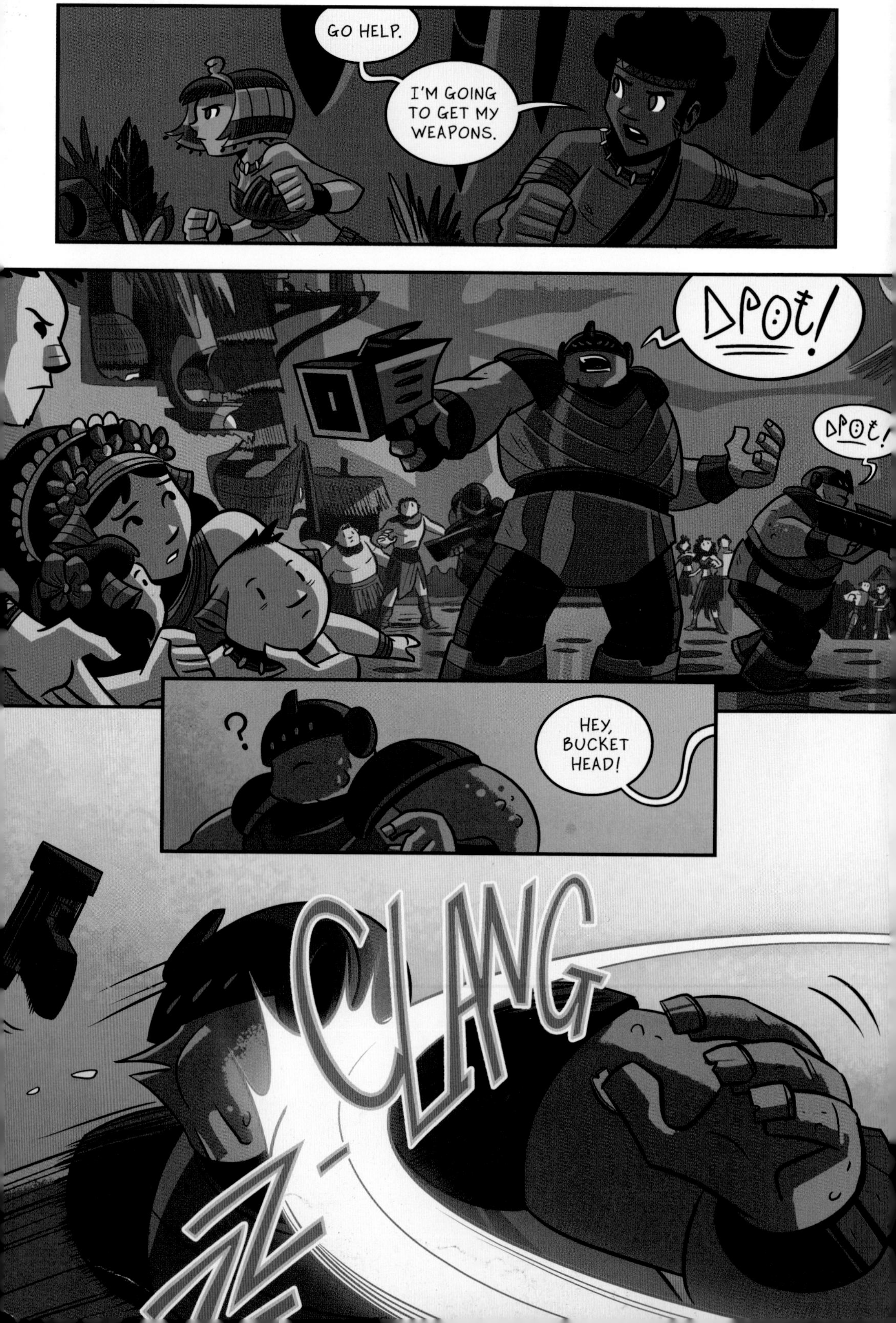

GO HELP.
I'M GOING TO GET MY WEAPONS.
DPOT!
DPOT!
?
HEY, BUCKET HEAD!
CLANG
ZZ-

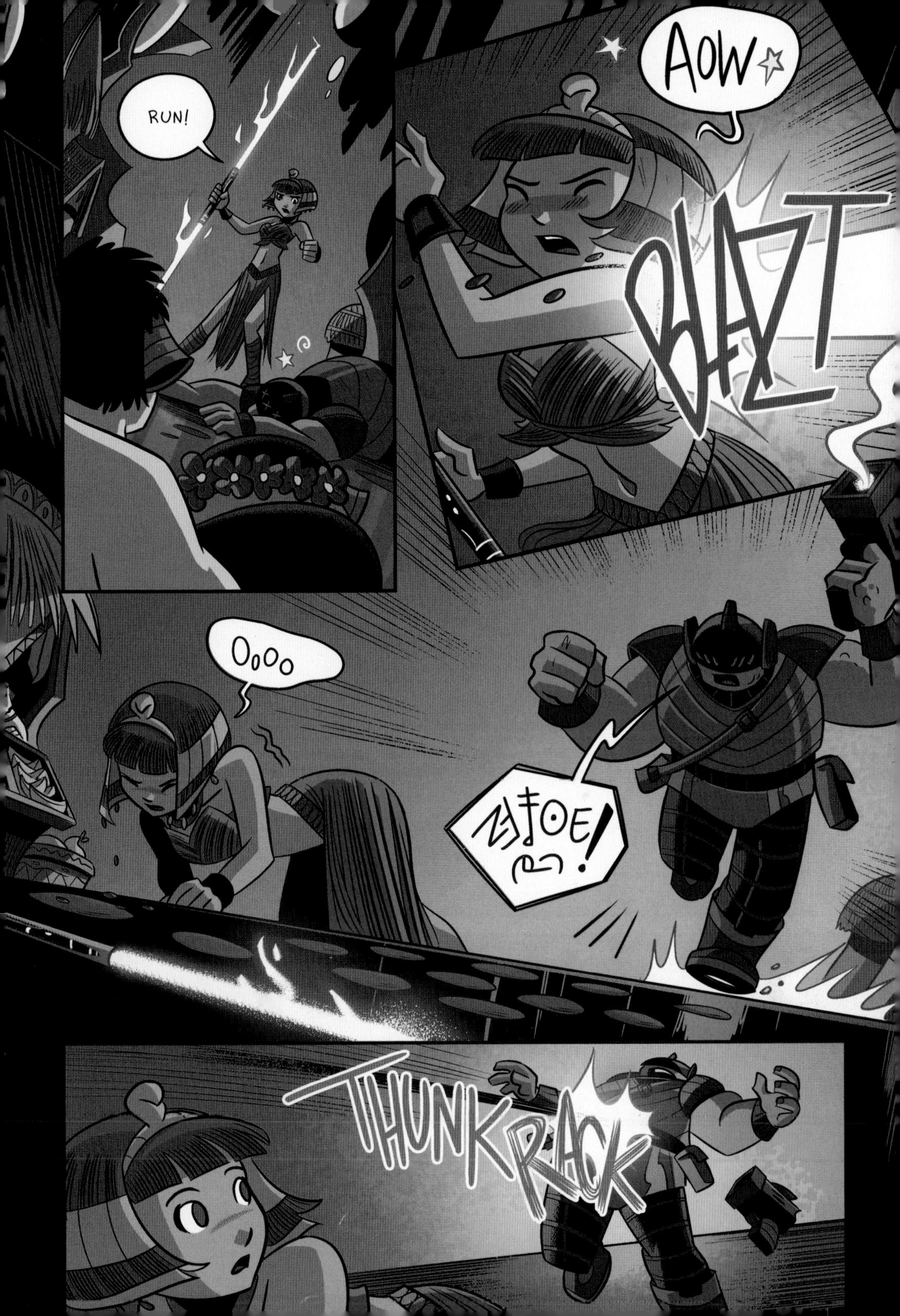
RUN!
AOW
BLAZT
Oooo
THUNKRACK

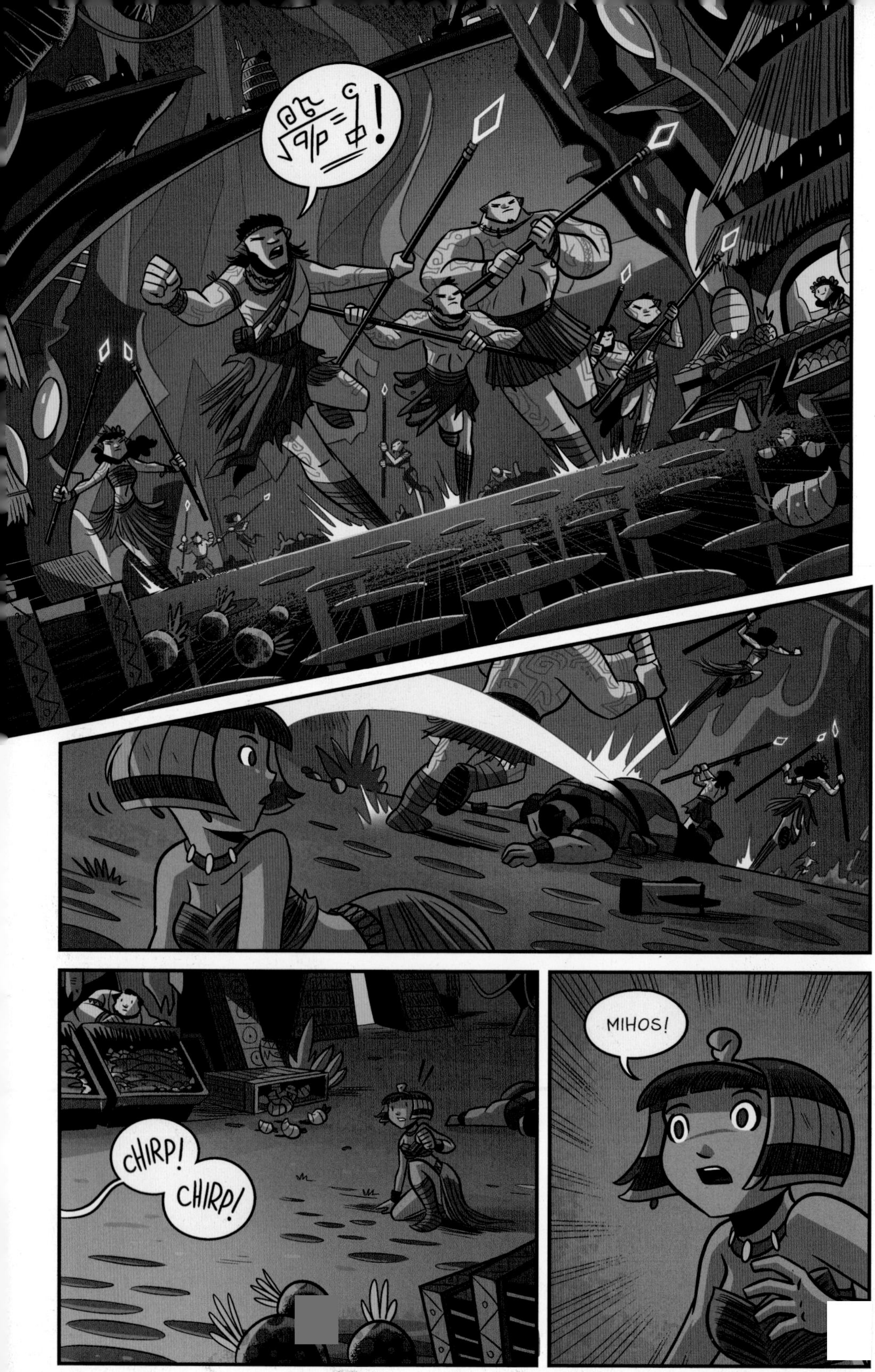
CHIRP!
CHIRP!
MIHOS!

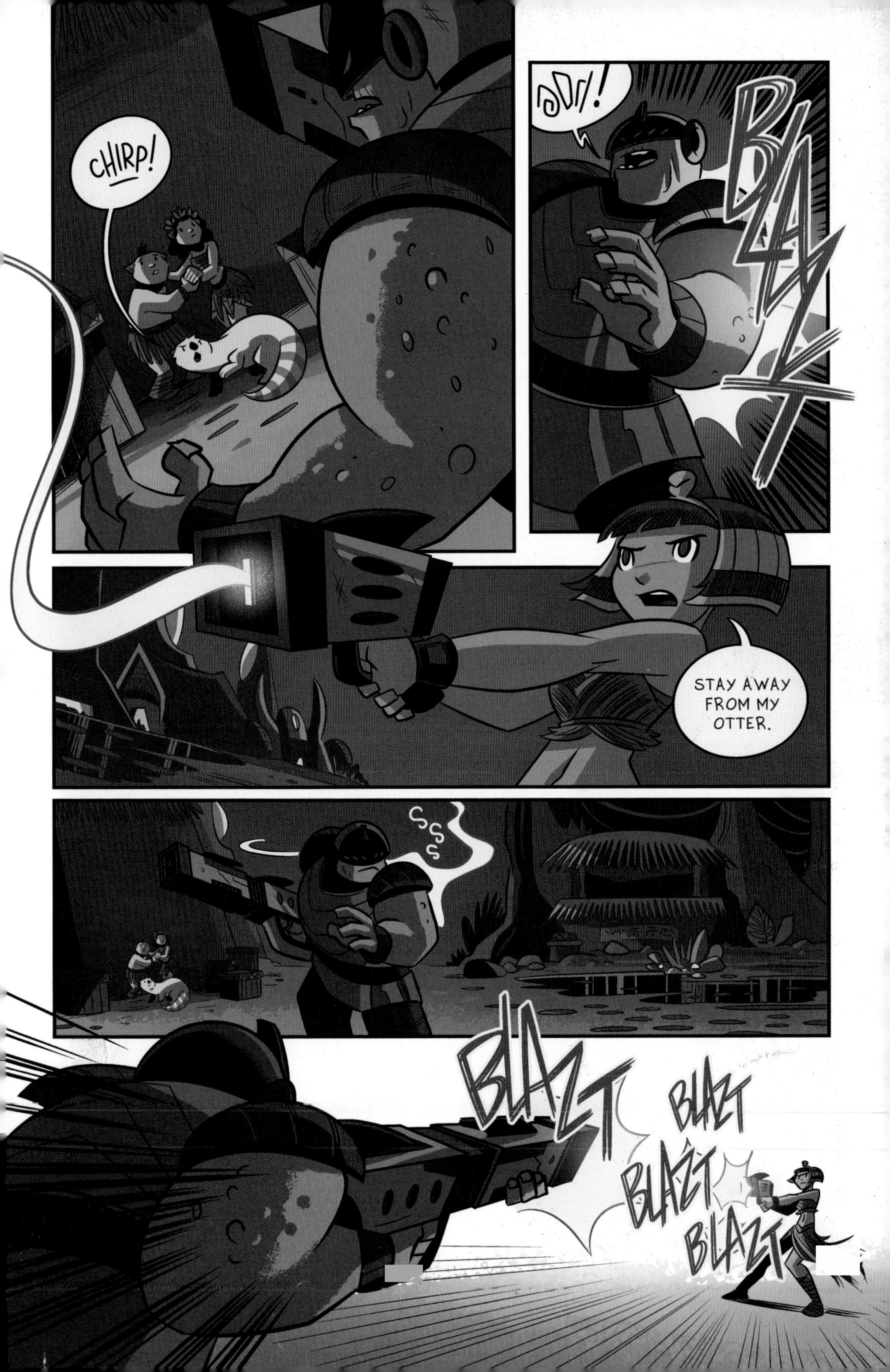
CHIRP!
STAY AWAY FROM MY OTTER.
SSS
BLAZT
BLAZT
BLAZT
BLAZT

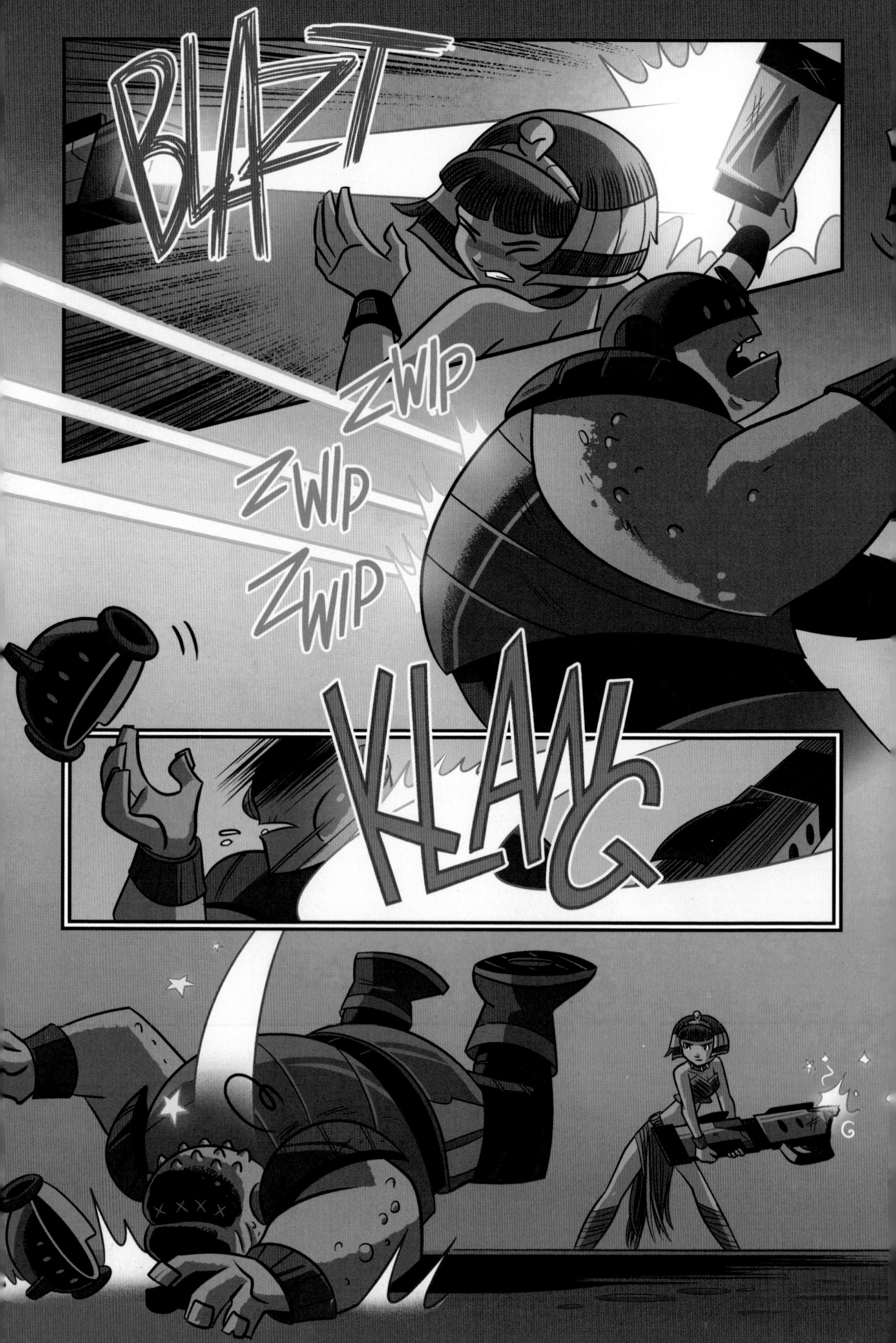
BLAZT
ZWIP
ZWIP
ZWIP
KLANG

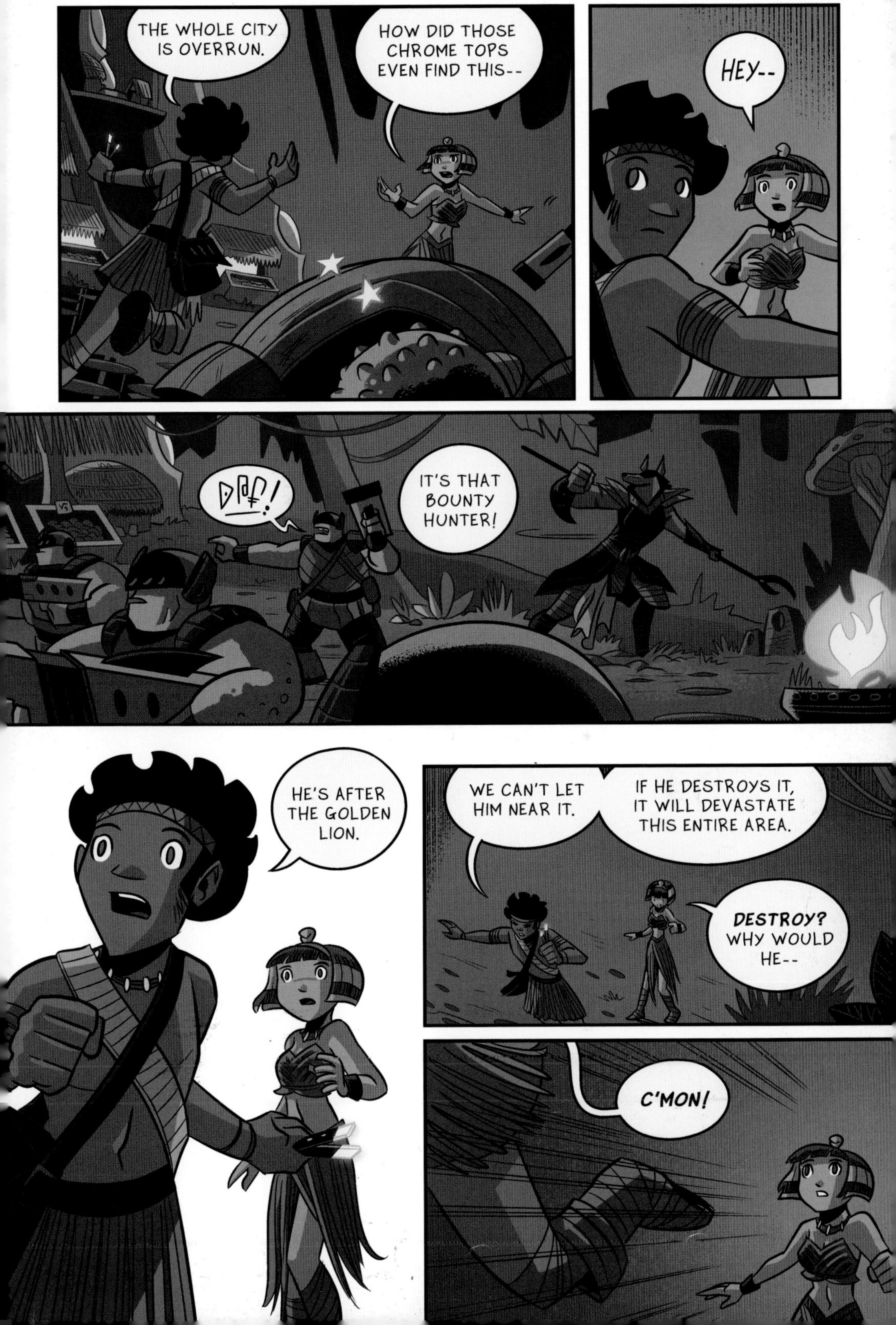
THE WHOLE CITY IS OVERRUN.
HOW DID THOSE CHROME TOPS EVEN FIND THIS--
HEY--
IT'S THAT BOUNTY HUNTER!
HE'S AFTER THE GOLDEN LION.
WE CAN'T LET HIM NEAR IT.
IF HE DESTROYS IT, IT WILL DEVASTATE THIS ENTIRE AREA.
DESTROY? WHY WOULD HE--
C'MON!

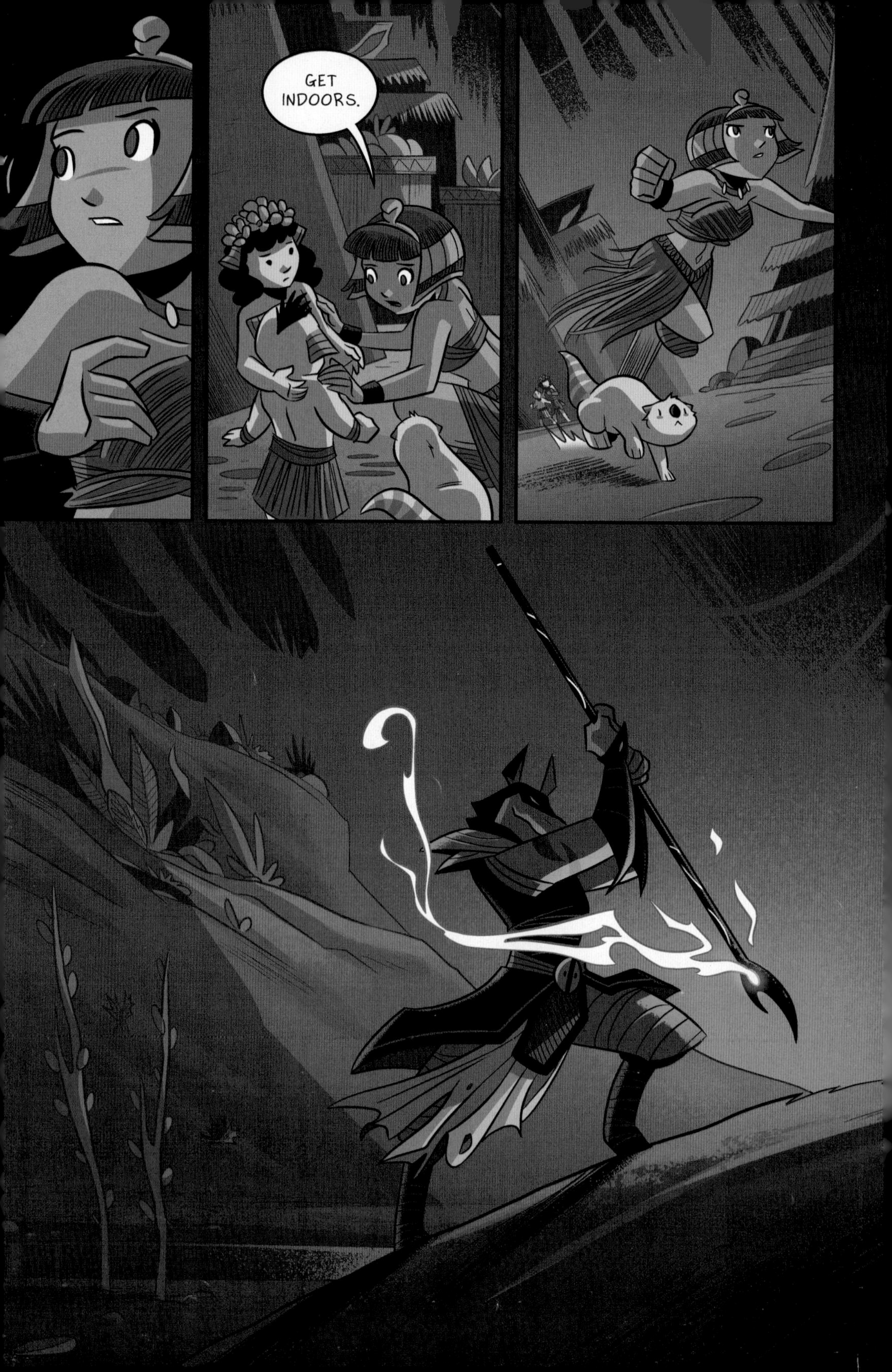
GET INDOORS.

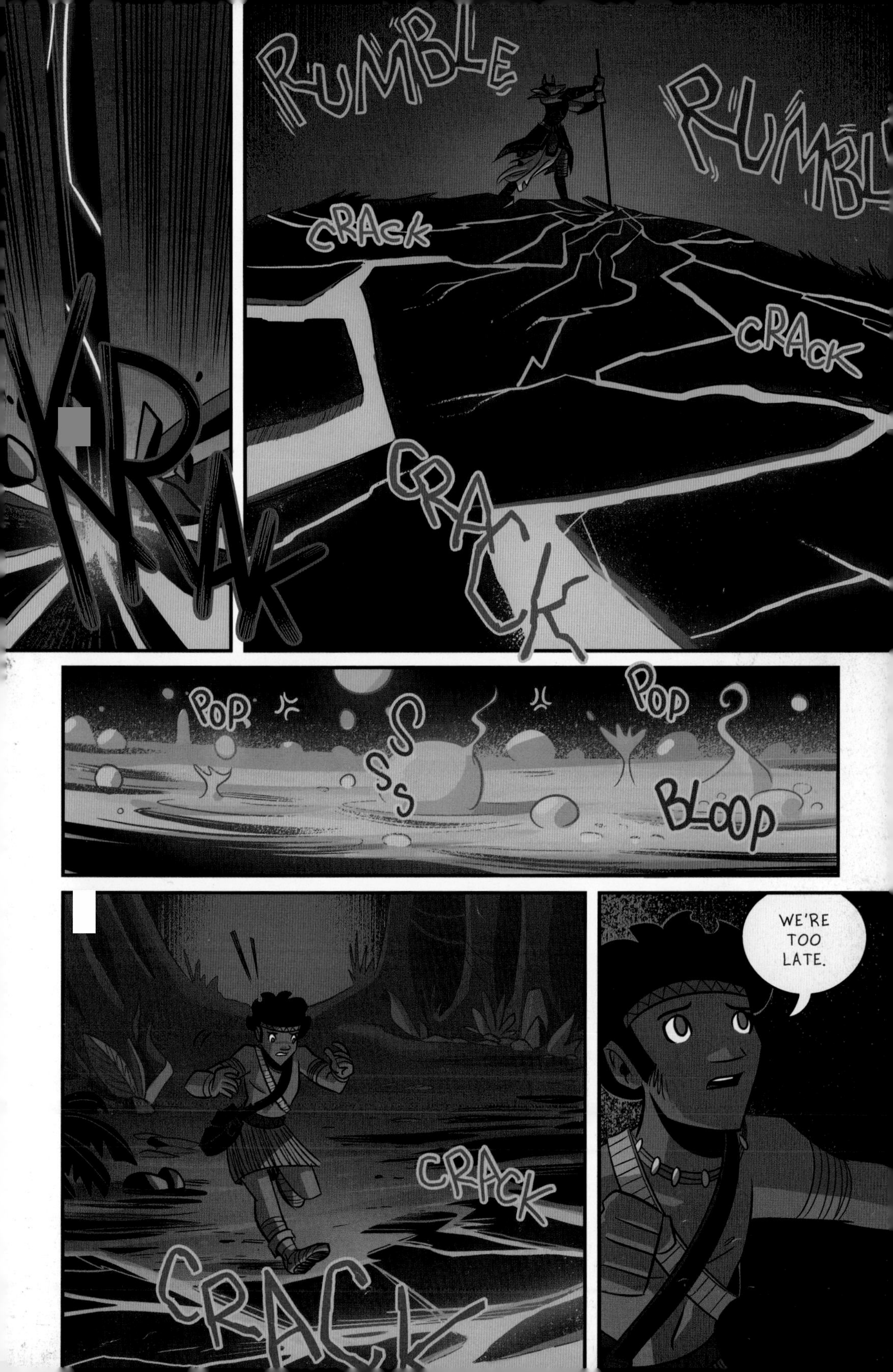
KRAK
RUMBLE
RUMBL
CRACK
CRACK
CRACK
POP
SSSS
POP
BLOOP
CRACK
CRACK
WE'RE TOO LATE.

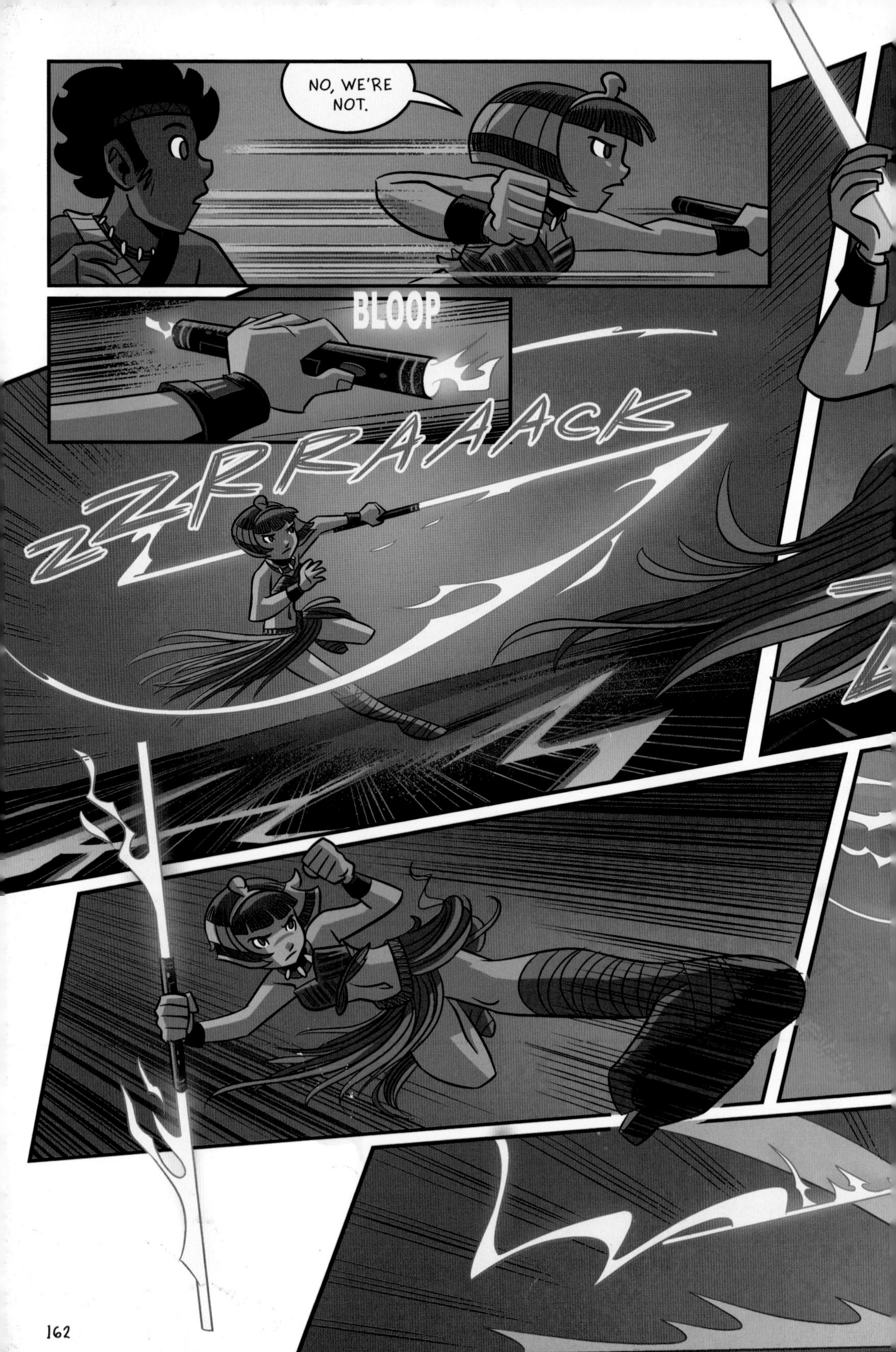
NO, WE'RE NOT.
BLOOP
ZZRRAAAACK

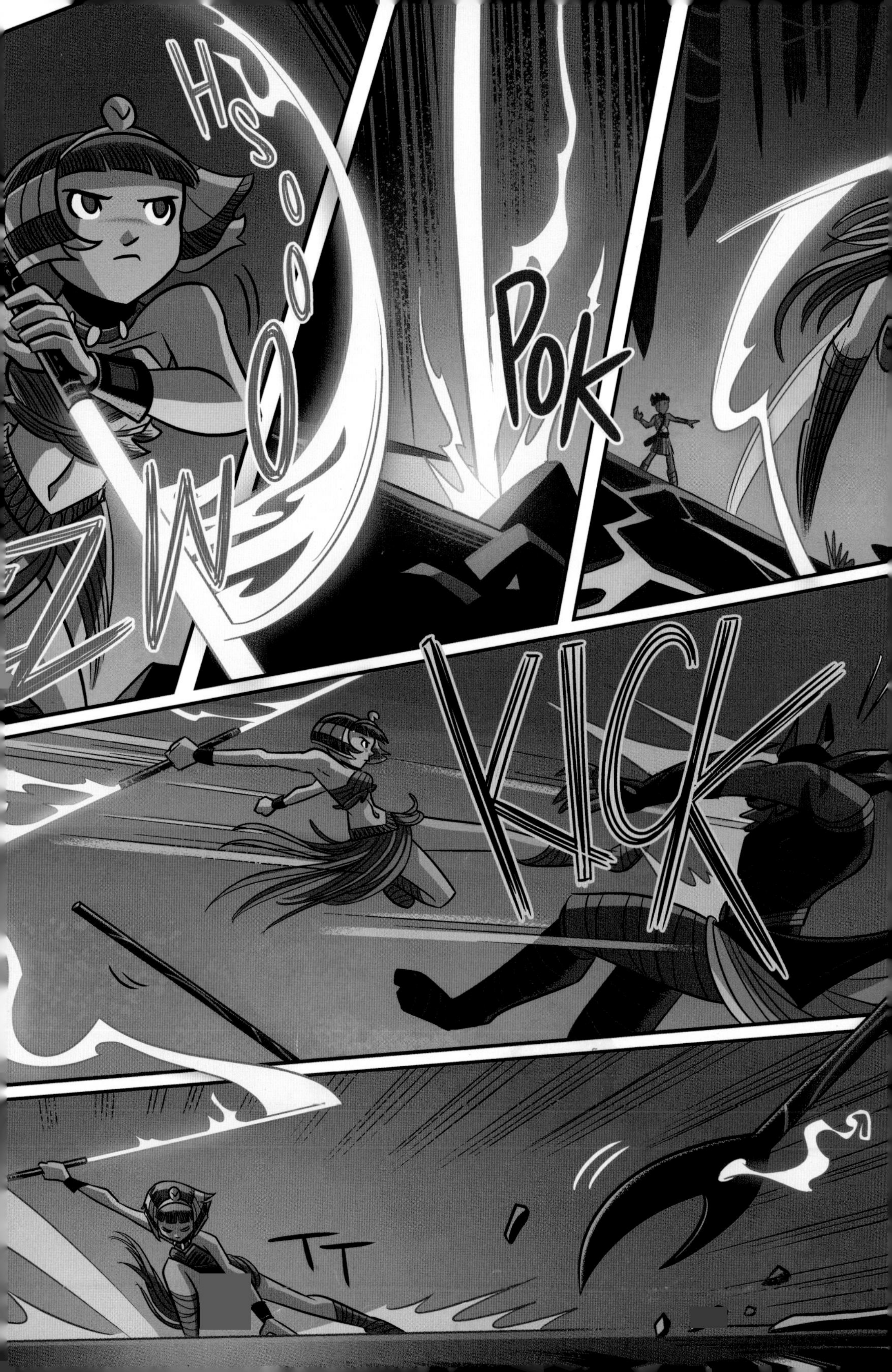
ZWOOOSH
POK
KICK
TT

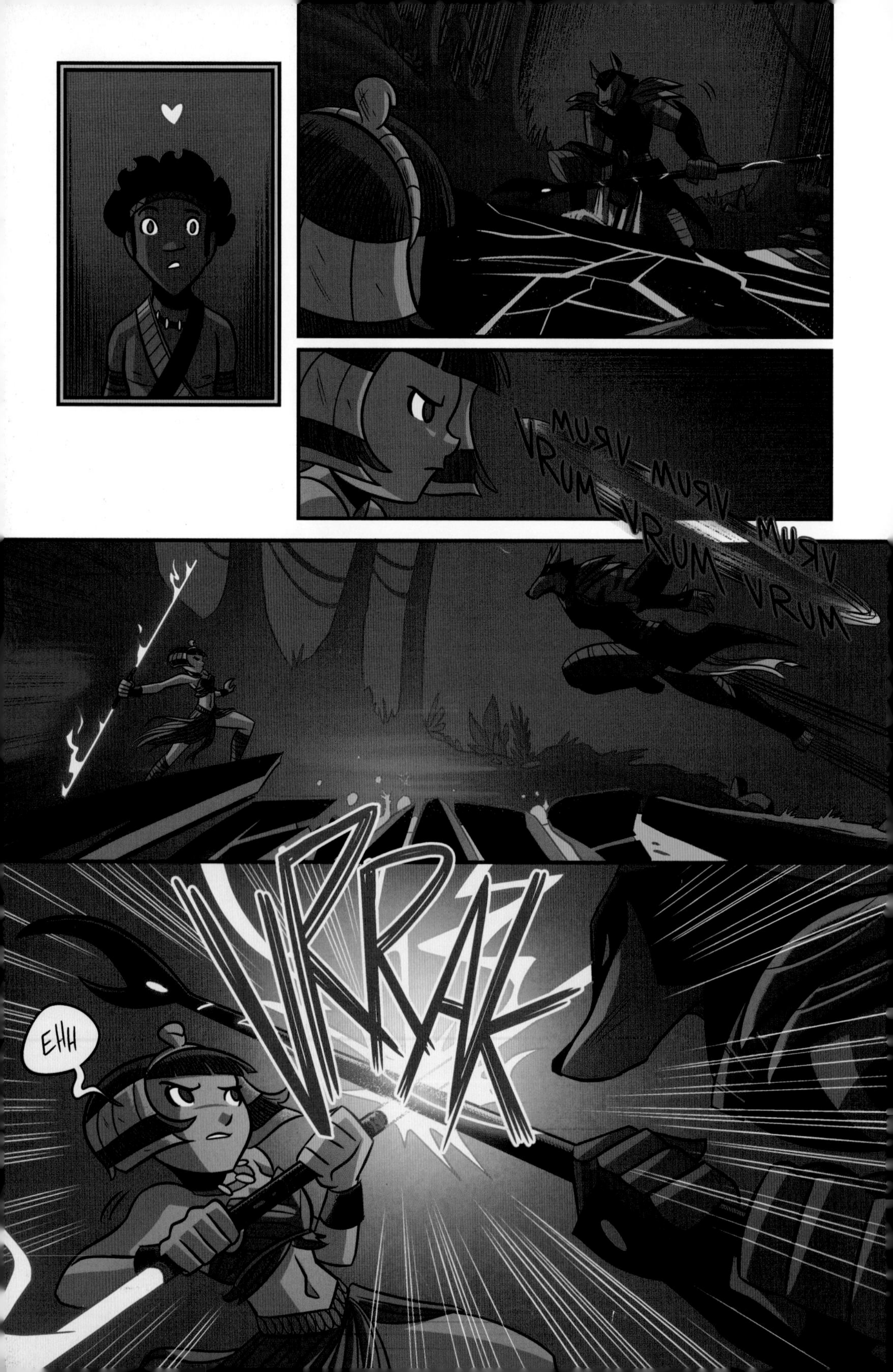
VRUM VRUM VRUM
VRUM VRUM VRUM
VRUM VRUM VRUM
VRRAK
EHH

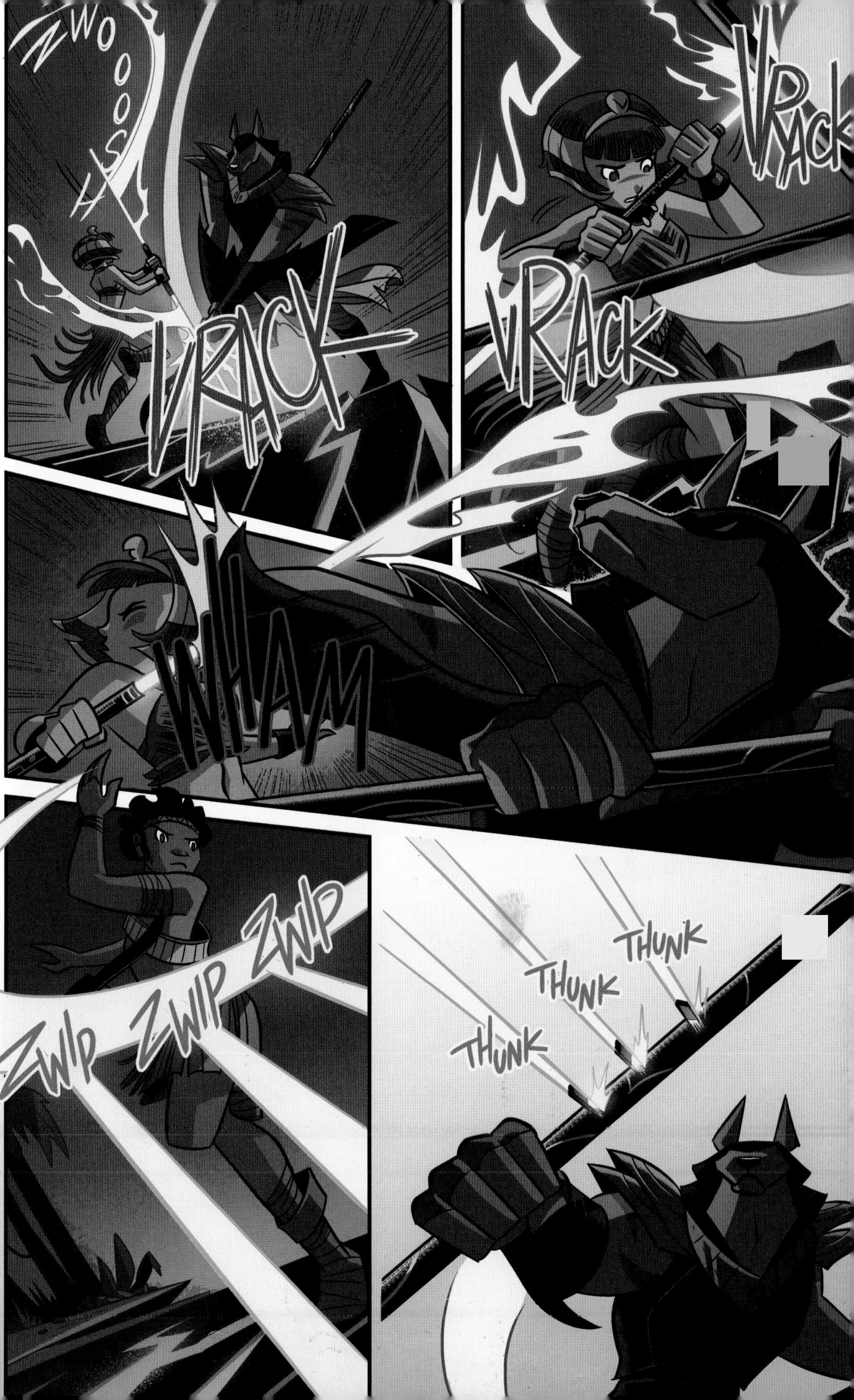
ZWOOOOSH
VRACK
VRACK
VRACK
WHAM
ZWIP ZWIP ZWIP
THUNK
THUNK
THUNK

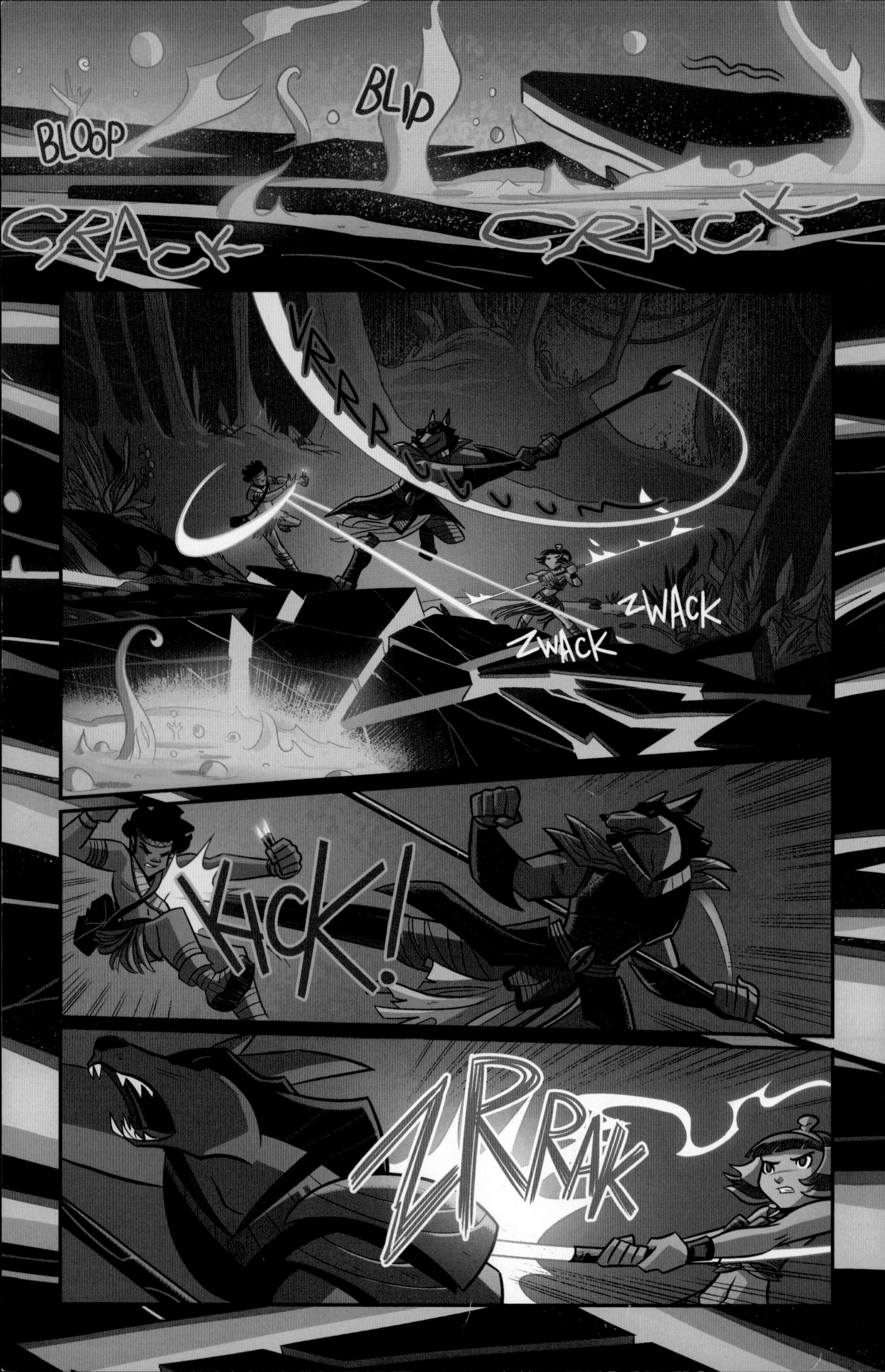
BLOOP
BLIP
CRACK
CRACK
VRRRRUUUUMM
ZWACK
ZWACK
YOICK!
ZRRAK

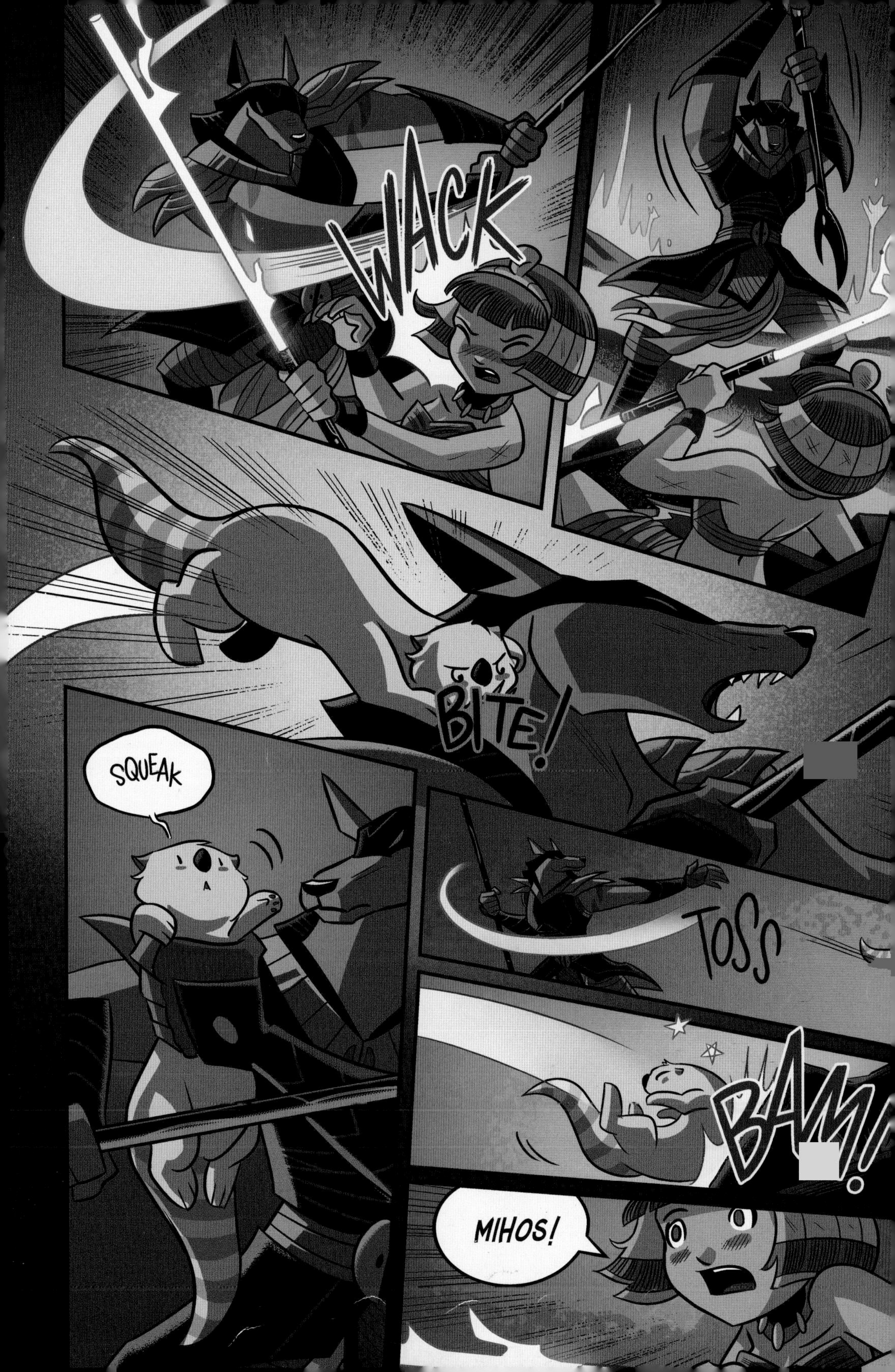
WACK
BITE!
SQUEAK
TOSS
BAM!
MIHOS!

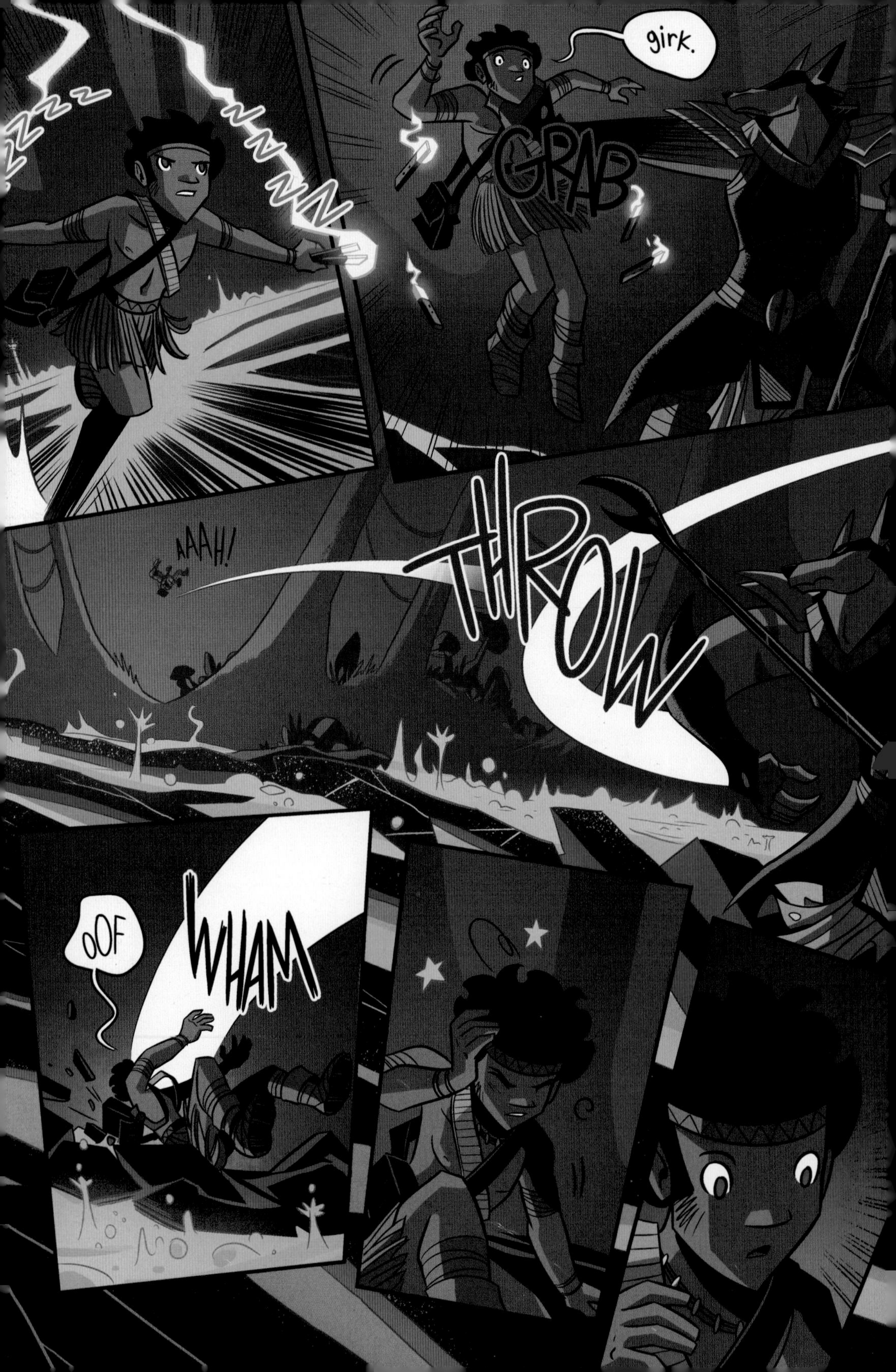
ZZZZZ
ZZZZZ
girk.
GRAB
AAAH!
THROW
OOF
WHAM

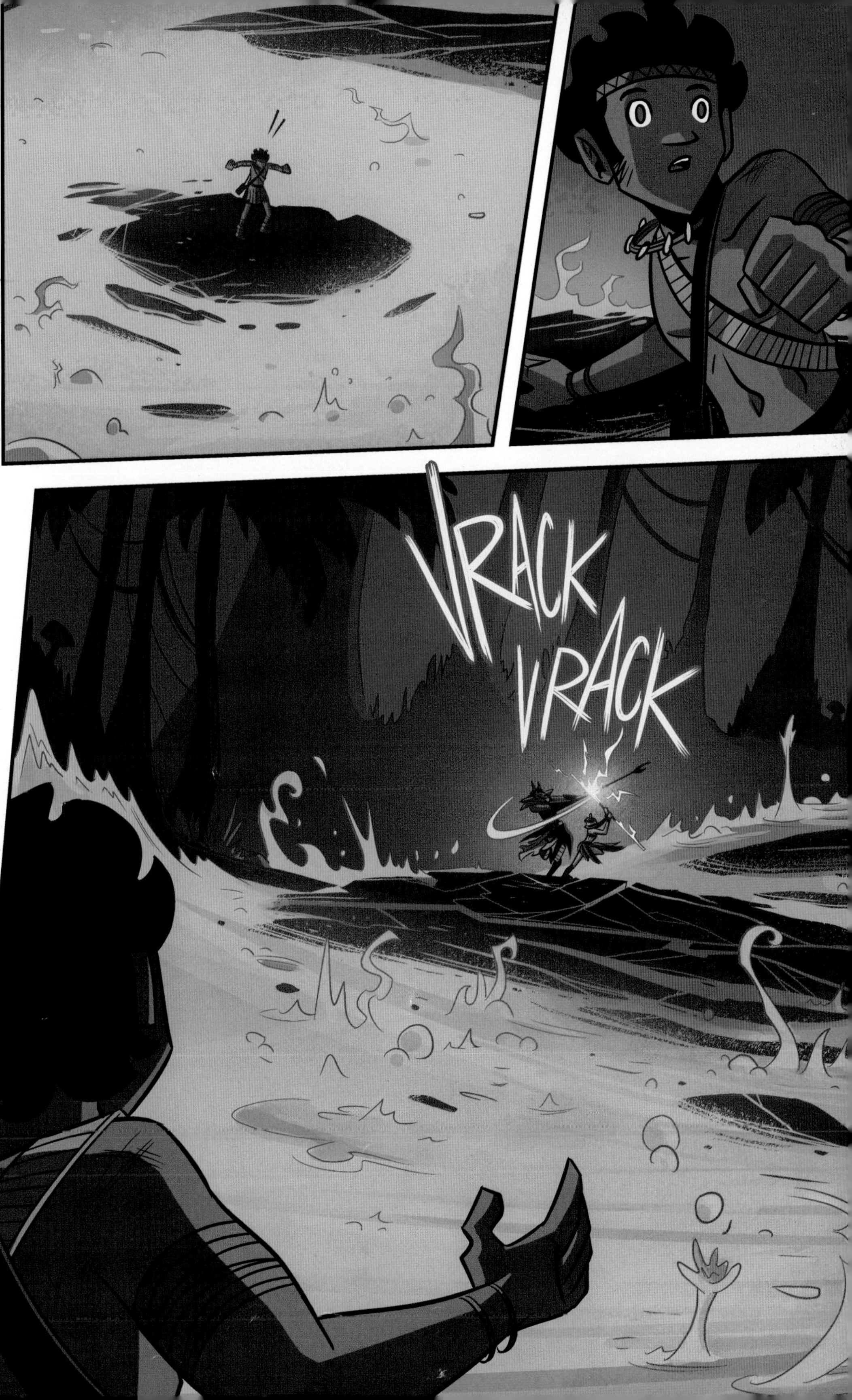
VRACK
VRACK

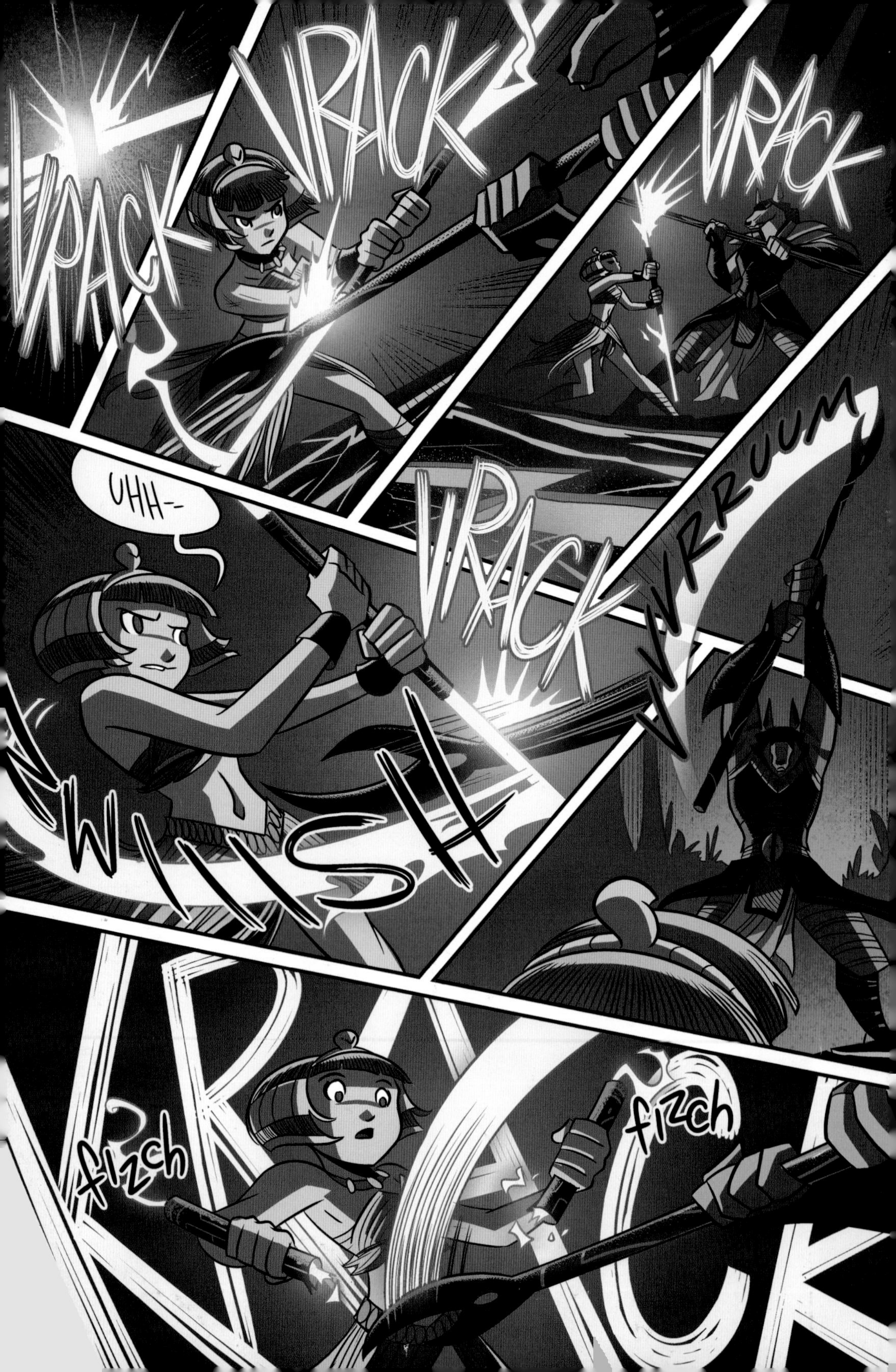
VRACK
VRACK
VRACK
UHH--
VRACK
VVRRRUUM
WHIIISH
fizch
fizch
VRACK

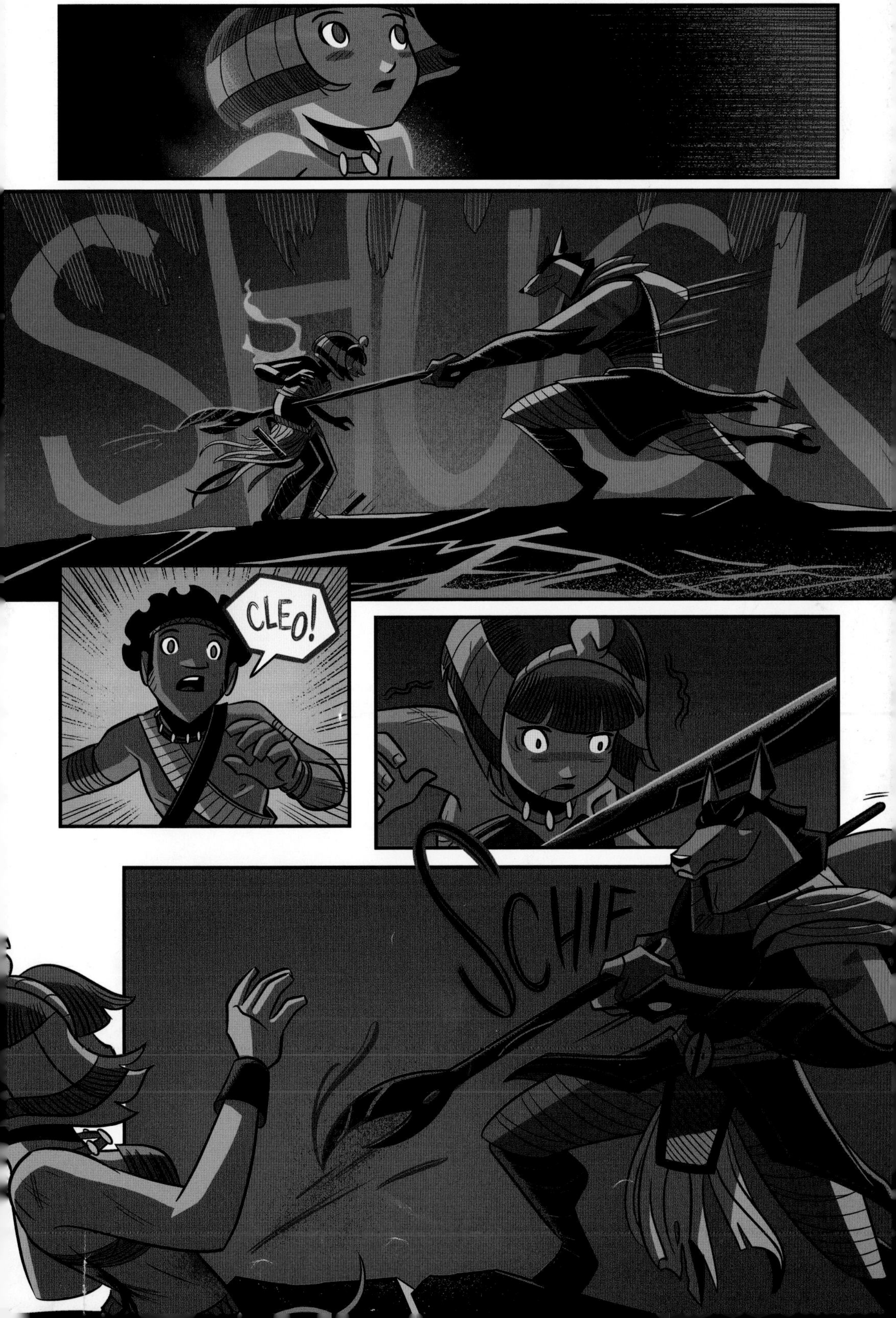
SHUCK
CLEO!
SCHIF

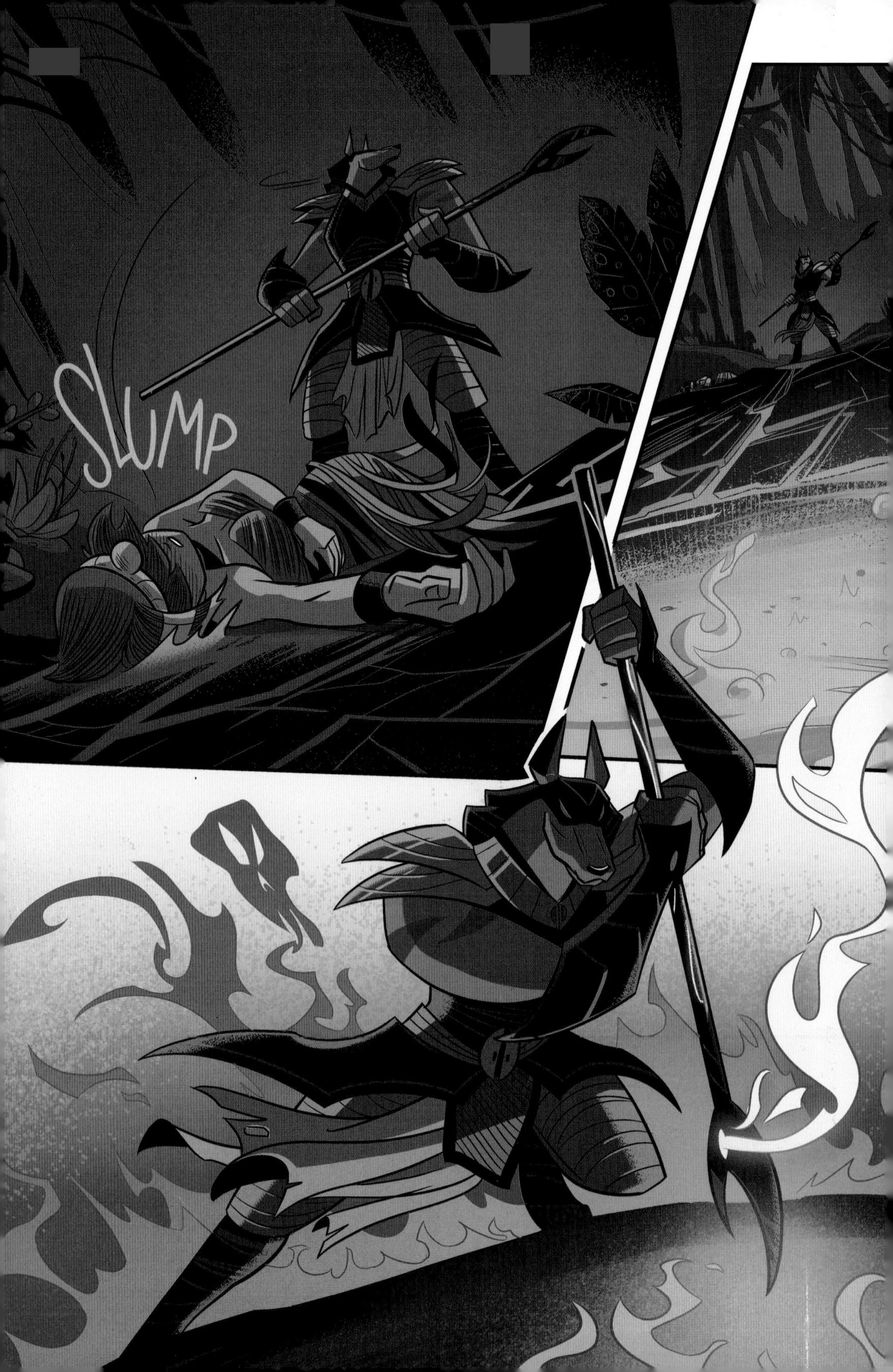
SLUMP

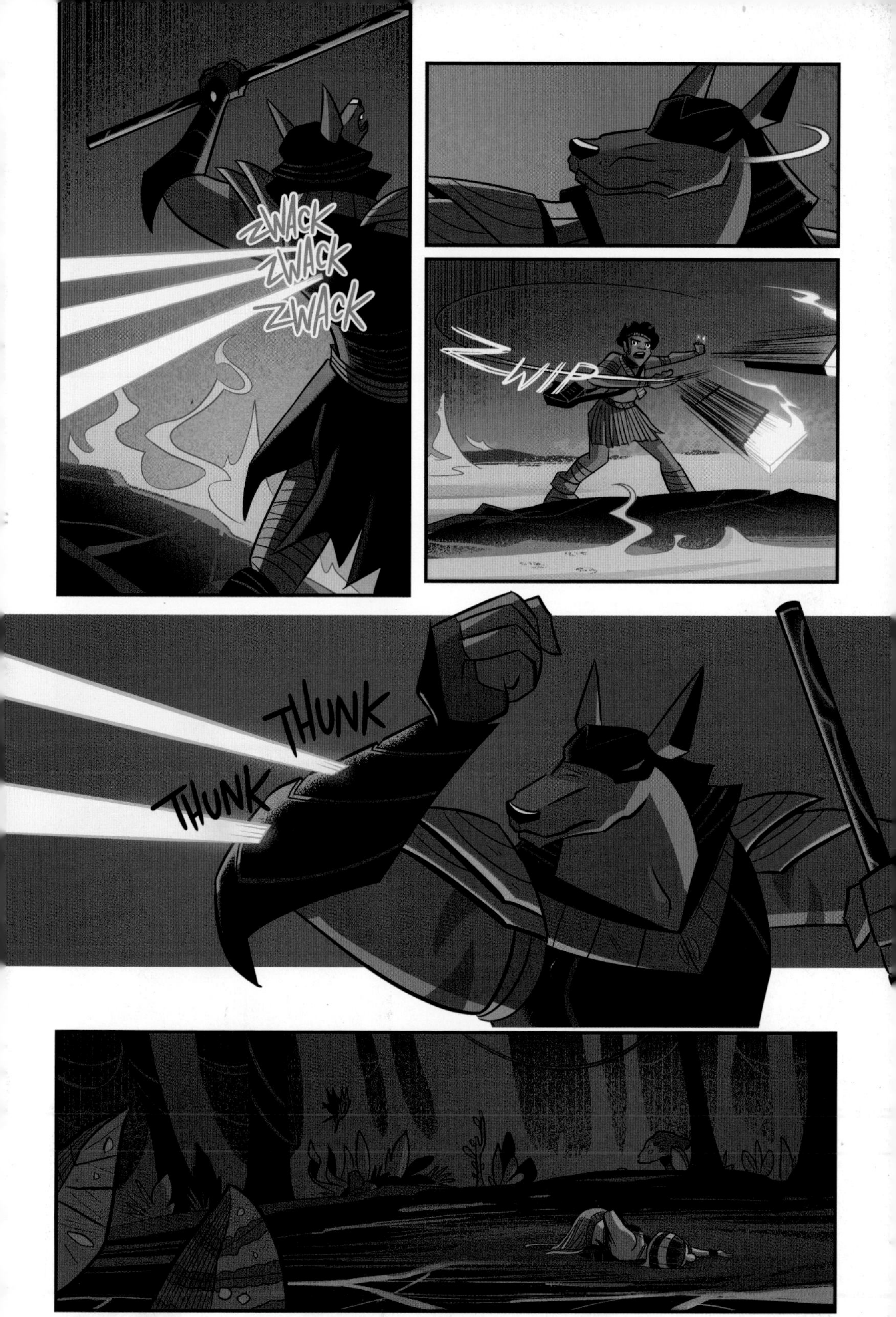
ZWACK
ZWACK
ZWACK
ZWIP
THUNK
THUNK

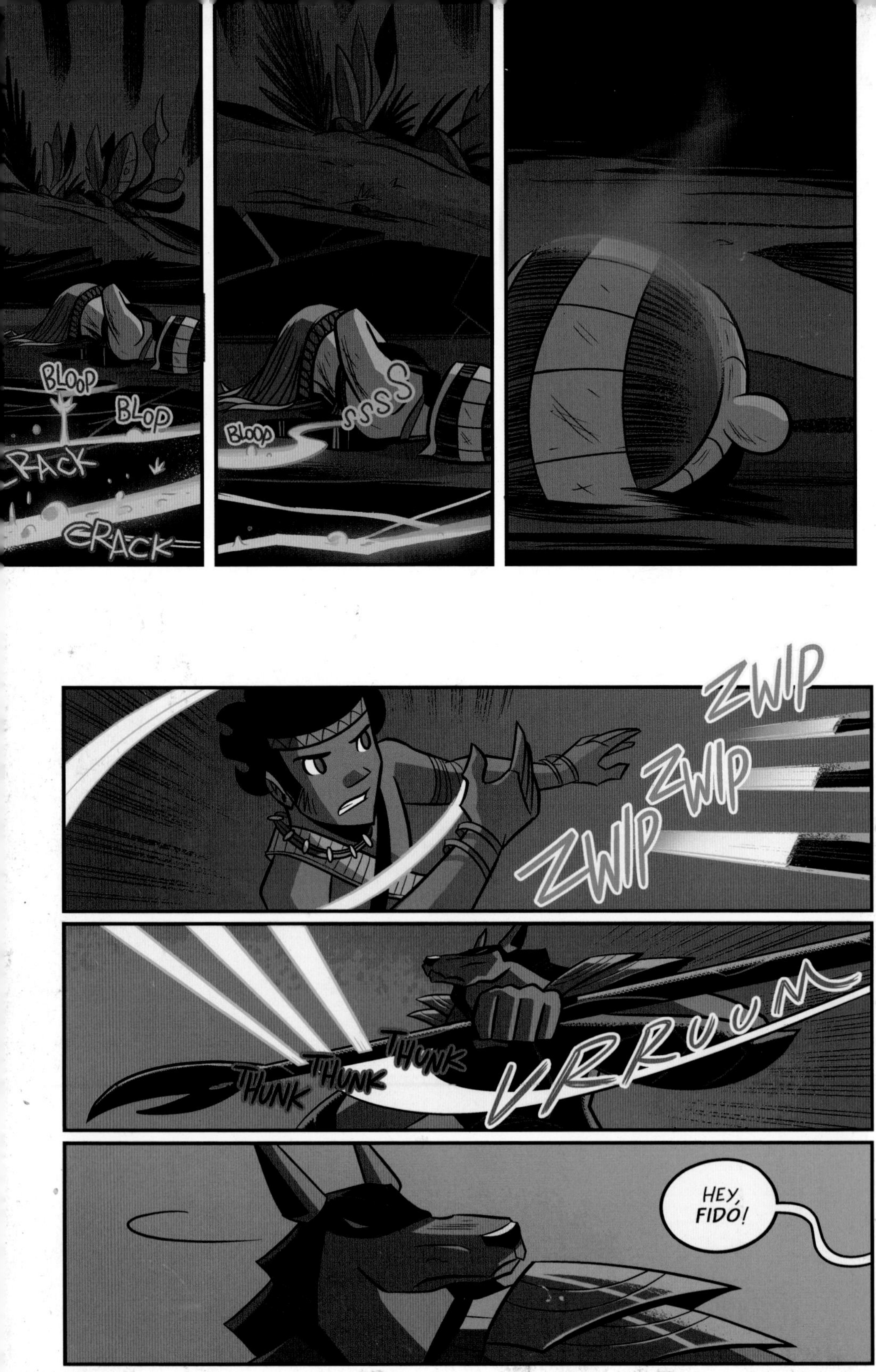
BLOOP
BLOP
RACK
CRACK
BLOOP
SSSS
ZWIP
ZWIP
ZWIP
THUNK
THUNK
THUNK
VRRUUM
HEY, FIDO!

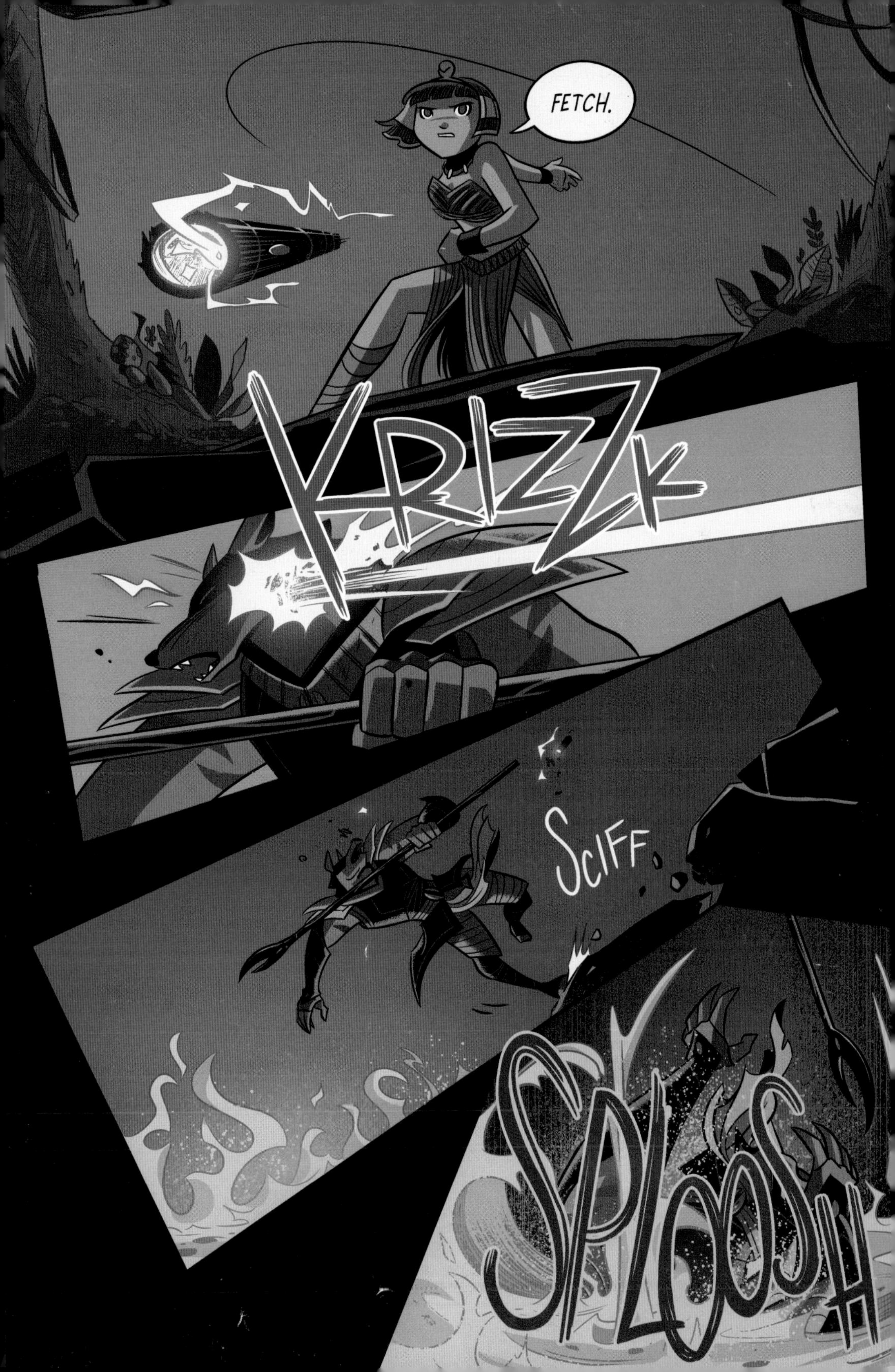
FETCH.
KRIZZK
SCIFF
SPLOOSH

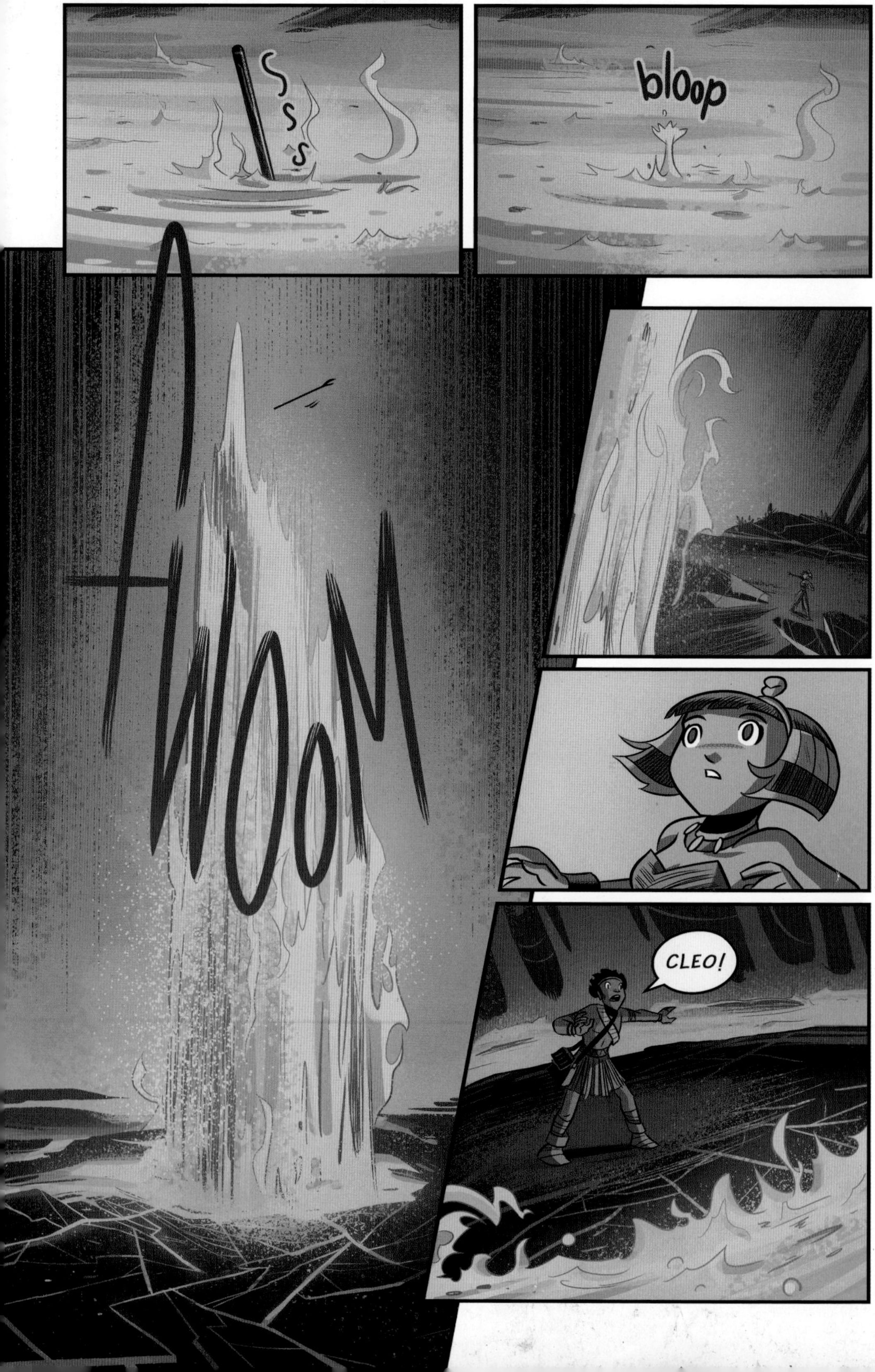
SSS
bloop
FWOOM
CLEO!

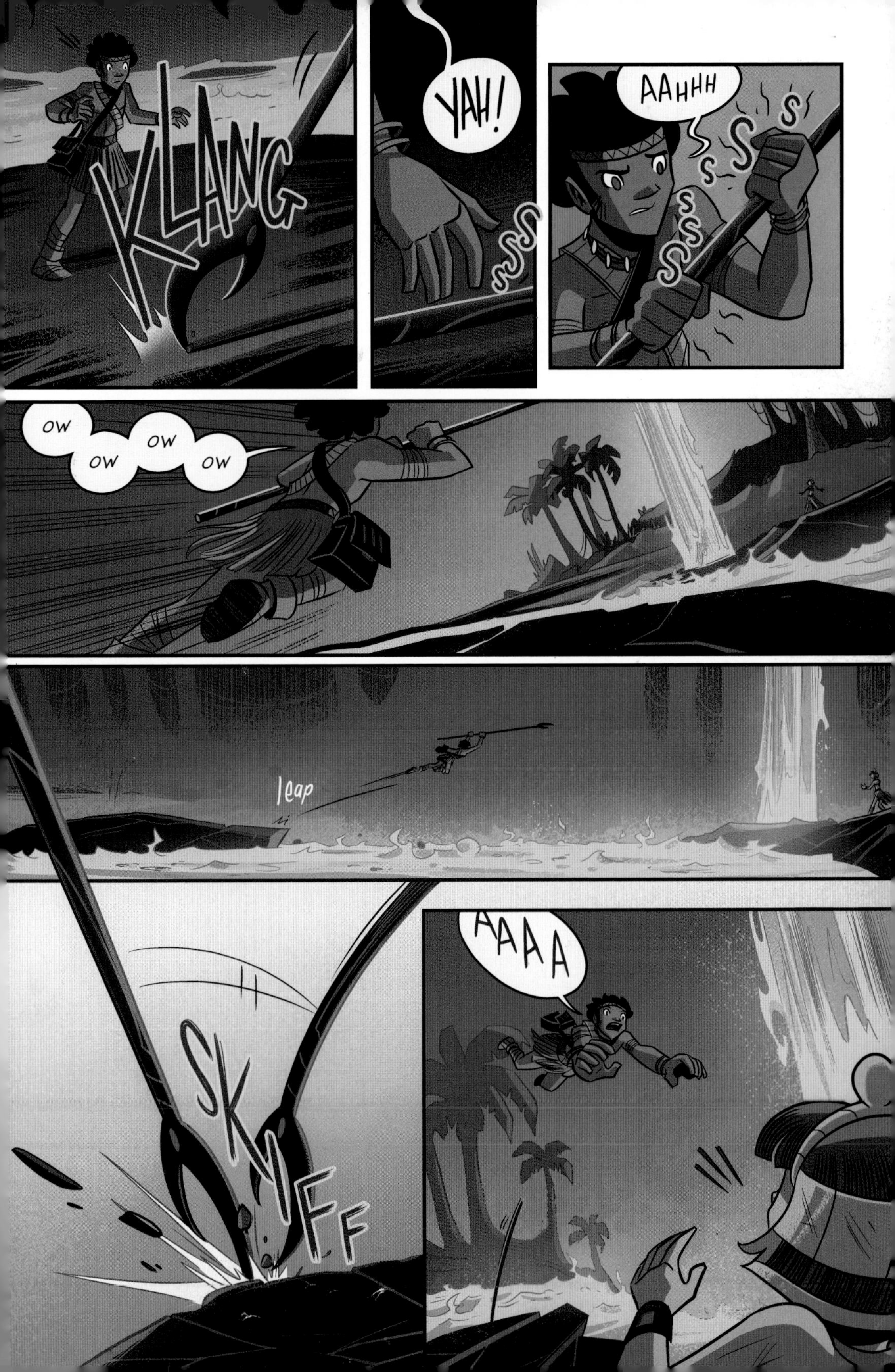
KLANG
YAH!
SSS
AAHHH
SSSSS
OW
OW
OW
OW
leap
SKIFF
AAAA

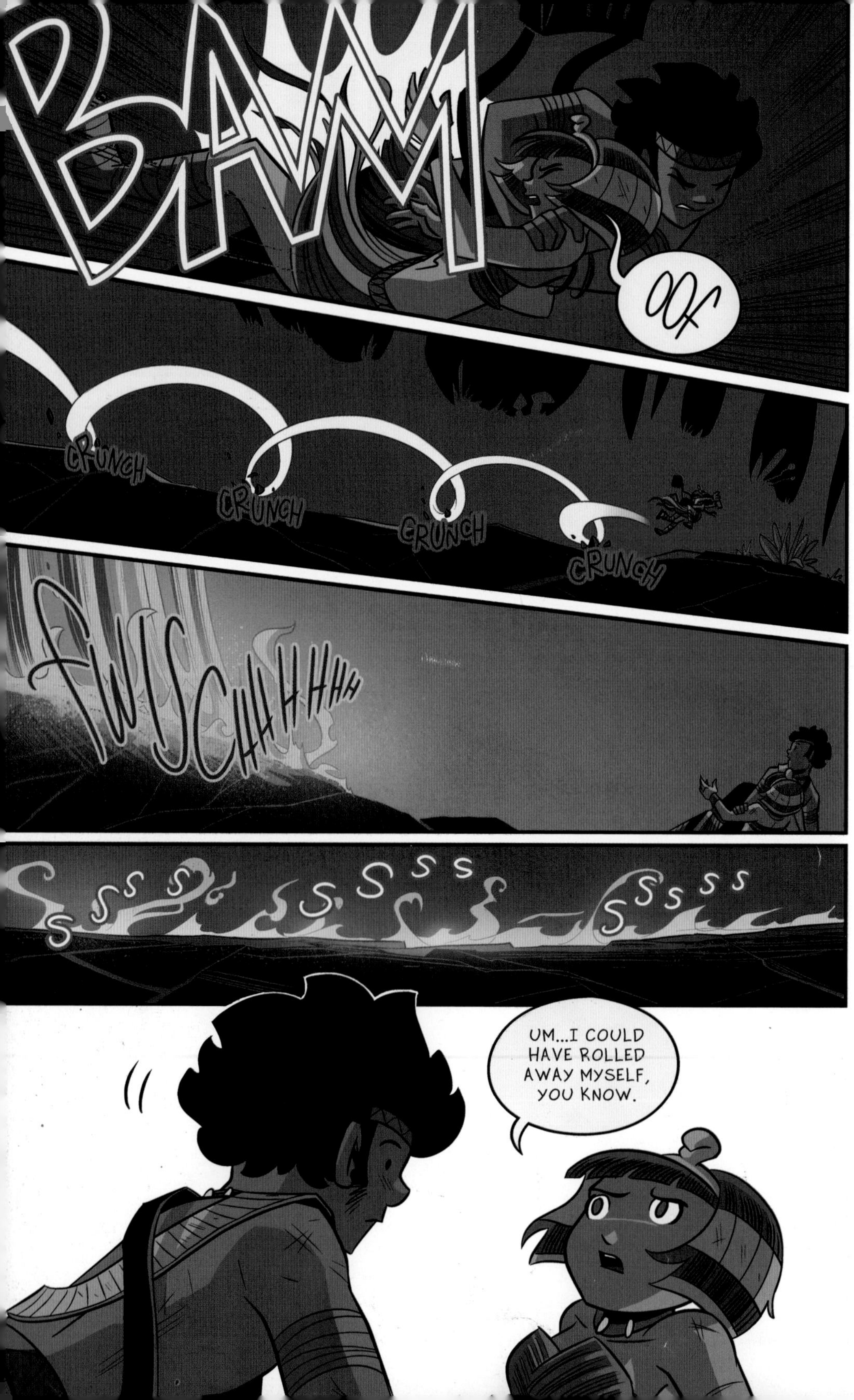
BAM
OOF
CRUNCH
CRUNCH
CRUNCH
CRUNCH
FWISCHHHHHH
SSSSSSSSSSSSS
UM...I COULD HAVE ROLLED AWAY MYSELF, YOU KNOW.

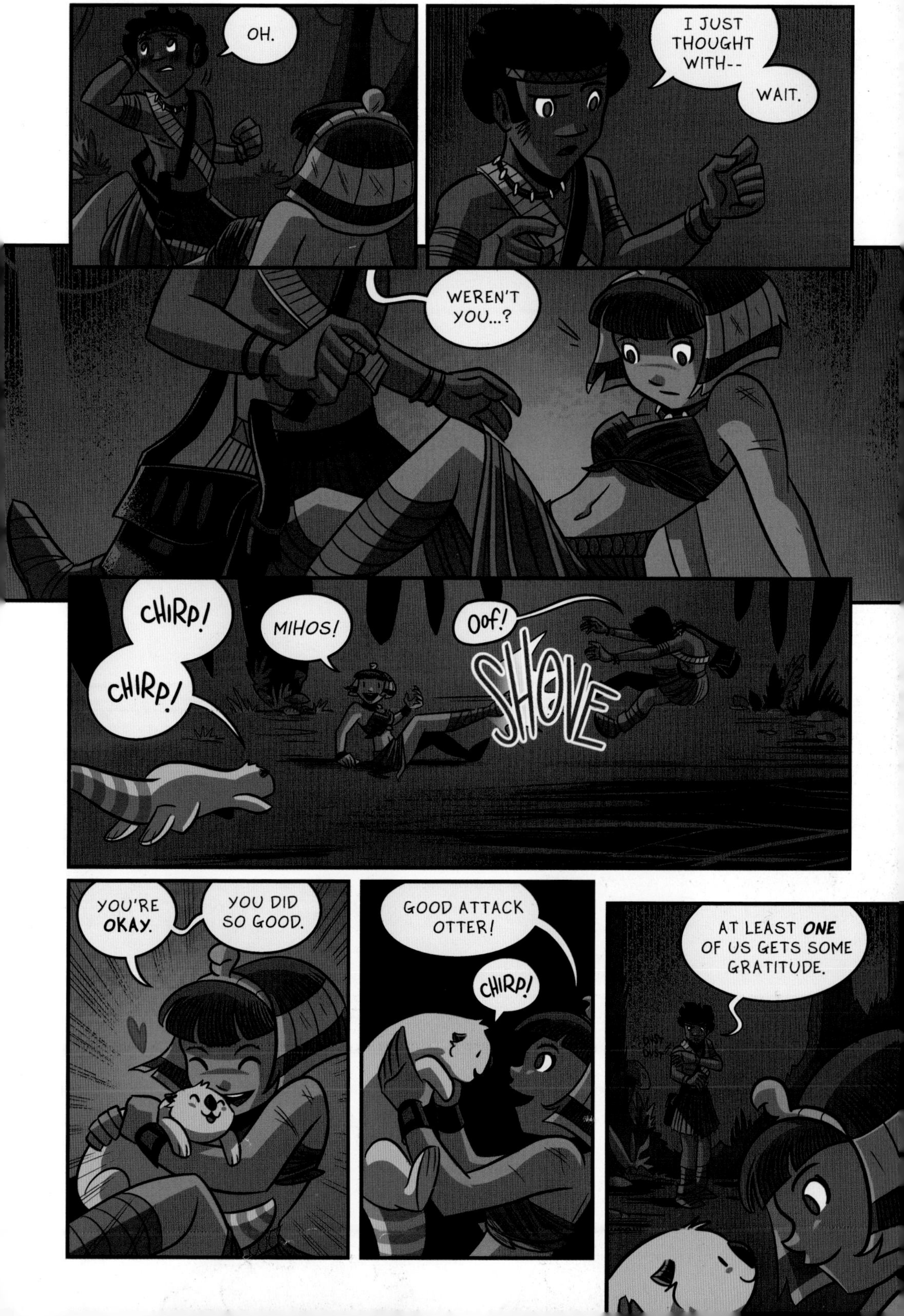
OH.
I JUST THOUGHT WITH--
WAIT.
WEREN'T YOU...?
CHIRP!
CHIRP!
MIHOS!
Oof!
SHOVE
YOU'RE OKAY.
YOU DID SO GOOD.
GOOD ATTACK OTTER!
CHIRP!
AT LEAST ONE OF US GETS SOME GRATITUDE.

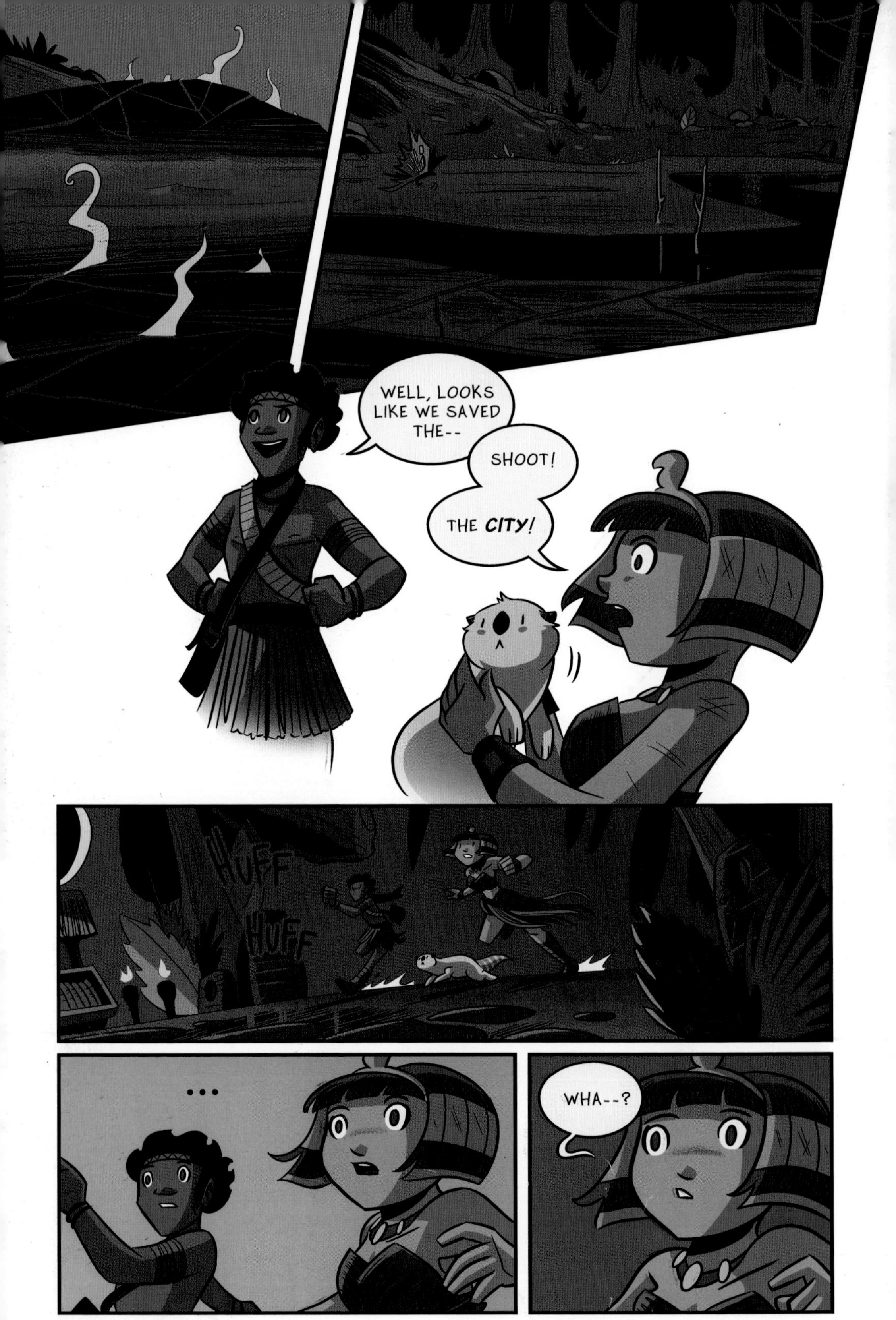
WELL, LOOKS LIKE WE SAVED THE--
SHOOT!
THE *CITY*!
HUFF
HUFF
...
WHA--?

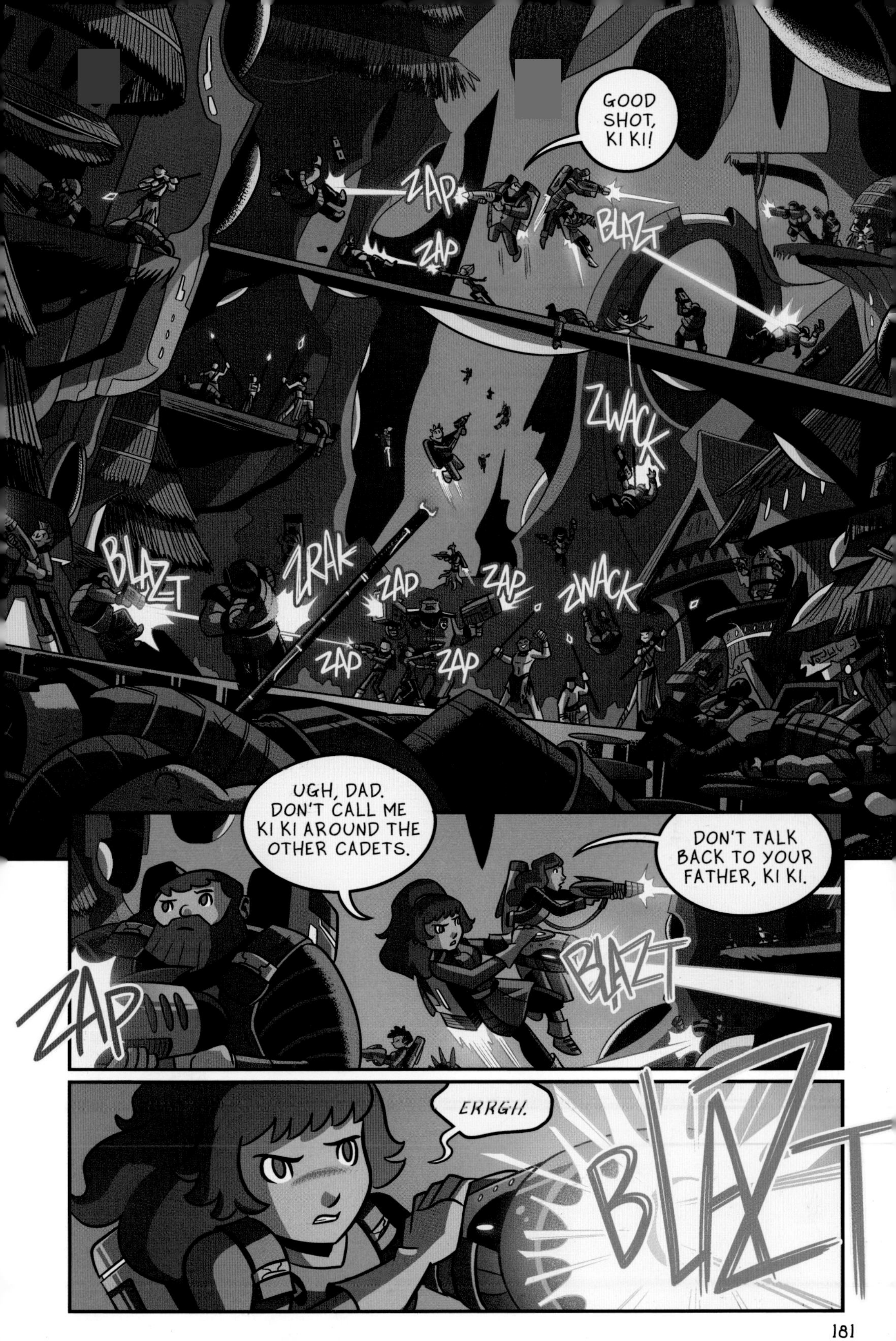
GOOD SHOT, KI KI!
ZAP
ZAP
BLAZT
ZWACK
BLAZT
ZRAK
ZAP
ZAP
ZWACK
ZAP
ZAP
UGH, DAD. DON'T CALL ME KI KI AROUND THE OTHER CADETS.
DON'T TALK BACK TO YOUR FATHER, KI KI.
ZAP
BLAZT
ERRGH!
BLAZT

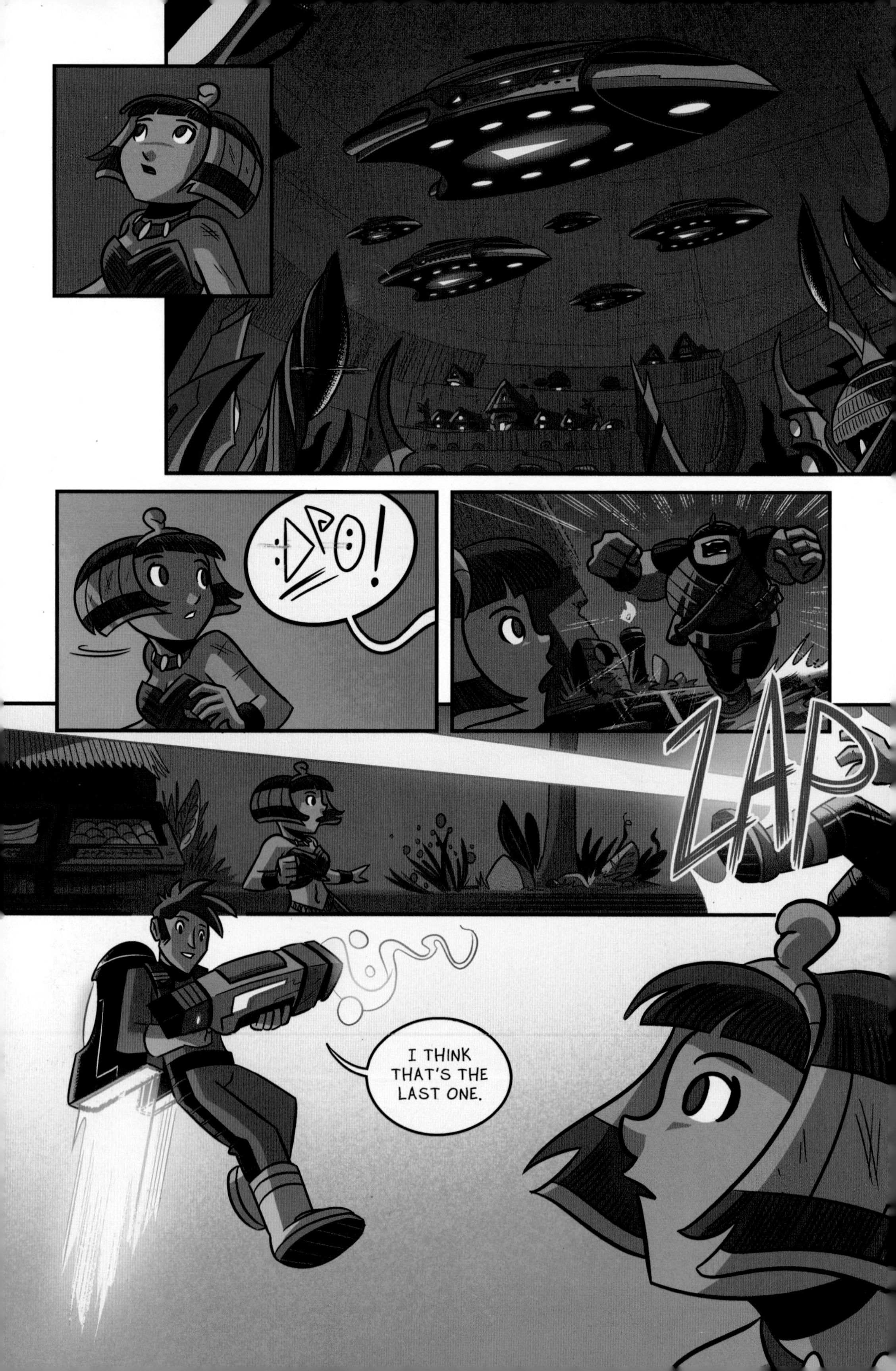

:DPO!
ZAP
I THINK THAT'S THE LAST ONE.

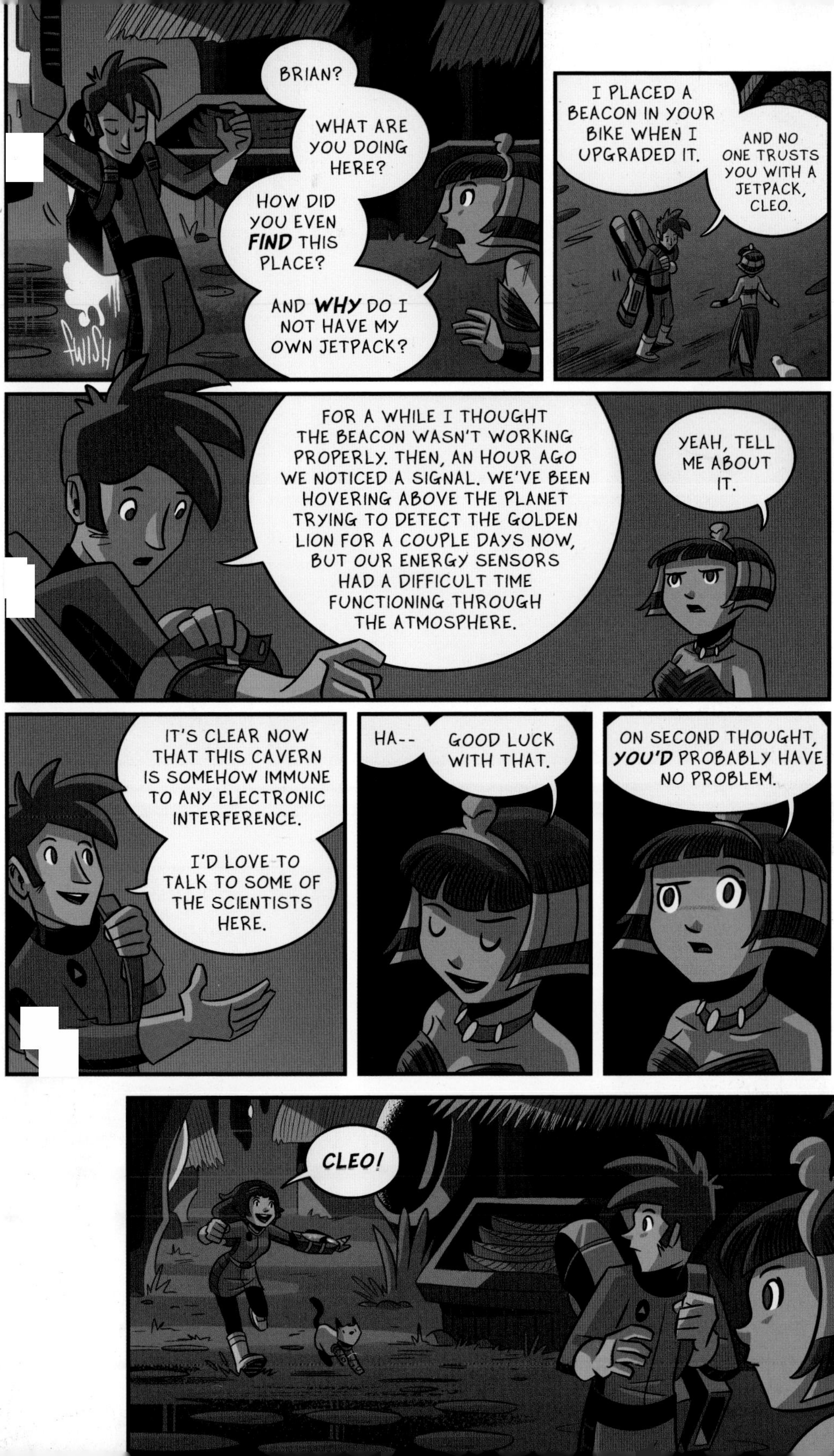
BRIAN?
WHAT ARE YOU DOING HERE?
HOW DID YOU EVEN FIND THIS PLACE?
AND WHY DO I NOT HAVE MY OWN JETPACK?
FWISH
I PLACED A BEACON IN YOUR BIKE WHEN I UPGRADED IT.
AND NO ONE TRUSTS YOU WITH A JETPACK, CLEO.
FOR A WHILE I THOUGHT THE BEACON WASN'T WORKING PROPERLY. THEN, AN HOUR AGO WE NOTICED A SIGNAL. WE'VE BEEN HOVERING ABOVE THE PLANET TRYING TO DETECT THE GOLDEN LION FOR A COUPLE DAYS NOW, BUT OUR ENERGY SENSORS HAD A DIFFICULT TIME FUNCTIONING THROUGH THE ATMOSPHERE.
YEAH, TELL ME ABOUT IT.
IT'S CLEAR NOW THAT THIS CAVERN IS SOMEHOW IMMUNE TO ANY ELECTRONIC INTERFERENCE.
I'D LOVE TO TALK TO SOME OF THE SCIENTISTS HERE.
HA--
GOOD LUCK WITH THAT.
ON SECOND THOUGHT, YOU'D PROBABLY HAVE NO PROBLEM.
CLEO!

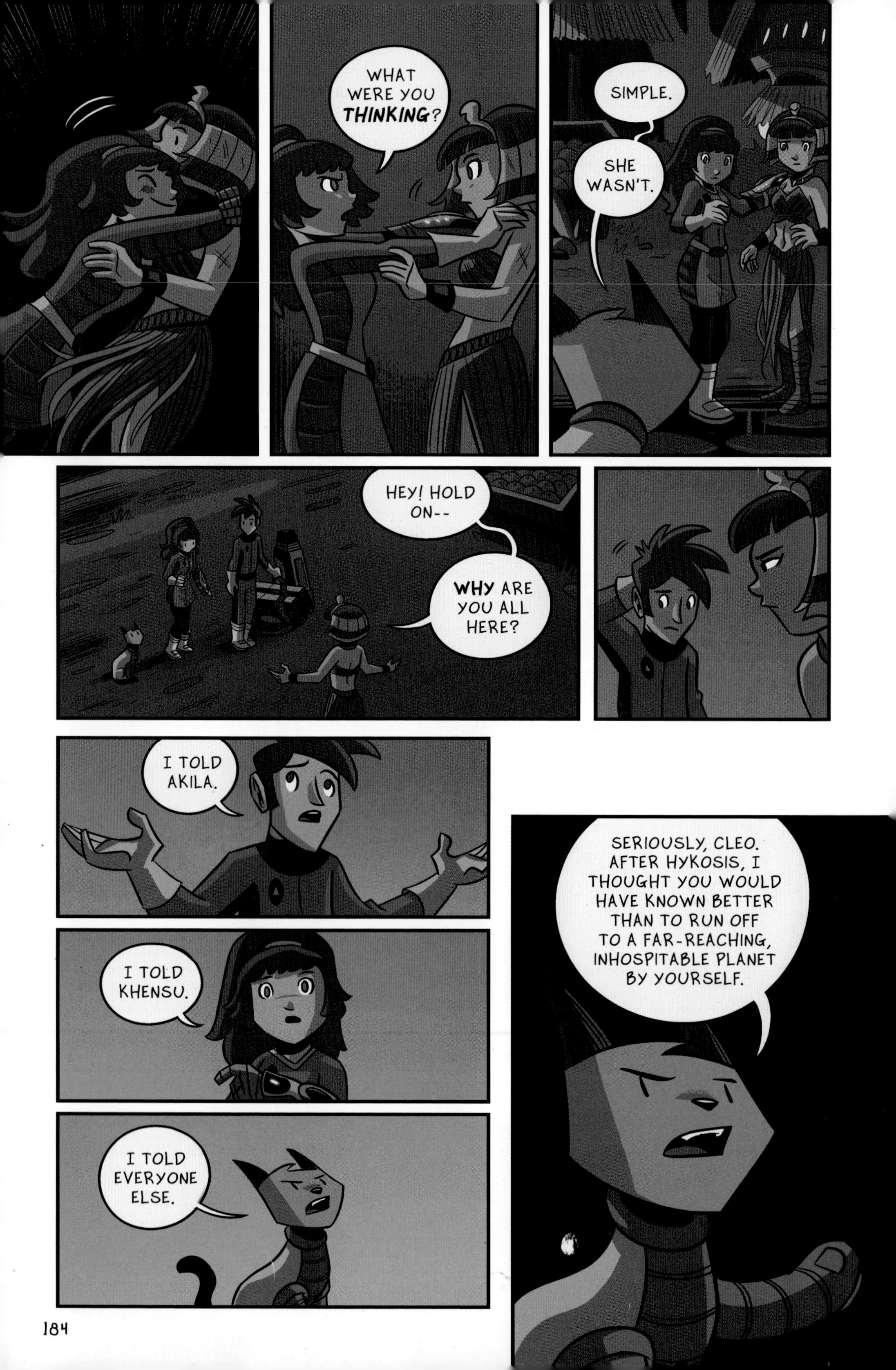

WHAT WERE YOU THINKING?
SIMPLE.
SHE WASN'T.
HEY! HOLD ON--
WHY ARE YOU ALL HERE?
I TOLD AKILA.
I TOLD KHENSU.
I TOLD EVERYONE ELSE.
SERIOUSLY, CLEO. AFTER HYKOSIS, I THOUGHT YOU WOULD HAVE KNOWN BETTER THAN TO RUN OFF TO A FAR-REACHING, INHOSPITABLE PLANET BY YOURSELF.

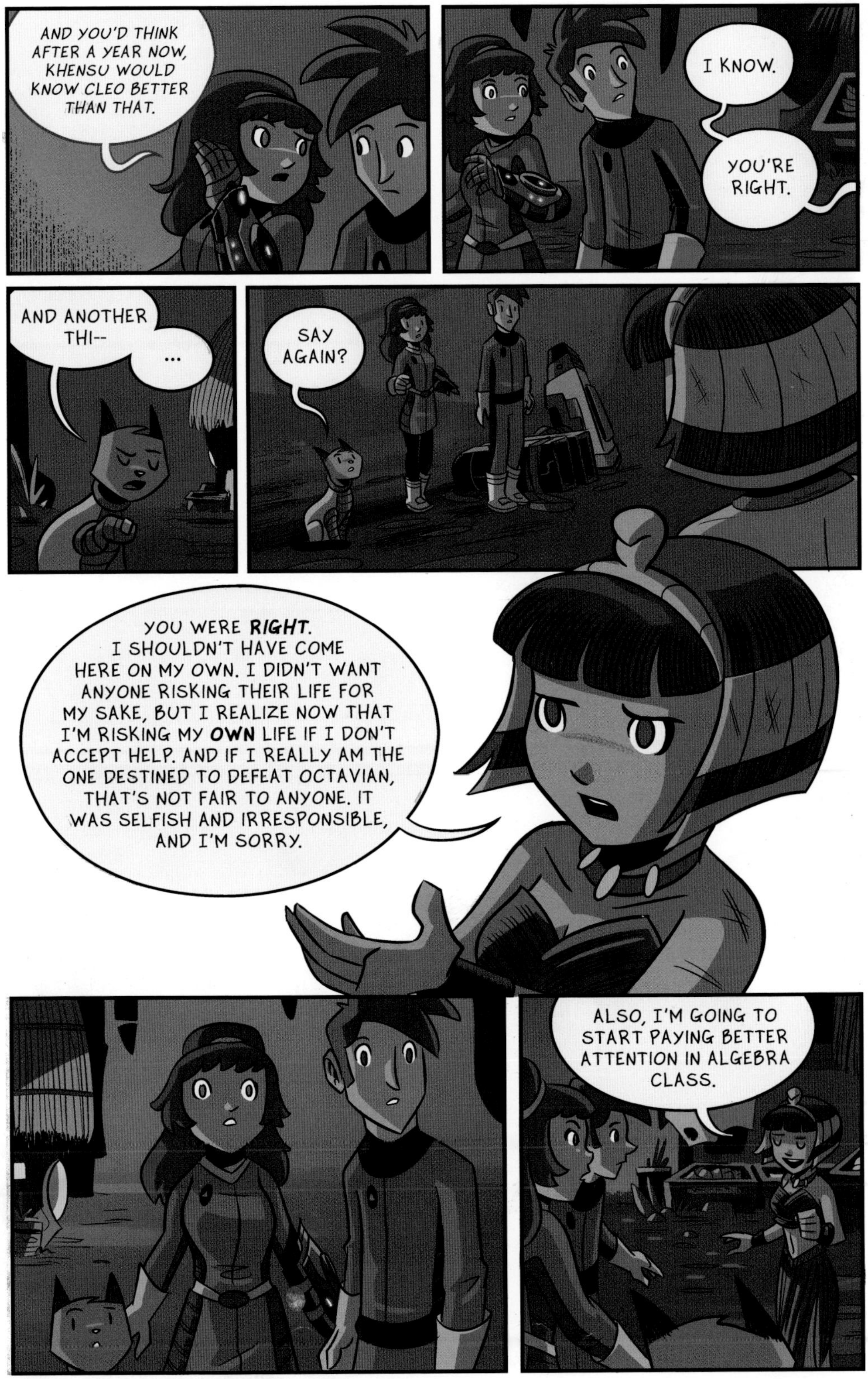

AND YOU'D THINK AFTER A YEAR NOW, KHENSU WOULD KNOW CLEO BETTER THAN THAT.
I KNOW.
YOU'RE RIGHT.
AND ANOTHER THI--
...
SAY AGAIN?
YOU WERE RIGHT. I SHOULDN'T HAVE COME HERE ON MY OWN. I DIDN'T WANT ANYONE RISKING THEIR LIFE FOR MY SAKE, BUT I REALIZE NOW THAT I'M RISKING MY OWN LIFE IF I DON'T ACCEPT HELP. AND IF I REALLY AM THE ONE DESTINED TO DEFEAT OCTAVIAN, THAT'S NOT FAIR TO ANYONE. IT WAS SELFISH AND IRRESPONSIBLE, AND I'M SORRY.
ALSO, I'M GOING TO START PAYING BETTER ATTENTION IN ALGEBRA CLASS.

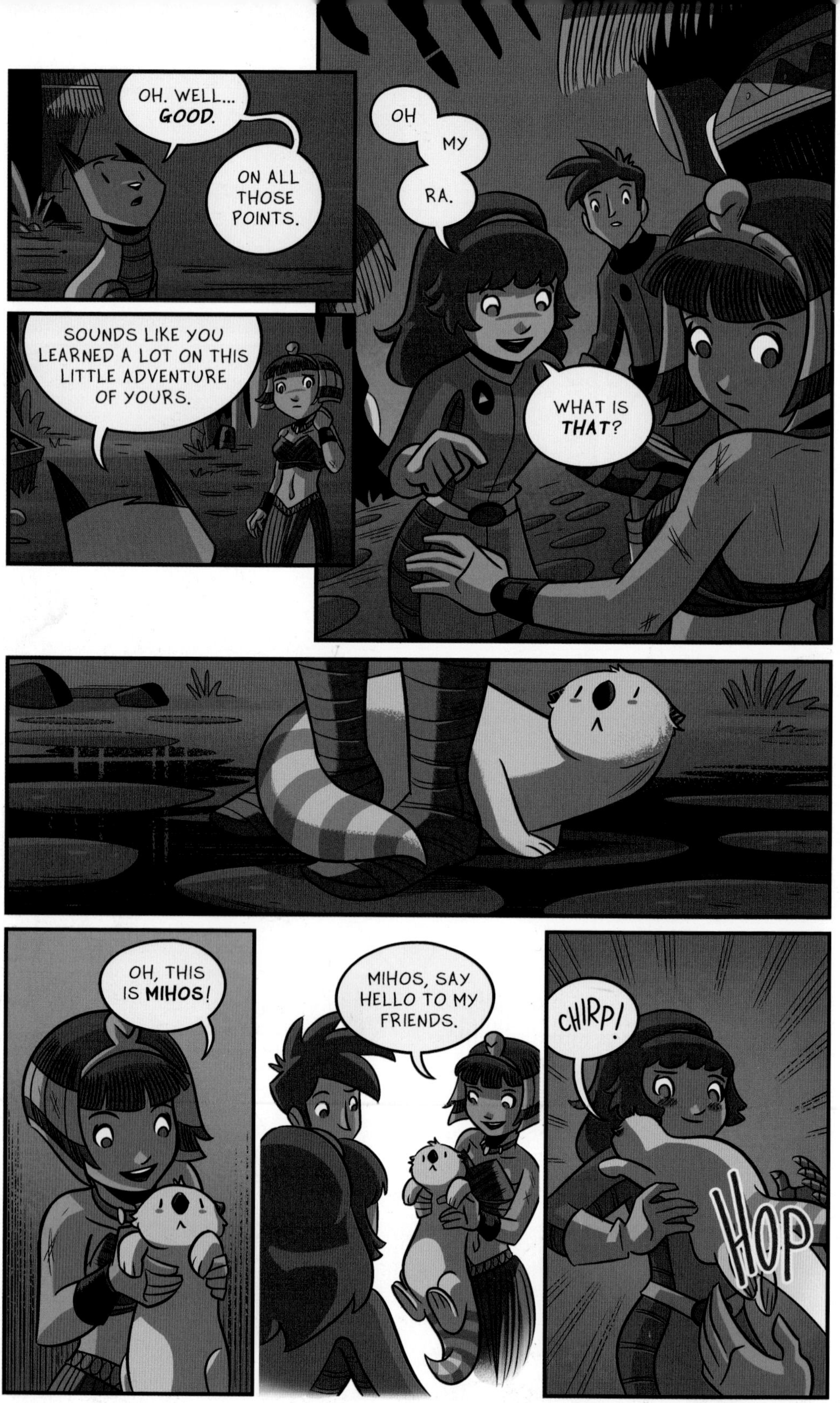
OH. WELL... GOOD.
ON ALL THOSE POINTS.
OH MY RA.
SOUNDS LIKE YOU LEARNED A LOT ON THIS LITTLE ADVENTURE OF YOURS.
WHAT IS THAT?
OH, THIS IS MIHOS!
MIHOS, SAY HELLO TO MY FRIENDS.
CHIRP!
HOP

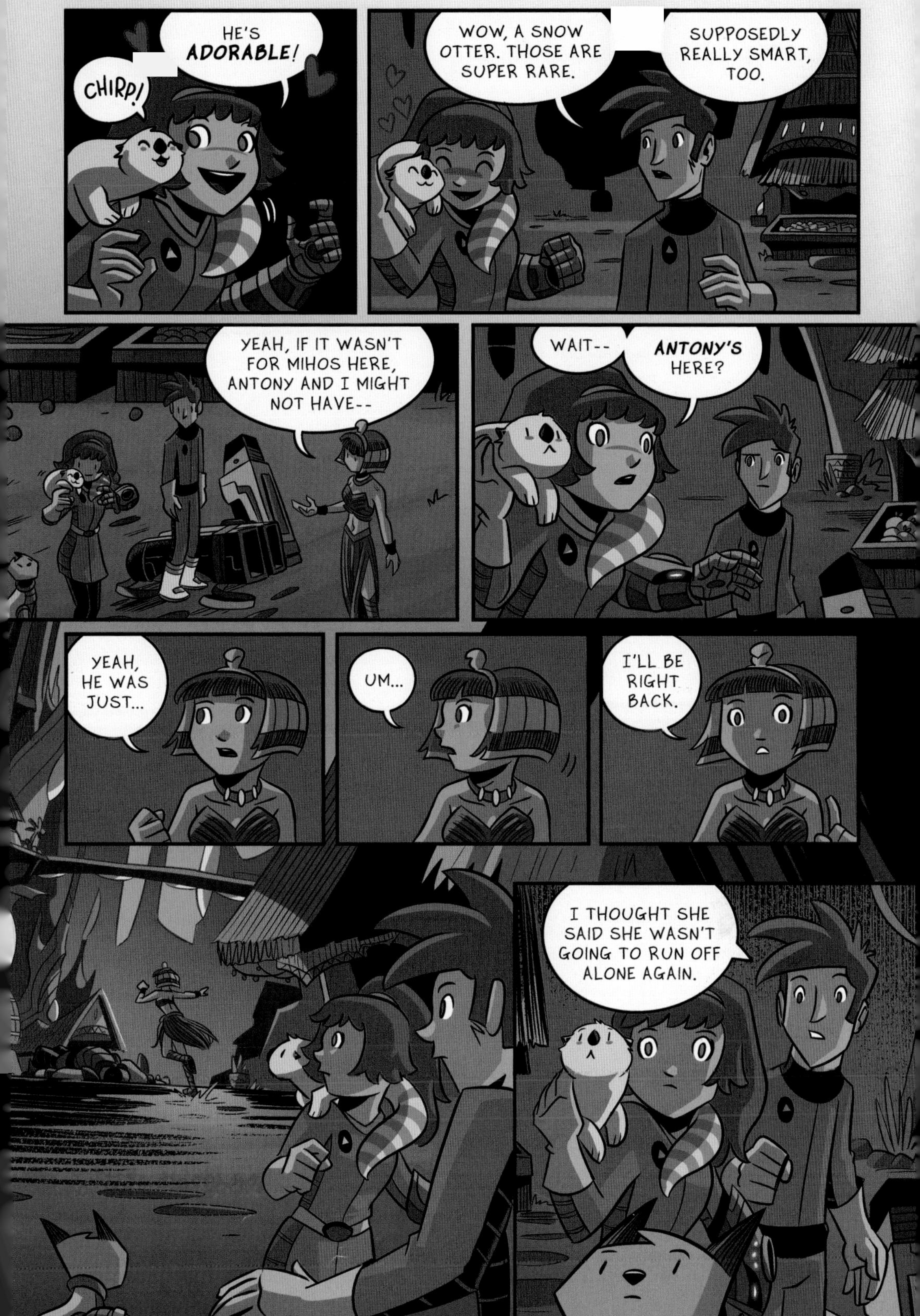
HE'S ADORABLE!
CHIRP!
WOW, A SNOW OTTER. THOSE ARE SUPER RARE.
SUPPOSEDLY REALLY SMART, TOO.
YEAH, IF IT WASN'T FOR MIHOS HERE, ANTONY AND I MIGHT NOT HAVE--
WAIT--
ANTONY'S HERE?
YEAH, HE WAS JUST...
UM...
I'LL BE RIGHT BACK.
I THOUGHT SHE SAID SHE WASN'T GOING TO RUN OFF ALONE AGAIN.

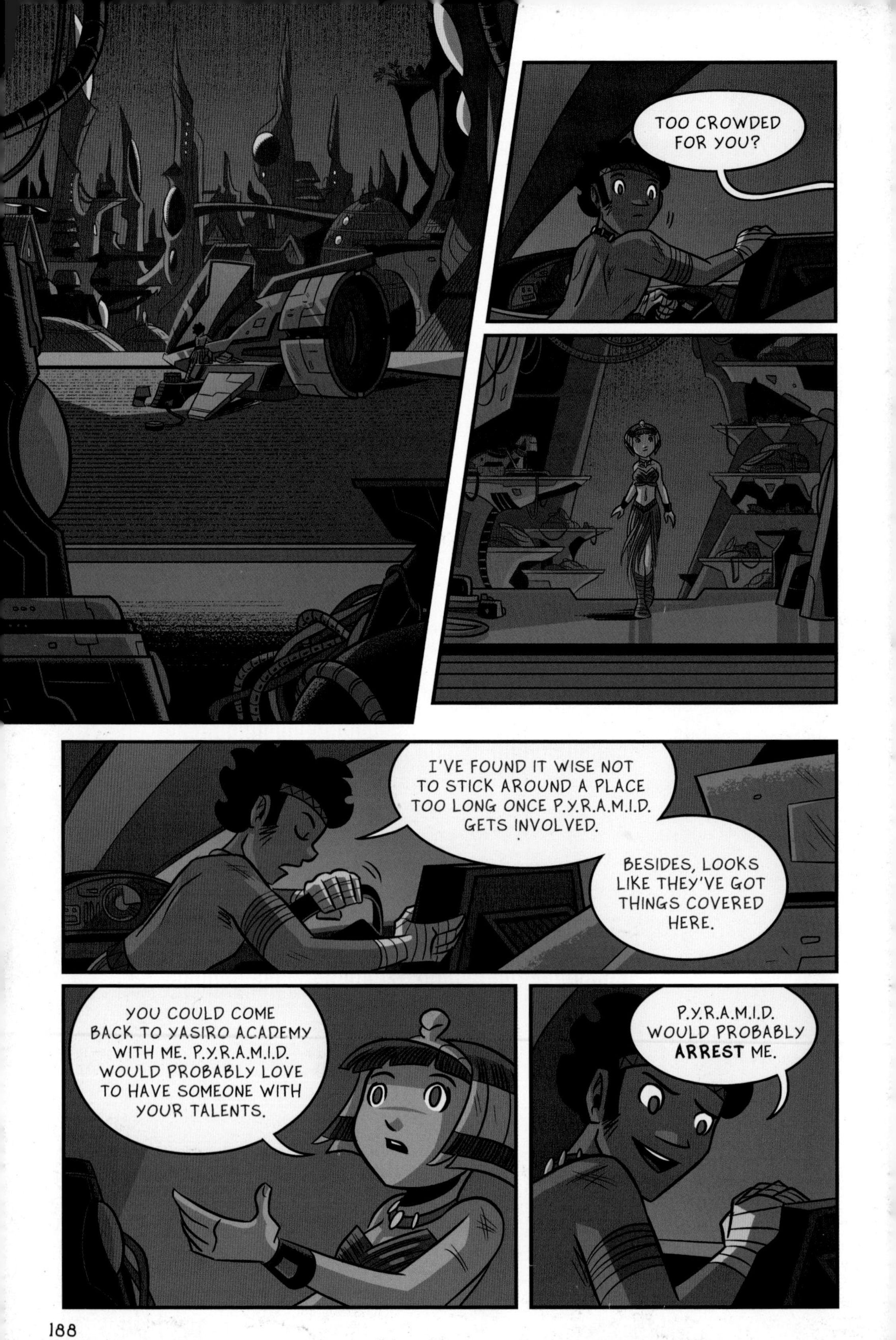
TOO CROWDED FOR YOU?
I'VE FOUND IT WISE NOT TO STICK AROUND A PLACE TOO LONG ONCE P.Y.R.A.M.I.D. GETS INVOLVED.
BESIDES, LOOKS LIKE THEY'VE GOT THINGS COVERED HERE.
YOU COULD COME BACK TO YASIRO ACADEMY WITH ME. P.Y.R.A.M.I.D. WOULD PROBABLY LOVE TO HAVE SOMEONE WITH YOUR TALENTS.
P.Y.R.A.M.I.D. WOULD PROBABLY **ARREST** ME.

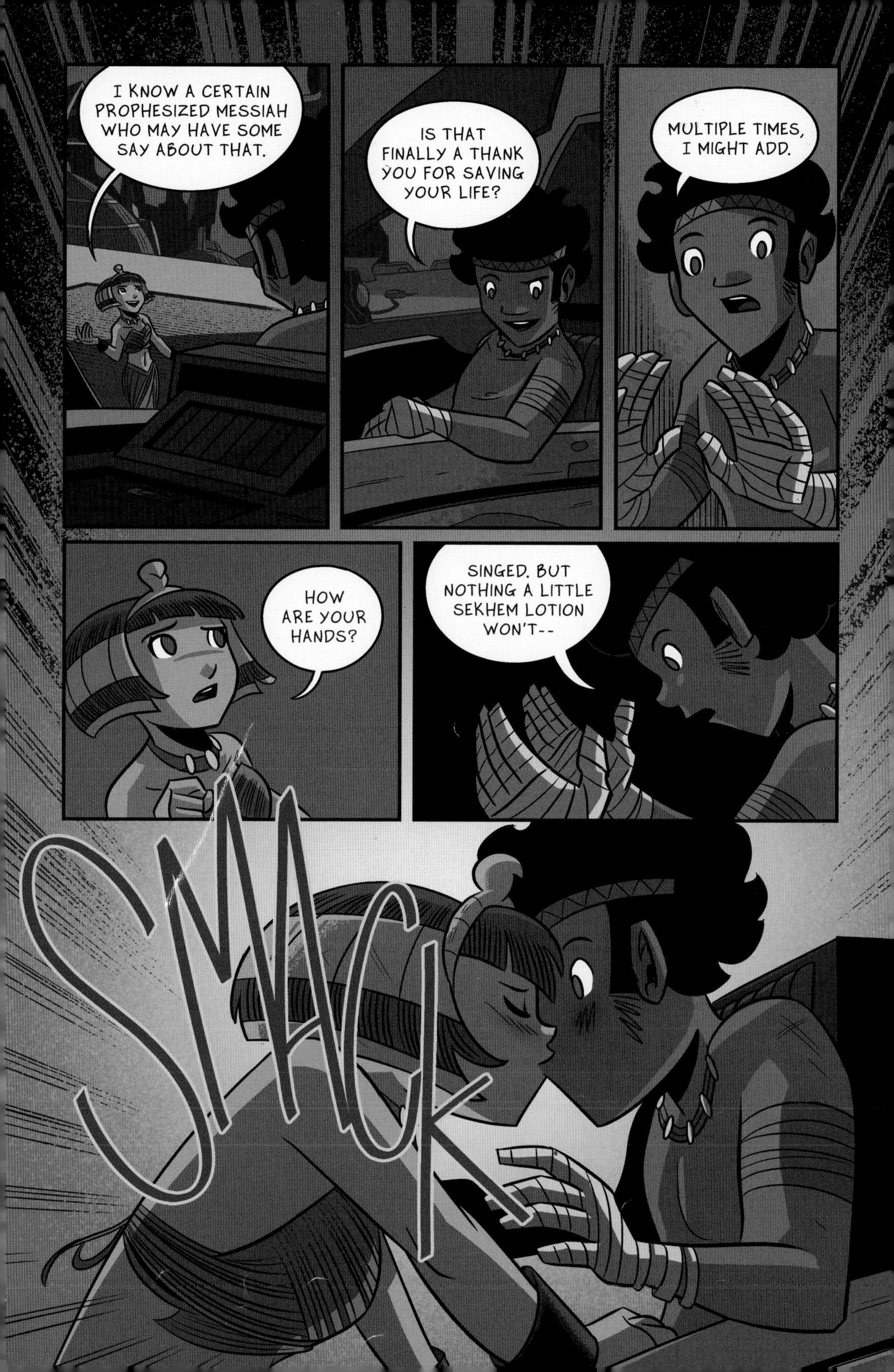
I KNOW A CERTAIN PROPHESIZED MESSIAH WHO MAY HAVE SOME SAY ABOUT THAT.
IS THAT FINALLY A THANK YOU FOR SAVING YOUR LIFE?
MULTIPLE TIMES, I MIGHT ADD.
HOW ARE YOUR HANDS?
SINGED. BUT NOTHING A LITTLE SEKHEM LOTION WON'T--
SMACK

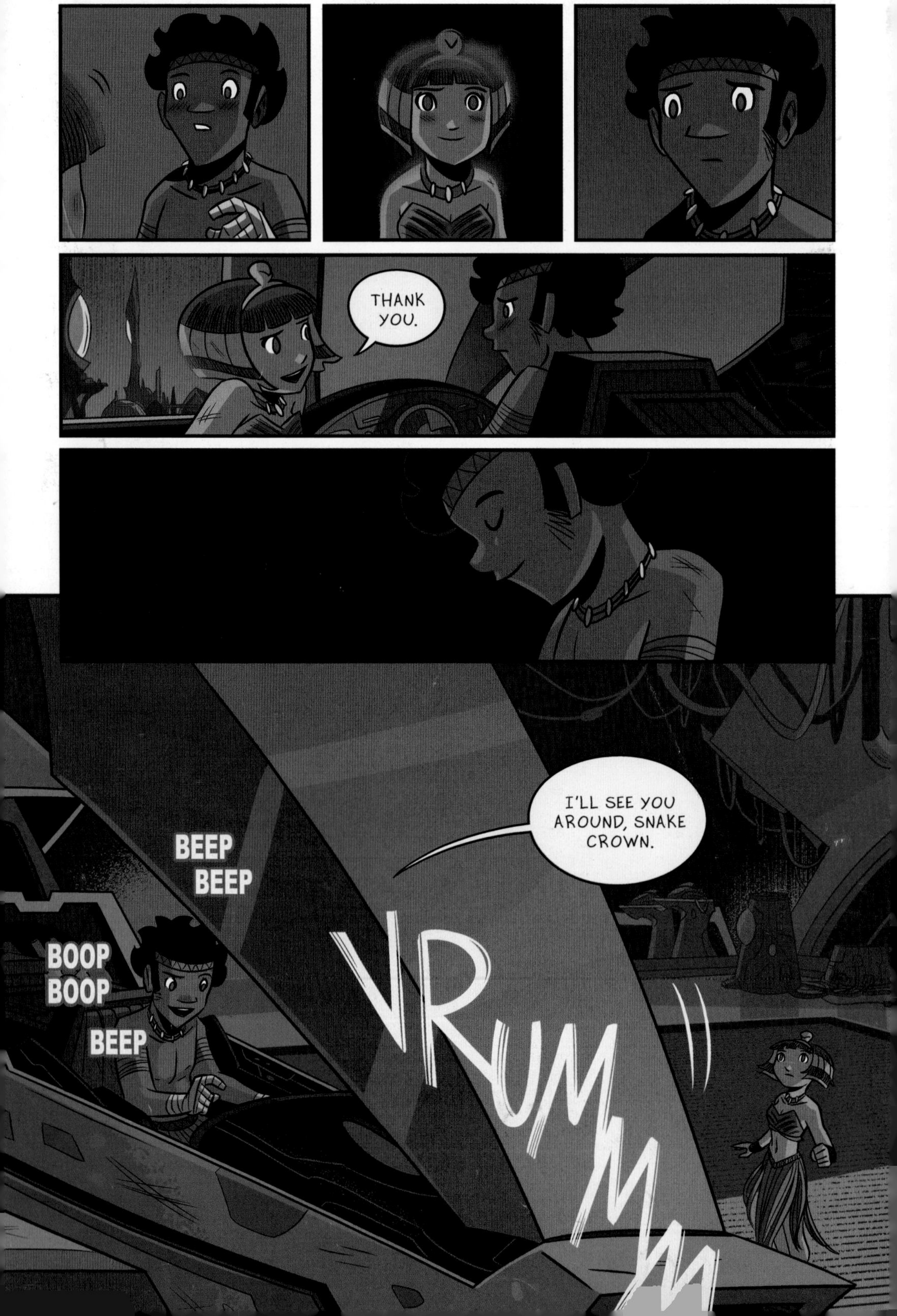
THANK YOU.
I'LL SEE YOU AROUND, SNAKE CROWN.
BEEP BEEP
BOOP BOOP
BEEP
VRUMMM

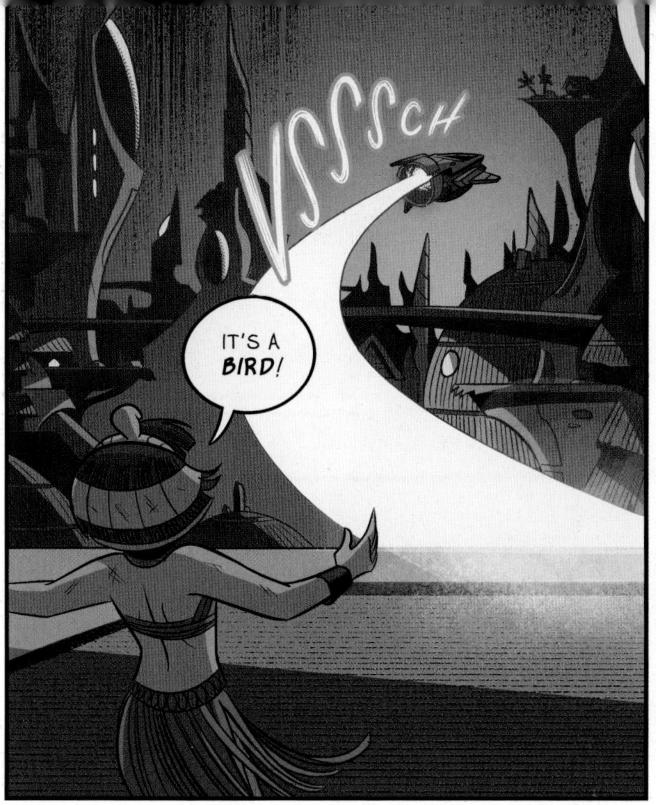
VSSSCH
IT'S A **BIRD**!

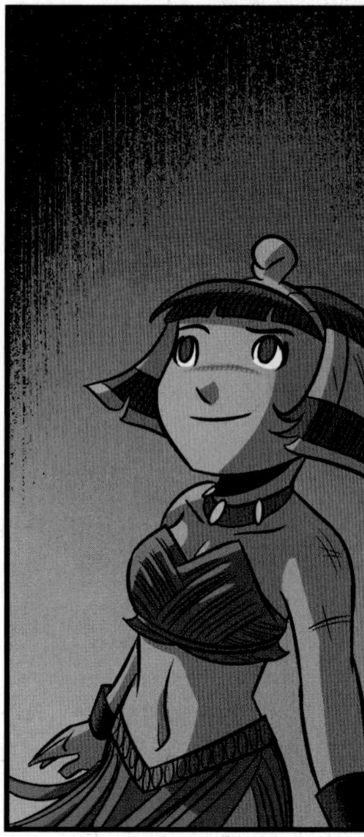

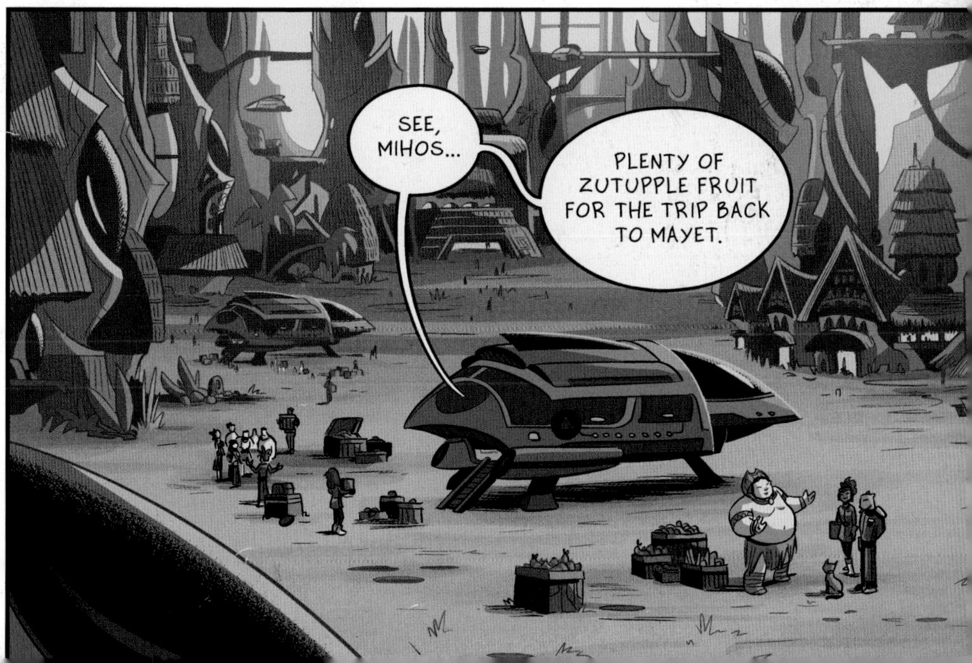
SEE, MIHOS...
PLENTY OF ZUTUPPLE FRUIT FOR THE TRIP BACK TO MAYET.

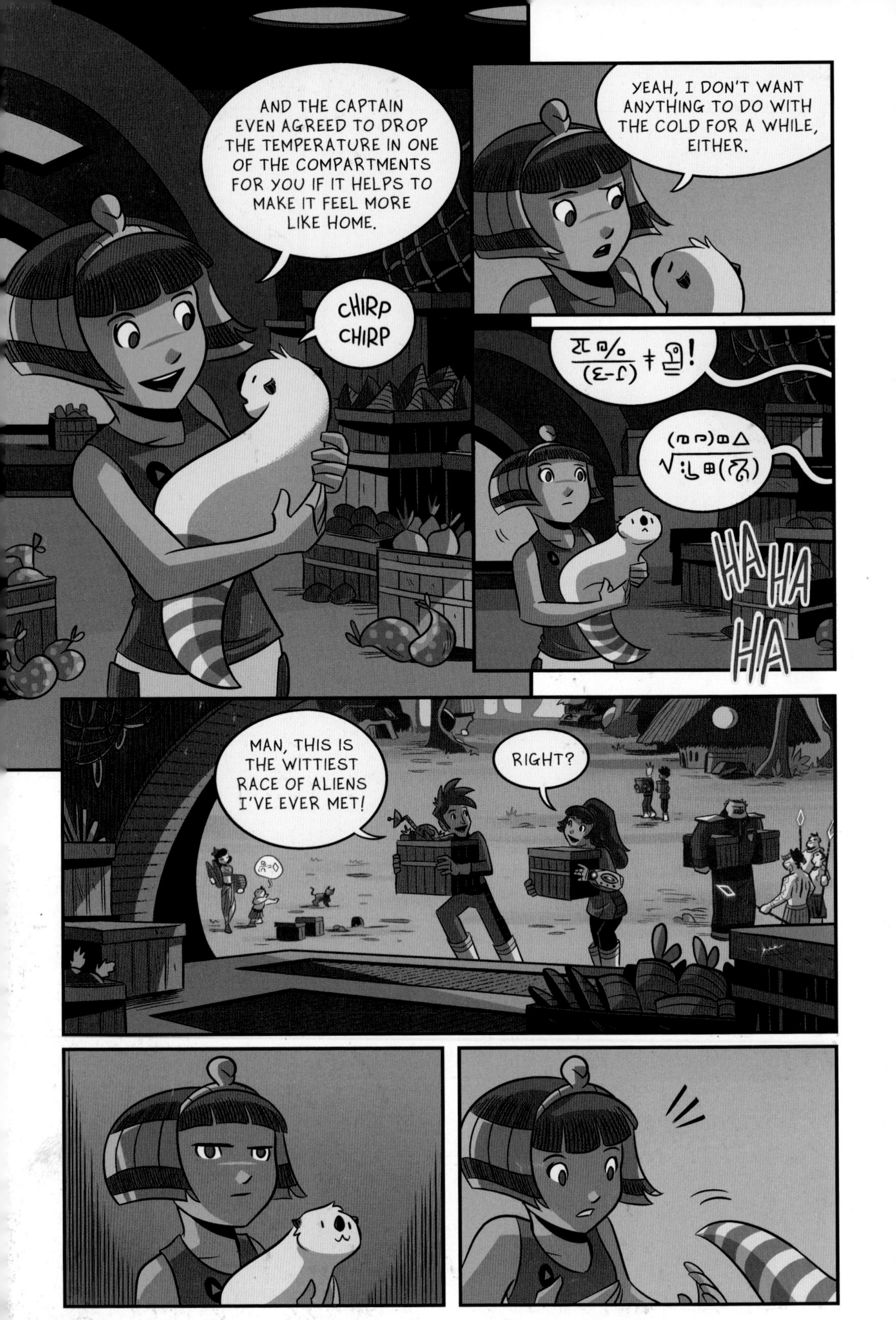
AND THE CAPTAIN EVEN AGREED TO DROP THE TEMPERATURE IN ONE OF THE COMPARTMENTS FOR YOU IF IT HELPS TO MAKE IT FEEL MORE LIKE HOME.
CHIRP CHIRP
YEAH, I DON'T WANT ANYTHING TO DO WITH THE COLD FOR A WHILE, EITHER.
HA HA HA
MAN, THIS IS THE WITTIEST RACE OF ALIENS I'VE EVER MET!
RIGHT?

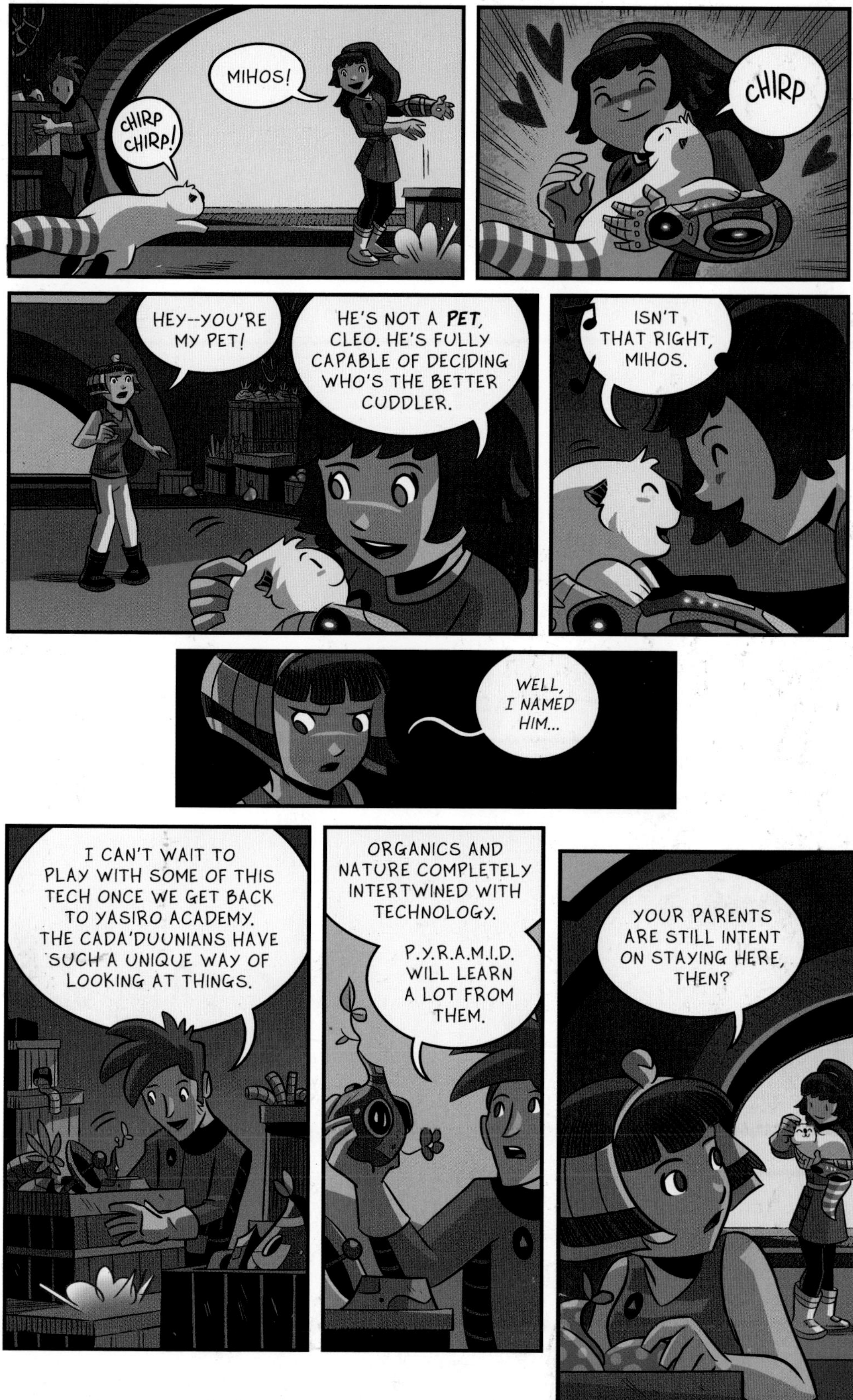
MIHOS!
CHIRP CHIRP!
CHIRP
HEY--YOU'RE MY PET!
HE'S NOT A **PET**, CLEO. HE'S FULLY CAPABLE OF DECIDING WHO'S THE BETTER CUDDLER.
ISN'T THAT RIGHT, MIHOS.
WELL, I NAMED HIM...
I CAN'T WAIT TO PLAY WITH SOME OF THIS TECH ONCE WE GET BACK TO YASIRO ACADEMY. THE CADA'DUUNIANS HAVE SUCH A UNIQUE WAY OF LOOKING AT THINGS.
ORGANICS AND NATURE COMPLETELY INTERTWINED WITH TECHNOLOGY.
P.Y.R.A.M.I.D. WILL LEARN A LOT FROM THEM.
YOUR PARENTS ARE STILL INTENT ON STAYING HERE, THEN?

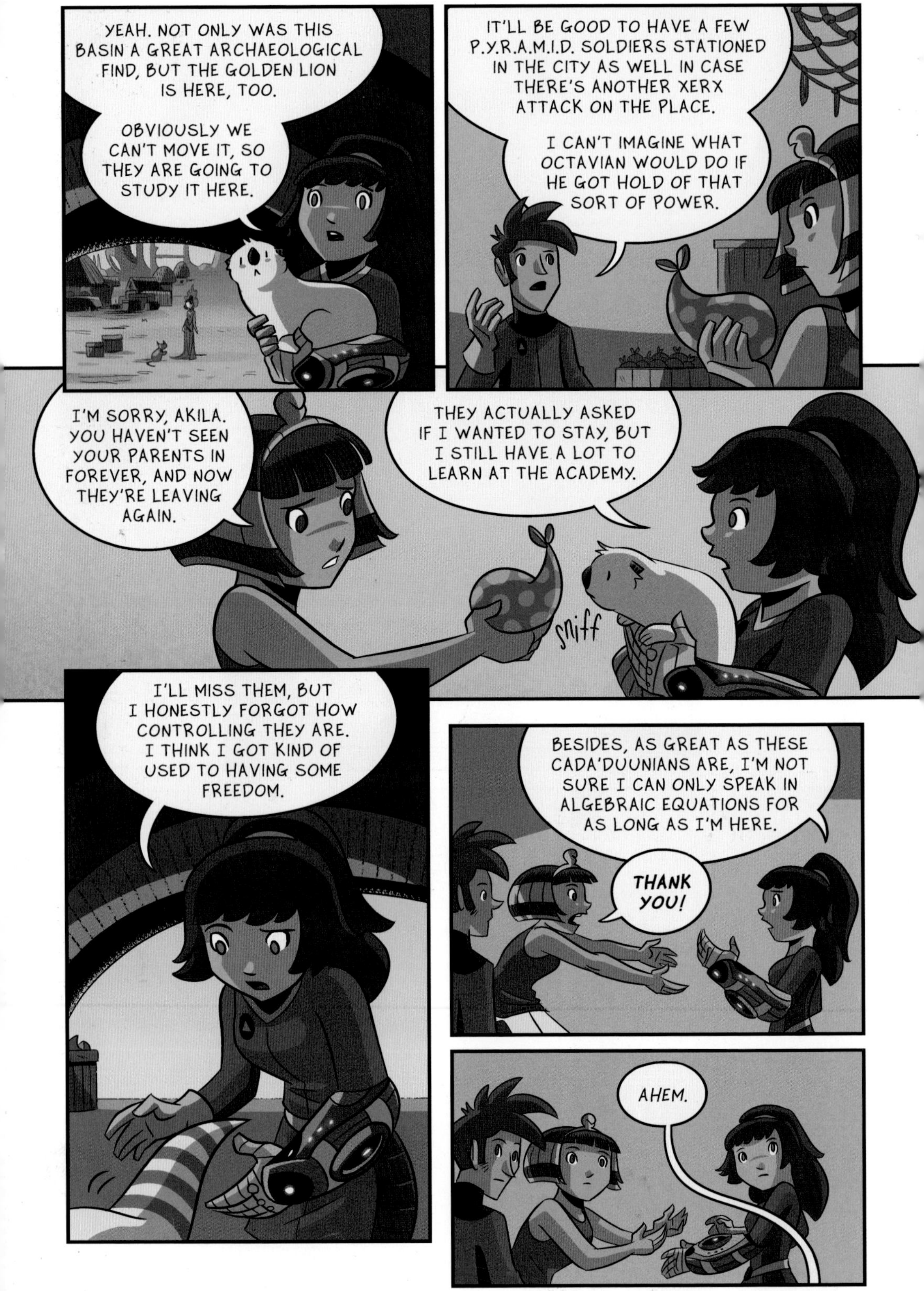
YEAH. NOT ONLY WAS THIS BASIN A GREAT ARCHAEOLOGICAL FIND, BUT THE GOLDEN LION IS HERE, TOO.
OBVIOUSLY WE CAN'T MOVE IT, SO THEY ARE GOING TO STUDY IT HERE.
IT'LL BE GOOD TO HAVE A FEW P.Y.R.A.M.I.D. SOLDIERS STATIONED IN THE CITY AS WELL IN CASE THERE'S ANOTHER XERX ATTACK ON THE PLACE.
I CAN'T IMAGINE WHAT OCTAVIAN WOULD DO IF HE GOT HOLD OF THAT SORT OF POWER.
I'M SORRY, AKILA. YOU HAVEN'T SEEN YOUR PARENTS IN FOREVER, AND NOW THEY'RE LEAVING AGAIN.
THEY ACTUALLY ASKED IF I WANTED TO STAY, BUT I STILL HAVE A LOT TO LEARN AT THE ACADEMY.
sniff
I'LL MISS THEM, BUT I HONESTLY FORGOT HOW CONTROLLING THEY ARE. I THINK I GOT KIND OF USED TO HAVING SOME FREEDOM.
BESIDES, AS GREAT AS THESE CADA'DUUNIANS ARE, I'M NOT SURE I CAN ONLY SPEAK IN ALGEBRAIC EQUATIONS FOR AS LONG AS I'M HERE.
THANK YOU!
AHEM.

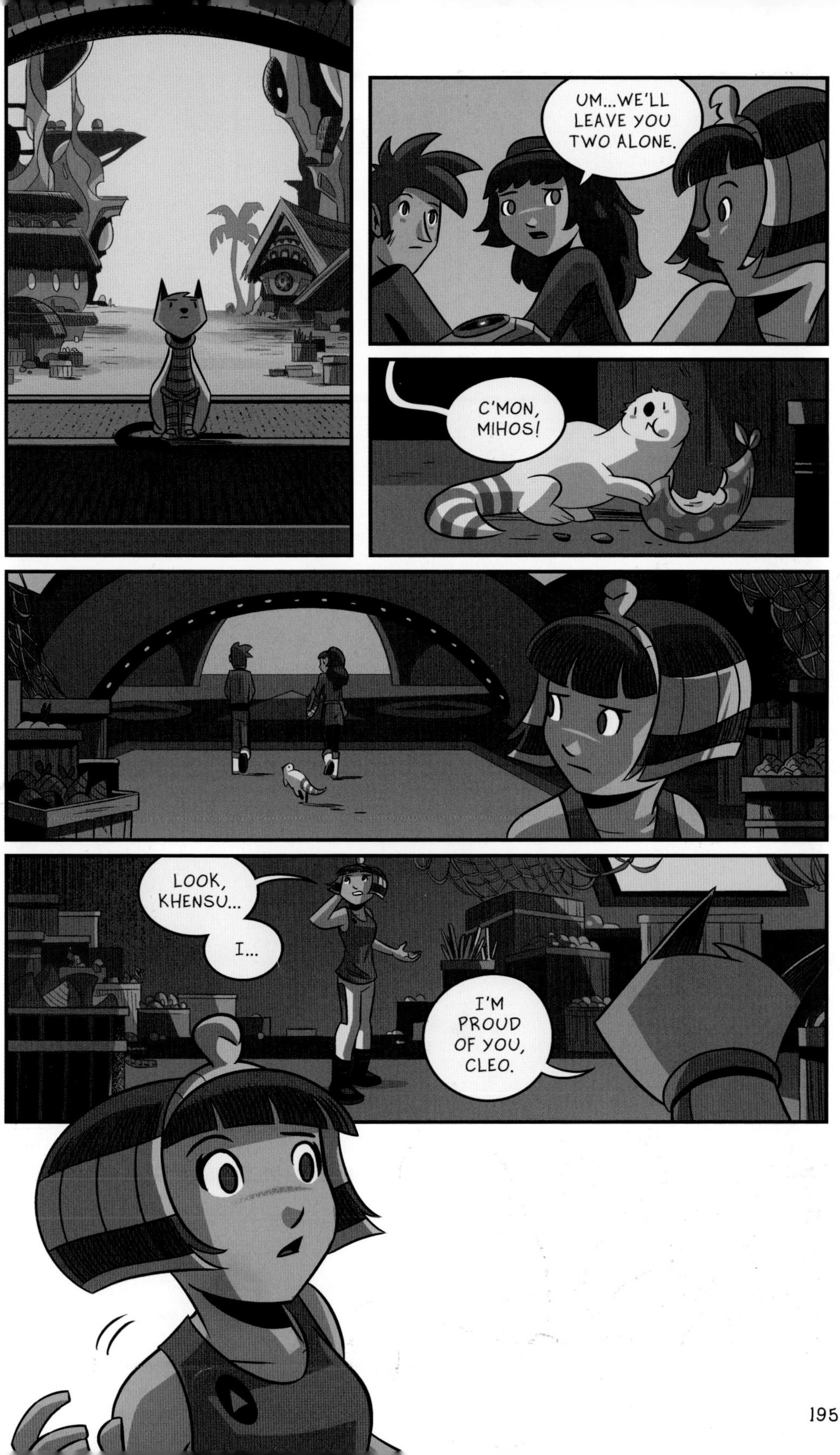
UM...WE'LL LEAVE YOU TWO ALONE.
C'MON, MIHOS!
LOOK, KHENSU...
I...
I'M PROUD OF YOU, CLEO.

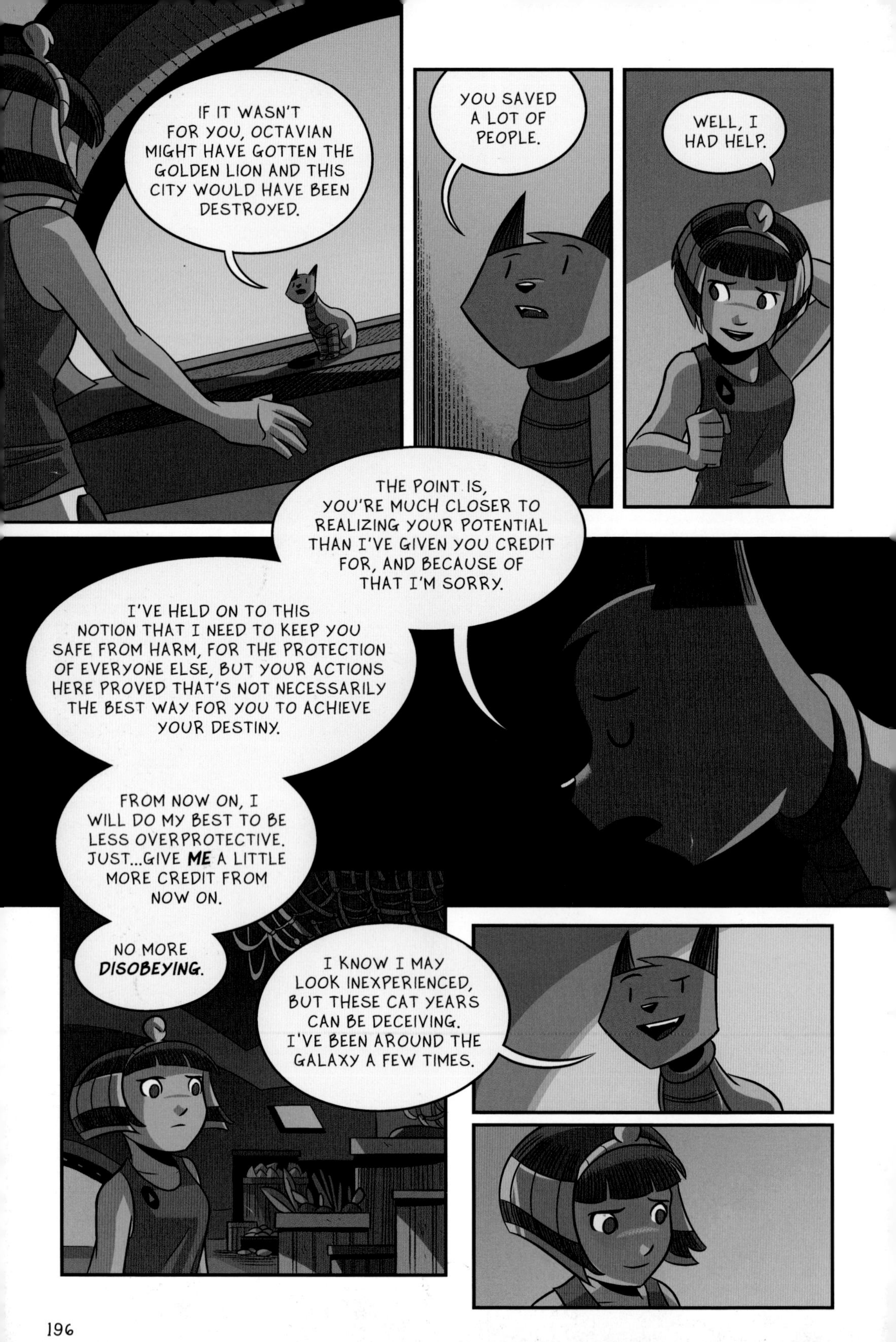
IF IT WASN'T FOR YOU, OCTAVIAN MIGHT HAVE GOTTEN THE GOLDEN LION AND THIS CITY WOULD HAVE BEEN DESTROYED.
YOU SAVED A LOT OF PEOPLE.
WELL, I HAD HELP.
THE POINT IS, YOU'RE MUCH CLOSER TO REALIZING YOUR POTENTIAL THAN I'VE GIVEN YOU CREDIT FOR, AND BECAUSE OF THAT I'M SORRY.
I'VE HELD ON TO THIS NOTION THAT I NEED TO KEEP YOU SAFE FROM HARM, FOR THE PROTECTION OF EVERYONE ELSE, BUT YOUR ACTIONS HERE PROVED THAT'S NOT NECESSARILY THE BEST WAY FOR YOU TO ACHIEVE YOUR DESTINY.
FROM NOW ON, I WILL DO MY BEST TO BE LESS OVERPROTECTIVE. JUST...GIVE **ME** A LITTLE MORE CREDIT FROM NOW ON.
NO MORE ***DISOBEYING***.
I KNOW I MAY LOOK INEXPERIENCED, BUT THESE CAT YEARS CAN BE DECEIVING. I'VE BEEN AROUND THE GALAXY A FEW TIMES.

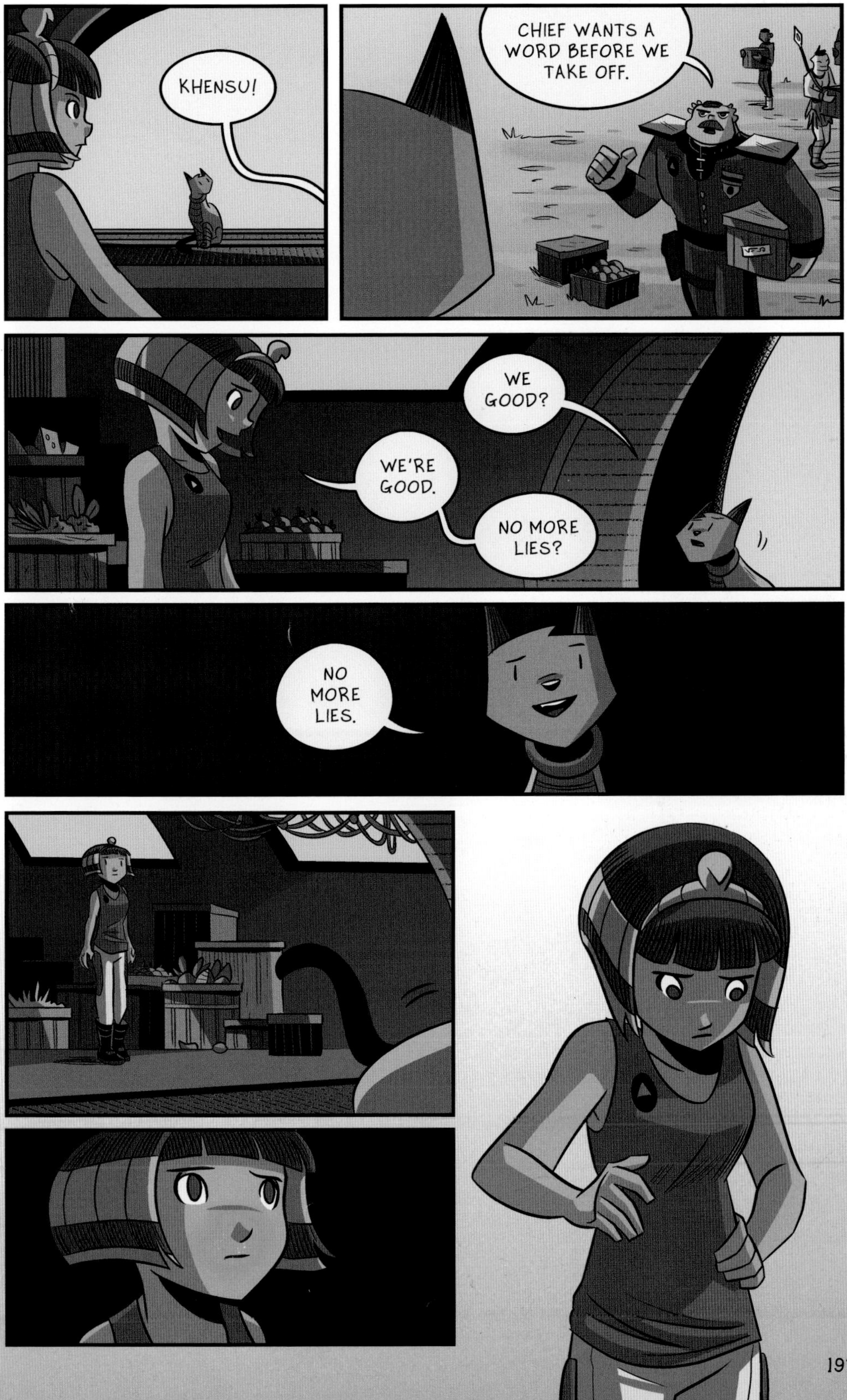
KHENSU!
CHIEF WANTS A WORD BEFORE WE TAKE OFF.
WE GOOD?
WE'RE GOOD.
NO MORE LIES?
NO MORE LIES.

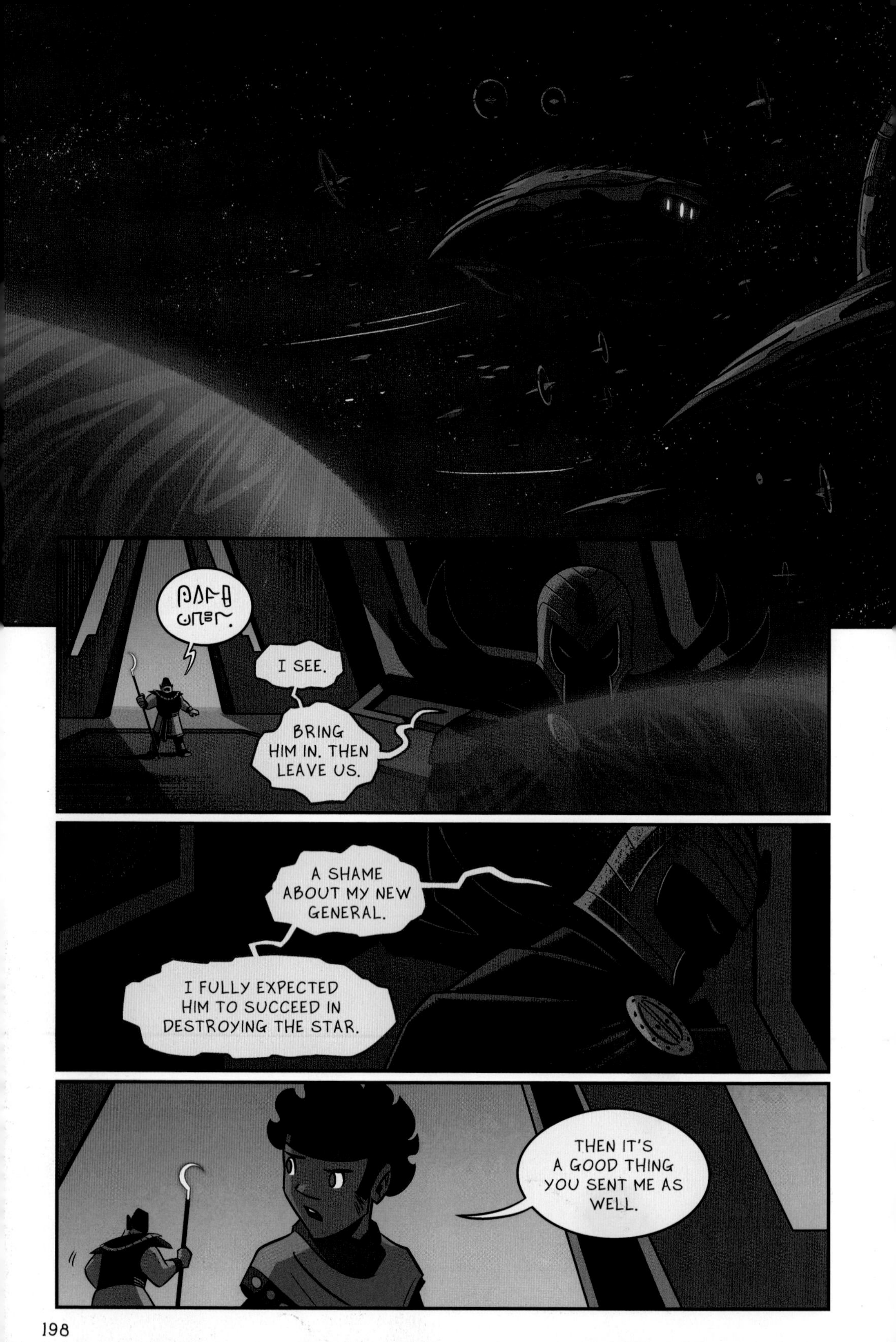
I SEE.
BRING HIM IN. THEN LEAVE US.
A SHAME ABOUT MY NEW GENERAL.
I FULLY EXPECTED HIM TO SUCCEED IN DESTROYING THE STAR.
THEN IT'S A GOOD THING YOU SENT ME AS WELL.

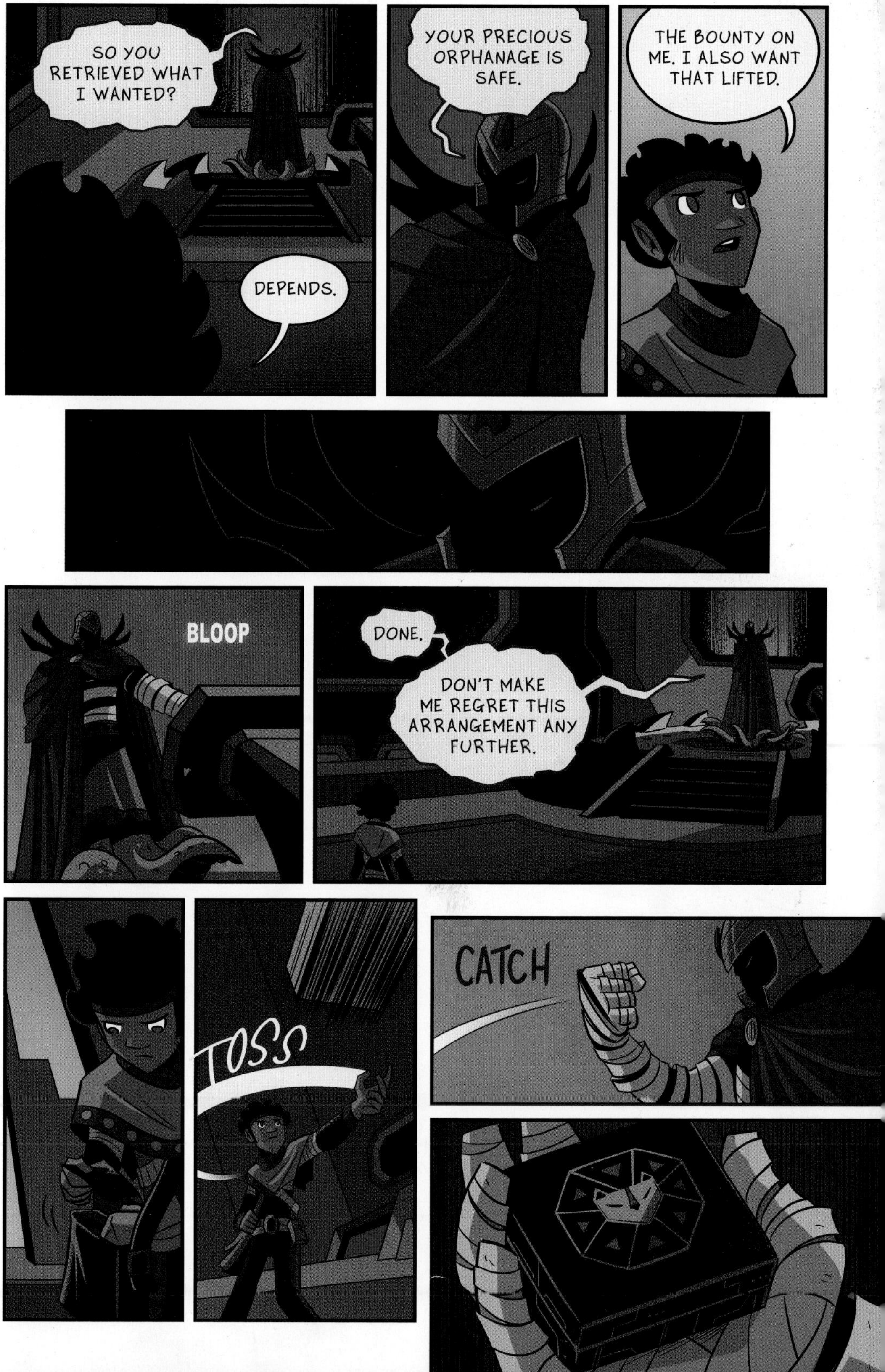
SO YOU RETRIEVED WHAT I WANTED?
DEPENDS.
YOUR PRECIOUS ORPHANAGE IS SAFE.
THE BOUNTY ON ME. I ALSO WANT THAT LIFTED.
BLOOP
DONE.
DON'T MAKE ME REGRET THIS ARRANGEMENT ANY FURTHER.
TOSS
CATCH

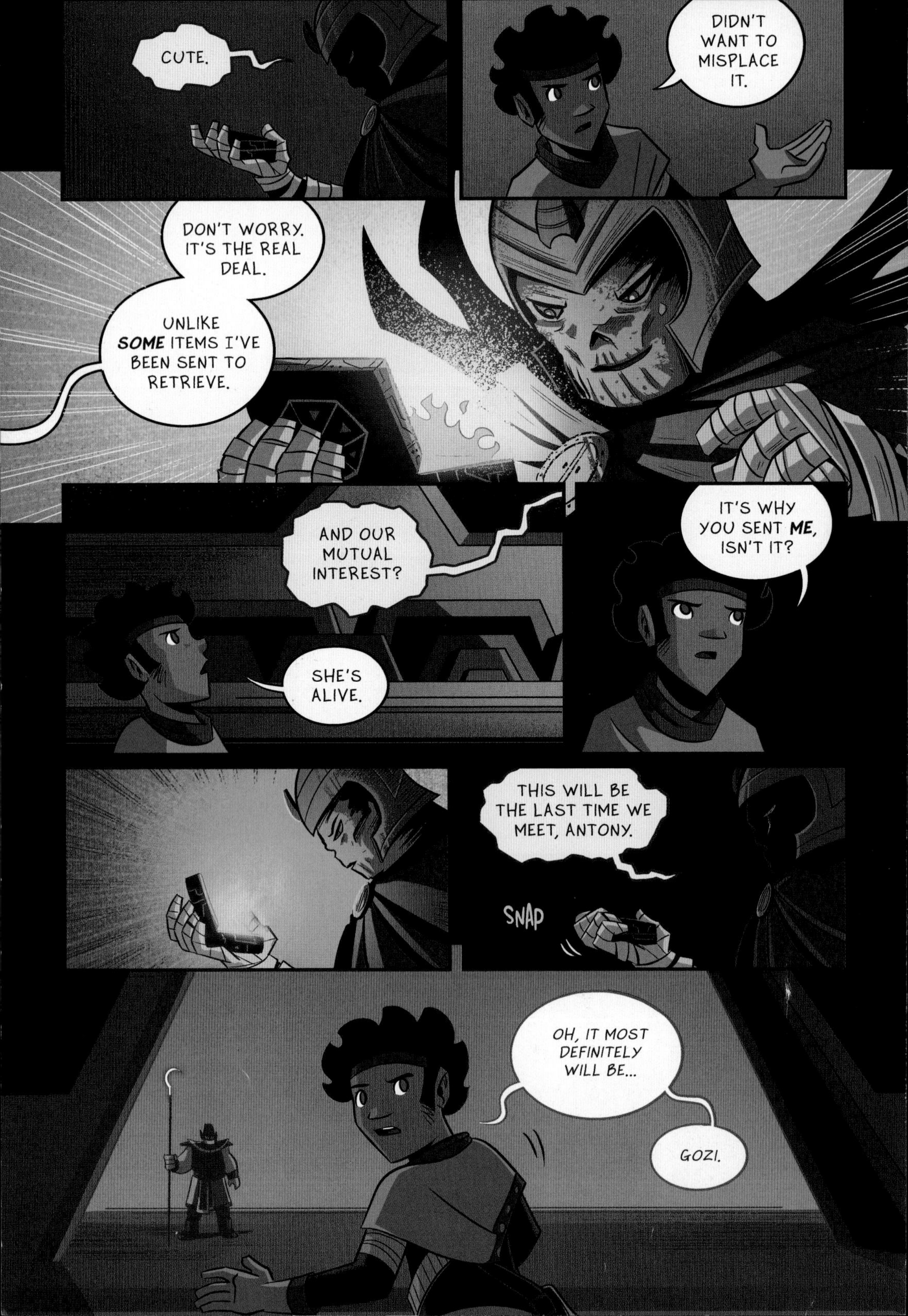
CUTE.
DIDN'T WANT TO MISPLACE IT.
DON'T WORRY. IT'S THE REAL DEAL.
UNLIKE **SOME** ITEMS I'VE BEEN SENT TO RETRIEVE.
AND OUR MUTUAL INTEREST?
SHE'S ALIVE.
IT'S WHY YOU SENT **ME**, ISN'T IT?
THIS WILL BE THE LAST TIME WE MEET, ANTONY.
SNAP
OH, IT MOST DEFINITELY WILL BE...
GOZI.

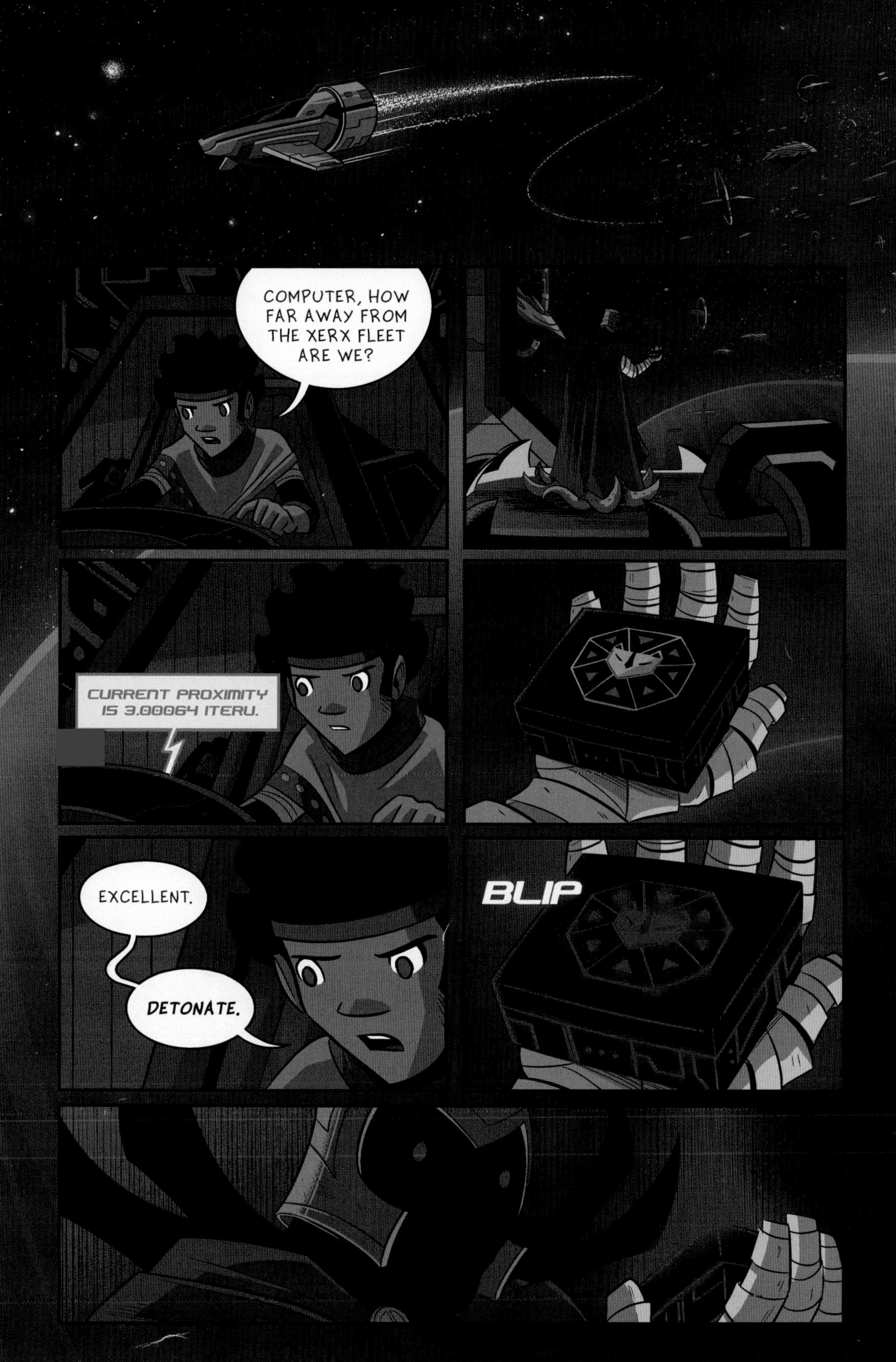
COMPUTER, HOW FAR AWAY FROM THE XERX FLEET ARE WE?
CURRENT PROXIMITY IS 3.00064 ITERU.
EXCELLENT.
DETONATE.
BLIP

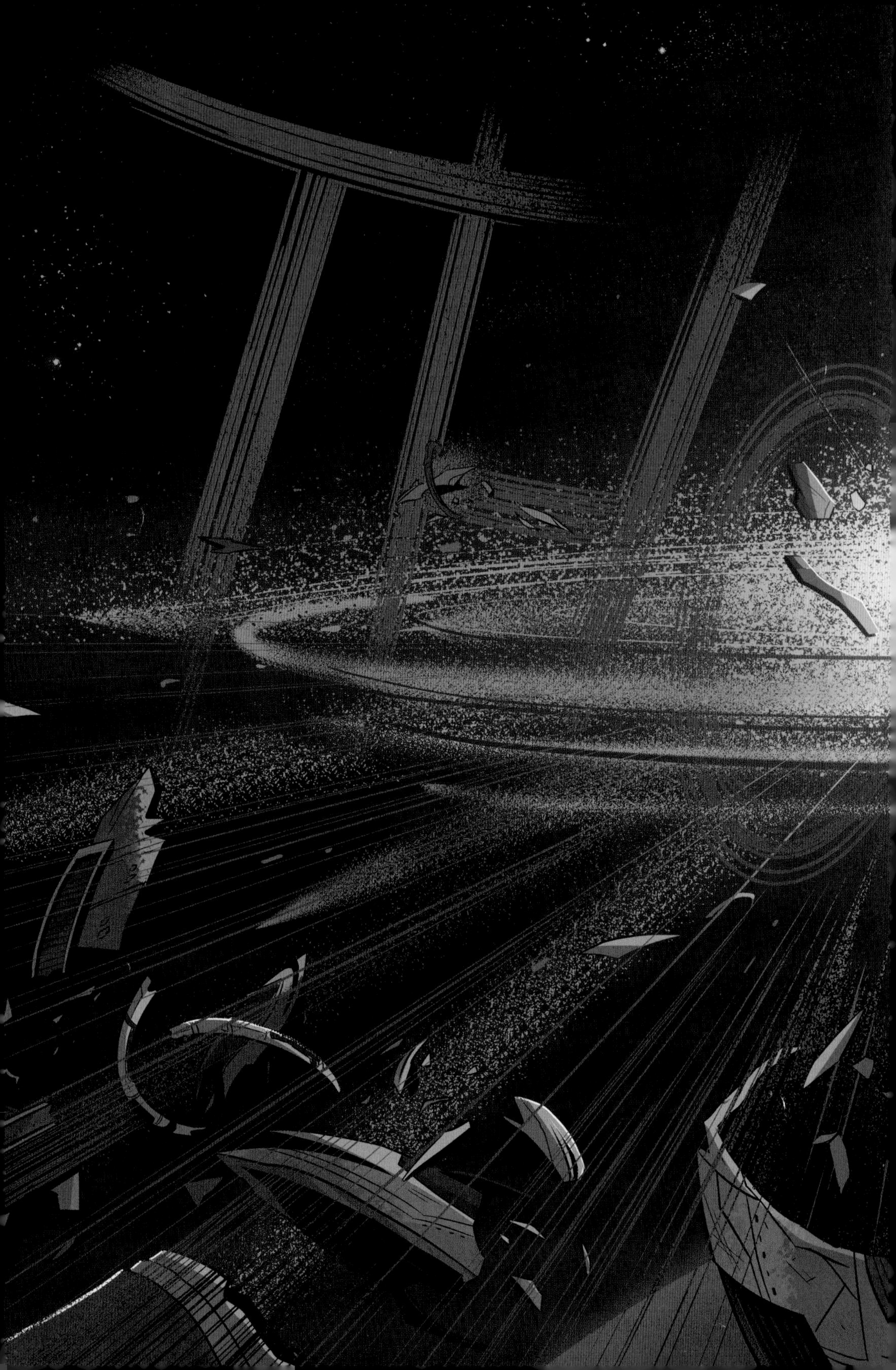

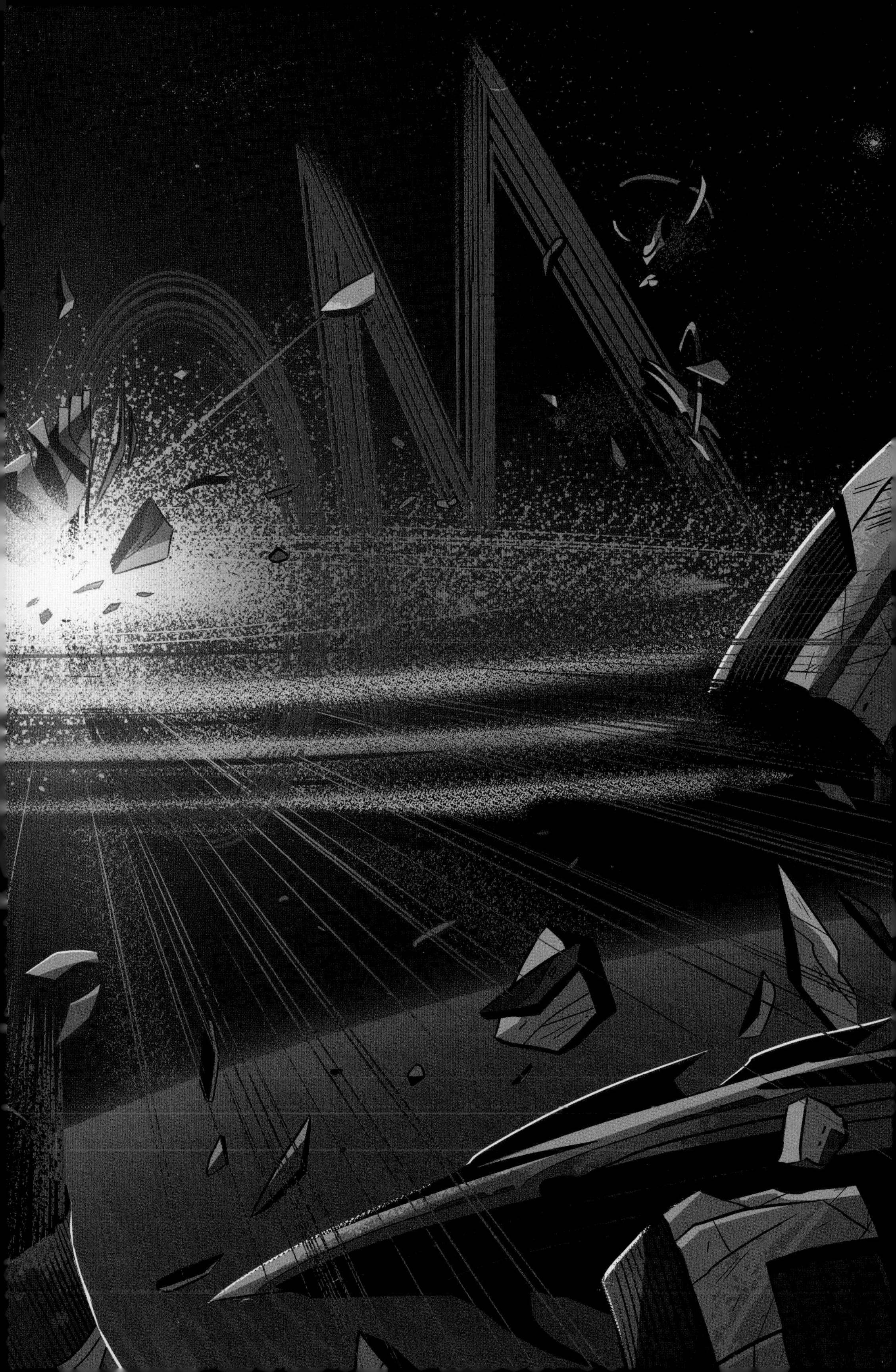

## SPECIAL THANKS TO:

My extraordinarily encouraging wife, Jen, whose patience and selflessness know no bounds.

My two boys, Oliver and Orion. I hope you enjoy these books one day. Also, please stop chasing the cat.

My cat, Misty, for putting up with Oliver and Orion while I was too busy working to save you.

The rest of my *incredibly* supportive friends and family. I am blessed to have so many of you in my life.

Cassandra Pelham and David Saylor for keeping this series steering in the right direction, Phil Falco for making it look so good, and Lizette Serrano, Sheila Marie Everett, Tracy van Straaten, Michelle Campbell, Antonio Gonzalez, Denise Anderson, Ed Masessa, and all the other wonderful folks at Scholastic for the amazing work you've put into it.

Judy Hansen, for your super heroics.

Dan Conner and Kate Carleton for once again helping to make sure this book got colored on time.

Christ, for Your guidance and the freedom to accept or ignore it.

And last but not least, the Internet, for the music and company.

## EXTRA SPECIAL THANKS TO:

All of the teachers, librarians, booksellers, parents, and readers out there who have supported Cleopatra in Space and/or given me high fives. CONTINUE TO BE AWESOME!

# ABOUT THE AUTHOR

A graduate of the Columbus College of Art & Design, Mike Maihack spends his time drawing comics and making sure his house doesn't collapse from the chaos that ensues from two boys bouncing around inside of it. He's contributed to several books, including Sensation Comics Featuring Wonder Woman; *Parable*; *Jim Henson's The Storyteller*; Cow Boy; *Geeks, Girls, and Secret Identities*; and *Comic Book Tattoo*. *The Golden Lion* is the fourth graphic novel in the Cleopatra in Space series, following the Florida Book Award–winning *Target Practice*, *The Thief and the Sword*, and *Secret of the Time Tablets*. He lives in the almost-tropical climate of Lutz, Florida, and is thankful that math isn't required to communicate with the locals.

Visit Mike online at www.mikemaihack.com and follow him on Twitter at @mikemaihack.

# ALSO BY MIKE MAIHACK

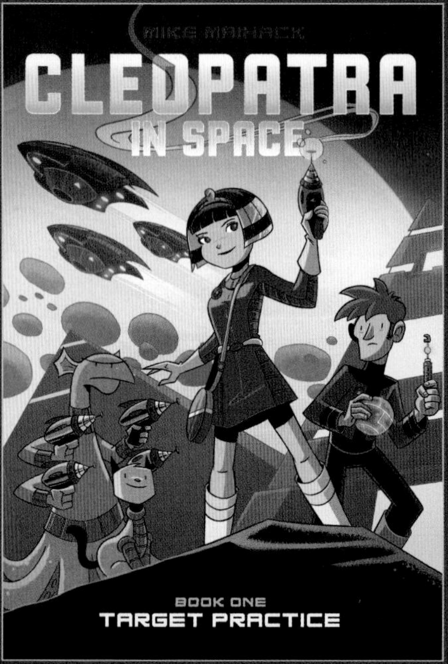
MIKE MAIHACK
CLEOPATRA
IN SPACE
BOOK ONE
TARGET PRACTICE

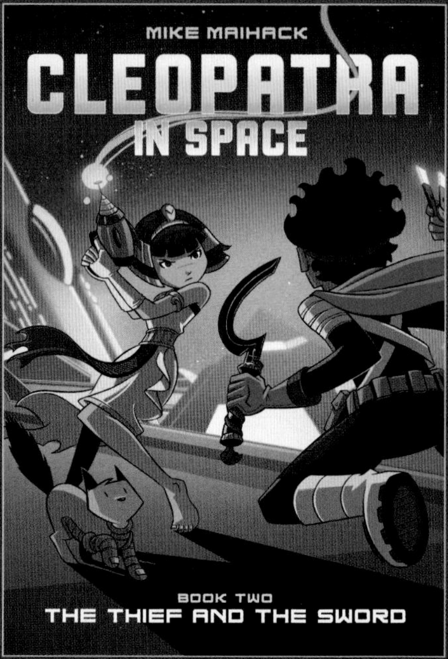
MIKE MAIHACK
CLEOPATRA
IN SPACE
BOOK TWO
THE THIEF AND THE SWORD

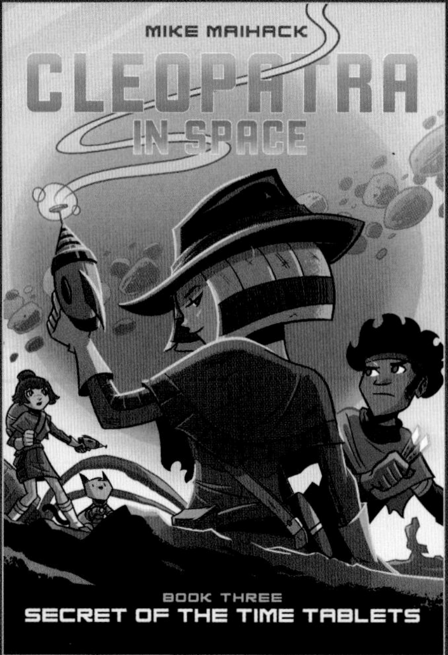
MIKE MAIHACK
CLEOPATRA
IN SPACE
BOOK THREE
SECRET OF THE TIME TABLETS